HIBISCUS LODGE

The Cousins – Part 2

by

Elizabeth Riding

Text copyright © 2015 Susan Elizabeth Mayer
All rights reserved

ISBN: 978-1516983773

This is a work of fiction. Names, characters, businesses, places, events and incidents are either the product of the author's imagination or used in a fictitious manner. Any resemblance to actual persons, living or dead, is purely coincidental.

Other books by this author: *Larkhill Manor, part 1 of The Cousins.* Available on Amazon Kindle or CreateSpace

Printed by CreateSpace, an Amazon.com Company

Contents

List of Characters   iv
Preface   vi

Chapter 1   Rupert returns   *1*
Chapter 2   London   *36*
Chapter 3   The music party   *57*
Chapter 4   Old and new friends   *78*
Chapter 5   Theft   *110*
Chapter 6   Coronation   *150*
Chapter 7   Secrets   *170*
Chapter 8   Hibiscus Lodge   *190*
Chapter 9   Another proposal   *225*
Chapter 10   Abduction   *244*
Chapter 11   Rupert to the rescue   *271*
Chapter 12   Larkhill Manor   *305*

Epilogue   *331*

Characters

In Larkhill

Harriet Larkhill aged 22
Sir John Larkhill, Harriet's uncle, the Squire
Young Clem, Sir John's grandson aged 5
Miss Humble, governess and family friend

Sir Charles Durrington, friend of the Larkhills
Lady Durrington (née Maria Denver) his wife
George Durrington, Sir Charles's son, recently retired from the Royal Navy
Juliana Durrington (née Denver), George's wife

Dr and Mrs Darymple, the Bishop of Salisbury and his wife
Mr & Mrs West of Bourne Park
Mr & Mrs Carter, tenants of Quennell House
Stanley Carter, their engineer son in America
Eliza Carter, their elder daughter aged 17
Jane Carter, their younger daughter aged 16

In London

Sir Hamish McAllister, senior legal adviser in the Home Office.
Lady [Elspeth] McAllister, his wife
Angus McAllister, their eldest son in Elrick Castle, Aberdeen looking after his father's properties
William McAllister, their middle son, barrister and Member of Parliament
Andrew, their youngest son, private secretary to Lord Glynn of the East India Company.
Miss Susan Finch, cousin and companion to Lady McAllister

Philipp Beaumont ('The Nabob'), wealthy Bombay silk merchant now retired to England
Philippa Beaumont, his daughter, aged 17
Marguerite de Lessups, a rich widow, Philippa's chaperone and Beaumont's fiancée
Captain Valentine of the Bengal Native Light Infantry, Marguerite's nephew, a rake

Sophia Darville, Dowager Countess of Morna (the 'Countess')

Gerald Darville, 4th Earl of Morna, her eldest son, a trifle slow
The hon. Ralph Darville, her second son, living in Italy
The Hon. Rupert Darville aged 31, her youngest son and man of science
Lord Patrick Darville (War Office retired), brother to the 3rd Earl, a jocular man of fashion.

Will and Catherine Hinton, friends of Rupert in Wiltshire
Emily Castlereagh (aka Amelia, Marchioness of Londonderry), Patroness of Almack's
Reichsgraf Ravensburg, Austrian diplomat in London for coronation with his wife, the Reichsgrafin Adelaide.
Lady Barbara Bixby, fashionable friend of Elspeth McAllister
Lord Stephen Everard, leader of fashion
Lord Frodingham, geologist friend of Rupert
Mortimer Shawcross, rotund, older Member of Parliament
Mrs Mary Somerville, famous mathematician
Miss Lavinia Snoddie, supporter of phrenology
The Cholmondley family, a jolly set of young people

Others
Annie, Harriet's maid, age 23
Dr Yardly, recommended by Austrian embassy.
Dunch, the Larkhills' butler
Figgis, the McAllisters' butler
Jacob, Rupert's 14yr-old native servant
Mr Jenkins, river pilot for the East India Company
Mr Tamar, Sir Hamish's man of business
Pole, the McAllisters' coachman
Ram Kumar, Mr Beaumont's Indian servant

Preface

The second part of The Cousins, *Hibiscus Lodge,* has taken me longer to write than expected but here is the continuation of *Larkhill Manor.*

Ten years on, my protagonists have grown in years and in experience and the raffish Regency era is morphing into the dynamic second industrial age. Against a background of exploration and scientific discovery, an age of unrest and shifting values, Rupert and Harriet gradually come to realise how they truly feel about each other. Nevertheless, wanting to write a sweet romance, I have used the age-old devices of coincidence and danger to bring my hero and heroine together.

Thank you to those friends and family who have offered encouragement, advice and information; I have written this for you. As ever, all mistakes are my own.

June 2015

CHAPTER 1   RUPERT RETURNS

It was Miss Humble who first saw the death notice. She was reading the paper to Sir John who, since his stroke, had been unable to cope with the confused misprints of *The Gazette* but nevertheless liked to keep abreast of events. The Earl of Morna was dead. The polite world had almost forgotten the earl languishing in his castle in Ireland with his compliant mistress. A stranger to both society and his rustic neighbours, only the dowager countess continued to visit twice a year to pester her spouse over her settlements and count the spoons.

Miss Humble decided to keep her discovery from the squire and continued to read the newspaper to him. As always, everything would be referred to Miss Harriet first.

Miss Harriet was making pastry in the kitchen and, at Miss Humble's urgent beckoning from the back stairs, she wiped her hands on her calico apron and followed her former governess up into the Great Hall.

"There, under Notices of Death, such a shock! My dear Miss Harriet, the Earl of Morna is deceased!" She pressed the folded newspaper into Harriet's hand. "I did not dare tell Sir John for fear of upsetting him." Since the death of his wife the squire had become more uncertain of temper.

"Yes, yes, quite right, Miss Humble," said Harriet absently. "Leave it to me. I will break the news to him, though I doubt if he can remember the earl very much." She was scanning the announcement. "The funeral will be in Ireland of course. I assume Mr Darville will attend, even if only for his mother's sake."

"Do you think he will break his journey here?" asked Miss Humble with hope in her eye. She could not think the callow Reverend Cusworth a fit suitor for Miss Larkhill and, while not daring to hope for an aristocratic alliance for Harriet, she would be happy to see Mr Darville at the manor again.

"Who can say?" said Harriet. "Larkhill is not on the Great West Road and there is no necessity for him to make a diversion. He has shown no desire to see Young Clem since his return."

"But Miss Harriet, are you not being a little unfair? Mr Darville has been away, sailing round the world braving great danger in the furtherance of knowledge. He was not *able* to come and see us."

Harriet thrust the newspaper back into her governess's hand.

"He has been back in Europe since last November and in London since January. I would have thought he could have afforded his old friends a few days of his company. Young Clem has not seen his guardian since he was three months old – as if a tiny baby can remember anything at that age!"

"Mr Darville must be a very busy man, and is a quite a famous one I have no doubt. His other commitments-"

"Precisely; he is too busy and too famous to come and see his ward. I think Mr Darville has treated us most shabbily. He might have at least come for Young Clem's fifth birthday."

"He did send that wonderful puzzle of such strange creatures." Miss Humble's grasp of exotic animals was rather hazy.

But that's not the same, Harriet's mind wailed, all the time knowing she was being unreasonable. She accepted Rupert's neglect as a bitter fact and resolutely turned her mind away.

"You may take the newspaper back to Sir John if you wish. I will write a letter of condolence to the Countess, though one can only suppose that she is relieved to be a widow at last. Now I must return to my pastry."

Not for the first time, the governess wondered if Miss Harriet was turning into a waspish old maid at twenty-two.

Once back in the kitchen, rolling her dough with unnecessary vigour, Harriet rebuked herself. She had been brusque because she was tired and worried, a condition that was permanent. Lady Day was but a month away and she would have to raise the rent of the tenant farms again – all of whom would protest or demand repairs to their properties that the estate could ill-afford. She twirled the apple pie on her hand, cutting away the excess pastry. The knife slipped and drew blood from her finger.

"Bind it up with a bit of cotton, Miss," said Janet, coming in with an arm full of dirty laundry. "Here let me take the dish, your hands are too small," she added, bustling her young mistress out of the way and finishing the job.

"And my mind is not on my work." Harriet went across to the shallow sink and pumped some cold water onto her finger.

"You shouldn't be doing this at all, Miss," said Janet shooting a look at Cook who was bent double rattling the ancient range with a poker.

"Nonsense Janet, I enjoy it. Where is Master Clem?" asked Harriet, ignoring the plaint she'd been hearing for years.

"At Home Farm. He wanted to see the lambs. Annie said she would have him back in time for his tea."

Harriet relaxed. Young Clem would be safe and happy playing with the Trottmans' ever-increasing brood of children. She would not have him repeat her own lonely childhood.

"Then we can depend upon it, there will be eggs and honey for tea," she said determined to put Rupert out of her mind and be cheerful. "Sir John will enjoy that. He hardly eats a morsel these days. I should take myself down to the farm tomorrow if I have the time. I must see if they are intending to sow oats or barley in the bottom field."

******

Two weeks later Harriet trotted the pony trap up the drive of Larkhill Manor to be confronted by a smart carriage standing on the gravel. A tall man in a many-caped driving coat was talking to Miss Humble and, standing on the barouche box, a young black boy with a topknot held up a birdcage with a squawking inhabitant. Young Clem was hopping up and down, tugging at Miss Humble's arm in excitement. "May I have him! May I have him, *please?*"

Harriet brought the pony to a standstill with a slight frown. She was about to climb down when the man turned round from talking to the governess and immediately came towards her. It was Rupert Darville, it could only be Rupert Darville! Broader, older, weather-beaten and smiling broadly.

"Miss Larkhill, my dear Harriet, at last I have found my way back to you all." He helped her down from the trap and bent forward to kiss her cheek. "You will forgive the familiarity, I am certain; we have been friends for so long."

Harriet looked up at him, blinking in disbelief. He was really here at last! She could not believe this assured, smiling man was the troubled soul she had last seen five years before. The almond eyes and high cheekbones had solidified into an arresting face under a profusion of dark windblown waves.

"Mr Darville, how wonderful! Why did you not write to forewarn us?" she exclaimed with pleasure. "I am so sorry to hear about your father's death. I wrote to your Mama. We are delighted to see you but on what a sad occasion and you have caught us quite unawares."

The parrot in the cage gave a squawk and Young Clem stepped back behind Miss Humble's skirts.

"Jacob, give Master Clement the cage. It *is* for him." Mr Darville turned to Harriet, "If you have no objection? I thought a monkey might be too disruptive and very difficult to house train," he smiled down at her. "The bird is an Amazonian blue-fronted parrot, rejoicing in the name of Captain Blood."

"How thrilling! I've always adored pirates! Clement, you must thank Mr Darville, and take great care of the bird."

The parrot squawked again as Clem clutched the cage to his breast. He didn't know what to look at first, the vivid green parrot, the shiny brown boy or this mysterious gentleman with the yellow face and eyes of a cat.

"May I keep him, Aunt Harriet?" begged Young Clem, breathlessly.

"Of course you may, but you must ask Mr Darville what he eats and how to take care of him. And you may teach him to speak – if he cannot already."

"I fear he may, but only in Portuguese, which will save all our blushes." murmured Rupert.

"Was he a pirate?" asked Young Clem turning to Rupert, blue eyes wide. He looked amazingly like Sylvia, and Rupert halted a little before replying.

"I won him in a card game *from* a pirate, in Brazil, but he comes from the deepest forest. I will tell you how I acquired him, tonight at your bedtime. Now, I believe he will need a drink, some water after his long journey. Take him to the kitchen and Jacob will show you what to do. Be careful of your fingers – the bird may bite!"

Harriet stood bemused as Rupert spoke a few words in some patois to the native boy and ordered the child and servant away.

"Jacob has only the rudiments of English," said Rupert, "but I find children communicate with each other very easily. You must forgive me Harriet for descending on you like this. I did write, from Castle Morna, but Miss Humble tells me that no letter was received. It can only be that the Irish mail service is as unreliable as always. I received your letters on the other side of the world but it seems we cannot rely on post to arrive here from the next island. Do not disturb yourself, I have rooms at the Three Crowns. Drinkworth regards me as a long lost prodigal and sees Jacob as something of an attraction to his establishment."

They had wandered into the vestibule where Harriet divested herself of her driving gloves, cloak and bonnet. She noticed that Rupert automatically ducked his head in the doorway as would a man who had spent three years avoiding overhead beams in confined spaces. Dunch relieved Darville of his coat and hat, beaming broadly.

Harriet suddenly felt shy of this imposing stranger. She made an attempt to sound grown-up. "We are familiar with negroes in Bath and Salisbury of course, but seldom in Larkhill. I hope your servant will not be too cold here, nor you, after three years in tropical climes. But that's nought to the purpose – you are with us again, and safe. Come into the hall. You will stay to dinner of course." Her mind raced over the contents of their scanty larder. On cue, Miss Humble, trailing behind them all smiles, vanished to the kitchens.

"Did you have a good crossing from Wexford?" asked Harriet.

"Tolerable. The Irish sea holds no fears for me after three years on a French corvette. If I look yellow, it's because I had a bout of fever in London some weeks ago. I would have come earlier but I had to give a paper to the *Academie des sciences* in Paris and then to the Royal Society."

She felt a pang of guilt at her unkind thoughts and instantly forgave him his tardiness. She earnestly enquired after the family and once again offered her condolences; Rupert was in deepest black, this time for his father.

"And you Harriet? The loss of Lady Larkhill was very sudden. I received your letter when I was in Sydney and felt for you all. You must miss her."

"A winter chill which she couldn't shake off. It went to her lungs and even our young Dr Makepeace could not help. I'm afraid the strain of recent years had weakened her considerably. But what of your own mother?" she said quickly, not wanting to dwell on her own grief. "How is she bearing up under the loss?"

"My mother remains at Castle Morna until my brother Gerald establishes himself," he replied absently not wishing to pursue that line of conversation either. He looked about him, smiling in satisfaction. The manor looked much the same as he had left it, except today a huge bowl of golden daffodils glowed on the brightly polished refectory table and a wooden pull-along toy lay abandoned at the foot of the shallow dais.

"You cannot imagine how often I have thought of this lovely old house. Remember how we used to throw chestnuts over the gallery at the servants?"

"You malign me, Mr Darville! You and Clement were the culprits; *I* was still in the cradle and am completely innocent of any such naughtiness. I trust you will not put any such ideas into Young Clem's head while you're here," she laughed and then, uncertain of how he would react to the mention of Clement's name, hurried on. "Will you be staying in Larkhill long?"

"A week or two at most. I have some business with Brownrigg for my mother, and intend to rusticate in the neighbourhood. Good English country air should set me up. But mainly I have come to look at my ward and see how you all fare at the manor."

"The Durringtons will be so happy to see you, and the Butterworths, but I hear Mr and Mrs Hinton have already gone to London for the season. We are so provincial here and hardly socialise at all. You must know so many more interesting people in London; all your natural philosophy friends and your mother's political acquaintances?"

"The Countess spends all her time racketing around Leicestershire when she's not scandalising my father's Tory friends in town. I found London a hurly-burly of noise and dirt but yes, I have been busy giving an account of my travels and I will certainly write a book about my findings."

"Oh how I would love to be your amanuensis, just like when we were children," said Harriet impetuously.

"Why thank you Miss Larkhill." He looked amused. "But I would not burden a young lady with sorting all my papers and scribbled notes and of course I shall go back to the Wren library in Trinity for any reference work. I intend to employ a secretary."

Harriet felt abashed at her outburst.

He strolled about the Great Hall examining the portraits and armoury on the wall. "Nothing changes, I see." He smiled at the ancient trout mounted in a glass case in the corner. "I would have posted down to Wiltshire earlier but for my father's last illness. He lingered nearly a month and my mother insisted on us all being at his bedside. I cannot tell you how good it is to be here again. And to get rid of that wretched parrot. It squawked all the way from Bristol."

"You may think nothing has changed but we are mainly confined to the ground floor rooms," explained Harriet. "Sir John can no longer manage the Grand Staircase; he has had several more slight strokes since Aunt Betsy died and we have changed the dining room into a bedroom for him. We take all our meals in the breakfast parlour now and hardly ever use the green drawing room."

Whatever his private thoughts, Rupert nodded. "What a very sensible idea. After living satisfactorily in a cabin no bigger than a broom cupboard, I wonder why we all need to encumber ourselves with these huge houses. Quennell House is a barrack of a place."

He looked at her once more. She was still small and brown with her hair wound around her head in a simple coronet of braids. Her dress was dark and serviceable, her figure filled out, her hands a little work worn as were his own. He was glad to see that her big brown eyes had not lost their youthful exuberance.

Dunch appeared carrying a tray with a decanter and glasses. "Shall I take the refreshment to the oak parlour, Miss Harriet?" He coughed slightly. "The master would like a word with Mr Darville as soon as convenient."

"Of course," said Rupert "I must pay my respects to the squire. How does he go on?" he asked Harriet in a significant tone. She had made light of her uncle's decline in her recent letters but Sir John was much changed since Lady Larkhill's death.

"He can walk when he chooses but the weather has been so bad of late-". She broke off and continued in a more positive tone: "He enjoys having the newspaper read to him and Young Clem can always rouse him. But he tires very easily and is inclined to become muddled and anxious. But I am certain your visit will lift his spirits."

"I won't stay with him long," replied Darville with a heartening smile. He strode off behind Dunch while Harriet ran upstairs to summon Annie and tell her the exciting news.

An hour later Harriet and Miss Humble met in the oak parlour. For Mr Darville's benefit, a fire had been lit against the cold spring weather. The ladies had agreed that they would dress for dinner in honour of the occasion. In Harriet's case this meant nothing more than changing her gown for one slightly less shabby and abandoning her fichu. Both ladies hoped that the meal sent up would not disgrace them.

"Cook has made a good soup, to be followed by veal pie and Mrs Trottman has sent up a dressed capon. There is young cabbage from the kitchen gardens and a dish of buttered asparagus. Janet whipped up a syllabub and we have stewed gooseberries from last year," whispered Miss Humble. "With cheese and some of Master Clem's sweetmeats – will that suffice, do you think?"

Harriet, conscious that Lady Larkhill would have been appalled at such a rustic offering, said in heartening tones: "I daresay Mr Darville has eaten nothing but hard tack and salt beef during his expedition; he will think this a feast!"

Dunch opened the door to admit Rupert.

"Forgive the informality of my dress ladies; I fear all my luggage is at the Three Crowns," he said indicating his top boots. "Thank you Dunch, yes I will have a madeira. This is very pleasant," he said looking about him at the chintz cushions and heavy curtains. One or two choice pieces from the green drawing room had made their way downstairs to brighten the wood-panelled parlour. "Only the piano forte is wanting. I was hoping you would delight us with some music this evening, Miss Larkhill. Will Sir John be joining us?"

"Yes, sir," said Dunch before either of the ladies could reply in the negative. "To mark your visit, sir, Sir John asked me to inform you, Miss Harriet, that he will join you in the breakfast parlour in half an hour."

"How splendid. Mr Darville, I knew your visit would be the very thing to bring him out of himself." Harriet smiled at him brightly, praying he would not refer to the piano forte again. She had sold it the previous winter to cover the loss of half the flock to a murrain.

"Miss Larkhill, do you think we could we throw convention to the winds and allow ourselves to address each other by our Christian names? Miss Humble, would you agree that there would be nothing improper in doing so? Lady Larkhill always treated me as though I were one of the family."

Miss Humble look flustered and gave Harriet a troubled glance.

"By all means, Mr Darville – Rupert, if you so wish it," returned Harriet evenly.

"Would you give us your sanction, Miss Humble? Miss Larkhill and I have known each other since we were children; we could be regarded almost as cousins."

"Of course Mr Darville," the governess hesitated. "How you and Miss Harriet address each other in private is no concern of mine or the world's. Except – perhaps – Larkhill is such a *small* town–"

"I understand. All the proprieties shall be observed in public, Miss Humble. Please bear with me; I have led a roving life for so long that I forget the requirements of polite society. The Countess tells me now that I am home I must settle down and find a wife to rub away the rough edges."

******

Rupert visited the Larkhills frequently and, as of old, never came empty handed. He would take the squire for a gentle ride in his barouche or put Young Clem up in front of him while he re-acquainted himself with the countryside on horseback. He did not trouble them by staying for dinner again. When it rained he played skittles with his ward in the Great Hall. He never once referred to Sylvia and it was as though the marriage and the duplicity had never happened. Harriet, busy with her own duties did not see much of him above a few chilly strolls in the Yew Walk when he would discourse at length on the expedition.

Young Clem was inseparable from his new playmate and in turn Jacob was in thrall to the blond cherub, refusing to leave him even during Miss Humble's lessons. Rupert hoped Jacob's English would improve by this arrangement and insisted on tipping the governess handsomely for her pains.

Rupert's gifts from his travels overwhelmed them. Harriet received a bolt of shot-silk in peacock blue shimmering with scarlet from Madagascar and a pair of gold filigree earrings from the markets of Montevideo. Everyone in the household was remembered.

"And Sir John is to have a barrel of brandy from Armagnac. I have arranged to have it sent up from Bristol, and yes I have paid the duty on it," he said. "Which calls to mind; I met Sir Hamish McAllister when I was in town. He has become a great man at the Home Department. Are you in correspondence with him Harriet?"

"From time to time," she said blandly. She had been in dire financial straits of late and had been forced to resort to him for advice but she had no wish to impart this to Rupert.

On Sunday, Rupert took them all to church in his barouche. The outing did Sir John good. Although the day tired him, he became animated when his neighbours greeted him with affection and concern. Harriet was touched by Rupert's care for her uncle and his reticence in public about his own adventures.

Rupert automatically took a seat in the Larkhill pew and amused himself by watching the young curate with the unfortunate rash cast curious glances towards the occupants. After a while Rupert grew bored and quelled the Reverend Cusworth's pretensions with a cold stare, which was unjust, because the young man was gazing at Harriet not the newly returned explorer. Harriet, after a brief acknowledgement, ignored her admirer and turned her attention to the pulpit. In deference to the squire, Reverend Butterworth cut his sermon short with the resolve to thunder on the Prodigal's Return next Sunday, if Mr Darville were still with them.

"But he is not exactly a prodigal, my dear," his wife pointed out. "He is a very personable and respectable gentleman who is merely making a visit to his friends. You would not wish to offend him by recalling to mind – anything that would rather be forgotten."

The Rector, while regretting the lost opportunity to display his oratory, was forced to agree and hoped they'd be invited to luncheon.

Greeting Rupert in the church yard, Sir Charles Durrington gave him a slap on the back, offered his condolences and invited him to dinner. "Come and eat your mutton with us one evening. George will have such a deal to discuss with you. He's at home with Juliana – she's not quite the thing this morning, in the family way, you know," said Sir John proudly. "George was in the West Africa Squadron until last year, blockading the slave ships. He's home now and setting up his own nursery, but to tell you the truth I think he misses his comrades and naval talk. And we must hear all about your adventures. It's not often we have someone famous in our midst."

"Thank you Sir Charles. I am by no means famous, but I would be delighted to exchange nautical experiences with George over dinner."

On hearing of her husband's invitation, Lady Durrington decided to hold a formal dinner party to mark Rupert's return, which threw Harriet into a whirl. Almost continuous mourning had left her with practically nothing in the way of evening toilettes, and those she had were woefully outmoded. Harriet had one good outfit, the costume she had worn for Juliana Denver's wedding to George Durrington the year before. With the removal of the long sleeves and the flounce of lace at the neckline, the cherry-striped gown would do for evening wear. Aunt Amelia's garnets suited the ensemble perfectly.

"Oh, Miss, you look lovely," said Annie standing back from her handiwork. Fond as she was of Master Clem, she longed to return to being a lady's maid.

"I look positively fagged," said Harriet without rancour. "But I own it *is* nice to have a pretty gown on one's back. Pass me the Gowland's lotion again would you; my hands are a disgrace. Where are the evening gloves that Lady Durrington gave me last Christmas? I never thought I'd ever have the opportunity to wear them", she added with delight. "And Aunt Betsy's Lisbon shawl. There is still a sharp wind at this time of year."

"I wish you'd let me curl your hair, Miss."

"Gracious, no Annie!" laughed Harriet. "It would take hours! We agreed it was no use at all to try and frizz and crimp my hair. The first sign of dampness sends it falling into rats' tails. My plaits will have to do." And then catching sight of Annie's disappointed face she softened. "But perhaps that bunch of artificial cherries and some cerise ribbon from the discarded sleeves could make my coiffeur more interesting?"

"Yes, Miss. I see just what you mean. If we wind your plaits up into a top-knot and pin the cherries at the side, to hang just so-"

Annie's efforts met the squire's approval when Harriet went in to bid her uncle goodnight.

"Enjoy your party, my dear and give my compliments to, to–". He paused, at a loss for the name of his friend of fifty years.

"The Durringtons, Uncle," prompted Harriet gently. "I'm dining at the Durringtons."

"But who is to take you?" he asked anxiously. "You cannot go alone. John Coachman will take you in the berlin but you must have a gentleman to escort you."

Harriet passed over the fact that John Coachman and the berlin had been dispensed with years ago and informed her uncle yet again that Rupert Darville was to drive her to Durrington Park.

"Not in that rackety phaeton of his, surely!" said the squire in growing agitation. "It is far too dangerous for a lady, and the roads are so very bad."

"No, Uncle, Mr Darville has hired a very comfortable barouche. You always said Rupert was an excellent whip and the sky is clear tonight," she soothed.

"Watch out for highway men. Has Darville his pistols? Take mine from the berlin, I always keep one there. Did I tell you when Sir Charles and I captured that gang from the Three Crowns-"

"Yes, Uncle and very exciting it must have been. I'll tell you all about the party tomorrow. Now you must sleep, and here is Dunch with your nightcap."

Still mumbling under his breath he released her hand and bade her be off. Harriet wondered how long she could cover up her uncle's deteriorating mind. She went up to the nursery to say goodnight to Young Clem.

She found him prancing on his bed in his nightshirt, a kerchief tied around his head and brandishing a toy cutlass in Miss Humble's direction "I'm a pirate, you can't come aboard my ship!"

"Master Clement! I will tell you one last time-". The governess looked exasperated.

"Good heavens, what is all this commotion, Clement? Put that down and attend to Miss Humble at once."

"Shan't," said the rebellious buccaneer. "I want another story – about pirates, not fairies" he added cunningly.

"I have quite exhausted my imagination, Miss Harriet," pleaded the governess suddenly looking worn out. "And I am not his nursemaid."

"Oh, Miss Humble, do forgive me! How selfish of me to keep Annie away from her proper duties. I believe she's in the kitchen preparing Master Clement's milk and should be here at any moment to settle this little monster down. Now do go and have your supper and leave him to me."

Miss Humble thankfully withdrew. Harriet fleetingly wondered if Young Clem was becoming too much of a handful for her ageing governess. This was another problem that would have to be dealt with, but not tonight.

Left alone with his aunt in her finery, the child said shrewdly: "Is Mr Darville coming? I want him to tell me about the shipwreck."

"Shipwreck?" asked Harriet in surprise, sitting down on the edge of the bed. "Was he shipwrecked?"

"Oh yes," replied Young Clem matter-of-factly. "And was nearly eaten by cannon balls. Only he was too thin and they let him go."

Harriet's gurgle of laughter was echoed by a cackle from Captain Blood. She got up to drape a cloth over the cage and returned to the bed where Clement was by now sitting down cross-legged ready to relate Mr Darville's nautical adventures.

"He shot a hippopotamus," said Young Clem. "Right between the eyes and the sailors shared it with the savages at a great feast instead."

"Where was this precisely?"

"I have forgotten," said Young Clem with unconcern. "But it was very cold and there were lots of penguins."

Harriet had doubts about the accuracy of the geography but only said: "And it will be very cold on your island if you don't slip under the bedclothes," she coaxed him in between the sheets. "Now see, here is Annie with your feast, a macaroon if I'm not mistaken."

The maid entered carrying a tray with a cup of milk and a biscuit for her charge. She also informed her mistress that Mr Darville was waiting below for Miss Harriet in his barouche.

"But what about my story?" pleaded Young Clem looking up at her with Sylvia's cornflower blue eyes.

"Mr Darville will tell you another one tomorrow. It would be rude to keep a gentleman waiting. Why don't you make up a story to tell him?"

"Because I have never been captured by pirates."

"You can pretend. Like we all do."

******

Harriet came downstairs closely wrapped in her heavy cloak and hood. Rupert was standing in the vestibule discussing the vagaries of hired horses with Dunch. He was booted and caped and smiled warmly as she came down the Grand Staircase. He handed her into the barouche, its half-hood up against the chill night air, he said: "Do forgive my not joining you in the carriage Miss Larkhill, Jacob is too nervous to get any speed out of these horses and is unfamiliar with the road in the dark. I must abandon you and take the reins."

"Oh," she said momentarily disappointed but continued: "Of course Mr Darville, you may safely leave me. I will feel even *more* like Cinderella going to the ball in such splendid isolation."

"I promise to have you home by midnight, the livery stable would not appreciate one of their vehicles being turned into a pumpkin, such slugs as these horses are."

He was about to close the door behind her when she leant forward and grasping a thick woollen blanket folded on the seat, saying: "Did you provide this rug? How thoughtful but do take it for poor Jacob, he is so unused to our March wind and I am perfectly snug in my cloak."

"I will not hear of it! Good English air will toughen Jacob up. You and Miss Humble pamper him too much, he is not a pet."

He tucked the rug around her knees firmly as if to silence her.

Dunch appeared at his elbow. "A horse blanket, sir – for the lad, as Miss is desirous of it." He held out a grey and malodorous blanket at arm's length.

Rupert pointed to Jacob on the box. "Give it to him." he said shortly. "And if I expire with the stink we will put it down to Miss Larkhill's misplaced charity."

"Ah, but the good English air will blow any obnoxious smells away," she said wickedly.

"I'll be as fast as I can on the road, there's enough moon to light us," said Rupert, choosing to ignore her and climbing up onto the box. Instantly the horses responded to his sure touch and pulled together down the gravel drive and onto the highway. The moon shone faintly behind scudding clouds and windswept branches while Jacob's lantern bobbed like a leading star. The wind whipped some colour into her cheeks and Harriet revelled in the speed with which Rupert drove the barouche towards Durrington Hall. Feeling rather daring and alive, she only regretted she had no opportunity to quiz him about the shipwreck.

They pulled up only once in order that Harriet could confirm the direction. As a youth, Rupert had ridden to Durrington Hall across the fields and down country lanes and after some years absence now hesitated over which carriage road to take in the dark. Jacob could not read the sign posts so Harriet obliged. Within half an hour they had reached the beautiful Jacobean hall of red brick and tall oriel windows. The clock on the cupola above the stables showed they were not more than ten minutes behind their time.

A clutch of local worthies stood waiting in the long salon. Rupert stiffened, obviously not expecting the gallery of faces turned to meet him.

"I thought this was to be a private dinner," he murmured.

"You must sing for your supper, Mr Darville," whispered Harriet. "You cannot expect to return from foreign adventures and not entertain your neighbours. What ever would we have to talk about without visitors such as yourself?" The approach of Sir Charles and his wife put an end to their conversation and Harriet was gratified to see Rupert greet his hosts with all courtesy.

Harriet moved among the guests with ease, all her friends complimenting her on her appearance, but Rupert was reserved, his former shyness surfacing at the introductions. He asked after the Reverend Butterworth's insect hunting and was about to dip into conversation when Dr and Mrs Dalrymple were presented to him.

The bishop and his wife were on an annual tour of their Salisbury diocese. This year, the Butterworths were the recipients of their short visit and Lady Durrington had naturally included them in her in dinner invitation. The bishop offered Mr Darville his condolences and when Rupert's voyage was explained to him, began to enquire about the Missionary Societies in Africa.

Harriet came under Mrs Dalrymple's scrutiny. She remembered Lady Larkhill with approval. "Wasn't there another, pretty young woman as I recall? Fair? A cousin of yours perhaps, Miss Larkhill? Certainly not a sister. Your aunt brought her to tea once, a most modest and well-behaved young woman. She married well I believe?"

Harriet shot a nervous look at Rupert, who thankfully seemed oblivious to anything but his own conversation. "Unfortunately deceased ma'am, many years ago. We do not speak of her."

The Rector, who had never uttered a word to his superiors on the 'Darville debacle' as he privately termed it, jumped in with both feet. "Ah these young ladies, ma'am they grow up and fly the nest before you know it. I have reason to hope that Miss Larkhill will find a coop not far from home," he said archly.

"You are mistaken, Rector. I have no intention of leaving the manor at present," said Harriet amiably.

At that moment two new guests appeared at the end of the long gallery. The Wests, again in possession of Bourne Park, were an ill-suited couple and strangers to Rupert. Horace West, short, stout and with a weakness for lurid waistcoats, compensated for his lack of inches by arrogance acquired from five years ordering his plantations in Jamaica. In his eyes nothing was to be compared with the elegance of Kingston society, the flora and fauna of the colony and the beauty of the ladies of whatever colour. He said quite openly, and with sufficient frequency to humiliate his wife, that it was only Mrs West's ill-health which had induced him to leave the island. Many of his neighbours wished he had stayed there.

George Durrington took the first opportunity to abstract his old acquaintance from the other guests. "Glad to see you back safely, Darville. Have you come settle in Larkhill? Back to England, Home and Beauty, eh?" The two men shook hands heartily in remembrance of boyhood days.

"No, alas. I have commitments in London at the moment and my future is uncertain."

George immediately plunged into questions about the voyage and exploration. "Have you the sea in your veins after three years afloat? Would you go on another expedition? How I envy you to be fancy free – not that I'm-"

"I'm sorry to disappoint you George; it's not the voyaging I care for but the thrill of discovering a new land mass and all the mysteries it holds."

"The whole world seems adventuring these days," replied Lieutenant Durrington with a small sigh. "If it ain't the North-West passage then it's the Arctic – but I prefer warmer seas myself."

"I hear Sabine is getting up another expedition to Africa and the Americas to take measurements with his pendulums. Unfortunately, my father's death has made it too late for me to apply."

"Ah, yes – my condolences, it must be a sad time for your mother." As everyone knew it was not, Rupert merely gave a polite smile and began to ask his friend about his time with the West Africa Squadron, blockading the slave ships.

"It's the only thing that puts Mrs Dalrymple in amity with me," whispered George, indicating the bishop's wife. "My mother-in-law and she are great supporters of Wilberforce, though I read in the newspapers that he has another bee in his bonnet now."

"Supporting the queen you mean? A lost cause. The king will never share the throne with her. The Milan Commission's findings were pretty damning I understand, though public opinion is sadly divided between the government and the mob. London was in turmoil when I left."

Horace West bustled up and barged into the conversation. "Ah, the travelling fraternity all together eh? Darville, I'll wager you'll find England too dull to hold you. I can imagine how you must feel, being back in the provinces. Three months from now I'll lay a pony you'll be aboard some other ship heading for the tropics. Did you touch on Jamaica? Fascinating place, best island in the world. I'd be back there now if it weren't for my wife's health – sickly woman, fancies herself ill at the slightest whim. I understand yours was a French expedition? You cannot compare the murderous chaos of French colonies with the profitability and order of our English possessions."

Rupert turned civilly to the intruder. "The *Neptune* berthed in many places, though I regret our route did not take us to the Caribbean. I assume you are referring to the troubles in Haiti?"

"I thought Haiti had declared for Spain, now that Toussaint is dead?" said George.

"All the better, nothing good comes of dealing with the Frogs," replied Mr West puffing out his chest.

Rupert's eyes widened in deceptive innocence. "On the contrary I found the frogs very interesting."

West looked affronted but Rupert continued: "A noisy breed of amphibian that one can never escape.

You are undoubtedly aware that there are over a thousand species of frog in the Amazon basin: the horned frog which can grow to an immense size and is aggressively territorial and has a voracious appetite and there is the blue milk frog, quite tiny in comparison, sometimes called the golden eye frog. Also not to be despised is the deadly poison-dart frog so called because of the savages' use of their toxic secretions to poison the tips of blow darts." He paused. "These amphibians are small but vividly coloured so one can take evasive action if necessary."

Rupert looked pointedly at the waistcoat. Mr West flushed and moved away.

"A bit hard on the poor man, weren't you Darville?" said George secretly pleased.

"Nothing can forgive that purple and yellow stripped monstrosity, a species all of its own. But I beg your pardon George, I was rude to one of your mother-in-law's guests."

"No matter. She can't bear him. She only invited him because it would look bad if we didn't and he inveigled an invitation from my father because he knew you were coming. If I have to listen to that man's tales of crossing the Atlantic one more time I'll swing for him." He broke off. "But I see your interests have widened since Cambridge; I thought you were a mathematician then an astronomer, now I see you have become a naturalist."

"Having seen some of the world at last, I find there is nothing that does *not* interest me. We did make significant measurements regarding the earth's magnetism but it was the rest of the work that opened my eyes! I am the living example of 'travel broadens the mind'. Botany, geography, hydrography, meteorology, entomology geological collections, tribal customs – they were all covered by our expedition's remit and I found it *all* fascinating."

"Then before you disappear from Larkhill I must hear all about your discoveries," said George. "Tonight is not the time to do them justice when you have to do the civil to the county. Come over when you can and we'll play a game of billiards and have a good jaw. I have some specimens from Sierra Leone that might interest you. Ah, I see that dinner is served. Now who should be taking my step-mother in, you or the bishop?"

At dinner Lady Durrington would have seated Harriet next to Rupert but precedence still held sway and the wife of a bishop ranked far higher than the niece of an impoverished squire. She rejoiced in seeing the girl sparkle as of old but she was forced to seat her between George and Mr Carter.

Her own daughters were safely married: Lucy was long settled in her vicarage; Mary had found a wealthy widower with three children and moved to the midlands; Juliana was in a promising way with her first pregnancy. She felt a little guilty about Harriet's likely spinsterhood and wondered how true were the rumours of the curate's interest.

Sir Charles, at first alarmed that George had succumbed to the conventional charms of his pretty step-sister instead of Harriet's practical boldness, had to concede that his son's union was for the best. The Larkhills had fallen on hard times and, with the adoption of Young Clem, Harriet was no longer heiress to the manor lands, such as they were. He was content that George was settled at home and producing a family to continue the line.

The bishop said Grace and Lady Durrington, after a few words of appreciation, turned to Rupert. She was apprehensive about introducing s*ervice a la russ*e and said as a distraction: "Do explain what precisely *was* your role on this wonderful expedition, Mr Darville? Enlighten our ignorance."

Rupert put down the menu and replied: "One of the tasks set by the *Academie des sciences* was to take astronomical and mechanical measurements to establish the shape of the Earth."

"But it is round, surely everyone knows that," broke in Mr West shaking out his napkin.

"Not precisely round," said Rupert. "By measuring the length of various pendulums in different latitudes over time, one can calculate the 'oblateness' of the Earth." He looked into several blank faces. "I mean the degree to which the shape of the Earth departs from a perfect sphere."

"And why would one need to know such information Mr Darville?" continued Lady Durrington, signaling to the footman to bring forward the soup tureen. She had a shrewd idea of the answer; Lieutenant George had explained all about the race to find longitude, but being a good hostess she wished to open the conversation to others. Harriet, who had already heard Rupert's lengthy explanations, hoped he would recognise the limitations of the company and confine himself to the simplest of answers.

She was to be disappointed.

"First one must understand that if the Earth were perfectly spherical and homogeneous, then longitude at a point would be the angle between a vertical north-south plane through that point and the plane of the Paris meridian. Everywhere on Earth the vertical north-south plane would contain the Earth's axis. But the Earth is not homogenous, and has mountains, which have gravity and so can shift the vertical plane away from the Earth's axis.

The vertical north-south plane still intersects the plane of the Paris meridian at some angle; that angle is astronomical longitude, the longitude you calculate from star observations."

Harriet felt her embarrassment rise at Rupert's obtuseness. The guests turned their faces towards the soup tureen as it made its way around the table, relieved to have an excuse not to comment.

"George tells me that calculating longitude is a method for establishing one's position either east or west of a certain point for which one needs accurate observations and measurements," said his hostess brightly, picking up her spoon.

Rupert turned an angelic smile on her. "Quite so Lady Durrington. You have it exactly. We English of course would site the prime meridian at Greenwich."

"The safety of shipping, the certainty of trade should be every man's concern," said Mr West, wisely deciding not to denigrate the French again. "When I was sailing back from Kingston, the captain showed me the marine chronometer. He hadn't much faith in it. Kept wobbling about, he said, with the movement of the ship. It was only the ship's navigator and his sextant which kept us on course."

Harriet cast a speaking look at George who, already alert, began talking about Harrison's clocks. Mr Carter stepped in to extol the new generation of inventors and engineers who were modernising the world, his son Stanley included. Thankfully, the talk drifted into innocuous topics while the soup spoons clinked.

"How did you manage on ship's fare, Darville?" asked Sir Charles, when the fish course was presented.

"Badly, sir. I particularly missed the refinement of a good cook such as yours, Lady Durrington." Rupert nodded a compliment to his hostess. "This bill of fare promises a banquet."

She was gratified. Entertaining an earl's son, let alone a scientific prodigy, had its own demands. She hoped seven courses would be thought sufficient.

"But the wine on a French ship must have been of the top quality? And you stopped in French ports on the way. Damme if I don't think it very clever of you to have gone on a French expedition after all!" Sir Charles signalled to the butler to replenish various glasses.

"The French officials did not lack for home comforts and the Portuguese court had every luxury shipped over from Lisbon. What the natives ate varied from tribe to tribe and what was available."

"I thought they ate each other!" said Mr West looking around the table and laughing hugely at his own joke. "I'll wager you're glad not to have ended up in a pot like Captain Cook. In Jamaica-"

"I regret having to disappoint you, sir, but Captain Cook did not end up in a pot," replied Rupert.

Mr West had a thick skin and continued: "How did you manage the savages? On my plantations I have the strictest overseers to keep the beggars in line. I went nowhere without a gun."

"Surely not, on such a well-run property as your own," said Rupert smoothly. And then speaking to the table at large: "*The Neptune's* was a purely scientific expedition; we were observers, not administrators or traders."

"That won't hold! You've brought a negro home with you – a quadroon is he? I hope you can whip him into shape. In my experience they're all lazy, treacherous beggars - apart from the women of course. Jamaica has the finest mulatto women in the Caribbean. What did you make of the native women?"

"I made nothing of them at all," replied Rupert.

"What? No dusky beauties on these islands? We have plenty of creole women in Kingston who know how to sway their hips and entice a man. No little dalliance on the way?"

Mrs West looked down into her lap. The bishop looked frankly embarrassed.

Rupert looked up. "None sir, that the present company would care to hear about."

A trickle of confused conversation broke out until Mr Carter's strong voice broke through the awkwardness. "Forgive me Sir Charles for using this evening as an opportunity, but perhaps now is the time, here where we are among so many good friends, to make the announcement that I have decided to remove my family to London at the end of the summer".

There was an instant outcry of disbelief and disappointment and the remainder of the course was occupied by discussing the Carters' plans and reasons for moving to the metropolis, accompanied by continual expressions of regret from their neighbours.

Lady Durrington hoped they would have the pleasure of seeing Mr Darville take up residence in his own home again but Rupert would not be drawn.

By the time Sir Charles had carved the side of beef, Mr West had regained his nerve. "Speaking of London, Mr Darville, will you be attending the coronation?" he asked, hoping to show his deference to the aristocratic classes.

"I doubt it, sir."

"But, the new earl – surely he will attend in some capacity?"

"I believe my brother and my sister-in-law have been invited to the Abbey."

In his youth, the late Earl of Morna had been a friend of the Prince Regent who, in a moment of nostalgia and gratitude for best-forgotten favours, had included his former friend in the festivities. Unfortunately no one had told him that the third Earl had died and his son, bearing the same name as his father, was now holder of the title.

"And will the new countess be wearing the Darville emeralds?" asked Lady Durrington, picking up the conversation in fear of Mr West's blunderings and instead committing one of her own. "I remember your Mama wearing them to your nuptial ball in Quennell House. Such a beautiful set of gems, an ancient family heirloom, I collect and so appropriate for the occasion."

"I am afraid I have no idea of my sister-in-law's sartorial intentions," said Rupert and bent his head to his beef.

Lady Durrington was silenced but Rupert was kind and addressed his next remark to her in the friendliest way, though he felt as uncomfortable as she. Harriet could have wept for them both but was relieved that Rupert had passed it off with unconcern.

As a respite to his hostess Rupert turned to Mrs Dalrymple, though he was not called upon to say much as she was more of a preacher than her husband and also a good trencher woman. She would later complain of the new-fangled way of serving dinner. He allowed her to bring him up to date with the horrors of the Peterloo riot and the industrial unrest in the north. For a woman who had supported the anti-slave trade movement she had little sympathy for the labourers of her own country; any other type of reform smacked of radicalism. Rupert suspected that Mr Carter, who still kept an interest in his grandfather's mills would give a more rational account, but he was entertaining Harriet with his views on the future of steam carriages.

Harriet was interested in everything. She remembered reading about Mr Trevithick's 'Catch-Me-Who-Can' when she was a girl. The prototype steam locomotive had been put on display in London in 1808 and had caused a sensation.

"I cut the illustration out of the newspaper and my uncle was so angry with me – the paper belonged to Sir Charles of course, who was a veritable saint over my vandalism." Her faintly flushed cheeks and animation gave her an allure that had been absent for a long time. Rupert looked down the table and fleetingly wished she had been his dinner partner.

When the company gathered in the long gallery, Lady Durrington invited Harriet to play something on the new broadwood. Card tables had been set up but she knew that Harriet could not afford to gamble even for the lowest stakes, and the men were inclined to be extravagant after the port. She also knew they would be tempted to increase their usual stakes in an attempt to impress a member of the nobility.

Harriet begged to be excused because truthfully she was out of practise. Juliana, in her condition, was not pressed to exert herself.

"But you know my dear that you can come here and use our piano at any time you wish. I have told you so often," said Lady Durrington softly. "It would benefit the instrument to be played regularly."

"I thank you, ma'am, I *have* no time. And indeed I do not miss playing. Juliana has much the lighter touch. I was never a virtuoso at anything and much preferred dancing."

"Ah, we would have had a dance but for Mr Darville's being in mourning for the late earl," said Sir Charles leaning over the sofa back.

"I don't think they knew each other very well," said Harriet. "Mr Darville had not seen his father more than once in a dozen years, I understand."

"All the same, we can't expect a man to dance two weeks after putting his father in the earth."

"No," agreed Harriet. "It would not do. Perhaps Mr Darville would not be averse to playing for us; he is a very good musician, or so I remember. I think he may be in need of rescuing."

Lady Durrington rose to extricate Darville from the clutches of the bishop's wife who, believing that cards were the toys of the devil preferred to tackle Mr Darville on the vexed question of Sunday travel. It had been whispered that he was a free-thinker and this she would not tolerate.

Rupert listened to Mrs Dalrymple politely and then said: "The Anglican Church may deplore travel on the Lord's Day but would you have had the captain becalm his ship every Sunday? We would have been home a year later in that case. According to the bible, God sends the wind, would it not be a sin to squander it?" asked Rupert lightly. "Forgive me madam, I see our hostess approaching." He rose as Lady Durrington crossed the long gallery. Mrs Dalrymple wondered if she had just received a set-down except that Rupert Darville's manner had been polite in the extreme. A moment later she remembered that she had never liked the Darvilles.

Rupert's performance was masterly. The Beethoven sonata shook his audience out of their commonplace conversation and drew their attention to the far end of the gallery. Coffee cups were suspended in mid-air, cards were put down as Rupert's long, strong fingers raced over the keys like a ripple of lightning.

He seemed lost in the music, a slight frown between his brows, his broad shoulders moving with strength and confidence under his black coat.

Juliana, relaxing with her feet up on a sofa, whispered to her friend: "Mr Darville is very accomplished is he not?"

"Yes, he has always had a natural aptitude for playing the piano forte."

"And he has so distinguished an air. Who would have imagined that such an odd-looking boy would have become such a handsome man?"

Harriet frowned. "His mother might think him handsome." She considered him dispassionately. "Striking to some eyes certainly –- but he looks too much like a cat to be considered one of Lord Byron's heroes."

"Will he marry again, do you think?" asked Juliana, setting down her tea cup.

"I have no idea," said Harriet, without thinking at all.

"Does he ever mention Sylvia?"

"Never."

"Not even when he sees Young Clem, who is her image?"

"I wouldn't say her image – he has her eyes certainly, but there are few here who would remember Sylvia's features particularly." The Durringtons knew the family secret but Harriet was unhappy that Julia had broached the subject in such company. "I must say, Young Clem adores him," she added to lighten the moment.

"You adored Mr Darville when you were twelve," sighed Juliana, "and followed him around like a puppy. I used to be quite jealous of the time you spent together. And of course, he *is* one step closer to being an earl now," she giggled.

"Juliana! Shame on you for such impudence!" laughed Harriet. "The death of his father puts Mr Darville even further beyond *our* sphere of society. Besides, I am not twelve and have a deal more sense," said Harriet. "And you know *you* will always be my particular friend. Am I not to be the little one's godmother?" She laid her hand gently on Juliana's swelling stomach. The conversation ended with the music and appreciative applause.

******

As they left Durrington Hall, Harriet was thoughtful. Rupert's behaviour troubled her. She had expected him to be the centre of the party and enthral his neighbours with stories of his voyage and fabulous discoveries, but apart from his lecture at the dinner table he had been reserved when questioned.

While he was polite to Sir Charles and his lady and voluble when talking to George or the Reverend Butterworth, their own easy intercourse of the past week obviously did not extend to the remainder of the local gentry. Rupert may have been civil to the Carters but they were Darville tenants, and Mr Carter a sensible man.

Admittedly Horace West had been a nuisance, but she had overheard the cutting interchange and felt uncomfortable. More to be deplored was that timid Mrs West had also heard and been horribly embarrassed by her husband's humiliation. Harriet also suspected that Rupert had been dismissive of Mrs Dalrymple. Where was the man who happily entertained his young ward and sat patiently listening to Sir John's repetitive ramblings?

At the card table Rupert's calls had been abrupt. He did not join in the casual conversation, preferring to concentrate on his hand. Harriet was well aware that this was his usual mode of play but to an unfamiliar observer, Rupert's silences bordered on rudeness. The fact that he had consistently won had not endeared him to his fellow guests.

Harriet could not believe that Rupert was proud; being the son of an earl had never weighed with him in the past. That he was a man of consequence was evident by the general deference shown to him, but Harriet had assumed this was because of his superior learning and experience. His position in society had never mattered to her when she was a child and she was surprised to find that it was of importance to her neighbours.

They had not gone further than the end of the drive when Harriet put her head out from under the carriage hood and called Rupert to stop.

"What's amiss Harriet, have you forgotten something?" He brought the horses to a standstill and twisted around to speak to her.

She stepped swiftly down from the carriage before Rupert or Jacob could assist her. "No, no, but *do* allow me up beside you Rupert, and I can give directions far more easily than Jacob. I know the road pretty well and we would be home much sooner."

Rupert started to protest but Harriet only tugged at Jacob's sleeve and pointed to the open door of the barouche with an encouraging look. She took the lantern out of his hand. "Look how cold he is, poor thing. He's shivering already. Let him travel inside. I promise to change places before we reach Larkhill, so as not to shock Dunch's sensibilities."

Rupert, who did not want to keep his horses standing, abruptly agreed. "I know the way back perfectly Harriet, but you must keep the rug, I won't have you ill with a cold because of some misplaced philanthropy."

"I have my own reasons for wanting to change places," she said climbing up and arranging the rug around her shoulders.

"You wish the feminine satisfaction of talking about your neighbours without any danger of your excoriating comments reaching their ears," he said and set the barouche rolling again.

She propped the lantern pole against the front board. "True, but I would need another woman to *really* enjoy a comfortable coze. Men are most unsatisfactory gossips. *You,* naturally, are too high-minded to indulge in any scandal." And then she cringed at the thought of his past and cursed her wayward tongue.

"I trust you enjoyed the evening?" he said glancing at her. Jacob had lain down on the soft seat, curled up under his horse blanket and promptly gone to sleep.

Harriet, ever one to take the bull by the horns, said: "Yes, it was a delightful party for me, but I fear *you* did not enjoy the company."

"The Durringtons are splendid people," he said.

"Lady Durrington is a much underrated woman. She has coaxed Sir Charles out of his wigs and skirted coats, but I miss that tricorne hat of his. Do you remember it?"

Rupert was silent. Harriet decided to be more direct. "You did not seem to like Mr West."

"The man is a fool."

"But a harmless fool. I fear he felt quite snubbed when you corrected him about Captain Cook."

"Then the man is a bigger fool than I thought."

"He is used to being a big fish in a small pool. You deprived him of the chance to tell his grandchildren that he once dined with a man who nearly ended up in a cooking pot," she teased.

"I rest my case - when the truth is far more interesting. The customs of the Ombay tribe are quite savage enough but we were never in any danger of being eaten. Only an idiot would believe such fairy-tales."

"You tell them to Young Clem, he believes them. I suppose you are used to a much better society than Larkhill can provide," added Harriet wistfully.

"Clem is five years old and even he knows they are only stories. And I find there just as many fools in London and Paris as there are in the country. Apart from my colleagues in the field, who can possibly understand the complexities of my scientific research?"

"Does that release you from the obligation of trying to explain things, simply, to your fellow man?"

"I was not aware that I was supposed to be a schoolmaster," he replied coldly.

Harriet was about to reprove him for being so poker-backed when, for the first time, she became conscious of who he was and the differences between them.

She hesitated and Rupert said suddenly: "The truth is I do not like discussing my work with those who cannot appreciate it. I feel that to do so degrades it somehow. Three men on the voyage died in the pursuit of such knowledge. I would not cheapen the outcome. Since my return I have seen too many blank stares and too many people edge away when I begin to explain. They lionise me and then retreat in incomprehension. You saw what happened tonight at table. My mother tells me that I am a bore, therefore I would prefer to say nothing at all."

"What nonsense, you do not bore me – us – any of us at the manor. You explain things to me in the easiest of ways."

"You have a superior understanding Harriet, which I fear eludes the majority."

He shook the horses' reins briskly and encouraged them into a trot.

Harriet, not knowing how to continue, said no more. The realisation was growing upon her that she did not know Rupert Darville at all. Her childhood adoration had been bestowed on a gauche and earnest young scholar. Of his life with Sylvia in London and Paris she knew nothing, and her mind shied away from any discovery. Of his life as a world traveller she knew only what his rare letters had imparted: colourful accounts of natural discoveries and the practicalities of shipboard life. She knew nothing of his character as a man, beyond his affability while at the manor, and that she had witnessed for a mere ten days.

He glanced down at her solemn face again. "You did not play cards tonight," he said. "Do you dislike whist? Or have you inherited Sir John's disapproval of gaming?"

"I would say that I am indifferent rather than disapproving. Besides I have no money to waste, though I do miss a good game of chess. Sir John cannot-". She paused and began again. "Miss Humble and I know each other's moves so well that we no longer find it a stimulation to play against each other."

"Then, if you will allow me, I will challenge you to a game – tomorrow."

"Why, thank you, I would enjoy that," she smiled, feeling a little easier. They were silent for a moment until Harriet said: "Let us star gaze as we did when we were children – if you are certain you know the road back to Larkhill in this darkness."

"Have you no faith in my navigation, Miss Larkhill?"

"Certainly, but I have more faith in the horses who want to be snug in their nice warm stalls. They are like pigeons and 'home' towards the livery stable."

He was betrayed into a laugh. "You are very right. Now, look up and see if you can pick out the constellations of Taurus and Gemini."

"What ever happened to Mr Herschel's telescope?" she asked suddenly.

"I sold it."

"Such a magnificent instrument; I am surprised you could bring yourself to part with it." When no answer was forthcoming, she continued: "I can see Orion's belt," she said, leaning into him. Her hood brushed the capes at his shoulder.

"And there is Jupiter nearby. Do you see it?" he responded.

"Oh yes – the star that does not twinkle."

******

To everyone's approval, Mr Darville extended his visit Larkhill for another week, by the end of which time he had a fair idea of how things stood at the manor. He was saddened but did not see how he could redress the financial situation beyond being generous with his purse in the matter of gifts and treats. An academic life in London beckoned. The child was happy and could be left safely enough with the women. However, Rupert felt it his duty to make enquiries as to his ward's future.

Finding Harriet pouring over the tenancy agreements in the library one morning, he asked for a private word. She looked up with a welcoming smile, though her mind was elsewhere. Lady Day was but a week away and she dreaded the necessity of putting up the rents.

She had just spent a wearisome hour trying to explain to Sir John the benefit of buying one of the new threshing machines for Home Farm. Two years of good summers had reduced the price of grain and Sir Charles had encouraged her to make the most of the wheat harvest she had. The squire nodded and agreed with all she said but refused to invest a penny in cultivating the land or buying machinery. He would sign nothing.

She again stressed the disgraceful state of the shepherds' cottages and the need for fertilizer for the farm. He looked blank at all her suggestions and started to hum softly to himself. Harriet played her usual card of 'keeping the manor lands in good order for when Young Clem came of age'. Today, to her dismay, even this ploy failed.

"I won't be around to see it," said the squire querulously. "I'll be long dead. Let him make his own way. He may not *want* to be a farmer," he looked cunningly at her from under his beetle brows. "He may go for a soldier like his father." His gnarled hand shook as he dabbed his mouth. "When's Clement coming home?" he said, staring at her as though she were a stranger. "Where's Betsy? Where's my wife?"

"They'll be here soon Uncle John, soon." She gave up, saying briskly. "What would you like you do today? Dunch will be here presently with your shaving water and to help you dress. Do you wish Miss Humble to read *The Times* to you this morning? Sir Charles has sent it over." She stood up to ring the bell and when Dunch appeared to do his valeting duties, she retreated to the library and began to think very hard.

She could see she would have to write to Sir Hamish for advice and perhaps ask the new young doctor for another consultation, disastrous though the last visit had been. Sir Charles had been urging her to 'take steps' for the past twelvemonth. But she could not bring herself to admit that the squire was incapable of managing his affairs, though she had been running the estate single-handed for more than two years. She put her head in her hands. She felt she had failed, and was failing her beloved uncle now if she took legal steps to override his authority. She doubted she could keep the estate intact until Young Clem reached his majority. She could not see where it would all end.

When Rupert knocked and entered she felt she was coming out of another world.

"Have you no agent to do this work?" he asked surveying the pile of audit books and legal papers.

"Uncle John dismissed him two years ago; he was not trustworthy. But Sir Charles helps me enormously; if ever I have a problem I turn to him. And Brownrigg knows as much about this property as he does your own." Harriet did not want to discuss her gloomy future in the short time there remained of his visit.

"Yes," he said absently. "He is a good man to keeps matters straight for my mother, though he seems increasingly concerned by the low price of wool."

Harriet said nothing. This was the perennial anxiety underlying all her troubles. "How may I help you Rupert?" she said, pushing the documents to one side.

"I rather think *I* can help *you*, if you'll allow me." He pulled up a hard-backed chair and sat opposite her across the cluttered desk.

"I cannot thank you enough for how you have taken care of Young Clem over the past five years. He is a delightful child and I realise what time and effort you and everyone here have–"

"It is no effort at all," she interrupted in surprise. "He is Clement's son. We love him. We should be thanking you for bringing him to us. His arrival brought great to happiness to my aunt's last years and his existence here is keeping Sir John on this side of the grave." She looked at him directly. "He is a Larkhill and heir to the estate."

"Perhaps I put the matter clumsily. I hesitate to raise the matter - what I meant to ask is, what will happen to you, Harriet? Have you given no thought to your own future? Surely you cannot wish to devote your life to someone else's child?"

"Why not? Hundreds of women do." She sounded amused. "Look at Miss Humble; she has devoted herself to many. And," she added, "I consider Young Clem almost as my own."

"But at what cost to you? You're a young woman; you deserve to have an establishment of your own. What will happen to the boy if you marry?"

"That is extremely unlikely, though I do not entirely despair." The Reverend Cusworth's pitted face swam before her and was promptly dismissed.

Rupert did not catch the irony in her tone. "What nonsense! You are intelligent, well-educated, a lady and, if you permit me to say, quite - personable."

Harriet gasped and then said a trifle acidly: "It may have escaped your notice but there is a generation of 'quite personable' young women who can never hope to marry because their future spouses were slaughtered on the battlefields of Europe." As if she hadn't enough to contend with, for Rupert to appear out of the blue and throw her spinsterhood in her face. Her nerves were stretched by Sir John's intransigence or else she would never have betrayed herself so bitterly.

Rupert was chastened. "Harriet – forgive me. It was most impertinent, but I think of you almost as a sister, and want only the best for you. I feel – have always felt - some guilt about saddling you with, my - responsibilities. Have there been any 'difficulties' about the boy's – parentage?"

"No. Only the Durringtons know for certain who his mother was. Others may suspect, but any likeness to Sylvia can be put down to Clement blood. And it has been years since you left Larkhill; people have had other scandals to talk about. Do not worry about the child. The responsibility for Young Clem lies only with his family. I am his aunt. *You* are not family." And then could have bitten her tongue out.

"You are *not* his aunt, merely a first-cousin once removed. But I am the boy's guardian and must consider my duty towards him and his future."

"Sir John is his grandfather! You're not about to take Young Clem away are you?" she said in disbelief.

"No, no, nothing of the kind! Don't be a goose Harriet. But my bankers in London tell me that Sir John has not touched the interest accruing on Young Clem's trust fund; this really will not do."

"He is a very proud man," replied Harriet trying to get a grip on herself.

"But I cannot have my ward, or any of you, suffer because of his misplaced pride. When I left Young Clem with you five years ago I thought all the financial arrangements had been agreed. I left your uncle with a *carte blanche* to draw as much as he wanted whenever was necessary."

Harriet said nothing. As the squire had grown frailer he had grown more confused and stubborn. After unpleasant scenes with his agent the squire became even more paranoid about laying out money. Since his wife died he had turned into a miser, trusting no one, allowing Harriet barely enough housekeeping to feed them all. But the scene earlier that morning had been a turning point; Harriet knew she would have to act, however unpleasant the consequences.

"You must at least pay Miss Humble's salary out of the trust," Rupert continued. "And Annie's too. She told me that she had no idea where her wages vanished to."

Harriet stiffened. "It will be Quarter Day soon and Annie will receive her usual increase."

"You misunderstand me. I have no wish to vex you. Annie made no complaint; it was merely something she said in passing. She was more concerned about her future, I believe. I hear that she and Jem are to be married in the autumn?"

"At Michaelmas. We intend to renovate John Coachman's old quarters above the stables for them." Where she would find the money from she had no idea. She had not been able to bring herself to sell any of the old-fashioned jewellery that Aunt Betsy had left her, mainly because she didn't know whom to approach on the matter.

"Would you let me send a sum of money every month direct to you? For Young Clem's upkeep and your comfort?"

"Good God No! You cannot *keep* us! The whole neighbourhood would know in a moment. It would do an immense amount of harm to my reputation let alone my uncle's. He is still the squire here," she said.

"Then I must persuade him to draw on the interest from the trust, or allow me to do so, and if that means harassing him then I'm afraid I shall have to."

"No, no, Rupert," Harriet begged. "Let me see what I can do. He is a sick man, you can see that for yourself. I will admit I was thinking of consulting Sir Hamish over my difficulties, but you need not tease yourself with our affairs."

"I hope you do contact him, Harriet, and I will make it my business to speak to him when I return to London. Perhaps *he* can persuade your uncle to release what's owing to Young Clem. As one of the boy's guardians, it is my duty to oversee his welfare." There was a pause.

"And in two years' time we must consider his schooling. It grieves me to say this Harriet, but you must be aware that Sir John is in no fit mental state to handle his own affairs."

After a moment's silence, Harried asked: "*Could* you send us some of the money which is due to Clem?" A faint hope momentarily cheered her.

Rupert shrugged. "There must be some way around this impasse. I am equal guardian with your uncle and a joint trustee. The sale of your Aunt Amelia's house in Milsom Street did not bring a vast amount but the sum was well invested by McAllister, and Young Clem was supposed to have the benefit of the interest."

"But Uncle John would have to agree to your drawing the interest. I remember Mr Tamar coming down from London and explaining it all to us when my aunt and uncle adopted Young Clem."

"Yes, I have tried gently cajoling him but he will not agree to the release of a penny. I fear he did not follow all I was saying. He insisted that he has plenty of money for his grandson."

"He has. He no longer trusts banks nor will have anything to do with them. It's all in a locked chest under his bed."

Rupert looked startled. "I had no idea."

"I am forced to resort to the chest from time to time," she said without shame. She was rather relieved to share her secret. "Dunch gives my uncle a double brandy before putting him to bed and I take the key from around his neck while he is asleep."

Rupert's cat's eyes narrowed in disapproval. "Is that really necessary? Cannot you have the chest removed to your safe keeping?"

"And risk Sir John having another heart-attack? Thief I may have become, but murderer I won't be. Miss Humble knows exactly what the situation is and I make her witness and note down what I have taken."

"Oh Harriet, this is too much – to compromise yourself and involve the servants! It is the most reprehensible conduct!"

"Miss Humble is not a servant, she is a good friend to this family!" Harried flushed, knowing that, seen in this light, Rupert was correct.

"She is a paid dependant who may feel she has no choice but to assist you in your – methods, at what legal risk to herself I dare not say. You have been grossly at fault, Harriet. Goodness knows what Dunch thinks of all this."

"Dunch has been with this family for thirty years and is completely loyal. And when did you ever take notice of what servants think?" She was furious.

"When they are put in a position of superiority over us by our own thoughtless actions." He looked very angry.

"I take very little money," Harriet protested. "My uncle counts his treasure from time to time. However feeble his mind he can still reckon and knows roughly how much should be in the chest, which means I cannot take more than a handful of coins each month to pay the servants. I just pray that guineas remain legal tender for the foreseeable future."

"Dear God, this cannot continue! Perhaps we should call on the services of a physician."

"I have already tried. Dr Makepeace says there is nothing we can do, 'tis softening of the brain and damage from frequent little seizures. Uncle threatened him with his stick and forbade him the house."

"Then you must have your uncle declared *non compos mentis*," replied Rupert flatly.

"I cannot! Would you have me declare him a lunatic? Have a coroner's enquiry and expose all our business! And who will run the estate then? Strangers?"

"My dear girl, you must do something or you will never survive! The property is on the verge of bankruptcy now, by what Durrington tells me."

"You have been gossiping about us with Sir Charles?" asked Harriet, horrified.

"Of course I have discussed the situation with him! We are your friends! Durrington has a profound concern for your well-being, and he *is* godfather to Young Clem."

How dare Rupert sit there and lecture her when she had been doing her utmost for years to hold the estate together while he had swanned off around the world. Something must be done, but no one would suggest precisely what, or how, or offer to take the responsibility from her shoulders.

Harriet swallowed her rage. "I agree we must release the interest for Clem's sake, but the rest of our – difficulties need not concern you, Rupert. I will write to Sir Hamish and see what he advises about Sir John."

Taking her continued silence for dismissal, Rupert rose to his feet, saying stiffly that he had promised to ride over to make his farewells to Sir Charles and Lady Durrington, and bade her good morning.

Harriet waited until she heard Dunch show Mr Darville out whereupon she put her head down on her arms and fought back the sudden tears.

******

The following weeks were hard for Harriet. Although Rupert had promised to write, she was resigned to his becoming engrossed by his London life and scientific pursuits. She felt a door had closed. Young Clem missed the company of Jacob but was happy to resume visiting his old playmates at Home Farm. He was consoled by Captain Blood once more escaping his cage and finding his way to the kitchen to wreak havoc among the lentils.

Rupert's letters came rarely, consisting of accounts of his lectures and ambitions for the new Astronomical Society of London which absorbed most of his time. He did not mention friends or leisure pursuits but reading between the lines she guessed he was the man of the moment in scientific circles.

The death of the Corsican Monster in May caused a great flurry of relief even in Larkhill; Harriet's news of Young Clem and Captain Blood's mischief seemed very tame in comparison. Nevertheless, the mere act of writing to Rupert gave her a sense of connection with the outside world.

One unexpected surprise was a packet from Sir Hamish, enclosing fifty pounds in Bank of England notes, seemingly a dividend made on Young Clem's behalf by the trust. However sceptical she might be, Harriet chose to accept the windfall. More surprising was a short letter in Elspeth McAllister's hand inviting Miss Larkhill to stay with the family in London for a few weeks in July for the coronation celebrations.

"I cannot go! We'll be selling the spring lambs, cutting the hay, the harvest may be early, and there's the late shearing! I cannot leave my uncle, and what about Young Clem? And there is Juliana's baby to consider. I am far too busy! How could Sir Hamish think of it?" Harriet looked up from the letter in distress.

Miss Humble assumed her old role of governess. "Don't talk nonsense Miss Harriet. Of course you can go. You have neither made nor received visits from any of your friends for a twelvemonth. And you know you have longed to go to London all your life!"

It was true, there had been no exchange of visits with the distant Mary Denver or any of her school friends since Lady Larkhill's death.

Miss Humble decided to press her advantage. "Mr Trottman has been taking the lambs to market before you were born, Mr Browrigg will oversee the harvest as he usually does and Sir Charles is always excellent company for Sir John. As for Miss Juliana - Lady Durrington has produced three healthy children without your aid, so you may safely leave your friend in the hands of her own mother. Unless you think I am incapable of teaching Master Clement or supervising the household?"

"No, no, of course not – you know I didn't mean - but - but, think of the expense! The idea is out of the question!"

"There is no need to make a martyr of yourself; it is most unbecoming in a young lady. Consider, my dear, you would offend Lady McAllister greatly if you refused her invitation, particularly when Sir Hamish has been so kind to you. There are many advantages to a sojourn in London and who could forgo the opportunity of seeing his gracious majesty crowned? You would not wish to be thought disloyal!"

Harriet did not look convinced but her natural common sense resurfaced.

"The season would be drawing to a close of course, you would be in London merely a month for the festivities," continued Miss Humble. "But who knows what benefits may arise," she added carefully. "Even from such a short period."

"I would so like to go to London," admitted Harriet, her mind wandering over the prospect of historic buildings, famous churches, glittering theatres and the beau monde. Even a short stay would nourish her spirits for what promised to be lonely days ahead.

"Then do so. You may never have this opportunity again and the McAllisters are held in very high esteem in the best of circles."

Harriet came out of her reverie. "Who told you that?"

"Lady Durrington. Have you forgotten that Mr George has a friend who is now private secretary to one of the Civil Lords of the Admiralty and he says the government consults Sir Hamish on every point."

Harriet pulled a face. "I had no idea. But that does not mean that they go into society very much." She yearned to dance and go to parties.

"Exactly so, you will mix with the elite of the political world, which means fewer dresses to find – and those only of the more sober sort," returned Miss Humble in blissful ignorance but determined not to be thwarted.

"Clothes!" started Harriet in alarm. "I have not a thing to wear apart from the cherry stripe. I cannot go. Dear Miss Humble, you must see that the whole scheme is impossible!"

"If you will allow me to suggest: Mr Darville's gift of the shot silk would make a perfect ball gown and Lady Larkhill left trunks of excellent dresses which I know she would be happy to see remodelled for your use. She loved you dearly."

Harriet looked down doubtfully at the letter. "How I wish Aunt Betsy were here, she would know exactly what I should do," she said, clearing her throat.

"Lady Larkhill would have insisted that you go to London," responded Miss Humble firmly. We must speak to the Misses Williams before they become too busy with the Summer Ball. If you can bear to, perhaps we could go through Lady Larkhill's wardrobe? You know you have been meaning to do so for some while and it is more than a year since-"

"Yes, you are quite right," said Harriet with decision. "I can put it off no longer. It must be done at some time, and for what better reason. When Young Clem has finished his lessons, we will go to Lady Larkhill's bedroom and contrive what we may."

The afternoon proved surprisingly happy and productive.

Lady Larkhill's Indian cotton dresses had long been reused for the daughters of the house but Miss Humble was convinced that enough material remained to produce a passable London wardrobe for Harriet. A bonus was the discovery of a clutch of feathers, carefully put by in tissue paper.

"If they can be dyed, they are just the thing to perk up some of your bonnets," said Miss Humble. "It was you who persuaded your aunt to buy them for her turban, do you remember?"

Harriet had sudden recourse to her handkerchief and blew her nose. "Goodness, how the dust does affect one so," she sniffed, and then stuffing her handkerchief back in her pocket, continued to delve.

At the bottom of one trunk, Harriet came across Lady Larkhill's jewel box. The two women spread the trinkets out across the bed. There were not very many pieces and no family heirlooms to speak of. The squire had not been able to indulge his wife in her extravagant tastes in his later years.

"They are very old-fashioned," said Harriet doubtfully, looking at a parure of dull purple amethysts set in antique gold. She picked up a set of pale-blue topaz in heavy silver, badly in need of a clean. "I would not wear any of these and I should really keep them for Clem's bride."

"Lady Larkhill left her jewels to you, Harriet. She would like to see you wear them in town. Let them grace a fashionable London salon as she was never able to do."

"I thought of selling them," confessed Harriet, "but perhaps I should wear them just once and then ask Sir Hamish's advice about what to do. But these pearls," she said with delight, holding up a long rope of perfectly graded orbs, "I *must* keep for Young Clem's future wife. I remember Aunt Betsy wearing them, more than once."

Conscience satisfied, Harriet tumbled the jewellery back into the box and brushed aside the vexed question of stockings, gloves and accessories. She knew she would have to have recourse to Sir John's treasure chest, if only for the coach fare and pin money, but she was determined not to embroil Miss Humble in her larceny ever again. Rupert's comments still stung.

CHAPTER 2   LONDON

The journey to London was uncomfortable but uneventful. Harriet's neighbours had plied her with advice and warnings about the metropolis and the danger of coach travel with the result that she had sewn Aunt Betsy's jewels into her stays and suffered for her prudence. Common sense told her that highway robbery was rare in these days of better kept roads and toll gates, but the future of the manor lay in the gems stitched into her corset and she was not taking any chances.

Harriet peered out of the coach window with curiosity. Since they had passed the last turnpike at Hyde Park the buildings along the road had thickened, the pretty market gardens left behind. Beside her Annie pointed out the sights that she could remember, often in error and then finally giving up in bewilderment. "This be all new, Miss. It's all changed since I was here as a lady's maid to Miss Sylvia and I never went far from the hotel when I came back to London with Master Clem and Mr Darville. I don't know where we are!"

"No, of course not, how could you - that was all years ago. I never imagined there would be so much building works," said Harriet as another cart laden with dusty stone blocks trundled over the cobbles towards a half-finished square of elegant town houses. The streets were full of jostling vehicles of every kind. Harriet marvelled at an irate old dame with feathers poking out of the window of a sedan chair, haranguing an obstructive crossing sweeper. The smell wafting from a pie man's tray made her stomach gurgle. The noise of wheels and cries of the street hawkers, the stench of horse manure and garbage in the streets was stunning. Shoppers of every kind, elegant women, tall footmen in livery and uniformed soldiers crowded the pavements, brushing aside the beggars that trailed after them. Harriet thought she had never seen so many people. Bath was nothing to this.

With a blast on the horn the coach rolled under the arch of the Swan Inn in Fleet Street and the sweating horses came to a standstill on the cobbles. The passengers climbed stiffly down into a mêlée of people and boxes. Luggage was taken off the coach and more piles of boxes and baggage thrown onto the roof. Travellers clustered in greeting, said tearful farewells, called for ale or demanded a room and their servants.

A tall thin young man in sombre black stepped out of the crowd. The sandy quiff above a thin and intelligent countenance immediately stamped him as one of Sir Hamish's sons, the family likeness was unmistakeable. He raised a silver-topped cane.

"Miss Larkhill? Allow me to introduce myself. I'm William McAllister, at your service." Harriet nodded to Annie who busied herself rescuing their trunk and portmanteaux dropped unheedingly from the roof of the stage coach. "M'father sends his apologies, some crisis in Whitehall has detained him, but I am to take you home to m'mother. Let the boy see to your luggage." He snapped his fingers at one of the inn servants.

"How do you do, Mr McAllister. How lucky you were at liberty," said Harriet shaking hands. "Have you come straight from court?"

"They're in recess until September. I've chambers in Inner Temple," he said leading her towards a large hackney coach and tossing a coin to the porter. They threaded their way through the bales and crates cluttering the inn yard. "I've rooms there, convenient for the courts and the Fleet prison you know."

Harriet stored away this piece of information. She was eager to learn all she could about the metropolis, conscious she would be here for little more than a precious six weeks. Once inside the hackney coach, William made sharp enquiries about the journey and seemed disappointed at its uneventfulness.

"That stretch between Slough and Maidenhead is notorious for hold-ups. Three men were transported only last week for highway robbery on that road." Harriet looked taken aback. "Forgive me Miss Larkhill, I shouldn't talk of such things to a lady. Forget where I am some times. Trust I haven't frightened you?"

"No, no, not at all," said Harriet. "But the driver did spring his horses across Hounslow Heath," she continued in an effort to console him. "And at least one passenger was very afraid of being robbed." The amethysts dug into her ribs most uncomfortably.

"Quite right too. Not surprised. Wittlestone, that is Lord Wittlestone, was held at pistol point on the Oxford Road only last week. Robbed of all his gingerbread and his wife had the diamonds ripped from her ears. "

Harriet winced but thought the lady foolish for travelling openly in her finery. "Surely these highwaymen will be caught? The Bow Street officers-"

William shrugged. "Don't know if the Runners have any leads on this particular crew. The informers will need a lot of rhino before coughing up. There are gangs of these miscreants come to London for easy pickings at the coronation. Lord, you've never seen so many beggars in the Mall, all on the buzz – er, pickpocketing."

At that moment the cabman let out a shout and the hackney swerved round a towering barrow of fruit being trundled blindly through Covent Garden. Harriet leaned out of the window in excitement. A burst of profanity ensued and Harriet withdrew her head smartly.

"The jarvey certainly knows how to control his horses," she admired.

"Not a district for a lady," apologised Mr McAllister. "We'll soon be in Southampton Row." Harriet's attention was caught by an imposing building with Greek columns and an ornate balcony. "Oh, that must be the Theatre Royal," she looked to William for confirmation as they trotted up Drury Lane.

"M'mother will take you there I'm certain. Kean is back from America. He's in something called *De Montfort.* Doom and gloom and gothick nuns – written by a woman of course." His fingers drummed on his knee.

"A man wrote the *Duchess of Malfi* and what could be more horrid than that!" replied Harriet. But William was leaning out to direct the driver as they reached Bloomsbury. Russell Square was not yet one of the coveted addresses of the *haut ton* but it housed several eminent lawyers and bankers and suited the discreet streak in Sir Hamish's nature.

As the cab turned into the square, Harriet was heartened by the sight of the statue of the fifth Duke of Bedford. The famous agriculturalist stood with his hand on a plough, sheep at his feet, surrounded by four figures representing the seasons.

The hackney pulled up at a substantial house, one of a row of identical white and brown brick houses with tall sash windows, narrow balconies across the second storey and railings around the area. Above the wide front door swung an oil lamp. William leapt out and ran up the steps to rap loudly on the door with the head of his cane. Harriet found herself clutching her reticule in apprehension. She was not timid but Lady McAllister was an unknown quantity and she could not help but be anxious. Harriet would have been surprised to know that her hostess viewed her visitor's arrival with the same uncertainty.

Lady McAllister had uneasy memories of Sylvia and regarded the Bath McAllisters as an unfortunate connection - and this was another cousin of sorts, doubtless on the hunt for a husband. Why Sir Hamish had invited the girl she had not been able to discover, but she had dutifully written the letter at her husband's command. Consequently she held out only two fingers in greeting and felt justified that she had not sent her town carriage to meet Miss Larkhill, who looked no more than a governess in her country bonnet and plain coat. She was relieved to see that her visitor was no golden beauty likely to inflame the passions of her unmarried sons.

Elspeth McAllister was a tall gaunt woman with the same wispy sandy hair as her husband. She wore a *pince nez* over protuberant eyes and carried herself with an air of consequence. She dressed with propriety but in a way that suggested thrift more than fashion. Under her arm she carried a small white poodle ennobled by the name of Cicero.

A befrilled and embroidered white gauze cap bestowed even more height and presence. Harriet thought she looked like an aristocratic heron.

Sir Hamish had married wisely. His wife had impeccable antecedents and all the self-importance required to further her husband's ambitions. At the age of twenty-seven her lack of fortune had made her grateful for a proposal of marriage from this rising lawyer with Scottish roots similar to her own. She had regretted their move from the more fashionable Mount Street some years ago but one could not deny that the house in Russell Square was more spacious for a growing family and the rooms more suitable for entertaining. Although basically idle, she saw herself something of a hostess as well as being occupied with good works. To no one's surprise, Sir Hamish enhanced his reputation for omniscience by correctly predicting that the ever-expanding metropolis would soon catch up with them.

"Figgis will show you to your room and then you will join me in a dish of bohea in the drawing room," said Lady McAllister in cut-glass tones. "I always take tea at this hour."

"Thank you Lady McAllister, tea is exactly what I should wish for," said Harriet, following the butler up the stairs. William effaced himself, duty done.

There was no time to unstitch her stays in the narrow bedroom assigned to her at the back of the house; a white room with an air of a religious cell looking out over a mews. Annie was to be accommodated in the attics with the other maids. Harriet quickly made herself presentable and followed the waiting housemaid downstairs to the drawing room.

Lady McAllister was seated on the sofa in front of her Worcester tea service, Cicero on a cushion on his own chair. Next to Lady McAllister sat a tiny, dowdy woman, busy with some netting. This lady was an impoverished relative, invited to live with Lady McAllister as a companion. She was overborne by her employer and overawed by the world but never ceased to reiterate her gratitude.

"My cousin Miss Susan Finch," said Lady McAllister dismissively. "She will pour tea."

Harriet shook hands kindly with the little companion and took her place opposite the tea tray before looking about her. The furniture, not in the latest style, was nevertheless good and solid but the carpet looked a little tired. Piles of books and periodicals lay scattered about the occasional tables. Several rather dusty pieces of Meissen adorned the mantle over which hung a rather misty oil painting.

"I see you're admiring Sir Hamish's family seat, Miss Larkhill. That is Elrick Castle, in Aberdeenshire. It is by Mr David Wilkie – an early piece. Not his usual style of course but he is favoured by the Prince Regent, by the king I should say."

Harriet dutifully admired the pile, much in the French style of architecture with its pointed turrets and narrow towers. In the foreground, various gillies and villagers gloated over a slaughtered stag.

"We are part of the Clan Leslie," continued Lady McAllister. "My eldest son Angus is currently in residence at the castle with his family. He is laird in all but name. I myself am a Montagu on my mother's side." She took her cup wordlessly from the companion.

There followed a detailed account of the intricacies of the McAllister genealogy going back to King Malcom III. The Jacobite rebellions were conveniently omitted.

As a slightly dazed Harriet could supply no reciprocal family information she commented on the array of fine embroidery embellishing the furniture and enquired whether Miss Finch were the skilful needlewoman.

"Oh, dear, no," simpered Miss Finch. "Dear Lady McAllister is the talented progenitor of such works. I merely occupy myself with netting a few little items for Coram's Bazaar. One does one's best, you know, for the poor little orphans. As one who has been so kindly been given a home, I feel I should return such Christian generosity in any way I can," her soft voice fluttered on.

"Cousin Susan adopts lame ducks." Lady McAllister did not approve. "I hold these persons take advantage of her good nature. She has a young protégé at the moment. He used to be a Coram's boy. Last year it was a young seamstress and before that a chimneysweep, if I recollect."

Miss Finch did not raise her eyes from her work. Harriet noticed that her hands trembled.

Lady McAllister continued: "I have long been an advocate of the aphorism that 'God helps those that help themselves' and while I feel it is one's duty to help the innocent, once these children are out in the world I see no reason why we should continue to cosset them. We have, after all given, them sufficient grounding in education and Christian principles to make their own way. My own involvement in the Society for Promoting Christian Knowledge means that there are plenty of bibles and literature to keep them on the right path. There is no need to devote one's valuable free time to individual persons."

It was plain that this subject was a bone of contention between the two women. Harriet returned the conversation to embroidery.

She confessed that she had no such skill; the upkeep of the manor had taken all her time and she had not polished what few talents she had. Lady McAllister looked askance and could only hope that the young woman's formal education had not been so neglected. As the daughter of a noted Bluestocking, Lady McAllister supported a wide education for women. On being assured that Harriet was a voracious reader, her hostess recommended Hookham's library in Bond Street.

"You meet everyone there. Do you read poetry? Lady Jersey, one of my dearest friends, and I were at Mr Clare's house yesterday – John Clare, the poet? Rather a strange person, but very sensible of the honour bestowed on him by the world. You may not be aware that he has recently brought out *The Village Minstrel;* not quite so beautiful a collection in my opinion as his poems of a rural life which were lauded by everyone. However, he gave me a signed copy of his new book, though I fear, for all his talent, I will forever regard him as the peasant poet. Perhaps you have not heard of him in Wiltshire?"

"We are not *quite* so out of the way in Larkhill, ma'am. A neighbour, Lady Durrington, very kindly lent me a copy of Mr Clare's works. I found the observations of nature very exact and although the gentleman feels deeply for the changing countryside he seems not to be overly sentimental, which is so refreshing."

As Lady McAllister had not yet read the poet's new book which was perched on the pile of improving tomes scattered artlessly around her drawing room, she abandoned the topic.

"I read extensively. Mr Scott's novels, of course, cannot be praised highly enough. Have you read *Kenilworth*?" She was mollified to hear that Harriet had not. "Biographies and history are to be encouraged and I recommend newspapers and political pamphlets, Miss Larkhill. Sir Hamish is much caught up in the question of the Malt Tax and I like to keep abreast of his work. My son William brings me a copy of Hansard whenever he can."

Harriet said all that was necessary. Another rather strained pause followed until Harriet, wishing to discuss the nub of her visit, enquired about the arrangements for viewing the coronation.

Lady McAllister obliged. "Sir William has obtained seats in one of the stands along the processional way. There will be a large party of us but we shall have a perfect view of the whole event. His Majesty is to cross from Westminster Hall to the abbey for the coronation and back again for the state banquet; His Majesty will pass directly in front of us."

"I assumed you and Sir Hamish would be attending the banquet," said Harriet innocently.

"I fear it is for gentlemen only; the ladies will be spectators in the galleries," replied Lady McAllister side-stepping the question.

"How unfair! And how dull it will be for the gentlemen without any female company!"

Lady McAllister privately agreed but did not think it suitable for a countrified young woman to voice such criticism of her betters.

"The company will be of the most select: peers of the realm, foreign royalty, ambassadors. I must console myself that only the presence of so many persons of consequence from the Continent – many of whom are known to me personally - means that His Majesty's truest supporters will be neglected in the hour of his greatest triumph."

"Ah," said Harriet correctly interpreting this to mean that commoners such as the McAllisters had not been included on the invitation list.

"Naturally we have been invited to the Devonshires' ball," continued Lady McAllister. "That is where the most select of society will be found; I have obtained an invitation for you, Miss Larkhill." She paused here to allow such condescension to impress her young guest.

As Harriet merely thanked her politely, Lady McAllister continued in frostier tones: "You will understand, I'm sure, that you cannot hope for Almack's vouchers in the short time you are with us, even under my aegis. The Marchioness of Londonderry is one of my dearest friends. The rooms will be crowded with all the foreign dignitaries – and these days I never attend myself."

Having no daughters to launch on society and two independent sons, Lady McAllister rarely made use of the entrée she had to the *ton's* most exclusive Wednesday balls and marriage mart. She was not going to bestir herself for this country nobody.

Harriet swallowed her disappointment. "I had no expectation of such an honour. I have come mainly to see the capital, and of course His Majesty." She hoped this didn't make the monarch sound like one of Rupert's exotic animals.

Eventually Harriet was dismissed to her room and bidden to rest until dinner at seven o'clock. She was met by a smug-looking Annie. "They've got offices, Miss, at the end of the passage. You crank a handle and a great woosh of water comes in."

"Oh, how perfect! Do show me! What it is to have modern comforts," she sighed when shown the porcelain bowl boxed in a closet. If Harriet could keep the roof on Larkhill Manor it was as much as she could hope for. Such modern luxuries as a water closet could not be thought of.

"There's a well in the garden, Miss, but the water do taste different from home."

"I suspect we shall find a lot of things different from life at Larkhill."

"And my lady's maid says that Lady McAllister has her morning chocolate in bed and dun't get up until ten o'clock – and you can do the same if you want, Miss."

Harriet, who was used to rising early, was not certain if she wanted this luxury but only said: "Then we will follow Lady McAllister's lead if she so wishes it and be fashionably lazy. But we must unpack, Annie, quickly, and see if there is anything that hasn't been crushed beyond wear and is suitable for dinner this evening. And I must unstitch the jewels from my stays."

"Don't you worry, Miss. I've already set a flat-iron on the coals in the kitchen. Cook says they don't dress when 'tis just the family for dinner."

Harriet wisely decided that what the McAllisters thought of as informal dress would not be her own. She chose her wardrobe accordingly. The cherry stripe would do as no one in this family had seen it before. Annie wound her mistress's plaits up into an elaborate knot and fastened a large oval locket around Harriet's neck.

"First impressions are so important," said Harriet, surveying herself in the pier glass. "Not the shawl, Annie, it is so hot in London, and then we shall brave the McAllisters."

Somewhere below, the dinner gong boomed. Harriet took a breath and entered the drawing room with a smile. Sir Hamish greeted his visitor with affection, taking his wife somewhat by surprise. "Ah, my dear Harriet! Welcome. You have grown into quite the young lady, I see. And you have realised your dream at last. You were always a child who knew her own mind." He bent over her hand with old-fashioned courtesy.

"My dream, Sir Hamish? What do you know of my dreams?" she asked roguishly. William looked interested as his father generally knew what he was about.

"I distinctly remember, when you were twelve years old, you said that you dreamed of going to London."

"And you promised that I would," said Harriet in delight. "I had quite forgotten. How kind of you to think of me after all this time. You cannot know how welcome this visit is to me."

"A man of honour never forgets his promises," said the diplomat. "And I felt I owed you something. Not quite the three hundred pounds you were dunning me for at the time – but a reward, of sorts."

"Three hundred pounds?" exclaimed his wife.

"Harriet had been playing pirates and found a treasure. She came to me and said that even pirates were allowed a share of the booty and that the government should give her a reward."

"What impertinence from one so young! How singular! I had no idea that little girls were mercenary," said the mother of three well-heeled sons.

Harriet turned to her hostess. "I can only agree, Lady McAllister; it was quite shocking of me! I have been told I was a wild child, but it was all for the manor, I assure you. And Sir Hamish *did* send Uncle John a very generous draft on the Bank of England." Harriet looked gratefully up at her host.

"Plus a promise that you would have your reward if ever you came to London."

"Coming to London *is* my reward! To see His Majesty crowned and be so much at the centre of things. What stories I will have to tell them when I go home!"

This led to a discussion of Larkhill news, lightly touched upon as no one else present knew those spoken of. Harriet noticed that Sir Hamish's hair was greyer and that despite his gentle teasing there was a strained look about his countenance. She enquired about his new position.

"Instead of spies I now catch agitators; it's pretty much the same," he said languidly. "So Harriet, be warned, no 'adventures' while you are with us. There promises to be enough upheaval in the capital without you adding to it."

Lady McAllister and Miss Finch looked shocked at Sir Hamish's levity.

"But you yourself said I had grown into a young lady," Harriet laughed. "I am merely a spectator of life in the metropolis. I cannot fall into mischief in a few weeks."

"How I would like to believe that," he smiled thinly. "Are you still as observant as you were as a child? If so, perhaps I *should* recruit you into the Home Office."

"I notice that you have cleverly diverted me from my original enquiry as to your work," she smiled back. "But I promise you I will investigate only the splendid buildings and monuments in my guide book."

Sir Hamish McAllister had moved on from foreign affairs. His duties under Lord Bathurst had led him into the maelstrom of the Congress of Vienna in 1815 at the end of the French wars. As a reward for his legal and diplomatic work with Lord Castlereagh and the triumph of the treaty he had been knighted and invited to become a senior legal counsel to the Prime Minister, Lord Liverpool.

If Sir Hamish had hoped for a less stressful career in peacetime he was disappointed. He no longer took on any private legal work as growing radicalism, Free Trade, the Corn Law unrest, emerging cries for Catholic emancipation were but a few of the problems requiring his incisive brain and discreet advice at the Home Department.

When colleagues asked why he did not enter politics himself, he merely smiled and said it was enough to have his son in Parliament. He had bought his second son William a safe seat and in exchange received grass-roots knowledge of the mood of the Commons plus a rising young criminal barrister at his command.

"William will escort you Harriet, if you want to see the sights," he said. "The courts are in recess. The devil makes work, you know, and there's no one more idle than my second son. You might teach him something of the more salubrious side of the capital – it will be such a novelty for him."

Lady McAllister's eyes bulged at this foolish notion.

"I can't help it, father, if my calling takes me into the seedier parts of London."

"I've never known a man enjoy his work so much," replied his father smoothly. "In my day, clients came to me. I didn't go in search of them around the slums of Porridge Island."

"Unfortunately William cannot frank your letters for you, Miss Larkhill, the House is not sitting, or won't be after the tenth," said Lady McAllister. "Miss Finch will take your letters to the post office, just leave them in the post bag on the hall table."

"Do you ride, Miss McAllister?" asked William in an effort to put himself in a better light.

"Indifferently, I'm afraid. I am much more comfortable with a gig or light chaise."

"Then would you care to accompany me in my curricle in the park tomorrow? I have the sweetest pair of ponies that a lady like yourself might care to drive, under supervision, of course. Midday is the fashionable hour. You will meet everyone in the Row."

"*I* will take Miss Larkhill out in the carriage, William. I have several errands to do and it will be an opportunity to show our guest the better parts of London. She wishes to visit Hookham's. There is no need to trouble yourself," said his mother in a tone that would not be denied.

At that moment the drawing room door opened to admit a huge square young man with a shock of rich auburn hair.

"Andrew, you are late. I have had dinner put back this quarter of an hour," said Lady McAllister. "Let me make you known to our guest. Miss Larkhill, this is our youngest son, Andrew, secretary to Lord Glynn of the East India Office."

The young bear bowed over Harriet's hand, murmured all that was required in a surprisingly soft and gentle voice and presented her with an open smile of welcome.

"Forgive me Mama, everyone, the traffic in the City is appalling. Some poor fellow was crushed by a dray in Threadneedle Street." He looked upset.

"We do not wish to hear of such incidents before going into dinner, Andrew. It quite destroys my appetite. Figgis, you may serve. William you may take Cousin Susan in."

"Am I your punishment for being late, sir?" said Harriet with a twinkle as Andrew offered her his arm.

"I would be late every evening if I thought I would always have such a charming dinner partner, Miss Larkhill."

Dinner was light and elegant, to which Harriet did much justice being used to country meal times. She made no effort to ingratiate herself with the young men but spoke only to ask intelligent questions of her host and give modest replies. Lady McAllister was gratified to see the girl treat Sir Hamish with the deference due to a man of his position. The young lady's dress was simple and Lady McAllister approved of Harriet's girlish adornments and classical braids. Elspeth McAllister found her hostility fading as she watched Harriet deftly peel and quarter a dessert pear, yet she had no intention of trying to foist the girl on the *ton*. Harriet was determined to be pleased and in doing so pleased those about her.

Later, in the drawing room, Lady McAllister took up her embroidery while Miss Finch disappeared into a corner with a candle and her netting. The gentlemen occupied themselves with various books and periodicals. Harriet begged leave to write a letter to Miss Humble apprising her governess of her safe arrival. Andrew furnished her with quill and paper from the study and brought a branch of candles to the rosewood table in the window. "The sun will soon have set completely but the gas lighter will not be round for another hour," he said lighting the candles from another taper. He retired to a chair near the empty fireplace and picked up a book.

"There was another burglary, father, did you read of it in *The Times?*" said William to the room at large, bringing his head out of the newspaper. "A reward of £100 is bein' offered by a Sir M—B-- of H--- in Bucks. Here for the coronation. Must be old Sir Mortimer Bulliphant, his daughter is to be one of the herb women in the procession. Had all his plate stolen, it says. Well, everyone knows he would never travel without it, so serves him right! He'll never get it back for that paltry sum."

"One can only hope that the gentleman is insured but I doubt whether his policy covers him for theft when the goods are off the premises," said Sir Hamish, dredging up some lawyerly interest. "I assume he was staying with his daughter?"

"In Berkley Square. The charlies have no leads – but then they never do! Best lock up your opals Mama and have James stand guard."

Harriet put down her pen and looked to her host. "Which reminds me, Sir Hamish, may I trouble you to keep my jewel box in your safe? I dare not have the Larkhill fortune going astray."

"Certainly my dear. I had no idea there *were* any jewels – of any value."

"No, there is none of any note. The settings are old fashioned, though I believe some of the stones are good. Lady Larkhill left them to me and I need your advice on the matter."

"Do you wish to have them re-set? Rundell and Bridge are the people to go to."

"The Regent's own jeweller, Miss Larkhill," explained Lady McAllister, pricking up her ears. "Lady Hartford had the prettiest set of aquamarines from them a week ago."

Harriet continued in reply to Sir Hamish's question. "Aunt Betsy, I know, would want me to dispose of them for the good of the manor and Young Clem. Perhaps I should have them cleaned. Of course I could always pawn them," added Harriet suddenly. "And if my fortunes changed, then I could always buy them back," she finished happily.

Sir Hamish smiled and wondered why he had not invited Harriet to London sooner.

"But what of your own jewellery?" asked Lady McAllister, disliking the mercantile tone of the conversation.

"Let me reassure you ma'am, no one would wish to steal *them*. They are quite valueless - apart from sentiment beyond price." Harriet's hand went to her neckline.

"Nevertheless, when you are not wearing them abroad, we will put them in the strongbox in my study Harriet," said Sir Hamish.

"Sir Hamish tells me you are an orphan. Did you know your mother, Miss Larkhill?" continued his wife. She needed to be clear on the girl's antecedents.

"No, nor my father, Sir John's brother. They died of the cholera when I was two years of age, but pray do not think it a sad story. I have no recollection of either parent and could have wished for no more loving family that my Aunt and Uncle Larkhill and my cousins."

From her dark corner Miss Finch gave an audible sigh of sympathy.

"But who were your mother's people?" asked Lady McAllister trying to place Harriet in her correct social sphere. The girl was obviously gently bred; before dinner there had been talk of a governess and the bishop's wife, and she knew all about Larkhill Manor. Sir Hamish steepled his fingers and waited, a glint of interest in his eye.

Harriet hesitated. It was not a subject she had ever thought about much and certainly not discussed beyond the family, but conscious that Lady McAllister had taken her blindly into her home at Sir Hamish's instigation, she replied: "Lady Larkhill told me that my mother was from Kent. An Emily Beaumont–"

"Beaumont?" said Andrew, looking up from his book. "That's the name of the Nabob."

"Andrew," chided his father gently, surprised at his placid son's interruption. "Please forgive him, Miss Larkhill. My son believes that the whole world revolves around the East India Company. Beaumont is a common enough name."

"I would not say it is a *common* name, Norman French I believe," said Lady McAllister and proceeded to recall the finest families with that appellation; she prided herself on a thorough knowledge of *Burke's Peerage*. When she eventually paused in enumerating her own connections, Harriet turned to Andrew and continued.

"My parents died in Ceylon, of cholera. My father went out with the first governor there. I believe my mother's family never forgave him for taking his bride with him. After they died I was sent home in the charge of a clergyman and his wife of the Baptist Missionary Society. I was only two years old at the time. But pray, who is the Nabob?"

"Perhaps you have a relative called Philipp Beaumont?" asked Andrew, closing his book and coming to sit beside her.

"I have no relatives at all, as far as I know. Uncle John gave me this locket on my twenty-first birthday. It has the silhouette of my mother on one side and of my father on the other," she said peering down at it. "I believe the Beaumont family are all dead now. Or so Sir John gave me to understand."

"Then I beg your pardon, Miss Larkhill, I did not mean to distress you. I only regret that Mr Philipp Beaumont does not have the good fortune to be related to you."

Harriet smiled at such a pretty compliment. "I am not the least distressed, Mr McAllister. My parents' life must be a sad story, but as I did not suffer in any way, I cannot claim any sympathy. But, please, do enlighten me as to this gentleman."

Andrew, nothing loath to talk about a subject dear to his heart, said: "Mr Beaumont made his fortune in silk and has lately come to town with his daughter. They normally live in Paris. Miss Beaumont is being educated in a convent there. Her father has hired a villa in Dulwich for the season. Lord Glynn, my superior, knows them well."

Sir Hamish and his wife exchanged glances. They had agreed that young Andrew had developed an interest in Miss Beaumont, who had substantial expectations. Lady McAllister chose to overlook how the Beaumont fortune had been made; times were changing and shy Philippa would be a malleable daughter-in-law. The young man had not yet spoken to them of his sentiments but all the signs were there.

"You will meet this gentleman and his daughter in a day or two, Harriet. They are asked to my wife's musical supper party. A small affair to introduce you to our particular friends," said Sir Hamish. He turned to his wife. "Have you invited Madame de Lessups, my dear?"

"Of course," she returned a little stiffly. "I cannot see why Mr Beaumont and his daughter cannot be invited alone; it will be a private supper. And of course Marguerite will bring her unspeakable nephew."

"Beaumont would not bring his daughter without Madame. Have the Darvilles accepted?" Sir Hamish continued.

"Naturally." Lady McAllister was slightly piqued. She knew Sophia Darville, but they were not intimates. She found Rupert entirely presentable if somewhat dour and Lord Patrick hearty to the point of frivolity. She had heard that the new earl was something of a lackwit and his wife, rumoured to be a Dublin barmaid, was kept well out of sight. Nevertheless, an earl, however impoverished and slow was not to be totally despised. "I believe you know the family Miss Larkhill?"

"I am acquainted with the dowager countess and R-- Mr Rupert Darville, they are old friends from Wiltshire. I have not had the honour of meeting any other member of the family," Harriet said, glad to claim someone as her own. "I assume the dowager countess is in town for the coronation?"

Lady McAllister could supply society details. "She is to accompany the new earl to the abbey but not to the banquet afterwards. His wife is expecting to be confined shortly and will not leave Ireland, though the best *accoucheurs* are to be had in London."

Sir Hamish continued in a warning vein: "I fear an evening of music may be too much for the earl, my dear; Morna's powers of concentration are not strong. I have no doubt he will slide away after supper."

"And then go on to some hell," said William not looking up from the *Police Gazette*.

"Is the earl a gamester?" asked Harriet in surprise.

"Dice and horses, so I hear. He can count up to twelve and manage the colours of the silks," said William. "God forbid he would try to add up a hand of cards. *Rupert* Darville on the other hand-"

"William, I will not have you disparage our guests," interrupted his mother. "At least the earl does not lay vulgar bets in the book at Whites."

"What do you know of such matters, Mama?" said William, startled.

She applied herself assiduously to her needle, unwilling to expose her middle son's recent foolishness in front of Harriet.

Harriet tactfully ignored this interchange. She looked forward to seeing Rupert and it had been some years since she had spoken to the dowager countess. The hapless Viscount Ardal and his dreadful wife had always been a source of speculation in Larkhill, and now that he had been elevated to the peerage and was invited to the coronation, her friends at home expected her to return with a detailed account of the new Earl of Morna.

Sir Hamish continued: "I met Lord Patrick in White's the other day. He says they're in a tight squeeze in the Albany. Rupert's instruments and books take all the space; he's given up his rooms in Brook Street to his mother and brother."

"Lord Patrick is the uncle, I collect?" asked Harriet. "Cannot the Darvilles go to an hotel?" She knew that the Darville's town house had been sold long ago.

"I'm told by a reliable source that there's not a room to be had for money or influence, Miss Larkhill. I was informed that visitors were sleeping head to toe in the Clarendon," twittered Miss Finch, naming one of the most exclusive hotels in London.

"The whole of Europe has come with their entourages and goodness knows what other riff-raff besides," sniffed Lady McAllister.

"A worry for you, father," said William putting his newspaper aside. "I presume the Guards will be lining the streets next Thursday s'ennight and your agents have smoked out any revolutionaries?"

"Sidmouth has the matter well in hand," said Sir Hamish dismissively. "Bye the bye Elspeth, the Castlereaghs have promised to look in on your musical soirée before going onto Carlton House."

"The Londonderrys, my dear," corrected his wife. She turned to Harriet. "The viscount succeeded to his father's title in April, but my husband cannot shake himself of referring to the marquess by his former title – they are such *old* friends."

"There Harriet, you will meet two Irish earls in one evening, that will be something to tell Larkhill," said Sir Hamish nodding to her letter.

******

Harriet was grateful for the cup of warm chocolate brought to her at nine o'clock by Annie. She had slept badly, unused to the sounds and the lights of the city.

Despite William's warnings to keep her window closed against intruders and the foul night air, Harriet could not bear to be shut in. After hours of tossing she succumbed and drew the heavy curtains against the gas lamps around the square and irregular chime of church clocks, with the consequence that she slept late.

Lady McAllister was waiting for her in the drawing room. One look at Harriet's walking dress, though acceptable, confirmed that she had a provincial on her hands, but she assumed that Sir Hamish did not wish her to bankroll Harriet for the short time the girl was with them. For a moment Lady McAllister felt a twinge of regret; she had never dressed a daughter, but her innate indolence and thrift soon caused her to dismiss the idea.

"We will go to Grafton House this morning. I am in need of embroidery silks and Cousin Susan enjoys plain sewing. Wilding and Kent's have cambric at a most reasonable price."

Miss Finch nodded shyly. "I sew handkerchiefs for the servants, Miss Larkhill, little Christmas boxes that I flatter myself they appreciate; in token of their many kindnesses to me."

"How thoughtful. I find one can never have too many handkerchiefs."

Lady McAllister examined Harriet's walking dress. "How unfortunate there will be no time to enlarge your wardrobe while you are here but you may like to purchase some fabric to take home with you. I have been told they have watered poplin at only five shillings a yard."

"Thank you ma'am but my London dresses will last me all my days in Wiltshire," returned Harriet without rancour.

"As you wish," said Lady McAllister picking up her gloves. "But come along; we are late as it is and the crowds will be insufferable."

Lady McAllister's town carriage deposited the three ladies on the corner of Grafton Street and New Bond Street where Lady McAllister sallied in and demanded to be shown every bolt of cambric in the shop. Miss Finch, relegated to dumb on-looker, dutifully accepted three yards of the cheapest. After twenty minutes of peering at the colours through her *pince nez,* Lady McAllister purchased one skein of embroidery silk. Harriet was happy to stroll about, arms behind her back looking up at this Aladdin's cave of buttons, beads and huge bales of cloth from all over the world. The squire's guineas weighed heavily in her reticule and she was tempted to buy. Being familiar with the bazaars in Salisbury and Bath, she had no fear of the crowds but longed for a friend to talk to. Miss Finch was busy by her employer's side and seemed too timid to voice an opinion of her own.

On an impulse of goodwill at a successful morning Lady McAllister purchased a lurid green fan and two pairs of cheap silk stockings, which she pronounced a bargain.

"You may have one pair Miss Larkhill, I suspect they will not last more than a few weeks at that price but they will suffice for your visit. My goodness, is that the time!" Lady McAllister looked at the fob watch at her waist and addressed her coachman: "It is gone noon already. Pole, Hyde Park! At once!" There was no time to stop at Hookham's library.

Rotten Row was noisy with elegant carriages and thoroughbred horses carrying the cream of society. There was much nodding and bowing of heads as Lady McAllister's carriage joined the throng. While dipping her head at various crested barouches and fashionable phaetons she favoured her young guest with an account of the illustrious personages in the slowly moving cavalcade. When this palled, little Miss Finch, sitting opposite, added her breathless mite.

Eventually Lady McAllister's coach drew rein at the rails on the south carriage drive. The footman was instructed to take Cicero for his walk. My lady sat her in her chariot like Boadicea waiting for homage; this was obviously her favoured spot for meeting her friends. At the sight of a particular group of horsemen approaching, she sighed with satisfaction and closed her parasol. Obediently, one rider on a strong-looking chestnut broke away and approached the carriage at a leisurely pace. Lady McAllister removed her *pince nez*.

The rider was a large gentleman, in his late thirties, round-faced and loose-limbed, of a build that would be prey to overweight in later years; he needed a big mount to carry him even now and schooled him well. The gentleman's lapels were rounded and the coat cut loosely to his figure, his riding boots gleamed and in his buttonhole he wore an exotic orchid. He was smiling pleasantly as he approached the carriage, touching the brim of his tall hat. He ignored the companion and looked at Harriet. He assessed her and dismissed her at a glance; Lady McAllister took all his attention.

"Good day Lord Everard. How fortunate I have seen you; I have been positively mobbed by so many people in the park today. You will forgive my detaining you, but would you be free to come to us after the coronation? A light supper, nothing more, among a few old friends. My sons are getting up a party to go to the Fête in Hyde Park in the evening; I wanted to be certain that we will at least have the pleasure of *your* company on coronation day, unless of course you will be dining with the Great Ones?"

"After the king's banquet I doubt if I'll be dining anywhere ma'am. Goodness knows what time that will end. If I had my wish I would take to my bed but duty calls. I fear I must decline your kind invitation; I am summoned to Carlton House in the company of the Duke of York."

Lady McAllister suppressed a sigh. "Of course, it was too much to hope. Sir Hamish has secured a number of seats in the processional stand but I hoped you would be able to tell us personally about the illustrious figures in the coronation procession and the ceremonies in the Abbey. Will we see you at the Duke of Devonshire's ball?"

"I hope to avail myself of that pleasure."

"Splendid! We shall *all* benefit from your company. Miss Larkhill is up from Wiltshire on her first visit to town and knows nothing of society." Introductions were at last made which left neither party any the wiser and Lady McAllister continued. "I myself will know most of those in the procession, but you, who have the ear of His Majesty, can enlighten us as to the origin of the costumes and ornaments."

"Of course, ma'am, it will be my pleasure. A lady of such discernment will appreciate the prodigious effort His Majesty has gone to in devising the occasion. I understand Sir Hamish's party will be quite extensive?"

"My sons of course. The Darvilles and the Beaumonts - and some others."

Harriet's lips twitched at her hostess's dismissive tone.

"How typical of your generosity ma'am. I wish I could be a simple spectator instead of being in the Abbey tricked out in velvet and ermine on a hot summer's day. And may I say how well that bronze silk becomes you. I am overwhelmed that you have heeded my advice and abandoned the blue – a rather cold colour I think, for one of your warm temperament."

Lady McAllister simpered a little while Harriet studiously admired a dashing couple cantering down the strand.

"My dear sir, what a wicked flatterer you are! To think I knew your mother! But we ladies depend on your eye for fashion. If the queen *does* dare to put in an appearance I wonder what she will be wearing."

"Widow's weeds, if she had her way," replied Lord Everard leaning down in deepening tones. "But do not breathe a word, ma'am, or I may end up in the Tower."

"Lord Everard, you are outrageous!" laughed Lady McAllister, treasuring up this *bon mot* to relate to her intimates.

"I hope I will have the pleasure of seeing you before the nineteenth? At the opera or the play perhaps?"

"My mantelpiece is quite thick with invitations! We will be having our own musical soiree tomorrow."

"Ah, I regret that I am engaged elsewhere, but I look forward to a happy meeting soon. If you will forgive me, ladies, but I see my friends are waiting for me. *A la prochaine!*" With another touch of his hat he wheeled his horse and trotted briskly after his companions.

Lady McAllister's triumph led her into mild indiscretion. "Dear Stephen. Charming, charming man," she sighed. "What address." She lowered her voice. "You must understand, Miss Larkhill, that Lord Everard is a great favourite, not to be crossed in any way – it would be social death. He is only a baron of course but of *such* a distinguished family, his mother was a de Montmorency; he is related to absolutely everyone. Did you see who was with him, on the bay? Mr Greville, recently made Clerk to the Council. The Grevilles are connected to us through the Montagues."

Harriet looked suitably impressed; she had never seen a man who had 'kissed hands' with royalty before. "I gather Lord Everard is what is called a tulip of fashion? A dandy?" she enquired, thinking of the orchid.

"Good Heavens, No! Never a Dandy! They are quite out of style nowadays – all frills and flounces and paint. No, Lord Everard *sets* the fashion. He is everything that is discretion and good taste. He advised me on the decoration of my drawing room when we first moved in to Russell Square. Lady Glynn is quite envious of my decorated cornices." She looked pensively after the retreating figure. "I wonder who will be invited to the reception at Carlton House. Poor man, he will have such a wearisome time with all those German Arch-duchesses. *I* enjoyed my time in Vienna but one cannot expect a gentleman of his exquisite sensibility to feel the same."

"And he is not coming to your party?"

"Alas, no. It will be a small select affair and one has to engage Lord Everard quite a month in advance. Everyone wants him. He is in constant demand in London when he is released from any royal obligations at Oatlands. Now we must be getting home. Where is Edward with dear Cicero? I have to attend to my arrangements for tomorrow."

"May I be of any help, Lady McAllister?"

Her hostess looked at her in surprise. "Miss Finch does all that is required." She turned to her cousin. "Susan? Could you make use of Miss Larkhill, to arrange the flowers perhaps?"

The little companion twittered her thanks and managed to convey that Miss Larkhill's so kind assistance would not be necessary.

"Ah, here is Edward with Cicero at last." She gathered the dog into her arms and prodded the coachman in the back with the tip of her parasol. "Drive on Pole, we are done here."

******

The afternoon was spent in making calls and leaving cards. Miss Finch was left to supervise the expected deliveries for the musical soirée the following day.

Lady McAllister preferred to mix with the wives of politicians and men of influence where Sir Hamish's writ ran strong. Harriet spoke little but observed everything in the fashionable houses they visited. The daughters were confident young women who had benefitted from a good education and travel and, this year, from the influx of foreign suitors. They generously welcomed Harriet into their circle; countrified Miss Larkhill was seen as no rival especially at the tail end of the London season. They were especially welcomed at the bustling house of the Cholmondleys, Elspeth's 'dearest friends'.

Mrs Cholmondley apologised for having to miss the McAllisters' musical evening; an elderly relative was due to arrive the following day for the coronation and they could not abandon their unexpected visitor so soon. Arrangements were made for Lady McAllister's guest to take tea with the younger Cholmondleys at Gunter's. Bertie Cholmondley, a fox-hunting young gentleman, was usually a reluctant chaperone to his sister Anne and her not-quite-committed beau; Miss Larkhill would make an unexceptional fourth. Bertie was partly reconciled to his brotherly duties by the sight of Harriet's cheerful face.

The dominant subject of conversation was Queen Caroline's outrageous behaviour. The previous year the king had made strenuous efforts to have his marriage dissolved and his wife barred from the throne because of her supposed adultery. The scandal had rocked Europe. So far, the king had managed only to have his wife's name omitted from the prayer book liturgy.

"And what would dear Maria think of all this?" sighed old Lady Winstan waggling her ear trumpet.

Lady McAllister had no sympathy for Roman Catholics but the sisterhood of abandoned women softened her attitude to Mrs Fitzherbert. "At sixty-five I would think she would be glad to be out of it all."

"Maria Fitzherbert was the best thing that happened to the prince – until that Frances Seymour got her claws into him." The old lady came from a less mealy-mouthed generation.

"You know perfectly well Prince George, the king I mean, had to get married, Mama. Lady Hertford had nothing to do with it," shouted her long-suffering daughter. "His Highness had to marry for an heir and before Parliament would pay off his debts."

"He was married to Maria Fitzherbert right and tight enough," grumbled the old lady. "And now we've got no heir at all!"

"Do you wonder I am so anxious to have Anne settled," whispered Mrs Cholmondley. "I cannot tell you the number of young men who have fled before Mama's outrageous pronouncements!"

Lady McAllister smiled thinly.

"I have great hopes for Anne but nothing is finally settled, so I will say no more." Mrs Cholmondley gave a sorrowful glance at her aged mother-in-law. "How I envy you, Elspeth, to have no daughters to worry you."

"I flatter myself that my sons will not behave foolishly or forget what they owe to the family name," replied Lady McAllister blandly. Nevertheless, she would not encourage them to loiter about the house during Harriet's visit. Thank goodness William had his own rooms in the Inns of Court and Andrew worked long hours in the City.

CHAPTER 3   THE MUSIC PARTY

After an aimless morning and meagre luncheon the following day, Harriet heard more sounds of activity below but Annie informed her that Lady McAllister had taken to her bed to gather her strength for the evening's exigencies and Miss Larkhill was bidden to do likewise.

"I cannot sleep in the middle of the afternoon!" protested Harriet. "What lazy hours we are expected to keep in London! Come Annie, I must have some exercise. Where is that guide book Lieutenant George gave me? This is just such an opportunity for exploring."

Twenty minutes later Harriet, with Annie in her wake, asked a disapproving Figgis to procure her a hackney for Westminster Abbey, "For we shall never be able to see inside on the big day."

The great gothic edifice was noisy with the sound of workmen hammering. Harriet marvelled at the wonderful fan vaulting in the Henry VII chapel, stood in reverence in front of the relics of Edward the Confessor and thrilled at the tomb of Geoffrey Chaucer. She read extensively from Lieutenant George's guide book until Annie's eyes glazed over.

The two adventurers returned sated by their excursion. "Goodness, I had no idea there were so many tombs," said Harriet. Annie hurriedly shook out a smart robe of cream satin decorated with green French knots while Harriet fell on the light supper that was sent up to her room at six o'clock. The gentlemen would dine at their clubs.

At eight o'clock, Harriet was the first to enter the drawing room. The last of the evening sun streamed across the carpet making the candles in the sconces and chandeliers dull in the twilight. The piano stood invitingly open with a music stand nearby. Rows of gilt chairs, hired for the occasion, were ranged around the piano.

The young gentlemen came downstairs. Andrew looked splendid in a moss green coat and high and complicated cravat. He carried his violin case in one hand. William had thrown off his workaday black for an exuberant mulberry swallow-tail and an orchid in his buttonhole. Both men wore buff-coloured pantaloons giving Harriet hope that the evening was not to be as formal as she had feared. The men were discussing the latest *on-dits* of the town.

"Dauntsey's just back from France. Brummell's in a bad way, I hear. The Drury-Lane ague is making his hair fall out."

At the sight of Harriet, Andrew squeezed his brother's elbow. "Hush, William! My compliments, Miss Larkhill, what a charming gown."

"Thank you Mr McAllister. But as to Mr Brummell, I am not shocked, sir, just regretful that I will not be able to see the gentleman now that he has left London. How sad that he has fallen on such hard times. Was he really as influential as they say?"

"More influential than he should be according to m'father. But we have Stephen Everard now to tell us what is all the crack," replied William.

An hour later Lady McAllister's drawing room was humming. Harriet was introduced to two members of parliament, Lord and Lady Glynn, a barrister colleague of William's carrying a flute, and a selection of her hostess's 'dearest friends' and their musical progeny. Harriet felt quite stimulated at being in such company, especially when shaking hands with Sir Thomas Lawrence, their neighbour from Number 65. As a protégé of the McAllisters, the guests treated Harriet civilly; beyond that, her own good manners and sunny interest ensured their goodwill. She was soon enjoying herself hugely, with the added relief that her costume did not look out of place.

However, Lady Bixby, all a-glitter in figured satin put her down as a country cousin and wondered whether Miss Finch were being put out to grass at last. Barbara Bixby was a scatterbrained woman of indeterminate years and girlish tastes, the perfect foil to Elspeth McAllister. They had been to school together and, inexplicable as their friends found it, had remained close. Tonight Barbara Bixby had come without her husband – a martyr to the gout - but chattered to anyone who would listen and there was plenty to talk about.

The ever-changing account of Queen Caroline's attempts to be recognised by her husband filled all the newspapers and every social gathering. Harriet found herself in a group of disputatious gentlemen and listened intently until moved to say: "Surely the queen does not expect to be reconciled after the revelations of the trial?" Then, slightly embarrassed by the sound of her own voice, added diffidently: "I beg your pardon, I should say 'enquiry'."

"Just so, Miss Larkhill, the 'queen's business' was merely a debate in the Lords," said the judicial Sir Hamish, whose grey hairs stemmed from the nightmare of constitutional politics the previous year. He knew the conflict was not yet over and the coronation only a few weeks away.

"The Lords would have given the king his divorce, only the narrowness of the majority prevented the Pains and Penalties Bill from being presented to the Commons. What a coward Liverpool was! What a fight it would have been!" exclaimed William with relish.

Mortimer Shawcross, M.P., a round and rosy-faced widower in his late forties, who was wise in the ways of the House, said sharply: "The government would have lost heavily had we presented the Bill to the Commons and we would have had a revolution on our hands! You more than most, young man, must be aware of the risk! Lord Liverpool was right to withdraw the Bill!"

Sir Hamish murmured to his son: "As a lawyer, William, you should know never to take on a fight one cannot win."

Their exchange was interrupted by Figgis announcing the Beaumont party. All eyes turned to the door; the merchant's *ménage* was something of a curiosity.

Mr Philipp Beaumont was slight and wiry as a greyhound with sharp darting eyes. His sunburned face was, as ever, unsmiling. Dressed in a well-cut coat with a large ruby pin in his cravat, he took in the whole room at a glance. As if to make up for her escort's severity, Madame de Lessups, petite, vivid in dark blue silk and sapphires, her black hair swept up under a cap of blonde lace that proclaimed her the widow, greeted everyone with smiles. Behind them came Captain Valentine in the red coat of the Bengal Native Infantry. He stopped on the threshold, well aware that he was the most handsome man in the room. Lazy-lidded with a thin dark line of moustache above a sensual mouth, he made several hearts flutter. Ushered between them stood Philippa, a tall, slight, painfully shy girl of seventeen in pale muslins and a spangled gauze shawl draped over her thin elbows. Her wispy ash-blond hair was scraped up on top of her head with tendrils falling in ringlets either side of her oval face.

Andrew hovered purposefully and then led Miss Beaumont away to the window. The girl cast an anxious glance at Madame de Lessups who gave a nod of permission and turned to her hostess apologising profusely for her nephew's presence. "He declares himself such a music-lover and would not hear of missing your delightful soirée this evening. As a penance you must ask him to sing, Lady McAllister."

Valentine bowed over Lady McAllister's hand saying: "Your musical evenings, ma'am, are renowned even among barbarians like myself. You will be kind and not turn away a rough soldier like me."

William snorted in derision. Lady McAllister, too well-bred to show her annoyance, merely stared behind her *pince nez* and handed the young man over to one of her dearest friends whose daughter blushed a deep scarlet.

Mr Beaumont was frowning; Lady McAllister's notions of a small private party obviously did not chime with his own.

He had come merely to examine this connection of the McAllisters who might prove to be a suitable companion for his daughter while she remained in London. If he could not snatch a word with the girl herself in this mêlée, he would have to trust to Marguerite's judgement. Sir Hamish had made this suggestion in his usual elliptical way, partly for Harriet's sake and knowing that any proximity with the family would bring Miss Beaumont further into Andrew's orbit. But Beaumont was no fool and while he was willing to consider a young friend for his daughter he did not wish to encourage suitors. Yet any diversion from Captain Valentine would be preferable.

He was distracted by Sir Hamish who pressed a glass of champagne into his hand and enquired for the latest news of Stamford Raffles and Singapore.

William, now standing beside Harriet said under his breath: "If Andrew can win the Nabob round and cut out the captain, then he is made for life. He looks to have caught the girl already and she's not yet made her first appearance. "

"Is Mr Beaumont so *very* rich?" asked Harriet.

"He's certainly 'shaken the pagoda tree' and I know he hasn't retired from trade, no matter what m'mother says. He's in the City at least three times a week. I've seen him m'self in the coffee houses, in Tom's mostly. He *enjoys* makin' money."

"How satisfying to know that the gentleman is so good at it."

"Good is not the word I would have applied to 'Bengal' Beaumont", he replied mysteriously. "Successful certainly and good for Andrew, if he can marry the daughter."

Harriet, who knew none of the parties well enough to comment, asked: "And who precisely is Madame de Lessups? And the dashing captain?"

"Stay away from Valentine, Miss Larkhill. The man's a bad lot, a nephew of hers on leave from India. He's rapidly becoming a four-bottle man. Beaumont only tolerates him for the widow's sake. She's the relict of the Collector of Ranjipur. They say he left her very plump in the pocket. She has a snug little house in Curzon Street and an *appartement* in Paris. She's seen everywhere. The quality of those sapphires beats Lady Conyngham's into a cocked hat - and at least they're *hers*," he added.

Harriet demanded an explanation. William, delighted to shock and inform, related what all the town knew. "Rumour has it that Lady Conyngham, the king's mistress y'know, is walkin' round with half the crown jewels on her head, includin' an enormous sapphire that was said to belong to the Stuarts."

"How very uncomfortable for her," murmured Harriet.

"Deuced comfortable for all her family – they all live in clover in Marlborough Row. The Conyngham woman will go too far one of these days. There was such a kick-up when she tried to put her man into some bishopric. I believe the cleric had been her boy's tutor. M'father had a devil of a time calming Lord Liverpool – the Prime Minister has the right of appointment of course - and then Liverpool had to satisfy the king. What a to-do! Some compromise was reached and face saved but the king will hold it against Liverpool, I'll wager. To think a woman like that can upset a government and she's not a whit better looking than the widow."

"Indeed, Madame de Lessups is lovely." Harriet studied the lady. Two dark brows flared over a heart-shaped face and her lips were carmine red in a complexion of milk. "Is she a particular friend of the Beaumonts?" asked Harriet carefully.

William hesitated. To his disappointment Miss Larkhill had not blinked when he had referred to the royal mistress but a *chère amie* in his mother's drawing room may be a step too far. "I believe Mr Beaumont and the lady have an understanding. She and her late husband were friendly with the Beaumonts in India. Bets are being laid in the clubs that they will marry." He hurried on as though on dangerous ground. "They need to be riveted soon so they can fire the daughter off into society next year. Unless of course the widow succeeds in snaring the girl for her nephew first."

William did the lady an injustice. Madame de Lessups disapproved of her nephew's wastrel life as much as Mr Beaumont did, but she did not wish to disown Valentine completely. The young soldier would be returning to India in a few weeks, to what fate she did not know. She also hoped that if the captain's flirtation took place under her eye, Philippa would come to no harm and may gain in womanly confidence.

If Elspeth McAllister accepted Madame de Lessups under her roof then not a scintilla of suspicion could be thrown on the lady's reputation, even though the nephew was frowned upon. This was sophisticated London where discretion was all. Harriet stared at Captain Valentine, a lock of raven hair falling over an arched brow as he leaned over a young lady with more *decollatage* than was seemly. Harriet felt a little frisson of excitement. She had never met a 'wicked' man before.

The footmen circulated with champagne flutes. Sir Hamish knew when to be extravagant even if his wife was parsimonious. William tossed his glass off in two mouthfuls and went off in search of more.

"Miss Larkhill?" A hard voice accosted her. She turned to find Mr Beaumont at her elbow. "What do you think of all this, eh?" indicating the gathering with his wine glass. For a slight man he exuded power.

"The company, sir? I find it very stimulating to be among such learned and worldly people – yourself included."

"You like such evenings? Music and talk and politics?" he frowned.

She opened her brown eyes wide. "Oh yes, indeed! Larkhill, where I live in Wiltshire, can provide any amount of entertainment," she explained, "but I confess we are somewhat limited in our society and are absorbed by the affairs of the county. Tonight is a refreshing change for me. However, I daresay London is but Larkhill writ large with its same scandals and concerns," she laughed.

"You have been out a great while I believe?"

Harriet was somewhat taken aback but replied politely. "Since I was seventeen. Family circumstances made it imperative that I take my place in the adult world."

"What circumstances?"

Harriet stared openly and then realised the question had some purpose behind it. "My uncle and aunt, with whom I live, were taken ill and the management of the manor fell on my shoulders."

Beaumont pursed his lips. "Have you no other family?" Harriet bridled at his impertinence. Beaumont shifted a little. "Forgive me, Miss Larkhill, I have been told I have no society manners, but I would not want *my* daughter to bear such heavy burdens so soon. She is still a child."

She followed Mr Beaumont's gaze and took up his thoughts somewhat diffidently. "Miss Beaumont will flourish under the right care, sir. A gradual taste of society under her friends' protection is, I think, a far kinder way to launch a young woman into the world, than a sudden immersion into the *ton*. I can appreciate your apprehension – and Miss Beaumont's, though I have not the pleasure of her acquaintance."

"Mmph. How long will you be staying with the McAllisters?"

"Until the coronation and then perhaps another fortnight. There is so much to do and see. I mean to take advantage of my visit. *You* are a world traveller, I understand, so must have a unique perspective on the attractions of the capital as compared with all the other cities you have seen." She looked at him expectantly.

"As you say Miss Larkhill, Lahore is but London writ small – unless one immerses oneself in the native culture, which I would not recommend any European to do."

"But I hope to take home a good impression of London. I have already visited the Abbey. The workmen were starting to put up the banners and decorations for the great day. It will be a wonderful spectacle."

"Some pantomime that the king has thought up no doubt! Do you not think it a waste of money Miss Larkhill; two hundred and forty thousand pounds, when one considers the state of the nation?"

"I regret I have not all the facts and figures, sir, and I am not well-informed enough to comment on the state of the nation. You would need to speak to Sir Hamish for that. But I would hazard that the expense of the coronation is a matter for parliament to decide. And the town is certainly full of foreigners – I saw myself today – which must bring in a lot of money and the goodwill engendered by the coronation must surely help stabilise the nation in these troubled times - and enhance trade?"

Beaumont sucked in the corners of his mouth. "We can only hope that you are correct Miss Larkhill." Harriet felt she had been too outspoken and subsided into maidenly silence.

"Have you tickets for Almack's?" Beaumont asked abruptly.

"Alas, No. Lady McAllister does not sponsor me for such a short visit, so I must forgo any hopes of making a dash in polite society," she said lightly.

"Do you wish to?"

Harriet held on to her manners. "I am not so naive as to believe I could," she said with a slight laugh. "Although I would like to mix with the cream of the *ton* while I am here and impress my neighbours when I go home, I will be content to see all the sights and be in *interesting* society like this," she indicated Lady McAllister's guests. "However, I understand that the Castlereaghs – I mean Londonderrys - are to make an appearance this evening. Perhaps I should do something *dazzling* and gain the marchioness's approval."

He frowned at her. "I trust you are far too sensible a young lady to attempt any such thing, Miss Larkhill."

Harriet felt herself snubbed and was relieved when Lord Glynn approached intent on discussing some matter of import tax with the Nabob. Beaumont eventually moved away, a little clearer in his mind as to the suitability of Miss Larkhill as a companion for his daughter.

"Been discussin' the Rajah's rubies?" said William, popping up again like a jack-in-the-box. "That looks like one of the beauties in his cravat!"

"The Rajah's rubies? No, not at all; the king's rubies maybe. Mr Beaumont is very direct but not very forthcoming. Why, what are the Rajah's rubies?"

"A mystery," he said in aweful tones. "No one has ever seen them, but they are said to be cursed. Stolen from a rajah's treasury during the Mughal Wars in the sixteen hundreds, and have brought bad luck to every owner since then."

"You delight in talking nonsense, Mr McAllister. How can you possibly know this if no one has ever seen them?"

"I can assure you it is true! Valentine, spoke of them over cards one evening. He swears the Nabob has this fortune in rubies stashed away somewhere. He's even got some monstrous Indian warrior as a body guard. Stands to reason the old man's brought the stones to London."

"Why should that be so? Miss Beaumont cannot wear them until she enters society, and rubies would not suit her at all; she is far too fair and delicate."

"Perhaps they're intended as a wedding present for the widow," he suggested with raised eyebrows. "Or a gift for His Majesty."

"Hardly, if they are reputed to be cursed! Has Captain Valentine ever seen these rubies?"

"He says not, but I think he's playing a close game. He was a trifle – disguised - at the time. A not infrequent event."

"I think he is making game of *you,* Mr McAllister. And you should not cast such aspersions on a gentleman's reputation."

"You cannot be taken in by a handsome face in a uniform, Miss Larkhill," said William looking piqued.

"No, certainly not. But neither am beguiled by nursery stories."

The Darville party was the last to arrive. Three tall men in mourning and the angular figure of the dowager countess entered the McAllister's drawing room. The new earl was a heavy man with a vacant face and lank hair; it was said he looked very like his late father. He had no social address and rarely smiled or spoke beyond a grunt. Lord Patrick, for all his twenty years seniority was a far more imposing figure.

Rupert, looking sleek and enigmatic, saw Harriet across the room among a group of chattering young ladies. He thought she looked happy but oddly in the wrong place. He gave her a brief nod before being taken away by Lady McAllister to meet the other guests.

Rupert had expected the McAllisters' invitation but was surprised at his mother's ready acquiescence to the idea. He had been responsible for Sir Hamish inviting Harriet to London when searching for something to brighten his young friend's life. Her outburst in the library at Larkhill had stayed with him. He had not truly expected Sir Hamish to take up this suggestion but found himself gratified when Harriet's letter arrived full of excitement and London plans.

"Ah, Miss Larkhill," said the dowager countess, descending upon Harriet. "All well at home I presume? I trust the squire is still with us? I could not come to Lady Larkhill's funeral; I was engaged to hunt with the Belvoir. Elisabeth will be sorely missed," she said thus disposing of a neighbour of thirty years.

Harriet allowed herself to be led to a distant sofa. She looked at her old acquaintance. To her surprise the dowager countess had not weathered well. Her face was still ruddy from a life-time of hunting the shires but she had lost the robustness that had overawed so many of her contemporaries. The once tight dark curls were white and sparse and there was a drawn look about her sharp face. Only the eccentricity of her dress - Harriet thought she glimpsed riding boots under the Countess's faded skirt and outmoded bodice - distracted from the hollowness of her cheeks.

In her turn Lady Darville took out her lorgnette and scrutinised Harriet without a blush. "You have grown into a sensible-looking young woman. Rupert was right. Certainly not a slave to fashion I see. You might get a husband yet, while you are here. I presume that is why you have come to town? Is Lady McAllister to launch you on the *ton*?"

"I was invited by Sir Hamish to witness the coronation. I am certain that Lady McAllister has no interest in what befalls me now or in the future - as long as it does not involve one of her sons," said Harriet with a dry smile.

The dowager countess let out a snort. "You always were a sharp child. Have you seen much of *my* son?" she added abruptly.

"Rupert?" said Harriet in surprise. "Good gracious, no. I arrived only two days ago. I could not expect the honour of a visit so soon; Mr Darville has so many calls on his time. I am delighted to see *you* here this evening, Countess."

"To be sure, Elspeth McAllister is no particular friend of mine but Lord Patrick and Sir Hamish are old cronies. I don't object to musical parties; we must be thankful it is not one of her literary evenings full of poets and puns and would-be-wits." She squared her shoulders and turned back to Harriet to say: "My son says he had a letter from you. He even cut a committee meeting of some learned society to be here; you are favoured." She looked across at Rupert who was talking to Mr Beaumont. "It would do you both good to go about together."

Before Harriet could voice her surprise, Lady McAllister called the room to order and, after the expected modest disclaimer, induced one of the young ladies to attempt a Haydn sonata.

As soon as the applause died away, the dowager countess was about to take up her subject again when Captain Valentine and another blushing belle were invited to perform. They sang a mournful love duet, much to the alarm of at least three mothers in the room. Several more guests produced sheet music and the music flowed on. Harriet admired the accomplishments of these sophisticates, regretting the sale of the Larkhill piano.

When Lady McAllister announced a short interval the dowager countess turned again to Harriet, only to be interrupted by Madame de Lessups with shy Miss Beaumont at her elbow. "Lady Darville, Miss Larkhill. May I make Miss Philippa Beaumont properly known to you? Philippa is new to London, as Lady McAllister says *you* are Miss Larkhill. I'm sure you two young ladies will have many first impressions to exchange."

Harriet obediently rose and held out her hand to Miss Beaumont. Whereupon Marguerite de Lessups gently drew the dowager countess aside with talk of the recent Gold Cup race at Ascot. "So amusing, don't you think, that the winner was called Banker," she said as she took Harriet's place beside the dowager countess. "The Duke of York must have been delighted, and Mr Greville too. You know he has taken over the supervision of the duke's stables? I did *very* well by Mr Beaumont's recommendation. I do hope you had a wager too, Lady Darville?"

"My eldest son has a very good eye for the turf," replied the Countess looking across at the earl who was staring vacantly into the middle distance despite Lady McAllister's efforts to engage him. Gerald Darville, the new Earl of Morna, could unerringly spot a winner on the flat which was about all that was keeping his personal finances afloat.

Meanwhile the two young women looked at each other and Philippa, as if reciting a lesson, said shyly: "How do you like London, Miss Larkhill?"

"Very well, by what I have seen of it, which is very little after only two days. Are you enjoying your season?"

"I have not been here for the *whole* season and I am not yet properly out. Papa sent for me just for the coronation and to see - to see - if I should like being in town before I am presented next year."

"How sensible. It is very much the same with me, though I will not have the happiness of returning next year, so I must enjoy it while I can. But Mr Beaumont, *he* has been here a great while I understand?"

"Oh yes, Papa rented a house in Curzon Street until I came, but now we also have a villa in Dulwich. It is so pretty," she hesitated not certain whether to continue with this rustic subject. Harriet gave her an encouraging smile. "It has a maze and a stream and a shell grotto. I can be quiet there," she added wistfully.

"*How* I understand. I come from the country and find the noise and bustle of London is quite overwhelming, but I'm sure we'll become accustomed to it in time."

"Oh, do you really think so?" said Philippa faintly. "Papa cannot conceive why I get such headaches in Curzon Street, but it is so noisy after the convent. He is busy in the City all day and if I have no engagements then I am quite alone and would prefer to be in the country," she said simply.

"Have you no companion to live with you?"

"No. Papa has no relations and I have come straight from the Sisters of Marie Claire. Madame de Lessups of course, lives a few doors away in Curzon Street. She is very kind and takes me about when I am in town." She looked towards Marguerite with a timid smile.

"Then perhaps, if you do not dislike it, *we* may go about together - if your Papa will allow it." She had been conscious of the gentleman's scrutiny throughout their conversation. Harriet had wondered at Madame de Lessups' motives at throwing her protégée into the company of a complete stranger, but began to have an inkling of Sir Hamish's schemes.

"Yes, yes, indeed. I'm sure Papa will not object." Philippa seemed relieved at a task fulfilled and although Harriet thought she may have been too forward, she decided to capitalise on a good beginning.

"I do so wish to go and see the Great Exhibition at Somerset House. Do you like paintings?"

"I – I have not seen many," stammered Philippa. "Only the pictures of the Holy Family in the convent."

"I have been told there is an art gallery open to the public in Dulwich." But when she observed Philippa's blank look she hurried on. "No matter. If you do not dislike the notion, we could visit the Great Exhibition, everyone does. There will be lots of new paintings to see; landscapes and sculptures and drawings. Perhaps Madame de Lessups would take us, or I could ask Lady McAllister?"

Philippa immediately turned to Marguerite and begged for her approval. Madame agreed, promised to ask Mr Beaumont for his escort and a day was suggested. The dowager countess eyed the two young ladies speculatively and continued to discourse on the likely entrants for Goodwood.

The girls politely tried to establish grounds for friendship, rather uneven though they were. Harriet ventured several topics but Miss Beaumont was as innocent and ignorant as snow.

She spoke perfect French, knew her bible and sewed exquisitely. When she wasn't practising on her harp she read poetry and had a penchant for novels which she had only just discovered on coming to England. It was plain she found Harriet's confidence and experience rather daunting. It did not take long for Harriet to realise that Philippa was no more than a child and she felt sorry for her.

It was a relief when Andrew picked up his bow and finding Philippa across the room turned in her direction. He played exquisitely. The violin sang under his stubby fingers. The cadences of a Telemann Fantasia rose and fell with a sweet longing of love. A storm of applause greeted the young man's performance.

"Who would have thought such a *large* young gentleman would have such exquisite sensibility," whispered Philippa, a little pink from applauding. "And he *adores* poetry, just like I do."

"From what I have seen of him on such short acquaintance, he is the kindest of creatures."

"How disappointing that he works in an office."

"Why? Being employed by the most powerful trading company in the world is a very honourable profession," said Harriet in amusement.

"Oh, do you really think so?" returned Philippa, naively. "I meant no disparagement of the gentleman; Papa talks of nothing but the Company. But Mr McAllister is so modest that one cannot help thinking of him as a – a - clerk, cooped up behind a desk all day. Like those poor men in Papa's counting house in Calcutta."

"Mr McAllister is private secretary to Lord Glynn."

"Yes, I know, but that's not quite the same as being a soldier or an explorer, is it? They lead much more exciting lives." She looked across at Captain Valentine standing picturesquely with one arm on the mantle, showing his figure to advantage.

Harriet was having none of it. "My cousin was a soldier. He said he was bored, uncomfortable and confused through all his campaigns and was certainly never his own master. And Mr Darville tells me that 'exploring' is much the same. We hear of their exciting findings only when they return, not the misery the collectors go through to collect their specimens or take their measurements. If you doubt me, ask him yourself. I see he's coming over." Harriet looked up, smiling in welcome.

"Miss Larkhill, how delightful to see you again," Rupert bowed punctiliously. "May I escort you to the supper room? And you Miss Beaumont? Lady McAllister has indicated that supper is served, but everyone is too busy talking to take any heed; the sign of a successful party I think."

"I thank you sir," breathed Philippa. "If you will excuse me, I see Madame de Lessups beckoning to me." She left them hurriedly.

"Mr Darville, how pleased I am to see you," beamed Harriet barely preventing herself from patting the empty place by her side. They sat for a few moments while Harriet told him of friends and family at home. She did not go into details for fear of boring him.

"I may have frightened away your companion," said Rupert.

"She seems a sweet girl," sighed Harriet. "Do you know her?"

"I was introduced to her at a concert in Hanover Square. Beaumont is a man of few words and the daughter even fewer."

"It was probably my unruly tongue that drove her away. I quizzed her on so many things that she knew nothing about and I did not mean to distress her. She is learning to play the harp and is a true music lover, so there is another accomplishment she has which I do not. But I find she has done *nothing* since she has been in London except go to small dinner parties and concerts."

"Isn't that what you want to do?" he asked, lips twitching.

"No, no, I wish to go to *large* dinner parties and dance till dawn! I hope I may do and see everything that London has to offer. I have a guide book that George Durrington gave me and already Annie and I have started to take the walks around London."

"Good Lord, don't let Elspeth McAllister hear you say that! No lady should go about unescorted, especially on foot, and certainly not while the town is teeming with strangers!"

Harriet's brow creased. "Ah, so that was why Figgis looked so disapproving this afternoon. But I have Annie with me and today we had a truly educational tour of Westminster Abbey. The guide was most informative and Miss Humble will so be pleased to know that I have paid homage to Mr Milton, her favourite, in Poet's Corner. We were not approached or accosted in any way and I cannot see the harm in such excursions."

But Rupert was serious; he would not answer for her safety or her reputation if she were to continue in her unchaperoned walks. Harriet, who did not wish to antagonise her hostess, was dismayed. "I agree a gentleman's escort would be desirable but I cannot think that Lady McAllister would permit William to accompany me, and Andrew has his secretarial position which occupies long hours. Perhaps she would lend me a footman?"

They both knew this was improbable.

Rupert, feeling under some obligation said: "I will take you about, Harriet - Miss Larkhill, but only if my professional engagements allow me the time. I am much occupied at the moment. My friend John Herschel and I are very busy setting up the Astronomical Society of London. However, if you promise to abandon the idea of exploring on your own I will take you to the British Museum, it is only a step away in Montagu house."

"Then you must on no account disturb yourself. I'm sure Lady McAllister will take me. She is related to the Montagues, you know," said Harriet with a twinkle.

"Then you do not need me at all," he shrugged, a little put out. He rose and offered his arm to lead her into the second salon.

Harriet took pity on him. "Mr Darville, for that most ungentlemanly remark I should banish you to find me a few little rout cakes, but I will come with you and chose my own. I find I am so very hungry even after dinner."

The double doors to the second salon had been thrown open where a selection of savouries, creams, jellies and little cakes were waiting. To Harriet's eyes the refreshments were skimpy. Perhaps such flummery was considered elegant in London society, but Harriet much preferred Lady Larkhill's generous bounty. Three bewigged footmen stood contemplating the decanters on the sideboard.

They found the Earl of Morna at the supper table, silently munching his way through a dish of quail eggs. Miss Finch was unsuccessfully trying to divert his attention with some pastries and becoming increasingly distressed as the earl, entirely oblivious, continued to pop one egg after another into his mouth.

"What a pretty floral centrepiece, Miss Finch. All your work I believe?" said Harriet admiring the peonies and stephanotis arrangement in the centre of an elaborate silver epergne.

"Thank you, yes Miss Larkhill. The florist was most accommodating of Lady McAllister's requirements, and one cannot help but produce something pleasing with such blooms." Thus relieved and appeased, Miss Finch faded into the shadows, leaving the earl to those with stronger influence.

Rupert introduced Harriet to his eldest brother once more. The earl showed no flicker of remembrance of having been introduced to her not an hour earlier and merely grunted. Harriet enquired after the new countess and was met by a blank stare. At first she thought she had been presumptuous until the dullness in his eyes showed he did not know and did not care about the condition of his wife.

Rupert led her to the far side of the table and whispered. "You see why my mother dare not leave him loose in London. Come and meet my uncle properly. He's the only presentable member of the family."

Lord Patrick sported velvet reveres and a square-cut waistcoat. The mutton chop whiskers and several rings and fobs proclaimed him a man of fashion. He was bluff, hearty, at ease with young women as only a life-long bachelor could be and they soon came to a very good understanding. Timid debutantes like Philippa left him at a loss but Harriet had countenance enough to tease and flatter him in response to his banter. After five minutes conversation he was ready to pronounce her a 'fine girl'.

Lady McAllister called everyone to the supper table once more in an attempt to prise the earl from the fast diminishing refreshments. But that gentleman, having cleared the last quail egg from the plate, approached his uncle and muttered something in his ear. Harriet could have sworn that the earl tugged at Lord Patrick's sleeve.

"Forgive us Lady McAllister, but we must tear ourselves away from your delightful repast. My nephew reminds me that he has another engagement and that I have promised to accompany him. We would not wish to interrupt the remains of your musical party and, if you permit us, we will take our leave now," Lord Patrick apologised.

A murmur of polite disappointment broke out. William caught Harriet's eye with a knowing look. Sir Hamish, ever the diplomat, was already ringing for Figgis. Lady McAllister turned to her remaining guests and begged them once more to sample her supper arrangements.

This time the company obediently moved from the other room, talking of the latest political news.

"I never know whether it is the Turkish Question or the Greek Question, they are just a set of horrid revolutionaries. Sir Hamish, I need you to explain it all to me," begged Lady Bixby rustling her fan.

"Alas dear lady, you must ask Lord Londonderry when he arrives. I now deal with only *English* revolutionaries."

Lady Bixby leant across the table to take an apricot from a hanging silver dish and narrowly avoided catching her loose bracelet on the branch of the epergne.

"What a pretty bracelet," said Harriet involuntarily as Barbara Bixby pushed the sparkling stones further up her arm. "I do beg your pardon, Lady Bixby," she said, fearing she had been presumptuous.

"Thank you, Miss Larkhill. I am never without it. They *are* particularly fine diamonds, so my grandfather told me."

She raised her plump white arm a little higher so the candle light now gleamed on the gems. "I *do* like the setting, and enjoy wearing the bracelet whenever I can but find it horribly inconvenient when I'm at table."

"I would be tempted to have it shortened. The extra stones would make beautiful ear drops," suggested the ever practical Harriet.

"Oh, there is no need of that; I have a complete parure," said Lady Bixby lightly. "Sadly, the necklace is even longer and the earrings so heavy I find it impossible to wear them with any degree of comfort. I am forced to wear this," she said fingering a delicate gold chain with a diamond pendant at her neck.

"I hope you keep your diamonds well secured," said William pulling up a chair between the two women. "These are dangerous times," he said with gravity.

"Tush, I have no faith in safes," returned Lady Bixby. "My husband's safe was robbed in '14 during the celebrations for the Peace Negotiations. Such a catastrophe, the whole library turned upside down, and a very good Kneller destroyed while the thieves were searching for our valuables. I regret the loss of my grandmother's portrait more than my jewellery. I have a much better hiding place *now*." She smugly turned the loose bracelet on her wrist.

"Which is?" asked William, his fork suspended. Rupert frowned across the table.

"Why, I throw the whole lot over the chandelier and no-one can see them amongst the lustres, especially when the candles are lit!"

Harriet and William went into peals of laughter, making everyone turn towards them.

"William, pray tell us the source of your hilarity?" asked his mother somewhat stiffly from the other end of the table.

Sir Hamish, who had caught the conversation, intervened. "A foolish joke of the young peoples' my dear. Do not mind them. This shaved ham is delicious, Lady Glynn, may I help you to a slice? Cousin Susan would you be so good as to pass the mustard which I believe is before you."

His wife returned to discussing the latest fashion of wearing little ruffs about the neck and the moment passed.

"You are not serious, Lady Bixby? What happens when the servants come to light the room?" asked William in an undertone.

"Oh the room is a back drawing room I hardly ever use. No one would ever dream of looking for my diamonds *there!* And my butler has been with me for years, he is most faithful and most discreet," she whispered back.

"As I trust *you* will be ma'am. You are among friends here but such quixotic behaviour is not to be noised abroad," warned Captain Valentine, a brandy glass in his hand. He quietly seated himself next to Philippa but otherwise deliberately ignored her. The tension was palpable.

"It was Lord Everard who suggested it," Lady Bixby looked surprised. "At just such an evening party as this."

"But only in jest, ma'am, surely?" said Rupert. "I do not believe he actually meant you to take him up on his absurd idea."

"But it is such a *good* hiding place. Who would think of looking for jewels in a dusty old chandelier?" Lady Bixby looked around the young people, very pleased with the sensation she had created.

"All the world would *now*," said William.

The soirée continued after supper with slightly less animation. It seemed natural for Rupert to seat himself next to Harriet.

"Will we have the pleasure of hearing you play for us Miss Larkhill?" asked Rupert.

"No," said Harriet drawing out the syllable. "At least Lady McAllister has given me no indication that I am to be called upon. She has her reputation to consider and as yet I am an unknown quantity. Has Lady McAllister captured *your* services?" She looked forward to hearing Rupert's masterly touch on the keyboard.

"Sadly, Miss Larkhill, since returning to London I have discovered that gentlemen are allowed to sing and play any amount of other instruments but, in the most fashionable circles, the pianoforte is considered the preserve of ladies in the drawing room."

"How silly," pronounced Harriet. "I will never understand London conventions."

Their conversation was interrupted by the arrival of the Marquess and Marchioness of Londonderry. The room stirred in anticipation of a new source of gossip closer to the seat of power. The Londonderrys were formally attired for a court ball, the lady in rich silk brocades and her husband in powder and knee breeches. They swept into the room. Harriet thought she had never seen a man so tired as the marquess but Emily Castlereagh, as she was still referred to by her familiars, talked enough for both and greeted Elspeth McAllister like the old friend she was. After introductions, the conversation inevitably turned once more to the predicament of Queen Caroline and how she would behave at the coronation.

"But she hasn't been invited!" squeaked Lady Bixby invariably stating the obvious.

"Lord Liverpool has advised her not to attend," said Sir Hamish soothingly. "She dare not disobey the first minister of the land."

"The woman's determined to be crowned! Prinny can hardly bar the doors of the Abbey against her, there would be a riot!" put in William.

"I believe that not *all* the queens of England have been crowned," said Harriet tentatively, "and I understand that no arrangements have been made for such an event?" The verger in Westminster Abbey had been most insistent on this point. She looked to Mortimer Shawcross, MP, for confirmation. He had declared himself a staunch royalist.

"Quite right Miss Larkhill. She did herself no favours by going in procession to St Paul's to give thanks for her deliverance from the House. The woman demands admittance to the Abbey only to cause a scandal and stir up the mob against the king." He flipped open his enamelled snuff box, took a pinch and sniffed with disapproval.

"We'll have the troops on hand to prevent any trouble from the crowd," assured Sir Hamish, with his usual urbanity.

"If you can depend on them! You don't want another uprising on your hands." Captain Valentine's remark was thought tactless in the extreme. Everyone knew of the previous year's unrest in the King's Mews, though the mutiny by the Guards had been contained and subsequently minimised in the newspapers.

"*Will* the revolutionaries cause trouble do you think, my lord?" asked Andrew, addressing Londonderry. The shock of the Cato street conspiracy and trial was still reverberating around the country. A year before there had been a plot to murder all the members of the cabinet and set up a Revolutionary Committee, after the French style. Nothing was said, but certain people in the room guessed that Sir Hamish's agents had been instrumental in foiling the plans.

The marquess looked agitated. "Lord Sidmouth has done his best with the Six Acts but I fear the queen gives the radicals her support at every turn. However, the mob is fickle. She only has to put a foot wrong and the people could turn their allegiance back to the king. Even Brougham thinks she has been unreasonable to refuse an annuity of fifty thousand pounds to return abroad."

"I'd live abroad for fifty thousand pounds a year," murmured William. Shawcross looked shocked at such an unpatriotic sentiment.

Lady Londonderry immediately broke in: "Forgive me, we are all tired of such talk, the drawing rooms are full of nothing but speculation on the queen's intensions. And there will be even more of talk of it at the ball tonight. Tell me Miss Larkhill how to you intend to occupy your time before we are all caught up in the coronation?"

Harriet was surprised at being addressed but rose nobly to support my lady's diversionary tactics. "I have promised my young nephew to visit the menagerie in the Tower. I have strict instructions to write to him all about the ferocious lions and tigers," she said. She could not have hit on a better subject.

"We have a menagerie at North Cray," said the marquess, suddenly. "My wife adores her ostriches; my favourite animal is the zebra. We have kangaroos, llamas, an aviary – all quite tame and safe, though none of them are used to our cold climate."

The talk ranged over wild animals seen and shot. Captain Valentine impressed the young ladies by recounting his experiences hunting the Sumatran tiger. Miss Beaumont looked at him in open admiration. Mr Beaumont showed a spark of interest for the first time in the evening, claiming that the Bengal tiger was the most dangerous of beasts. The captain would not contradict the older man in public and had to be satisfied with causing several young ladies to shudder in horror at his exploits. Harriet took it all in, hoping Mr Beaumont would disclose more of his life in India.

Sir Hamish asked Rupert for an account of dangerous beasts he had encountered on his travels.

"A few alligators and snakes, nothing more. However I would recommend my public lecture at the Royal Institution - for those who are truly interested in the flora and fauna of the south Americas."

An awkward silence fell before Harriet piped up. "Is it true that you shot and ate a hippopotamus when you were shipwrecked, Mr Darville?" She would not have him appear churlish despite his own indifference.

Rupert gave her a quizzing look. "An elephant seal, I think you must mean, Miss Larkhill."

"Shipwrecked!" said Sir Hamish. "You're a dark-horse, Darville. You said nothing about shipwreck to me!"

"A few days on one of the Falkland Islands, the Malvinas as the Spanish call them. We suffered no hardship to speak of. The elephant seal Miss Larkhill refers to was quite an imposing specimen."

He would elaborate no further, despite the company's curiosity. The marquess talked of his own acquisitions and breeding regimes on the farm. Philippa shyly admitted to a fondness for lambs, while Harriet discoursed knowledgeably on various breeds of sheep she had encountered. "Jacob's sheep are very pretty with their black faces if one is careful of the horns; they provide very tender meat for the table, but the Cotswolds are even better for their wool." There were a few titters and raised eyebrows at such a rustic topic.

"How very singular that a young lady should acquaint herself with such things," said one of the Members of Parliament behind his hand. He spoke just loud enough for all to hear.

Harriet turned to stare. "My uncle is a landowner and we farm. I must know my flock as I presume you must study to know your electors, or how else will you persuade them to vote for you?" said Harriet unabashed.

"Bravo, Miss Larkhill," whispered Shawcross, leaning forward, brushing snuff from his coat. "I'm a landowner myself. I have vast flocks of Leicestershire long-wool sheep. And *his* voters show far less sense than the average hogget."

At last the chiming clock on the mantle brought Lady Londonderry to her feet.

"Good gracious, we are expected at Carlton House this instant, my dear." She shook out her panniered skirts. "Elspeth," she said, kissing Lady McAllister's cheek. "What fascinating guests you do gather about you. We *do* so enjoy the company of young people. Not alas that we will enjoy any more tonight – all those fusty Hanoverians, though I must not say it and many are our good friends."

Lady McAllister, who would have sold her eyes to be among the 'fusty Hanoverians' countered with: "Emily, a delight to have your company. Pray be so obliging as to give my compliments to the Princess Anastasia and the Countess of Metz-Colmar. They cannot have forgotten the charming times we all had in Paris and Vienna and I hope to give myself the pleasure of calling on them very soon." She followed her guests downstairs into the hall where Londonderry took Sir Hamish aside for a private word.

As Figgis draped Lady Londonderry's heavy satin cloak about her shoulders, she said: "I cannot promise, but I will do my best to get vouchers for Almack's for your guest."

"Oh."

"She is some relation of yours as well as the Darvilles is she not? Sophia informs me the young woman is the daughter of their local squire."

"Niece."

"Robert took to her at once. She has presence of mind and pretty manners."

Lady McAllister thought Harriet had been disastrously forward, but Emily was still talking. "I must consult with Sally and Dorothea of course," she said naming the other patronesses of the exclusive assembly, "but I have hopes of getting my way. There are so many people coming to Almack's this season that one more is of no consequence, and for such a short time too – that is, if you so wish it?"

"Why, yes – yes, I had every intention-" replied Lady McAllister faintly.

"Of course, if you do *not* wish it, then we will say no more on the matter. I had assumed *you* would be attending the rooms to meet our embassy friends, and would wish to bring your niece."

Lady McAllister chose not to correct any of her friend's misapprehensions.

The departure of the Londonderrys signalled the general break-up of the evening. Rupert made his punctilious farewell and promised to call when he had the time. Philippa made shy adieus. She was not used to late hours even though they were not to attempt the drive home to Dulwich but stay the night in Curzon Street.

"But *where* in Curzon street, I wonder," murmured William *sotto voce* to Harriet who had risen to make her farewells and confirm their appointment for the visit to the Summer Exhibition.

Harriet frowned. "Mr McAllister, I am forced to believe that if Mr Beaumont enjoys making money then *you* enjoy making mischief!"

CHAPTER 4   OLD AND NEW FRIENDS

"The Dowager Countess of Morna," announced Figgis opening the door to the dining parlour.

"Ah, Harriet," said the dowager. "I am glad to find you alone."

Despite the late night, Harriet had risen at her usual time and had eaten her breakfast with the gentlemen of the house before they dispersed. She was still at the table examining the *Morning Post* for the latest arrivals for the coronation.

"What an unexpected pleasure, Countess," said Harriet rising and holding out her hand. "I regret that Lady McAllister has not yet come down, but if you wish I will send a message-". She folded the newspaper away.

"All to the good. These fine town ladies she will lie abed of a morning and it's you I wanted to see. You may pour me some coffee. I have been bumped like a sack of potatoes all the way from Brook Street."

"Did you come in a hackney?"

"I find I cannot ride one of these hired nags amid all the traffic," the dowager countess said avoiding Harriet's look of surprise. Harriet had assumed that Lord Patrick would have put his chaise at his sister-in-law's disposal, not realising that the dowager was on a private mission.

Harriet indicated a seat and looked expectantly at her visitor. She seemed pale and agitated but determined. Harriet got up to ring for fresh coffee, thought better of it and when Figgis appeared, asked him to bring the sherry. They chatted of the previous evening until the butler had left the room whereupon the dowager bluntly changed the subject.

"I meant what I said, Harriet, last night. Now that I have seen you in London I think it a good notion that you go about with Rupert while you're here. He can lend you consequence among young men of learning – I know you like that type of thing. Rupert tells me you can converse sensibly on any topic of the moment, not like most flibbertigibbets. A serious-minded man would suit you, support you, help you run the manor and Rupert knows a great many clever young men, most of them clergymen but don't let that put you off. And even if an older man offers for you, you have the spirit to manage him. I always think a man should have an absorbing pass-time to distract him from being a nuisance to his family."

Harriet raised her eyebrows and tried not to laugh. "I thank you for your concern Countess but I am in no hurry to find myself a spouse. And how precisely would Mr Darville benefit from squiring me around the scientific salons?"

"Ah, I would expect you, in return, to introduce my son to suitable partners at Elspeth McAllister's social engagements. Sir Hamish, I hear, rarely appears at these things unless half the cabinet attend. But *you* will accompany Lady McAllister to the best and most elegant political soirees and dinners and whatever nonsense is being held for the coronation."

"But I am not going to be presented at a Drawing Room! Lady McAllister has not even obtained vouchers for Almack's for me and you know without those I have no hope no of an entrée into the best social circles."

"Nonsense! No one cares about being presented these days – they're such a dreary lot at court. Amelia Castlereagh, Londonderry I should say, is one of Elspeth's friends. She should procure you vouchers for Almack's, though I hear that isn't what it once was."

"I found Lady Londonderry very kind but surely you will need Mr Darville as an escort to your own engagements?" said Harriet desperately.

The dowager countess shrugged. "I am forced to attend the coronation in the abbey as my daughter-in-law has decided to cub at last – such dreadful timing, but then she is a dreadful woman. The earl needs my support. After that I must return to Castle Morna with him, to take charge; Gerald will never cope alone. Let us hope we'll have an heir at last."

Harriet murmured her understanding and continued. "And while you are away I am to introduce Mr Darville to suitable young ladies?" she said faintly.

The dowager shot her a look. "But they must be rich Harriet. I'm sure you're perfectly well aware of our circumstances. I will not mince matters, we cannot depend on the present earl to restore the family fortunes; you saw how he is yourself. He has been 'touched' since birth, I daresay you have heard. My late husband always blamed me because I would ride until the seventh month." Her eyes glazed over with memory and then she snapped back to the present.

"I have no compunction in admitting that I still find Rupert something of a dry stick, and I daresay many women do. Unfortunately, three years adventuring around the world do not appear to have made him a whit more interesting to the ladies. He looks well enough but that don't signify and he has only his grandmother's money and mine when I go."

She took a mouthful of sherry. "I confess I was never more surprised than when he married your cousin, but they were both very young at the time." She shuddered at the recollection. "I should be thankful he at least did show some interest in women-". She stopped, seemed annoyed at herself and then went on.

"I am not asking you to arrange a marriage Harriet, just bring my son into the way of like-minded young women of good birth and fortune. Prevent him from becoming a hermit, forever at this new Astronomical Society of his. Why he could not join White's like his father and brother I do not know! Lord Patrick has offered more than once to put him up."

"I thought you were a staunch Whig, Lady Darville!" teased Harriet.

"Whig or Tory, what do I care? As long I can see my youngest safely married to money before I take my last fence, that's all that matters." She stopped, seeming a little out of breath, and took another mouthful of sherry.

"Flattered as I am by your confidence in me, Countess, I must know: is Mr Darville aware of your schemes?"

"Good God, of course not! I have merely suggested that he take you about a little, as our families are so long connected. You must not breathe a word of this conversation to anyone, least of all my son. It would be just the way to set hares running."

Harriet chose to be amused, though she felt a sting in her heart and could easily have taken offence. Rupert as an escort would be a mixed blessing; she yearned to be frivolous while she was in London and, as his mother said, she feared he was correct to the point of prudery. As for finding him a bride, she had her doubts. She would have to form her own circle of friends first and she was under no illusion that she could make any kind of mark on society, especially this season. London was crowded with the cream of English and European aristocracy and she had no idea how far - or how little - Elspeth McAllister's influence stretched.

She found out a few days later when Lady McAllister appeared in the drawing room with an envelope in her hand. Her hostess announced, unbending a little with her own importance. "You will be flattered to hear, Miss Larkhill that I have procured vouchers for Almack's in your name. Sir Hamish says he will pay for the subscription. The tickets came this morning, all thanks to Emily Castlereagh. I knew I only had to mention it and she would grant me this favour, we have been such dear friends for so long."

Harriet was amazed, knowing the annual subscription was ten guineas, and wondered at Sir Hamish's generosity in paying such a sum for a mere few weeks. Philippa would not be allowed to attend a public ball and Harriet wondered if Sir Hamish was aware of this – but then he knew everything and she would not question her own good fortune.

******

Despite the humid weather, Harriet and Annie elbowed their way along Piccadilly. They stuck tightly together, Annie's basket imperiously shoving at anyone who came too close. Harriet admitted to herself that Rupert had been right; a teeming London was no place to be on foot. She much preferred the luxury of Lady McAllister's coach and the escort of a footman when shopping. There was little respite in the new Burlington arcade and she was about to steer Annie towards a milliner's when a commotion in the crowd ahead forced them to stop.

"*Hilfe! Hatet den Dieb!*" came a strident cry. Harriet peered ahead, to be nearly knocked flying by a youth dodging among the crowd and disappearing into the throng. Harriet, making a clutch for her bonnet, saw no more. Her attention was held by the clamour from the victim. She pushed through the spectators to find a large lady in rich brocades sprawled on the pavement, sobbing and clutching her wrist. Standing over her was a gaunt maid, directing the uncomprehending crowd in Prussian military accents which stunned them into immobility. Several gentlemen hovered helplessly on the perimeter of the drama. The maid, standing sentry, would let no one approach her mistress but fired blistering orders to all and sundry.

Harriet cleared her throat and gathered what little schoolgirl German she could remember. "*Gnedige Frau,*" she said coming forward to kneel by the weeping figure on the pavement.

"*Reichsgrafin Ravensburg von unt zu Neufreistad!*" snapped the maid, rigidly on guard.

"*Madame, let me be of assistance to you.*"

Hearing Harriet's simple words in her own language the large lady looked up to meet Harriet's smiling open face. The lady clutched at Harriet's arm and gabbled something in fear, her pale blue eyes streaming and red in her round puffy face.

"*Please would you speak a little slower, Madame. Can you rise? We will go into this shop.*" She looked up at the maid and ordered: "*Help your mistress to her feet. Into the hat shop.*"

The Reichsgrafin held out her soft fleshy arm to show a deep scratch and red marks of a cord bitten into her wrist. "*My eyes, they sting and he hurt my arm,*" she whimpered like a child. Neither she nor her abigail made any effort to move.

"Some cutpurse bungled his aim, Miss, with the knife and pulled the lady's arm something wicked." An elderly man in a pea coat and peaked cap of a waterman stepped forward. There were various insignia on his uniform.

"I saw it all and will tell the constables if they ask. I hope the beadles got the rascal. It's all these foreigners coming yur that make the streets unsafe for a decent woman." There was a murmur of assent from the onlookers.

"Thank you, I'm sure you're right," said Harriet ignoring this illogical but well-meant statement. "If I could trouble you to take this lady's other arm. We should get her inside away from the crowds."

The spectators flowed on, happy that someone else should take responsibility now the excitement was over. Putting aside his distaste of foreigners, the elderly man, who had instantly recognised the authority in Harriet's voice, hastened to oblige. He stooped down to comply, whereupon the fierce maid thrust him out of the way and hauled her mistress to her feet with a stream of fussing words. Annie pushed the remaining loiterers aside and the procession tottered into the seclusion of the shop. Madame Delphine, the proprietor, who had been watching the scene from her bow window hurried to bring a chair for the Reichsgrafin.

"How terrible this should have happened right outside my establishment. I can assure you we have only the best of clientele here. A glass of water, Madam?"

"Wine, I think would be preferable, if you would be so kind," said Harriet. "And some water to wash the lady's eyes. Her wrist too must be bound. Have you a bandage or soft scarf?" Madame Delphine signed to her minions and Annie, seizing a fan of ostrich feathers from the counter began to cool the Reichsgrafin's red face. Madame Delphine snatched it from her with a glare and replaced it on the counter.

Hearing a discreet cough, Harriet turned to see the elderly waterman hovering in the doorway clutching a lady's battered hat. It was covered in dust and had evidently been trampled upon.

"Why thank you, Mr-?"

"Jenkins, Miss, barge pilot for the East India Company," he said touching his cap. "If I can be of further service?"

"Thank you Mr Jenkins. A lady should never be separated from her hat. Madame Delphine will soon put all to rights, I'm sure. If I could trouble you fetch a beadle or a constable? Perhaps the lady can give a description of her attackers, or else we may have to rely on your testimony alone."

"I think they threw snuff in her eyes, Miss. It all happened so quick. I only saw some young lad pushing through the crowd. It's a typical trick: one throws the dust and the other robs the mark. I'll fetch one of the beadles, he'll know what to do." The pilot set off with determination.

Harriet turned the key in the lock of the shop door to allow the lady time to compose herself. As the lady was unlikely to move into the back premises, it would never do to be interrupted by customers. Harriet returned to the Reichsgrafin to find the tears still flowing and thought it was for the best. *"Your tears will clean your eyes,"* she said. Annie held a bowl of water while the Prussian maid dabbed at the cut on her mistress's arm. Madame Delphine, with a mind to future custom, produced a length of fine lawn for a bandage and offered a selection of silk scarves to support the injured arm, though she made no effort to assist the lady.

"If you could repair the Reichsgrafin's hat, I'm sure she would be eternally obliged," suggested Harriet, holding out the crushed concoction of brocade and ribbons and receiving a glass of hock in return.

"It's not one of *my* creations," sniffed Madame Delphine, "but I will do what I can to make it presentable." If this disaster was what they were wearing in Vienna she had no fear for her reputation as a leading milliner to the *ton*. She disappeared into the stock room.

Harriet passed the glass of hock to her new friend and began her ministrations. *"Drink this, it will do you good. You will soon recover from this sad adventure. The cut is not so very deep. Where are you staying, Madame?"*

"The Clarendon. My husband is the Reichsgraf von Ravensburg. We are here for the coronation. This is a terrible city, such lawlessness. My reticule, the cross! It is a gift for your king! What will I do? My husband! Why did Lord Everard not come with me? Will there be a revolution? We are cousins to your queen!"

"Lord Everard?" said Harriet in surprise. She ignored the remainder of the statement; most of the Austrian rulers could claim to be cousins to the Royal Family. But the mention of Everard and a jewelled cross made her ask: *"Do you always carry your jewellery about with you?"*

"Nein, nein! It is not mine! A link was broken on the chain. I trust no one with this jewel, no one!" The Reichsgrafin's sobs turned to anger and then back to self-pity. *"I was taking it myself to – ach I forget the name of the shop. It is so valuable, my husband is to present it at a levée! My husband will murder me!"*

"Your husband will be pleased to see you safely returned," soothed Harriet, hoping the Reichsgrafin was exaggerating. She stepped back to admire her handiwork. *"Where is your carriage, Madame? Why did you come on foot and alone?"*

The Reichsgrafin gulped and said sullenly. *"Lord Everard recommended the establishment; it is in the new arcade he said. My carriage will be waiting for us somewhere. I do not know where the fool of a footman is. He was to protect me!"*

Harriet hoped that the footman had gone in pursuit of the thieves. She produced her handkerchief from her reticule and silently passed it to the Reichsgrafin to continue mopping her eyes. After a thoughtful pause Harriet asked: *"Did Lord Everard know you would visit the jeweller today?"*

"I do not know," replied the lady pettishly. *"I may have told him – and he did not offer to accompany me! My husband is too busy with diplomatic affairs."* She sounded more outraged by this neglect. *"The repair was urgent! My husband must present the cross to your king in a few days."*

"How did you know which jewellers and where to go?"

"The English coachman knew the direction, of course," said the Reichsgrafin looking affronted. *"Why do you question me young lady? Who are you? Where are the authorities to take charge of this matter? I wish to be taken back to my hotel at once and the Commissioner of Police sent for! I wish to lay information! My husband is in negotiation with Viscount Sidmouth and will be enraged that I have been treated in this way!"*

"At once Reichsgrafin," said Harriet. Recognising the name of the Home Secretary in this tirade, she scribbled the Russell Square address on the back of one of her calling cards and gave it to the now irate lady. *"Sir Hamish McAllister of the Home Office is – related, and if I can-"*

The Reichsgrafin started. "Chevalier McAllister to us is known," she said, hesitantly attempting English for the first time. She looked at Harriet doubtfully.

Harriet beamed. *"How delightful – then we are acquaintances already."* She looked up to see Mr Jenkins, accompanied by a splendidly liveried figure in boots and top hat, beckoning through the bow window. She unlocked the door.

"Now I see Mr Jenkins has found a beadle. He will take the details and then we will leave."

There followed an exasperating twenty minutes of fruitless interrogation with Harriet translating as best as she could. A policeman arrived. Harriet and Mr Jenkins repeated everything once more. The constable took a cursory note and could only suggest a later visit from an Inspector to the lady's hotel, so busy were they with the spate of housebreaking in the metropolis. He did not sound hopeful as to the recovery of the article. A sweating footman appeared saying he had chased the thief and then lost him in the crowds.

The appearance of a worried coachman in search of his passenger decided Harriet to put an end to the matter. "I think we have told you all we can, gentlemen, and the Reichsgrafin must recover from her ordeal." She turned to the bewildered woman. *"Here is Madame Delphine with your hat. Doesn't it look modish? The buckle looks just as pretty as your rosette which was sadly ruined. We will go home now."* She gently tied the strings of the now respectable hat under the Reichsgrafin's many chins while the Prussian maid looked on jealously. She raised the Reichsgrafin to her feet and escorted her trembling to the door.

"Thank you Mr Jenkins," she said to the pilot who was opening the door wide. "I will mention your kind offices to Mr McAllister of the Company." She slipped him a treasured half-sovereign from her purse. "You may know of him? Now I won't keep you from your work or your dinner any longer, you must be dreadfully late."

"Yes Miss. I know Mr McAllister very well; he's always round the warehouses checking things. Proper gentlemen he is." He stood aside with a touch of his cap.

It took another hour to locate and explain the situation to the Reichsgraf. The Imperial Count sported a huge moustache, a wasp waist and a vile temper which sounded even more ferocious in German. His rage at the loss of the jewel was a wonder to behold and Harriet felt deeply for his quaking lady who was near to hysteria.

A physician arrived, recommended by the Austrian embassy. Doctor Yardley spoke fondly of his student days in Tübingen, approved Harriet's bandaging and administered a composer to the Reichsgrafin. Harriet thought the lady's husband needed one before he burst out of his corset. When his wife had been allowed to retire in the care of her Prussian maid, Harriet quietly rose to go. The Reichsgraf turned to her and gathered the rags of his manners.

"I cannot understand it, Fraulein Larkhill, the piece is but a copy of the original cross, at the moment safely in Ravensburg Cathedral in Neufreistad. The copy is set with several fine rubies and sapphires, but they are modern stones of no great note. It is the symbolism of the original piece that gives it its value." He paced up and down the room. "The original cross was made to celebrate one of the many victories that my ancestor, Leopold I, had over the Turk in 1514. It embodies the heart of the Reich, the spirit of our people. I admit the pearls are rather fine in the replica but I cannot believe that the thieves could find a buyer for it, the Ravensburg Cross is too well known as it stands."

"Perhaps the thieves are unaware of its fame, or that it is a replica," said Harriet tactfully. "Or they may intend to break up the piece or reset it."

"Yes, yes, but the tragedy is that I am to present it to His Majesty at a reception in three days' time – a gift for the coronation. The *scandale,* the shame, that it is lost to admit!" said the Reichsgraf, momentarily losing his grammar under pressure.

At that moment an inn servant knocked and entered. "A letter for you, sir. Urgent, the boy said, no reply needed."

Harriet once more made to go as the Reichsgraf begged her indulgence and opened the note. The contents seemed to shock him and Harriet hovered, uncertain what to do.

All at once he turned to her as if surprised to see her still there. He had a certain bewildered look in his eye. "But *gnedige fraulein*, forgive me. We have detained you too long. I must set enquiries in motion. You have our heartfelt thanks for rescuing my wife." He clicked his heels and bowed and uttered a dozen more protestations of obligation all the while ushering her to the door. "Now, my coachman will take you back to Russell Square. Ah, here is your maid, waiting so patiently for you. Please give my compliments to Sir Hamish and his lady, and my apologies for imposing on your good nature. Please do not trouble yourself about this matter, and if I might beg another favour?"

Harriet assured him of her compliance.

"That you say nothing of this distressing matter to anyone. I would not like to be the cause of upheaval on the eve of the coronation. Tongues can wag so maliciously and make profit from others' misfortunes. If you are questioned, we will say that my wife merely had an unfortunate fall in the street. Say nothing of the theft. Much can be achieved discreetly, Sir Hamish will tell you. And it is most likely that we will recover the cross eventually."

"Certainly, sir, if you so wish it." She had no intention of revealing Mr Jenkins' help in the affair to the Reichsgraf, and hoped that he would not bruit the incident too widely. She placed no reliance on Madame Delphine's discretion but trusted that the shopkeeper did not understand German.

Harriet and Annie arrived back in Russell Square exhausted. Lady McAllister too had been out most of the morning at one of her charitable committees and had not noticed Harriet's absence. Figgis, after a surprised look at the crested carriage which brought Harriet to the door, saw that Miss Larkhill was going up in the world and altered his manner accordingly.

******

"Susan, I have decided that you shall come with us to the Great Exhibition. I will need you to read the catalogue to me while I examine the paintings. William will accompany us," said Lady McAllister.

There was a splutter of protest from behind the newspaper. "Dash it all mother, you know paintins ain't my interest."

"It pains me to admit that any son of mine would show no appreciation of Fine Art, but I place no great dependence on Mr Beaumont's attendance. Like you, I suspect the gentleman has *no* artistic sensibility and would not appreciate such modern masterpieces, but we cannot go unaccompanied. I need your escort."

"If Beaumont don't show then I'm certain Valentine will," said her son crumpling the paper beside him. "The widow will make sure he's always hoverin' in attendance."

"Then that's all the more reason why *you* should attend," she returned with a warning in her voice that was not to be ignored. She would have said more but for Harriet's presence.

The parties met in the expansive courtyard of Somerset House among a jam of town curricles and phaetons. Lady McAllister was correct in her prediction; Mr Beaumont was nowhere to be seen. She peered over her *pince nez* at the inevitable appearance of Captain Valentine and whispered sharply. "William, you will stay close to the young ladies at all times."

"The man ain't goin' to do anything outrageous in public, Mama!"

Madame de Lessups approached and smiled charmingly. "My dear Lady McAllister, ladies. Mr Beaumont sends his deepest apologies; he has an important matter of business today and regrets he cannot accompany us." Madame de Lessups turned gaily to the scarlet-coated figure beside her. "However, Richard was providentially free and will take care of us beautifully I am sure."

"I'm sure my son will provide all that is required in an escort," responded Lady McAllister in arctic tones.

"Of course, Lady McAllister. How delightful that he should come. We ladies are spoilt in having *two* dashing young men to point out what we must like and what we should dismiss as not worthy of attention."

William rolled his eyes and caught Valentine's sardonic look. The captain gave a mock salute. "All present and correct ma'am. If you will allow me to take the lead." He offered his arm to Philippa but she slipped to Harriet's side and slid her hand beneath her friend's elbow. Captain Valentine made a quick recovery and smilingly offered an arm each to the two elder ladies, leaving Miss Finch to trail behind with William.

"Come ladies, I will be the envy of all; such fair companions as yourselves will surely challenge what society beauties there are on the walls."

Lady McAllister was not pleased at this mode of address but she had the satisfaction of knowing that Miss Beaumont was temporarily in Harriet's charge. There was a little hiatus at the ticket desk as the captain, well-provided with funds by his aunt, proceeded to pay for the whole party. Lady McAllister rustled her reticule, protested but subsided soon enough.

The Exhibition Room took Harriet's breath away. Rows upon rows of paintings climbed to the ceiling curving forward on their hangings until they looked about to topple onto the gazer. There was not an inch of wall to be seen between the frames. Summer light streamed in from the windows above, casting a shadow on one side of the large room. Harriet did not know where to look first. Philippa remained clamped to her side at the sight of so many fashionable people and scarcely peeped from beneath her bonnet.

Captain Valentine fell in beside the young ladies and by dint of his superior height and decidedly unartistic commentary soon had Philippa giggling at his descriptions of the new paintings. There seemed a surfeit of bourgeois landowners and their stiff-faced progeny posed in vast parks with their newly built mansions in the background.

"I wish I knew who some of these people were," mused Harriet staring up at yet another painting of a rising landowner and his family. "I like a story in a painting, something to stir the imagination."

"If only you had been in London last year Miss Larkhill, you would have seen Gericault's *Raft of the Medusa* – there's a story for you! It was not shown here of course but in the Egyptian Hall – more space you know. It's monumental, more than twenty feet wide! It showed all the horror of the catastrophe," said William with relish.

"*The Méduse?* I remember hearing a little about the tragedy when I was in school," said Philippa. "The nuns said the shipwreck was very terrible and they said special prayers for the souls of the poor drowned people."

"They were the lucky ones. Sooner drowned than murdered," said William.

"Murdered? Whatever do you mean Mr McAllister?" Philippa looked alarmed.

"Mr McAllister exaggerates-" began Harriet.

"I can assure you I do not, Miss Larkhill. It is well-known that of nearly a hundred and fifty people only fifteen survived. Crazed, parched and starved after two weeks adrift on a collapsin' raft, what else could they do but eat each other?"

Philippa gave a little gasp, looked to see if Mr McAllister were teasing, saw that he was not and moved a little closer to Captain Valentine. He patted her hand soothingly and made no effort to silence William.

"A shocking tale, it quite curdles the blood," said Valentine a decided glint under his lazy lids.

Harriet frowned at William. "I collect that the artist chose his subject for fashionable effect, which you, Mr McAllister, and the rest of the sensation-seeking world have succumbed to. Famous and shocking the depiction may be, but Miss Beaumont and I prefer more subtle subjects and the delineation of the truth – and neither do we value our canvases by the yard."

Suitably snubbed, William bowed and dropped back.

"A spirited defence, Miss Larkhill, leading to a comprehensive rout," said the captain appreciatively. He had not relinquished the heiress's hand.

"Mr McAllister can be very – imaginative at times," said Harriet feeling a trifle guilty.

"But he cannot have *really* meant that the castaways survived by – by - cannibalism?" said Philippa.

"No, not at all," replied Harriet briskly. "I suspect it was the English newspapers that wanted to put the French government in a bad light and added those false and dreadful stories to a sad tale. Mr McAllister delights in putting people out of countenance."

Philippa seemed puzzled but relieved and the captain drew her attention to a charming Landseer painting of a litter of pointer puppies. Before long Philippa was standing on tiptoe, using Valentine's arm as a support.

William soon returned to mutter over Harriet's shoulder: "My brother should take some leave and attend to his own affairs, or the heiress will slip through his fingers." He tapped the silver head of his cane to his teeth in disapproval.

"Then you shouldn't drive her into the arms of the first sympathetic gentleman she meets."

The thought flashed across her mind as to whether her new friend might make a suitable partner for her old – and then she berated herself for her disloyalty to her hosts and specifically to Andrew McAllister.

By the time the party moved on, the captain had Philippa's arm in his and was whispering wicked comments about the other visitors. Lady McAllister consulted Miss Finch on every canvas until, to her pleasure, she was accosted by a group of smartly dressed people. After a few moments of listening to gossip about people she did not know, Harriet drifted back to examining the pictures. William had vanished.

"I like that painting of the English countryside," said Philippa shyly, indicating a study of a hay wain bearing two rustics, standing in a shallow river. "The little dog looks so pretty."

Harriet consulted her catalogue. "It is by Mr Constable. 'Landscape: Noon'," she said. The countrywoman in her thought it rather lowering. "There looks to be a thunderstorm looming."

"Oh, do you think so?" One glance at Philippa's crestfallen face made Harriet repent her remark.

"Let us hope they emerged from the river safely and had a bumper harvest."

"Miss Larkhill has such amusing interests," said Valentine. He might as well have called her a country bumpkin.

"Now, this is what I call a real picture!" he pronounced, halting before a battle scene of immense proportions. He approved of the accuracy of the uniform and horses and chose to enlighten Miss Beaumont. "The insignia is the most difficult detail to get right. A chum of mine took me to see Mr Ward's *Allegory of Waterloo* last week – I didn't understand it. I daresay you would have done with all your fine education! But to a simple soldier like myself, well, it was nothing like the real battlefield!"

"Were you there Captain Valentine? At Waterloo?" asked Harriet quietly.

"Well, er, no, not actually there. I was fighting in India; the Bengal Government was forced into a war with Nepal at about that time. We gave a good account of ourselves. Thrashed the beggars soundly."

Seeing Harriet's stony face he turned back to an admiring Miss Beaumont. "Shall we explore the ante-room Miss Beaumont?" he said offering his arm. "Only second-raters in there, but we'll be away from the crowds."

Harriet ignored the hint and followed behind, stopping to look at some architectural drawings. Marguerite had been waylaid by one of her many friends from Paris and thinking that Philippa was in the company of Miss Larkhill, had taken her eye off her charge.

A little while later, in the half-empty ante-room, Harriet found Valentine and Philippa staring up at a marble sculpture of an amorous Mars embracing a voluptuous Venus. Philippa was looking decidedly pink and uncomfortable.

"Ah, Miss Beaumont. Madame de Lessups is enquiring for you. She has discovered some old friends of yours from Paris and knows you would like to renew your acquaintance." Harriet indicated the main salon and Philippa hurriedly turned away from the suggestive statue.

Unperturbed, Captain Valentine let her go. He had made enough progress with the shy heiress for one day, and now he felt in need of a drink. He shot a sardonic look at Harriet. "Classical nudes not to your taste Miss Larkhill? Or do you prefer nymphs and shepherdesses?"

"In their place if there are no wolves about, Captain."

She turned and rejoined the rest of the party who were admiring Sir Thomas Lawrence's latest portrait of a society beauty. After a while, when Harriet was beginning to feel a crick in her neck, she heard her name spoken. "Why it *is* Miss Larkhill," A handsome-looking couple accosted her in surprise. "Mr Darville mentioned that you were coming up to town. We were hoping we would meet you."

"Mr Hinton, Mrs Hinton," she said shaking hands with pleasure. Introductions were made, approving glances exchanged and Harriet fell into easy discourse with her Wiltshire acquaintances. They were a fashionable couple, Will Hinton being a clubbable man who bred horses and managed his estate profitably. He was known to be something of a connoisseur in matters of art. Mrs Hinton was a fair beauty of lively temperament who had been the toast of the town a few years previously but was now a contented spouse. Contented, because Mr Hinton had the sense to bring his wife to town every season and entertain frequently when in the country.

By tacit consent the Hintons joined them. Mr Hinton discoursed knowledgeably on the painters of the day while Catherine Hinton and Madame de Lessups found they had several mutual friends. Elspeth was more than happy to add this smart couple to her list of acquaintances while Miss Larkhill was staying with them.

Lady McAllister had strained her eyesight more than she had intended and now satisfied that there were no more of her dearest friends to be accosted, decided it was time to leave. Having discovered what the world was thinking of this year's collection she had seen enough to voice a contrary opinion and promote her reputation as a woman of independent views.

The whole party made their way towards the foyer and were about to make their adieus when Harriet caught sight of a figure in black on the stairs. It was Rupert. He ran briskly down towards them explaining he had just come from a meeting of the Royal Society, established in a few cramped rooms in Somerset House.

After general greetings the others politely moved a little distance away from the four friends.

"Have you seen anything to tempt you, Hinton? I thought you were more concerned with selling? Have you found a purchaser yet?" asked Rupert.

Harriet looked from one man to the other in enquiry.

"Alas, Miss Larkhill, I have come to town not to buy but to dispose one of my father's paintings," explained Mr Hinton.

"Oh, surely not the Stubbs? The horses look so splendid in the gallery at Hinton Hall," said Harriet.

"Good Lord No, I would not part with 'Thunderbolt', we are not quite so destitute as that," laughed Mr Hinton. "But I have some drainage works in hand and there's an obscure little Velasquez that my father never liked. I have no scruples about parting with it."

Mrs Hinton leaned conspiratorially towards Harriet. "Papa-in-law won it in a game of faro when he was in Florence as a young man. It is rather ugly. You must come and see it. Yes indeed you must come to tea very soon for we have not had the pleasure of seeing you for many months and I long to know the latest news of our Larkhill acquaintances. Mr Darville does not gossip and indeed seems to have no interest in his neighbours at all."

"But they are not my neighbours. I live in London."

"Yes, yes, of course," beamed Hinton. "My wife is right. Better still, why not *all* come back to Park Street with us now?" He encompassed the whole party with a gesture. "We would be delighted to offer you luncheon and then you must have a tour of my treasures. I have several oriental pieces that I feel sure you could advise me on, Madame? Captain? With your experience of the East. And you Darville, I need your opinion on some new Polynesian masks I have acquired. You must all come and have luncheon with us."

Hinton, who liked nothing better than keeping open house, would hear of no excuse. He had every faith in his housekeeper to produce refreshment for eight extra people, and his wife warmly added her pleas to the general invitation.

Like most impromptu gatherings, the lunch party was a success. Lady McAllister was disposed to be entertained and Marguerite's calm good nature ensured an ease among the young people.

The Hinton's town house was all light and pastel with pink Chinese wall paper and bright Brussels carpets. The rooms embodied good taste, elegance and harmony; everything necessary for a young couple of fashion. Harriet found it beautiful in comparison with the ancient furnishings of Larkhill houses. After the guests had partaken of cold meats, prawns, peaches and a thin claret, Will Hinton showed them his treasures.

The Velasquez, displayed on an easel in the little salon, was deemed to be not one of the artist's best works. It was a small study of an aged beggar woman which appealed to none of the ladies except Miss Finch who openly pitied the old crone in her destitution. "One must remember that not all have been as fortunate as myself to have found shelter in their old age."

"A worthy sentiment ma'am, but the brush work is very poor. It may even have been done by an apprentice in his studio, though my father swore it was a Velasquez. I have advertised of course and put the word around among some people I know," said Hinton turning to the others. "I do not despair of finding a buyer among some of the European royalty before the end of the season. But come, let me show you my porcelain collection. My wife likes the pale green celadon ware but I prefer something more striking. I would value the opinion of the world travellers among you."

Hinton took a key from his waistcoat pocket and brought out from his japanned cabinet a small round bowl with a highly coloured floral motif on a pink background. After a brief look, Captain Valentine drifted towards Philippa who had hung back. He had drunk freely of Hinton's claret and felt mischievous.

"Not as fine as your Papa's collection, I'll wager," he whispered. "He keeps all his treasures in Hibiscus Lodge does he not? And will never allow a philistine like me near them." He gave her a slow wicked smile.

She blushed in pretty confusion. "I am sure Papa would be pleased to see you at Dulwich, whenever Madame de Lessups choses to visit." She felt this wasn't quite true but did not want to appear rude to her chaperone's nephew. The chaperone at that moment was occupied.

"Have you seen an example of this before, Madame de Lessups?" asked Hinton.

The lady received it carefully with a smile of recognition. "Yes, I believe I have. If it is authentic, it's an example of Peranakan ware from the Malacca Straits. Chinese in manufacture but made for the wealthy Malay inhabitants. My late husband brought some back from his travels. A pretty piece," she said turning it over in her hands. "The peony and dragon are traditional symbols in Chinese culture but I fear I cannot tell you what they denote. I am more familiar with the Hindoo."

Rupert broke off from his scrutiny of some fearsome tribal masks and came across. "Chinese dragons traditionally symbolise potent and auspicious powers, particularly control over water, rainfall, hurricane, and floods. The dragon is also a symbol of power, strength, and good luck for people who are worthy of it." He took the bowl from her hands.

"Thank you Mr Darville. I knew we could rely on you to inform us," said Marguerite with a gleam of amusement in her eye.

"And the peony?" asked Harriet brightly.

"It is the flower of riches and honour. A member of the rose family and considered to be the king of flowers in China."

"How odd it is the 'king' of flowers," said Lady McAllister. "Surely the *queen* of the flowers would seem more appropriate, Mr Darville. I consider the peony such a showy plant, don't you agree, Madame? Almost vulgar. But then it *is* foreign. I would say it merely bears a *resemblance* to the rose with its heavy scent and extravagant bloom but without its English purity." She looked around with a slight smirk, secure that her audience would understand her allusion to the despised Queen Caroline.

"Mama is trying to be clever," whispered William.

"Which is not wise where Mr Darville is concerned," returned Harriet in some anxiety. To her relief, Rupert seemed indifferent to Lady McAllister's clumsy attempt at wit. He returned the bowl to Hinton and proceeded to examine several exquisitely carved jade figurines.

"Allow me to show you the pride of my collection," said Hinton. "The ladies will particularly appreciate this. Catherine, would you ring the bell, my dear." He despatched a message and several minutes later a long box packed with tissue paper was brought in by two servants. Hinton carefully unwrapped the contents to reveal a robe of brilliant green silk, heavily embroidered with two white cranes flying across a vivid sunset sky.

With the eye of a true connoisseur, Lady McAllister went into raptures over the needlework and Philippa shyly endorsed her every compliment.

"The sleeves, the cuffs! What minute stitches! How exquisite! I would go quite blind over such work. My poor efforts cannot compare with such an accomplishment," said Lady McAllister boldly examining the inside of the garment.

"Take care ma'am," Hinton spoke hastily. "The fabric is very fragile. It is over two hundred years old."

"The silk is of the very best quality," said Marguerite knowledgably.

"The work undoubtedly took years to complete." Elspeth peered myopically at the thousands of tiny stitches woven across the front panel.

"My dear Lady McAllister you do yourself an injustice, when your own work has been admired by the highest arbiter of good taste."

"Hush, Susan! Lord Everard cannot have seen the work of art we have before us when he so kindly praised my mediocre attempts."

"On the contrary," said Hinton. "I had Everard here only the other day. No matter what one thinks of the man, he appreciates quality when he sees it."

Hinton gently extracted the robe from Lady McAllister's grasp and held it up so his visitors could admire it more easily. "He professed to know little of the Orient but recognised at once that this was the robe of a minor court official of the Ming dynasty."

"It must be worth a fortune," commented Valentine.

"No so much," replied Hinton leaving the ladies in raptures as his wife packed the robe away in its box. "The agent tried to tell me it was an emperor's robe, but I'm not such a fool; the Chinese would never allow a garment as sacred as the emperor's out of the country. However, I'm satisfied I made a good bargain. Everard confirmed it was likely to be robe of a high-ranking civil servant. It will look well in the gallery in Hinton Hall."

"I trust your servants are armed and on the alert, Hinton," said William. "I don't know what your place is like down in the country but London at this time is a nest of thieves."

Mr Hinton was confident in the vigilance of his footmen – all his own people from Hinton Parva, he assured the company. William McAllister looked openly sceptical at this rustic naivety.

As the party prepared to depart, Lady McAllister and Philippa found themselves talking quite naturally of the demands of black branch work as opposed to needlepoint. Rupert helped Harriet and Miss Finch into their carriage.

"Have you enjoyed your day, Miss Larkhill?"

"Enormously, thank you."

"It was none of my doing," he said with a faint awkwardness. "But I'm glad you have met the Hintons here, they will enlarge your acquaintance while you are in London."

"I have no intention of neglecting my *old* friends, Mr Darville," she said teasingly. "I trust I will have the pleasure of your company again soon?" She was mindful of the dowager countess's request.

Miss Finch looked shocked at such forwardness.

Rupert smiled. "I will send tickets round to Russell Square for my lecture at the Royal Institution. I am asked to speak on Friday morning. How many tickets will you need?"

Harriet broke it to him gently that only herself and Lady McAllister would be attending from Russell Square, although Madame de Lessups had promised to bring Philippa, and surprisingly, Mr Beaumont had decided to accompany them.

Rupert was unperturbed and bade both ladies a civil farewell.

******

Harriet's visit promised to be full; every social encounter led to another and more. London was *en fete* and Harriet intended to make the most of her opportunities. However, she found it was not within her gift to absolutely decide on her own entertainments; Lady McAllister drew the line at a masquerade ball at Vauxhall Gardens. No lady of virtue would be seen there nowadays, however fashionable the pleasure gardens might have been in her youth. Harriet had wanted only to see the thousands of lamps and dance among the trees but bowed to her hostess's superior knowledge.

In compensation, Lady McAllister took Harriet to the British Museum. The weather was fine for the short walk to Great Russell Street so there was no need to call out the carriage and the entry was free. Elspeth McAllister was starting to realise that it was not enough to be aware of fashionable literature and *beaux arts*, one also had to be conversant with the latest discoveries and movements in natural philosophy to retain one's reputation as a woman of worth.

In the ten minutes it took to walk round from Russell Square to the great seventeenth century mansion, Lady McAllister gave Harriet a detailed account of the first and second Montagu House which had stood on the site, the fluctuating fortunes of its extensive gardens and the sad departure of the second Duke of Montagu who abandoned his father's house to move to Whitehall.

"My only consolation is that, as a distant member of the family, I am privileged to live nearby even if the house will never be a domestic residence again. It was a third cousin of my mother who sold it to the trustees of the museum."

"The collection is based on that of Sir Hans Soane, I believe?" ventured Harriet. She had been reading her guide book again.

"And many others. You will see the Townley collection of classical antiquities and the Parthenon Marbles, brought back by dear Lord Elgin. But I fear it is mainly books and manuscripts, which my poor eyesight does not allow me to appreciate as I should wish. However, Cousin Susan will read out the labels on anything that interests us."

"Of course, Elspeth," breathed the little lady bobbing at their heels.

They entered under the arch into a spacious quadrangle and crossed to the imposing façade with its prominent mansard roof and dome over the centre. Once inside they signed the visitors' book and looked about them. Lady McAllister hoped to see an acquaintance she could impress. Several parties of visitors were making their way directly up the wide stone staircase. Lady McAllister led her charges forward.

Lady McAllister was the kind of woman who liked to have her money's worth whether the occasion was free or not. There followed an hour of exhaustive bending and staring, with poor Miss Finch trapped by her employer into deciphering each exhibit card.

Harriet soon left her companions behind and found herself in the wonder of the Egyptian room. There were so many glass cases to examine that she would have to return for several other visits to absorb it all. There was so much to tell Young Clem; the mummies stacked three deep in pyramid-shaped display cases, the hieroglyphs and friezes painted on the walls, the shining sarcophagus and carved heads of Egyptian kings. She wished Rupert were there to explain it all to her.

Her conscience made her go in search of her companions. She found them about to mount to the second storey, Lady McAllister looking impatient and Miss Finch exhausted.

At the top of the wide stone staircase Harriet gave a gasp; three giraffes towered above them looking down their noses. Next to them, stuffed in all its glory stood a rhinoceros. Miss Finch leaned over to read the card. "Rhinoceros, is a group of five species of odd-toed ungulates in the family *Rhinocerotidae*. Two of these species are native to Africa and three to Southern Asia. What a horrid horn it has! And its skin looks as though it does not fit. I hope it does not frighten the little children."

"Children are not allowed inside the museum," returned Lady McAllister with approval.

"Which seems foolish for an institution devoted to enlightenment," murmured Harriet and added quickly: "I wonder if Mr Darville encountered one of these beasts on his travels."

Ahead of them, a small, fair lady with bright eyes turned at the sound of Harriet's remark. She started, said a word to the well-built young woman at her side and came forward with one gloved hand outstretched and a glance of enquiry at Harriet.

"Why, Lady McAllister, how well met!" said the lady in a soft Edinburgh brogue. "I intended to call on you tomorrow, and never expected such a happy meeting in the British Museum."

"Good morning Mrs Somerville," returned Lady McAllister with frozen politeness. "I refresh myself with visiting Montagu House frequently. The property once belonged to an ancestor of mine."

But Mary Somerville was a modern woman. "Indeed? However, I must apologise for not coming to your musical soirée. Dr Somerville and I returned to town only yesterday with a young family friend from Edinburgh, and found your kind invitation. My husband was mortified to have missed the evening. May I present Miss Lavinia Snoddie."

Here she beckoned to the young woman. "She insisted on coming here at once, though we have been home but a few hours."

Elspeth McAllister did not know Mrs Somerville well but her academic credentials were impeccable. She had thought to invite the Somervilles to her party as her husband was widely travelled and known to Sir Hamish.

"I do beg your pardon but did I hear this young lady mention the name of Mr Darville, Mr Rupert Darville?" continued the lady, looking from Elspeth to Harriet.

Explanations were given and Mrs Somerville beamed. "Mr Darville is a great friend of ours, too. You must know that I spend every free hour studying mathematics and he has been an enormous help to me regarding my algebra. Are you mathematical, Miss Larkhill? I hope he will give Lavinia similar encouragement in her studies, he is such a widely-read gentleman."

Harriet was impressed and slightly overwhelmed, but Elspeth made the decision that Mrs Somerville was worthy to be added to the select group of her dearest friends. Harriet eyed Miss Snoddie doubtfully. She was a round-faced, haughty-looking girl with pale eyes and a stubbornness about the jaw. Her clothes were smart and she filled them to capacity.

"Will you be attending Mr Darville's lecture on South America, tomorrow? At the Royal Institution?" asked Harriet looking from one lady to the other. "It is not about mathematics but is certain to be interesting."

"Sadly, no, Miss Larkhill. My husband is engaged at the Chelsea hospital and I must collect my children from school, which is great pity as Lavinia would enjoy the lecture immensely I am sure. Her interests are not mathematical."

Lavinia remained unsmiling but Lady McAllister could not ignore the suggestion in Mrs Somerville's voice. "We would be happy to take Miss Snoddie as one of our party. It would be no inconvenience at all for me to send the carriage for her – early." Lady McAllister would not stir until the last moment, by which time Pole would have fetched Miss Snoddie.

Gracious thanks were given and the elder ladies moved on, talking together. Miss Finch was forgotten, much to her own relief.

"What is your opinion of the exhibits?" asked Harriet with her usual enthusiasm as she fell in beside Miss Snoddie.

"A prodigious collection of note but sadly illogical in its arrangement," returned Miss Snoddie. "Mrs Somerville is endeavouring to find a connection between everything in nature so must enquire into everything, but I fear she has set herself an impossible task. For myself, I am sadly disappointed; I did not find what I came to see." She had a low breathy voice with a hint of Scotch.

"What did you come to see?"

"Skulls."

"Skulls! Why?" asked Harriet in surprise.

"I am a student of Dr Gall."

"I'm afraid I do not know who that gentleman is."

"Then may I recommend his work on the Physiognominal System? He is the father of the only true science of the mind, phrenology. I am interested in whether the mind is dependent on the brain's physical qualities."

"Oh, the *reading* of skulls!" said Harriet with interest. "In order to discover someone's nature? I have seen something about it in *The Quarterly Review*." She had heard of an extremely derogatory article on the matter and knew of popular lectures on the subject given in Bath.

"Quite so. The skull takes its shape from the brain therefore the surface of the skull can be read as an indication of the various organs of character."

"It does seem logical," said Harriet politely. "Wasn't it Aristotle who held that fancy resided at the front, reason in the centre and memory at the back of the brain?"

Miss Snoddie looked down her nose. "The study of phrenology is not so simplistic. Dr Gall's pupil Dr Spurzheim has taken the theory further; he holds that there are thirty-seven innate faculties of the mind which can be discovered from reading the skull. My papa has just helped to found the Edinburgh Phrenological Society. He is an eminent physician and is very highly thought of by his colleagues. I had hoped to look at the skulls of the Egyptian Pharaohs while I was in London."

"But they are all wrapped, or in sarcophagi, surely?" said Harriet surprised that Miss Snoddie should be unaware of this.

"The average visitor will not know that many Egyptian kings had their heads shaved. I have read that wigs were frequently worn. I think I might have been granted access to at least one skull."

"I think it is extremely unlikely that the custodians of the museum would allow anyone to handle the exhibits," said Harriet.

"I don't understand why not. I would do them no harm. My papa is a well-recognised practitioner of the science and has taught me the rudiments of phrenological examination. He wrote a letter asking for permission on my behalf, but was refused. It must be because I am a female and considered untrustworthy. Such prejudice is abominable when it obstructs the study of the only true science of the mind."

Harriet thought this an exaggeration but commented from experience: "I fear the organ of benevolence is not well developed in elderly gentlemen who are trustees. Do you intend to see the coronation while you are in London?"

"Of course! It is the perfect opportunity of seeing exemplars of the leading families of Europe. I welcome the chance of personally examining the Hapsburg lip and the elongated chin at first hand. These royal houses are so interbred. My papa intends to write a paper on the physiognomy of the different social classes, so I must take careful notes."

"How fascinating." Interested though she was, Harriet resisted the temptation to enquire further, sensing Miss Snoddie would abuse a willing audience. Conversation wilted while Harriet's mind wavered between the suitability of Miss Snoddie as a mate for Rupert, and a suspicion that the young woman might be a bore.

At last the ladies separated, Mrs Somerville waving and Miss Snoddie climbing into the carriage without a backward glance.

"Mary Somerville is a highly intelligent woman, so Sir Hamish tells me," commented Lady McAllister as they walked back to Russell Square. "Scottish of course, a notable beauty in Edinburgh when she came out. She made a disastrous first marriage but is settled happily enough now. I wonder whether Miss Snoddie is worth cultivating?"

******

The Darvilles invited the McAllisters to the opera at the Haymarket and afterwards to supper at Rules. Lord Patrick had borrowed a box from an old friend for the latest musical sensation: 'The Thieving Magpie'.

"It will certainly be a change from that interminable German stuff we have been plagued with over the years. I do not refer to Mr Handel of course," said Sir Hamish. "What would His Majesty do without Mr Handel?"

"The man is a genius and almost British," confirmed his wife.

"You sound like Mortimer Shawcross, Mama," said William casting a sly look at Harriet. They were playing backgammon in the drawing room when the invitation arrived.

Much to William's glee and Andrew's puzzlement, Harriet had a suitor. Since Lady McAllister's musical evening, Mortimer Shawcross had become a regular caller in Russell Square. Sir Hamish wondered if his old friend had serious intentions.

Harriet ignored the young gentlemen's teasing and enjoyed Mr Shawcross's company.

He was of respectable birth, possessed an easy fortune, had good manners and if one could ignore the corset and the snuff, dressed with style. He took extra pains with his appearance, to which he fondly believed only his valet and coiffeur were privy. The fact that he had three quarrelsome daughters and a host of sponging relatives in a mouldering pile in Grantham made no difference to Harriet as she had no wish to marry him.

She also believed that Mr Shawcross had no intention of making her an offer. He was amusing himself with a pretty girl for a few weeks, nothing more. Besides, she got on famously with older men, it was always the younger ones who were a problem. She would be returning to Larkhill when the season was over and until then it would be pleasant to have a reliable escort. William had no interest in sightseeing and Rupert came and went on a whim. Besides, she felt she was now duty bound to throw Miss Lavinia Snoddie in his way.

Harriet was excited at the prospect of a visit to Almack's rooms that evening. Lady McAllister too had mellowed with the prospect of meeting some of her foreign friends again. Andrew declined to attend knowing Philippa would not be there but William was agog to catch up on the latest court news, though Almack's was too respectable to be the source of much scandal.

Harriet felt she was presentable in her chartreuse silk and, in a fit of generosity, Lady McAllister lent her the green fan. Lady McAllister had sensibly eschewed feathers in her headdress and wore a flat turban with trailing ribbons of silk. The gentlemen were all in dark knee breeches and stockings.

The stairs up to the ballroom were crowded but the major domo gave their party a quick scrutiny and waved them in. Lady McAllister had not expected such a crush and on this occasion her height proved an advantage; she soon spied out the company, swooping towards a group of dowagers like a heron in flight. William disappeared toward the card room while Sir Hamish was taken aside by young Mr Peel.

Harriet was chastened to discover that Elspeth McAllister was indeed remembered and claimed as an acquaintance, if not a friend, by several *grandes dames*. "*Chère Elspet, bienvenue! Combien de temps depuis Vienne?*"

Their costumes ranged from the old-fashioned to the bizarre but all sported the choicest lace and the best tiaras. The ladies displayed the dignity of their rank and after a few nods and stares, ignored Harriet, but Lady McAllister would not be dislodged.

Harriet was wondering if she would ever reach the dance floor when Mortimer Shawcross brushed past her.

"I beg your - Why Miss Larkhill, what a pleasure to see you here." He took in the circle of dowagers. "Let me rescue you from *Mittel Europe* and beg the honour of the next set." Lady McAllister, distracted by her friends, gave a nod of approval, and was happy to be relieved of her charge.

Shawcross proved to be an excellent dancer for a man of his years. Harriet was grateful when he pointed out the leading figures of the *ton*. She was surprised at how many older gentlemen wore wigs, adding to the formality of the evening. The babble of foreign tongues made her head turn. The swish of silk, bobbing plumes, dazzling candles and jewels delighted her. The musicians in the gallery struck up a quadrille and Shawcross led her into a square set. Despite William's tutoring, Harriet was so busy concentrating on her steps that she had no time to take much note of her partners until the ladies formed a star and she came face to face with Barbara Bixby.

The lady hesitated for a moment. "Miss Larkhill, isn't it? Such a pretty name. Elspeth's little – cousin?" The lady looked tired and strained but elegant enough in straw-coloured silk. To Harriet's disappointment, the lady was wearing heavy amber jewellery. Where were the famous diamonds?

Harriet could only smile and acquiesce as the figure of the dance moved them apart again. She had the delight of being acknowledged by Lady Londonderry and received a civil word from the marquess, though several ladies quizzed her with curiosity. She recognised one or two of the young ladies who had been at Lady McAllister's musical evening and envied them their ease of entitlement. Eventually, Mr Shawcross returned her to Lady McAllister and disappeared to the card room with the promise of another dance later. Lady McAllister had moved on from the dowagers to Lord Everard who was twirling his lorgnette in boredom.

William came up to do his duty. "Enjoyin' yourself Miss Larkhill? What's wrong? You need stamina when in town, you know. We'll be footing it until four in the morning. Would you care to stand up with me and put our practice to the test? I take it you waltz? Or may I escort you to the card room? I warn you it's pretty tame stuff. Or are you feelin' tired already?"

"Tired? No, not at all. I was merely disappointed that Lady Bixby is not wearing her famous diamonds tonight."

"Diamonds, with yellow?" came a pained voice from behind them. "Shame ma'am, have you *no* sense of colour?"

She turned to find Lord Everard at her elbow and bristled slightly. "I was advised that diamonds could be worn with any shade, my lord."

Everard put up his lorgnette to her, turned to the room and murmured "In dress perhaps, but complexion no, and dear Barbara is looking distressingly wan this evening. Your pardon ma'am." He moved languidly away through the scented crowd.

"Ignore him Miss Larkhill," advised William, secretly admiring Everard's lofty demeanour. "I hear he'll be a bankrupt before the year is out, for all his supercilious manner."

Harriet's face lit up as she caught sight of Rupert in dark velvet swallow tails and extravagantly tied stock. He was talking to the Hintons and a group of military men. A stern gentleman with a strong nose who was in the company of the Countess Lieven was holding forth. Rupert broke away from the group with a bow and came towards them.

"Good evening McAllister. Save me from the idiocies of military men. Come dance with me Harriet."

William looked scandalised. "You cannot talk of the Saviour of Europe in such terms!"

"Is that the Duke of Wellington?" gasped Harriet in awe and a little disappointment. William had revealed that the great man treated his wife cruelly.

"It is. Will you dance, Miss Larkhill? But you must not complain if I tread on your toes; I have not waltzed in a year. I dare not ask any other lady to partner me this evening."

"Mr Shawcross-" she began.

"Will not miss you; he's playing vingt-et-un with Frodingham."

Harriet turned an apologetic face to William who was happy to be released.

"Thank you Mr Darville, such a compliment. We will dance very carefully then. Did you dance in Rio de Janiero? At the Portuguese Court? Or at any of the Governors' houses on your travels?"

"Infrequently." He took her in his arms with decision.

Harriet was intrigued. "Were all the ladies tropical beauties with languorous eyes and flashing teeth?" she teased.

"The Creole women, yes. Did you know there were eight ranks of mulatto?"

"I'm sure you told me so in one of your letters, and you must tell me again tomorrow, but not now as I have to take care of my feet or we'll come a-tumble."

After a moment's silence Rupert said: "I do believe this is the first time I have ever danced properly with you Harriet."

"Indeed, I think you are right," said Harriet knowing full well it was.

"You do it very well."

"Thank you."

"You did not come to my–"

"Your nuptial ball?" she completed his broken off sentence calmly.

He twirled her round, a slight frown between his eyes. "Why was that?"

"I went to school," she replied easily.

"How odd." And with a sudden masterful lead he swept her away from the McAllisters. "I did not expect to see you here tonight. Elspeth McAllister must have exerted considerable influence to obtain a voucher for you."

"You are *most* uncomplimentary Mr Darville! However, I can only put it down to the sheep." He looked puzzled. "I'll wager Lord Londonderry approved of my sheep, which made Lady Londonderry approve of me," she said with satisfaction.

He gave a bark of laughter and held her tighter.

After a moment Harriet said: "Lady McAllister and I intend to come to your lecture tomorrow. May I beg an extra ticket for a friend?"

"Not Miss Beaumont? I doubt if she would find my talk of any interest."

"Well she *will* be one of our party, and you are unjust to poor Philippa, who has a very good understanding, of some things, but I have recently met a Miss Lavinia Snoddie who, I am told, is an original 'thinker' and wishes to hear you speak. Do you know her?"

Rupert frowned. "My talk will be about the flora and fauna of the Amazon, nothing classically philosophical."

"She is Mrs Somerville's connection and has an interest in phrenology."

"I believe there is a link with the body and the mind, but not through reading lumps on the skull! What nonsense!"

"What a fraud you are Rupert!"

"What do you mean?" he retorted.

"Was it not you who told me to question everything?"

"Of course - except anything *I* tell you. It is the motto of the Royal Society," he added grudgingly.

"Then I will keep an open mind on the subject – as should you, until it is proved to be nonsense."

Rupert shrugged. "Mary Somerville is a truly remarkable woman, so one has hopes of any connection of hers. By all means include Miss Snoddie in your party, Harriet. I will leave tickets at the door. I'm glad you have made another new friend."

As expected, Miss Larkhill's first appearance in society made no impression on the *ton* whatsoever. With this she was perfectly content. It was enough that she had danced at Almack's and that Rupert had sought her out. Her letter to Juliana would be worth the two pence postage, especially as she had the opera night with the Darvilles to relate.

******

Jacob was waiting for them at the foot of the red-carpeted staircase beaming at the sight of Harriet. He looked splendid in his green livery and swelled with importance.

"How Master Clem, Missarriet?" he said, leading the way up the stairs and treading on the heels of a slow and stout gentleman.

"How nice to see you again Jacob. Master Clem is perfectly well and sends his remembrance."

"And the parrot, Missarriet? How Captain Blood?"

"Thriving. Master Clem has taught him to say 'Avast me hearties'. I will tell him I have seen you when I next write to Larkhill."

The McAllisters mounted through crowds of jostling people to the middle tier of boxes. Jacob piloted them towards an open door where Lord Patrick stood ready to welcome his guests. Cloaks were removed, seats arranged and at last Harriet had leisure to take in the fabulous King's Theatre. Four tiers of velvet and gilt-encrusted boxes rose to the roof, each one occupied by some scion of the nobility and their friends. All was a shimmer of gold and red, illuminated by a giant gas-lit chandelier suspended from the domed ceiling. A rising susurration of voices drew Harriet's gaze to the audience.

She was amused by the young bucks in the pit ogling the fair ladies in the boxes. Several men in military uniform were threatening to start a fight. She was appalled to see Captain Valentine among them and quickly averted her gaze, thankful that Philippa was not here. As she turned to the boxes her eye was caught by a rotund gentleman, making a bow in her direction. After a swift glance about her to ensure she was the intended recipient she raised a tentative hand.

"Good lord! Is that Mortimer Shawcross," said Lady McAllister, flapping a glove in his direction.

Sir Hamish confirmed the matter.

"Charming man, such good manners." She took a look at Harriet and then up at her husband. "You must invite him to our box in the first interval, Sir Hamish." Lady McAllister turned to Rupert. "You will not object, Mr Darville, if I send your page with a message?"

"My dear, this is Lord Patrick's evening, we cannot invite all and sundry," said her spouse quietly.

"Nonsense Hamish, invite who you like," broke in Lord Patrick. "The more the merrier, I say. 'Tain't my box but Winterbourne's. Shawcross ain't a damned Whig, so no harm done."

Jacob was despatched and Lady McAllister continued to bow to her acquaintances. Her long-sightedness gave her a distinct advantage and she was satisfied that a night at the opera would provide conversation for a month.

The dowager countess leaned across to Harriet. "I don't mind opera in general. Morna has cried off as usual and I can't say I blame him. I'm not sure I will be able to last the course myself. I find the ballet at the end more than tedious, but needs must."

Harriet decided to ignore the countess's needs for this evening and said: "This is my first visit to the opera; I am so grateful that Lord Patrick had this notion to invite us, and hope the evening isn't too disagreeable for you, Countess. Mr Darville," beamed Harriet, turning to Rupert. "How did Lord Patrick know I wanted to visit the opera?"

"He didn't. It's more the tyranny of returning invitations. Sir Hamish has been civil enough to entertain me more than once since I have been back in England. Good manners dictate that I reciprocate."

"Oh, so this was *your* scheme? How cunning! An invitation to the opera will ensure you a place at Lady McAllister's table for the rest of your days," said Harriet matching his incivility.

"I thought Lady McAllister would not refuse an evening at the opera, though I seldom see her here. *You* were a music lover as a child; I knew your interest persisted even in the depths of Wiltshire. And you said you wanted to take in all the sights."

She was prevented from replying by the orchestra striking up the overture. For the next forty minutes Harriet sat enraptured by the music but more carried away by the spectacle. The dowager countess closed her eyes.

Mr Shawcross was prompt in his attendance at the first interval. He commented on the success of Lady McAllister's soirée, passed a snippet of political news to Sir Hamish, offered Lord Patrick a pinch of snuff, complimented Rupert on Jacob's manners and offered his services to Harriet as an escort if ever she needed one.

"If you like spectacle, Miss Larkhill, as I surmise you do – forgive me but I was watching you during the performance - then I'm certain you would find the entertainment at Astley's Amphitheatre to your taste. It's a good old fashioned English performance – plenty of horses and chasing about. None of this foreign how-de-do. I would be perfectly happy to make up a party to include all the young people."

He looked around him for support.

Mr Shawcross's generous invitation was accepted by Lady McAllister on behalf of her absent sons and Miss Larkhill, which meant that Miss Beaumont must be asked and Madame invited as chaperone.

The dowager countess spoke up. "Darville here appreciates horseflesh. He took us when Morna and I first arrived in London. The trick-riding is extremely neat and some feats of horsemanship would not disgrace the battlefield, I'm told. Why don't you go with them?" she said turning to look up at her silent son.

"Then perhaps I might ask Miss Snoddie to accompany us as well; she is new to London," added Harriet impulsively.

Shawcross, who saw his pleasant evening with Harriet ballooning into a gala, hesitated. "Who is Miss Snoddie?" he asked politely.

Lady McAllister enlightened him. "Miss Snoddie is visiting the Somervilles; she is a very intellectual young lady from Edinburgh. Miss Larkhill is acquainted with her. The Somervilles are very good friends of ours, are they not Sir Hamish? You must have heard of Mrs Somerville, a mathematical genius and friend of Mr Darville."

Shawcross knew when he was beaten. "Then by all means, we must include Miss Snoddie."

It wasn't until the second interval that Harriet had a chance to talk to Rupert again. He offered his arm to her and suggested a stroll in the corridor outside the box.

"Do not tease yourself about coming with us to Astley's, if you would rather not," said Harriet. She was slightly regretting her enthusiasm.

"I very much wish to come to Astley's again. My mother is right; the horses are most beautiful to watch, and I am glad of the excuse to see another performance."

"Poor Mr Shawcross, he has landed himself with a circus before we even get south of the river."

She was just about to enquire whether he had found himself a suitable secretary in London when a loud party of noisy people swept round the curve of the corridor. Coming directly towards them in deep magenta silk was Lady Bixby on the arm of her portly husband. The gentleman was grimacing and limping slightly. Across Lady Bixby's plunging bosom lay a magnificent swathe of diamonds. Great dull drops hung from her ears. The pretty bracelet rattled around her wrist. Lady Bixby laughingly turned her head to respond to some comment from her friends and did not notice Harriet's round-eyed stare.

Harriet blinked in appreciation and breathed. "At last I have seen the famous Bixby diamonds." Her eyes sparkled.

"And how did they seem to you?" asked Rupert with a hint of amusement.

"Dirty!"

"Harriet, you are incorrigible!" he laughed aloud. "Someone may hear you."

"But truly, the settings looked quite grubby and the stones particularly dull. Of course it could be because of their great age and the antique setting, but I would have thought her maid would have had them cleaned for such an occasion. But that's what comes of keeping them in the chandelier I suppose – such awkward things to dust. You must know I have been on the fret to see them! Miss Beaumont will be *so* disappointed to have missed this opportunity. We can only hope Lady Bixby will wear them to the coronation festivities."

"I didn't imagine you hankered after fine jewels, Harriet."

"What woman does not? But no, I will not have you think me mercenary. I merely wished to see if they were as wonderful as I had imagined. Lady Bixby was not wearing them at Almack's last night. She did not seem at all herself at the assembly. I do not quite understand the etiquette of such things; perhaps the diamonds would be considered too extravagant for such an evening?"

"I regret that the niceties of ladies' dress escape me. However, I trust your imagination is now satisfied?"

"Entirely so." She gave a mock sigh of pleasure.

"I do not know why women go into raptures over what after all are merely lumps of quartz."

"Rupert, please do *not* talk geology to me this evening. I wish to have one night in fairy-land and a visit to the Italian opera house is the nearest I will ever come to it."

Harriet's excursion into fairy land happily continued beyond the end of the opera. She even approved of the ballet finale and was pleased that William was not there to spoil the spectacle with sordid gossip about the prettiest of the dancers.

Supper at Rules was everything she had hoped. Lord Patrick was adept at entertaining and had reserved a booth where they could see and be seen by the other diners. He was known to the proprietor and the service was prompt and discreet. The food melted in Harriet's mouth – she was always hungry in London - and by the end of the evening her head buzzed with good champagne.

Lady McAllister divided her time between the menu and claiming acquaintance with the other diners. She declared the evening perfect after Lord Everard stopped by their table and exchanged pleasantries.

Harriet and Rupert chatted easily, Lord Patrick occasionally interjecting. The dowager countess started to flag and contributed little apart from a few frowns. Only when they were parting did Lady Darville take Harriet aside. "Don't forget what you promised me, Miss Larkhill," she said gripping her arm.

Harriet did not pretend to misunderstand. "I wasn't aware that I had *promised* anything, Countess. I merely said I would do what I could."

"I'm relying on you to see my son safely settled!"

Harriet was about to make a sharp retort – the champagne had made her bold – when the countess's drawn features caused her to relent. "I have just met a young lady who *may* be a - congenial partner for your son. Mrs Somerville's connection, the Miss Snoddie we spoke of. She is very 'scientific'."

"But is she rich?" snapped the Countess.

"How can I tell! I have met her but once. She will be one of our party at your son's lecture." Harriet resisted removing the dowager's hand from her arm. "If you intend to be there you can discover her prospects for yourself. I can do no more than introduce you."

This exchange slightly soured the evening for Harriet but she clung to the thought that every day brought exciting new experiences and soon she would be going to the Royal Institution to hear Rupert speak.

CHAPTER 5   THEFT

Philippa quailed at the steepness of the tiered benches in the Royal Institution and begged to be seated at the front. Her father offered his arm to help her up the steps when a party of gentlemen, seeing her pretty face, gallantly rose to give up their places to the ladies. Lord Everard was amongst them and Lady McAllister, seizing the moment, made introductions, only to discover that the Nabob and the leader of fashion were already acquainted. Lord Everard shook Miss Beaumont's hand with the familiarity of an old friend.

"How very enlightened of you, Miss Beaumont to attend a lecture on natural philosophy – and on such exotic places. What would the nuns think if they discovered you were imbibing the new thinking? Be careful not to shock them with any blasphemous notions of the origins of the world when you return to school."

Philippa blushed at his teasing but said: "Nature is all part of God's work. Papa would not allow me to come to anything improper. Miss Larkhill says that Mr Darville is only to talk about the animals and the flowers of Brazil. I am sure the Mother Superior would not object."

"Then I defer to Miss Larkhill's knowledge of the speaker."

Miss Snoddie broke in: "My friend, Mrs Somerville knows Mr Darville *very* well. They dine frequently and he consults her and Dr Somerville on almost everything. There will be nothing heretical in his lecture."

"How gratifying," murmured Lord Everard raising his lorgnette.

Mr Beaumont, uncomfortable at this exchange, brusquely ordered his daughter to sit down. He took his place at the end of the front row like a sentinel of a harem as Lord Everard leisurely mounted the steps to join his friends.

"There, we will see and hear Mr Darville comfortably now," said Harriet. She twisted round to look up at the balcony. "He's attracted a great crowd." She acknowledged the Hintons some way above them. "I cannot see the Countess but there is Lord Patrick. Lord Everard is part of a very grand set."

Elspeth McAllister was gratified to recognise several notable members of society scattered about the lecture room. She was pleased that she had made the effort to attend; she would refer to the occasion in conversation as soon as possible. Miss Finch had begged the morning to visit her charity case so she was forced to rely on Harriet for companionship.

"What is that strange contraption?" asked Lady McAllister pointing to a small table directly in front of them. "And why is there a sheet on the wall?"

She indicated a tall metal box with a stubby tube on the front and a chimney at the top. Certain mysterious objects lay on the table in preparation for the speaker. Jacob stood guard, an attraction in himself with his bristling topknot and scarred face.

"It is a magic lantern. Mr Darville brought the device from Paris," whispered Harriet. "The paintings are most realistic he assures me. He puts a light behind them and shows them on the wall, on the white sheet."

"Paintings?"

"Of animals and plants and the natives," she explained. "The expedition's artist on the *Neptune* provided them. He had some copies of the official illustrations painted on glass, especially for Mr Darville. The device is all the rage in France."

None the wiser but unwilling to reveal her ignorance, Lady McAllister said no more.

At last Mr Faraday, the newly appointed Assistant Superintendent of the Royal Institution, appeared and introduced the speaker.

Wearing his usual dark coat, with his black curls brushed into some semblance of order, Rupert waited for the applause to die down. After giving his friends a quick smile of recognition Rupert spoke surprisingly well. The elder ladies were, on the whole, informed and entertained. Philippa, used to spending many quiet hours in the convent, had no problem sitting still, her eyes occasionally downcast. Harriet was as enraptured by the lecture as she had been by the opera but Miss Snoddie, after one calculating stare at Rupert, allowed her gaze to wander.

At one point Rupert called for some of the shutters and curtains to be closed. Jacob took up his position by the contraption, ready to push the slides through the aperture at his master's command. Rupert moved from the lectern to the small table in front of the auditorium and lighting a strong candle slid it into the body of the apparatus. He moved an oil lamp closer to his notes.

"I have seen such a demonstration before," whispered Miss Snoddie. "A professor of anatomy gave a lecture using one of these machines, at Edinburgh University. They are nothing new."

Harriet was surprised that ladies had been allowed to attend such a lecture but did not challenge Miss Snoddie's statement. She was far more interested in what Rupert was saying about the rain forest.

The magic lantern slides were a revelation. The ladies gave a shriek of alarm when a ferocious jaguar leapt to life on the wall opposite. Huge fronds of green foliage flickered over the white sheet. The toucan with its great beak caused great amusement and the length of the anaconda caused even the gentlemen to shudder.

"Miss Beaumont will have nightmares tonight," whispered Miss Snoddie with a smirk.

Rupert spoke briskly, only occasionally misplaced his notes, produced some specimens where he could and painted slides when he could not. If there was a trifle too much Latin or Greek, his audience felt flattered and bestowed generous applause when he finished an hour later. His friends crowded around him with congratulations. Will Hinton urged Rupert to publish his findings.

"Where is the Countess?" asked Harriet.

"A slight indisposition," replied Lord Patrick enjoying his nephew's reflected glory.

"Capital, Darville," said Beaumont shaking the younger man's hand as the audience dispersed. "Another continent for trade maybe, if we can wrest if from the Portuguese and the Spanish. The maps were a masterpiece. Dashed cunning to 'throw' your pictures on the wall like that."

Lady McAllister stepped forward. "Quite magical, Mr Darville. What a clever instrument. I feel one ought to be *au fait* with the latest manufacturing inventions." Jacob was packing away the contraption with great care into a wooden box.

"It is more a matter of understanding physics, ma'am," said Rupert. "The magic lantern is merely the vehicle. Physics encompasses the study of the properties of light."

"Quite so," replied Lady McAllister and then turning to the young ladies said: "Miss Snoddie, may I introduce our friend Mr Rupert Darville to you?"

Harriet was surprised to see the haughty Miss Snoddie drop a demure curtsey and say breathily: "What an honour it is to listen to someone with your experience and fine mind, Mr Darville. Dr and Mrs Somerville would have found your lecture *most* enlightening and send their regrets and apologies for their absence."

"I'm flattered you thought it interesting, Miss Snoddie. I understand that you have an interest in matters of the mind?"

"In my own modest way." She seemed in no hurry to expand on this. "I was hoping you would discourse on the various tribes you had come across on the expedition. Did you find them so very different from the European lower orders?" She looked at Jacob as if he were an interesting specimen.

"Ah, there is matter enough there for another lecture perhaps."

"How I would love to hear your theories on the different behaviours of the brutish native and our own labouring classes."

Rupert was prevented from replying when more of his colleagues came up to congratulate him. Lavinia remained beside Rupert and turned her shoulder on the rest of the party.

As they left the hall, Philippa said to Harriet: "The south Americas sound a fearful place do they not, Miss Larkhill? All those wild beasts and poisonous plants."

"Extremely. Mr Darville's letters did not convey any sense of danger to us, only excitement and discovery. But one cannot be entirely ignorant of the risks such expeditions suffer."

"He wrote to you?" asked Philippa in wonder.

"Yes, we received several letters over the years," she smiled at her friend. "Mr Darville's observations have given me much food for thought."

"He rather frightens me," said Philippa with a nervous glance ahead. Miss Snoddie appeared to be in fine flow. "Mr Darville talks of the oddest things and I never know how to answer."

"Then you must ask questions," Harriet responded. "Gentlemen *always* like telling one things; it makes them feel superior to a mere female."

"Oh, do you think so?" said the wide-eyed Philippa.

"Invariably," replied Harriet promptly. "When you find a gentleman who will *listen* to *you,* then exert yourself to marry him."

Philippa said with some insight. "*You* are not afraid of Mr Darville – will you marry *him*?"

"He is still at the talking stage I fear," mused Harriet watching the animated couple ahead of them. "And not exclusively to me. But that's as it should be. I *do* hope she doesn't talk to him about phrenology. I am not at all certain of the gentleman's manners."

******

Harriet had more to think about than Lavinia Snoddie's pursuit of Rupert. The season and her own popularity meant that she would have to go shopping for ribbons and beads to transform her dresses; expenditure on another gown was out of the question despite her hostess's hints. Another day of jollity was promised. Tea at Gunter's with Cholmondleys and then a select card party in the evening with Lord and Lady Glynn. She hardly had time to write home.

To Harriet's relief there had been no report of the theft of the Ravensburg Cross in the newspapers. William would have called attention to it immediately even if she had missed it. She assumed that the Reichsgraf had successfully used his influence to keep the incident out of the public eye.

Sir Hamish detained her at breakfast. The young gentlemen had gone to their respective appointments: William to exercise his horses and Andrew to Jackson's boxing saloon in a rare morning of liberty. Sir Hamish dismissed the footman.

"I am pleased to have this moment alone with you Harriet. No do not run away. I was speaking to Count Ravensburg last evening," said Sir Hamish conversationally. "I had no idea you were acquainted with him, my dear. He was somehow under the impression that you were my niece."

Harriet looked awkward and tried to explain.

"No matter - I hear you did a singular service for his wife the other day."

Harriet picked up the coffee pot and poured him another cup. "Anyone would have done the same, sir. I accompanied the Reichsgrafin to her hotel when she had a fall in the street. She was very shaken. I do hope the lady has recovered from the incident – and her husband. I have never seen a gentleman so distressed."

Sir Hamish's looked serene as he helped himself to a piece of ham. "It appears that all is well; the Imperial Count was at great pains to make light of the matter. In fact he was under the impression I knew all about it. Such a little thing, too insignificant to mention I suppose?" Hamish looked at her enquiringly

"It was a matter of no moment, sir, a small accident in the street. I had quite forgot the matter. And I have not had the pleasure of seeing you for three days," she replied sweetly.

"The Reichsgraf wished to reassure me that there would be no diplomatic repercussions." Sir Hamish gave her an old-fashioned look. "I warned you Harriet, no adventures. I can only assume that you didn't want to tell Lady McAllister that you were abroad unaccompanied. Not that we can prevent you, you are a grown woman, but the streets can be dangerous – as you must be aware from this unfortunate encounter. Nevertheless the Reichsgrafin herself sends you all compliments and a message that the lost reticule has been found and that all is as it should be."

"*Found!*" Harriet stared at him open-mouthed.

"I thought that would surprise you," he said dryly. "I of course have no idea of the significance of this message, and thought it wisest to make no enquiries. But yes, indeed, the Count was in fine fettle at the reception last night. He was presenting the king with a charming replica of the famous Ravensburg Cross, as it happens. So the matter is closed."

"*Where* was the reticule found? When? Who found-?"

Sir Hamish held up his hand. "A lucky co-incidence it seems. The Reichsgrafin's reticule was found in the gutter in Oxford Street where it was discovered by an 'honest citizen', who was suitably rewarded - I am told."

Their eyes met: Sir Hamish's bland, Harriet's disbelieving.

"Quite so, my dear but unless you wish to provoke a diplomatic incident, I would leave well alone."

Harriet, puzzled and dissatisfied, sipped her coffee and wished she could confide in Rupert. There was something odd about the whole business; Sir Hamish's elaborate unconcern proved it. If the Reichsgraf had spoken about the incident to Sir Hamish, surely *she* was now permitted to speak to someone? She would be discreet of course, but the danger of scandal was over and Rupert, she was sure, would be able to rationalise the incident.

******

The aroma of horse dung, sawdust and sweating bodies permeated the auditorium of Astley's Amphitheatre. Harriet was surprised at Rupert's being at ease in such surroundings; she had assumed this popular entertainment would be beneath his notice. Shawcross had taken a box where his guests had a perfect view over the circus ring and the stage above it. Madame de Lessups took a discreet seat at the back of the box and Mr Shawcross, a man of perfect manners, felt it incumbent upon him to keep her company.

As he inhaled his snuff his eyes strayed to Harriet, happy in conversation with the young gentlemen. As usual Andrew squired Miss Beaumont. Harriet had half expected to see Captain Valentine, especially as the spectacle was to include a re-enactment of the Battle of Culloden, but Mr Shawcross had refused to increase the party further and was well aware of the captain's louche reputation.

Miss Snoddie examined the audience crowded on benches around the ring. She put her handkerchief to her nose. "I am so relieved Mr Shawcross obtained tickets for the evening performance," she whispered. "Imagine what it would be like in the afternoon with even more screaming brats! Why the lower orders have to take their offspring with them wherever they go I cannot imagine." She looked with disdain at the riotous benches around the ring, squashed with families eating and scolding their children.

"Oh come now, Miss Snoddie, that's a little unreasonable, surely? Labourers have no time to come during the day, and who would take care of the children? Astley's is a family entertainment. My young nephew would adore it! But I can see why it is not to some people's taste."

"I'm not sure *I* should be here at all; but it is an opportunity to study the antics of the lower classes." She produced a tiny box of comfits and offered one to Harriet. When Rupert took the remaining chair on her other side, Miss Snoddie soon reconciled herself to the vulgarity of the spectacle and between bonbons and *bon mots*, made herself most agreeable.

The feats of daring were truly remarkable. The ladies applauded the performers' pyramids, the slack-rope vaulting, the juggling and tumbling and tricks of balance. The gentlemen appreciated the Spanish horses. William declared undying devotion for a young lady in spangled tights and ballet skirt who rode round the ring poised on one leg on the back of a pony. Philippa was captivated by the manége display of a magnificent white horse; a favourite with the crowd, half kneeling in curtsy to applause.

In the first interval Mr Shawcross seized his moment to sit next to Harriet. They would have had an amicable conversation but for Miss Snoddie's continual abrasive remarks.

"Do you enjoy the spectacle, Miss Larkhill? Such clever fellows to climb like monkeys and twist about so. Or do you prefer the jugglers?"

Miss Snoddie interposed. "I have been told that such performers have an enlarged faculty for the calculation of weight and resistance. This allows them to be more aware of the specific gravity of objects, especially when such objects are handled. My papa examined a troupe of these Italian jugglers in Edinburgh last summer."

"By jove, is that so?" said Shawcross, not quite sure what else to say.

"It still looks exciting and dangerous," said Harriet, not wanting to offend Mr Shawcross. "I was quite alarmed when the last poseur balanced so precariously on the highest chair."

Shawcross gathered his wits and spoke across Harriet to Miss Snoddie: "Such a knowledgeable young lady! You are a proponent of the new science I take it?"

"Oh I quite dote on phrenology. An examination of the brain and its faculties would explain all human behaviour, I am convinced of it. I long to understand why people act the way they do."

"Greed and foolishness ma'am, if my fellow Members of Parliament are anything to go by. They're venial, disloyal and stupid for the most part. I refer to the Whigs of course, though some of our own people ain't as sound as I would like."

"If ladies were allowed to stand for Parliament there would be a much more sensible arrangements in the country."

To her own surprise, Harriet found herself in tacit agreement.

Shawcross guffawed. "Women in the House! Whatever next?"

"Women in the professions? I can assure you women are every bit as intelligent and capable as men."

"I don't doubt it ma'am, especially the present company," replied Shawcross. "Yet I understand there is a modern theory that the female brain being smaller than the male's is far less capable of rational thought. Where is Darville, he will back me on this." And then recollecting his duties to his guests added: "But I am constantly amazed at how clever young ladies can be nowadays."

Miss Snoddie turned with a look of contemptuous despair to Harriet who could only smile in sympathy.

Rupert returned with a waiter and refreshments. He went and sat beside Lavinia and began to talk of George Coombe's *Essays on Phrenology*. Harriet did her best to fix her attention on Mr Shawcross's account of the horses in his Lincolnshire stables and his prowess on the hunting field.

The second act was announced. The programme had changed from Rupert's first visit only a few weeks before and the master of ceremonies proudly presented the 'Amazing Spectacle of the Glorious Victory of the Hanoverians over the Jacobite Rebels'.

"In honour of the coronation, I presume. How patriotic," approved Shawcross.

As no one had the slightest idea of what the real battle had been like, the audience was happy to accept the flouting of the wild red-bearded men in their plaid kilts and gave rousing cheers to the red-coated cavalry charging into the ring. Trumpets blared, fireworks rocketed to the ceiling and the scene was cloaked in smoke from the firing of the flintlocks and rifles.

Philippa clung onto Andrew as the horses thundered frantically round the ring. She was even more afraid when a glossy black stallion reared up and struck out with his hooves. Harriet had her hands clapped to her ears and was forced to admit she hated loud bangs. Madame de Lessups retreated behind her fan while Miss Snoddie kept dipping into her comfit box and chortled whenever she thought appropriate.

When the smoke finally cleared and the 'corpses' of the defeated Jacobites were dragged from the arena to the boos and hisses of the crowd, the cavalry horses took their bow. Philippa came out of McAllister's arm and Harriet was touched to find Rupert's warm hand on her shoulder.

"There Miss Larkhill, the noise is all over."

"Foolish, I know," she smiled ruefully up at him.

"Not foolish at all," he replied. And by the kindness in his face she knew he was remembering her childhood experience up at Lud's long barrow.

"Are you afraid of thunder, Miss Larkhill? There's no need to be. It is only the noise of the gas explosion which reaches us after we see the lightning." There was a shade of contempt in Miss Snoddie's voice.

"Yes, thank you Miss Snoddie," replied Harriet weakly.

The second interval gave the ladies a chance to recover themselves. Madame de Lessups, fearing she had not been sufficiently vigilant as a duenna, moved to the front of the box. Andrew made way for her and went to procure sherbet for the ladies. William and Rupert discussed the likely bloodline of the horses.

Rupert enjoyed the raw slapstick comedy of the pantomime. Harriet enjoyed watching his normally expressionless face relax into laughter. She thought life would be better if he laughed more often. Miss Snoddie laughed a fraction later than everyone else.

******

Early on Sunday morning Will Hinton rapped loudly on the door of the Albany. A sleepy porter allowed him entry and directed him upstairs to Lord Patrick's rooms.

"Is Mr Darville at home? I must see him urgently."

Jacob took Hinton's hat and cane and indicated the sitting room.

"Good morning Will, what brings you here so early?" said Rupert rising from the sofa among a shower of manuscripts. He wore a deep red quilted dressing gown and looked tousled. A haze of blue tobacco smoke hung about the room.

"Where's your uncle," asked Hinton absently shaking hands with his friend.

"Taken my mother and Gerald to the early morning service. Nowhere fashionable I am certain."

"I hoped as much. I knew *you* wouldn't be in church, that's why I came at once so we could be private. Though goodness knows I need all the prayers I can get."

"Sit down man and tell me what's brought you here. No catastrophe I hope?" Rupert moved to the decanters and poured a generous helping of brandy. "Here, drink this."

Will sank down, took a mouthful and said dramatically. "I've been robbed!"

"Of what precisely?" said Rupert unmoved.

"The Velasquez – and the jade pieces from my collection."

"Last night? Have you informed the police?"

"A fat lot of good they were! Some dolt of an inspector said 'there was a lot of this about' and they'd do what they could to find the perpetrators. Of course I should have put bars on my window, he said. Dammit I'm three floors up! Or at least I should have kept the Velasquez somewhere more secure. Thank God the mandarin's robe was locked away in the cellar."

"I'm flattered that you have come to me for sympathy, but why this early morning dash across London? Do you expect me to join in a hunt around the Minories to get your belongings back for you?"

"My God, you're a cold fish, Rupert. If you must know I can get the Velasquez back whenever I want – if I pay five hundred pounds for its safe return."

Rupert's almond eyes widened. He sat down opposite his friend. "Now you *do* interest me. Tell me everything from the beginning." He helped himself to a thin cigar from a silver box.

Will took another swig of brandy. "Catherine and I were at the Glossop's ball last night. We came home late, I got waylaid in the card room. Everard was losing a lot as usual and I stayed to watch the outcome – d'you you know he's almost bankrupt? When we got home, about three in the morning, most of the servants had gone to bed. On my way up I noticed the door to the little salon was ajar and felt a draught. I went in, found the window smashed, glass everywhere, the doors of my treasure cabinet swinging wide and the Velasquez gone from its easel."

"The servants heard nothing?"

"No. It was the cook's birthday and they were all celebrating in the kitchen – on my best burgundy. I sent for the constables of course, who were no help. Dammit the room is thirty feet from the ground, with no nearby tree or drain pipe. The man must have been a monkey to climb up there!"

"And then? What made you come to me? How are you to get your treasures back? Where does the five hundred pounds come into the business?"

Will nursed his glass between his knees. "At about six o'clock my butler brought me a note that one of the maids had found, pushed under the back door." He reached in his pocket and handed Rupert a stained and crumpled piece of paper.

Rupert read it aloud. "'If you want to see your valuables again send five hundred pounds in bills, within three days, to John Smyth Esq. c/o the Receiving Office, Bristol.'"

"Admirably succinct, you must agree," mused Rupert as he handed the note back. "The handwriting is crude, probably disguised. The note paper looks like a scrap of an old invoice with the company heading torn off. What do you propose to do?"

"I don't know. That's why I've come to you, for advice. Catherine said you were the best person to ask."

"I'm flattered by your wife's confidence. How much do you – did you – hope to get for the Velasquez?"

"About two to three thousand pounds."

"And the jade pieces?"

Will thought. "It would cost me about another thousand if I wanted to replace them."

"You are not insured against theft I take it?"

"No." Both men fell silent.

"Let me lend you the five hundred. It might take a while-"

"No, no," burst out Hinton. "Dear fellow I have not come to you for money; I know you haven't a farthing to spare. I can raise the wind myself, but of course cannot get to my bankers until tomorrow. I could go to the Jews; I'm sure they would do business with me any day of the week. But what I need to get clear in my head is whether I should give in to this blackmail at all!"

"Extortion not blackmail."

Will's lips tightened and he took another slug of brandy.

"Whatever you call it, what do you advise I do? How do I trace my property? I cannot just let it all go yet it is impossible to go posting down to Bristol and mount a twenty-four hour guard on the receiving office. And I cannot ransack the mail coach at The White Horse in Piccadilly! It leaves from there."

"No. But perhaps there is no need to." Rupert paused for thought. "*If* there is an accomplice in Bristol what's to prevent him running off with the money when it arrives? It is too risky I think for the London thief. If the instigator *lives* in Bristol what control has he over his London associates who could easily vanish with the goods?". Rupert got up to pace the room, his eyes narrowing in concentration. "Even if there were 'honesty among thieves, which I do not believe there is, the rogue in Bristol would have to send a letter back to London informing the thief that the money had arrived. Somewhat laborious don't you think? And such delays would allow more time for discovery."

"So it's just one man, then? The constable kept referring to a 'gang'."

"Well, certainly there is probably more than one person involved. The thief may have climbed the garden wall and the back wall of the house easily enough, but how did he get out again, with the painting under his arm? Can you be sure he didn't leave by any other means than the broken window?"

"My butler swears the front door was locked all evening and indeed I had to knock and heard him draw back to bolts when we returned from the Glossops. The servants were awake and drinking until the small hours; they would have seen any intruder below stairs. The window frame in the little salon was thrown right up when we found it."

"So unless the thief risked tossing a valuable painting thirty feet to the ground, which would surely damage it, then he lowered it to an accomplice. Or lowered it down on a rope. However I think it is likely he would have needed someone as a lookout even at that time of night. I assume you've questioned the night watchman?

"The police inspector did. He saw nothing."

"Would you allow me to come and look over the premises?"

"Yes, yes, I was hoping you would come back with me. Catherine will be relieved to see you. But what of the Bristol business? Are you certain it is a ruse?"

"I'm not certain at all but it seems an unnecessary distraction. I suspect that the thief either works at the Lombard Street Post Office or his accomplice does. *I* certainly would not risk five hundred pounds in notes to the mail coach!"

Within the hour the two men were examining the little salon in daylight. Mrs Hinton provided breakfast, though she and her husband were too upset to join Rupert in anything but coffee. The maids had swept up the broken glass but otherwise the room had not been touched since the inspector's departure.

Rupert ran his hand along the outer window sill. "There is a great gouge in the plaster, here Hinton. Can you recollect whether it was always so?"

"No. When does one ever examine one's window sills?"

"But we had the exterior of the house painted two years ago," said Catherine, peering over Rupert's arm. "And I cannot think what would have made such a deep gash."

"A grappling hook. I have seen them on board ship. And this one has taken the weight of a man, by the depth of the claw mark."

"So the thief is a sailor?" surmised Catherine hopefully.

Rupert shook his head. "Nothing so simple as that Mrs Hinton. Any man may go into a chandler's shop and purchase a grappling iron. But it might take a sailor, or an army man, to use it with confidence, there's a considerable drop down into to your garden."

Rupert peered over the window sill at the small slabbed terrace dotted with some tired-looking urns and an area of neglected grass. Beyond the garden wall lay the mews. "Did anyone search the garden?"

"Yes but it was hardly daylight and the intruders had long gone."

"It will do no harm to take another look."

He found nothing except scuffs on the wall.

Returning to the dining room, they found Mrs Hinton looking fagged and anxious. "But what are we to *do* Mr Darville? Should my husband pay the money or not?"

"That's a decision only he can make," he said gently. "If you would be so good as to show me the note again."

Hinton handed it over. Rupert scrutinised it and held it up to the light. "Whoever it is has pretensions to gentility. Did you notice the demand for an 'Esq' on the return packet? And the spelling of the name? Not the common 'Smith'." He lowered the instructions to his nose. "Cinnamon I fancy. This paper has fallen among spices as well as among thieves."

"Then I bet my life they're connected to the docks; it *must be* a sailor," said Will.

"Possibly, or someone connected to a spice mill, a cook shop, restaurant, or a street trader or any one of fifty warehouses on the river, not necessarily a ship. No, I'm afraid this note in itself will not lead us to the thieves. I regret that, if you want your painting back, I suggest you pay the ransom money."

Hinton swore. "How do I know I can trust them?"

"You can't, but I suspect they want to get rid of the painting quickly. They guessed it was valuable by the fact you had it displayed on an easel, but they don't quite know how much it is worth or they would have demanded more for its return. And they certainly don't know how to, or do not dare to try to, sell it for a profit."

"And the jade pieces? Will I see them again?"

"I doubt it; they're small, portable and unidentifiable. The thieves will easily find a buyer or a fence for them."

"Damnation!" said Will pacing about the room. "But you're only telling me what I already know."

"And if we rely on the police or advertise offering a reward for information?" suggested Catherine.

"I believe they would destroy the painting sooner than draw attention to themselves. Time is of the essence."

The three of them sat in silence until Rupert broke out. "I wonder if this truly is a serendipitous affair?" He looked at his friend. "Who knew you had the Velasquez in town?"

Will blinked his way back to the present. "The servants of course, but they are all our own from the Hall; I could not possibly suspect them. They would have had enough chances to steal it when we were at home. Naturally I have informed a number of art dealers who have been putting the word about for me. Friends knew. I have not kept it secret, Darville, but then I have not broadcast it from the rooftops."

Rupert pinched his bottom lip. "This may not be their first attempt at extortion. They may have tried it before and been successful. The very nature of the crime means that no one will come forward." Something niggled at the back of his mind, something connected with Harriet, but he could not put his finger in it.

Eventually he slapped his hands on his thighs and rose. "I'm sorry Hinton, not to be able to throw more light on the matter. If you *do* decide to pay, then let me know. You have three days." He held out his hand. "Meanwhile I will make some discreet enquiries regarding the General Post Office."

An hour later Rupert called at Russell Square. As luck would have it, Sir Hamish was alone; Mr Shawcross has escorted the ladies to listen to the charismatic Henry Venn preach at St Dunstan's-in-the-West, Fleet Street. William had escaped to his chambers and Andrew was spending Sunday with the Glynns knowing the Beaumonts would be there.

Rupert did not waste words. "Forgive me for breaking into your day of rest sir, but I have a problem which is somewhat urgent. I think I should tell you of it and ask your advice. Though it seems you never do stop work." Rupert looked pointedly at the bundles of documents tied in pink tape in front of him.

"When is any problem not urgent?" sighed Sir Hamish. "But I'm pleased you've called, I need to discuss some domestic matters with you. And I need a rest from this." He indicated the paper-strewn desk. "We hope to get the king away to Ireland as soon after the coronation as possible." He stopped himself from saying more. "Tell me, how can I be of service to you?"

Mindful of the Hintons wish for privacy, Rupert gave the bare bones of the extortion plot. "What you *should* be aware of, sir, is the involvement of the General Post Office. Could you alert the authorities, or place one of your agents on the inside to watch the employees?"

"*My* agents? *I* have no agents," said McAllister.

"I sincerely hope you *do,* sir, and that the country is a safer place because of them."

Sir Hamish gave Rupert a bland look. "I'll certainly have a word with Francis Freeling and see what we can do. I can promise no more than that. I agree, we cannot have anyone interfering with His Majesty's mails - at least no one unofficial. When is your friend to deliver the parcel of money to Lombard Street?"

"He will send me word, but I think it will take him a day to collect the banknotes together."

"That should give us enough time. Tell him to take a record of the numbers of the notes; it will help trace them. You were wise to come to me and not try to outwit this fellow, this gang, yourself. And I concur with your theory that the Bristol address is all gammon. But if your friend does want his property back, the money must be real, no fake bundles of paper or suspicious wrapping or the thief will take fright. By the way, I assume there were no indications from the ransom letter as to its provenance?"

"Nothing of merit," said Rupert noncommittally. He had done his duty in getting a message to the Secretary for the Post Office to safeguard his friend's money. Tracing the Velasquez was between himself and Hinton.

They discussed the problem, its approaches and possible outcomes, before Sir Hamish led Rupert onto his own concerns.

"You have been seeing a deal of Miss Larkhill while she is here in town?"

Rupert shrugged. "Occasionally. When I have time to spare from my committees and talks. Why do you ask?"

"Oh, do not misunderstand me, Darville. There is not the least objection. She comes home full of the latest findings and the famous speakers you have introduced her to at the Gresham rooms."

"Harriet was always a keen observer, even when she was a child."

"You were right to advise me to invite her to London. I had no idea the situation at Larkhill was so dire. She has blossomed like a flower in the few weeks she has been here. But now we must talk about the future of the manor and that young relative of mine."

Rupert stayed to luncheon. Mortimer Shawcross was engaged elsewhere. Harriet was pleased to see her old friend. Apart from wishing to avoid Lady McAllister's critical analysis of the sermon, she wanted to know if Rupert had seen much of Lavinia Snoddie. He admitted to a visit to the Pall Mall picture galleries with the Somervilles to see John Martin's gigantic painting of *Belshazzar's Feast.*

"A shilling well spent, I take it?" asked Lady McAllister.

"A very dramatic portrayal ma'am."

"Did Miss Snoddie approve of the painting?" asked Harriet.

"I believe so."

"What's this Harriet?" asked Sir Hamish. "Do you want to see the writing on the wall or have you already written it yourself?"

Harriet wondered what and how much Sir Hamish knew of her agreement with the Countess.

"I must go myself," said Lady McAllister into the silence. "Only the best people exhibit there, unlike at the Royal Academy. One must not entirely neglect the old in the pursuit of the new. The British Institution may be considered a trifle conservative but one should not abandon a body which has the king as its first patron. Harriet, we must consult our engagement books."

"Yes, ma'am." She was more touched by the term of address than her hostess's intentions.

Harriet favoured Rupert with a vivid account of her recent visit to the gas-lit Theatre Royal in Drury Lane. Harriet had gone to the theatre with the easy-going Cholmondleys and a large party of their young friends. London belonged to the young people in this time of festivity.

"I loved our visit to the opera but I prefer spoken drama," she said tucking into her sweet omelette. "And this one was very funny."

Lady McAllister looked over her *pince-nez*. "You saw nothing unseemly, I trust?"

"Sheridan's *The Rivals*. Aunt Amelia took me to see it in Bath, but I never tire of listening to Mrs Malaprop."

The reference to Sir Hamish's unfortunate sister-in-law, deceased though she may be, made Lady McAllister's eyes bulge. Harriet scolded herself for her tactlessness. Rupert remained silent.

After luncheon Sir Hamish, with a nod to his guest, disappeared into his study to write a letter to the Secretary of the General Post Office. Seizing the moment, Harriet asked Lady McAllister for the key to the Russell Square gardens.

"Oh I would not advise taking Cicero for his walk in this heat, Miss Larkhill. Edward can take him out when it is cooler." The poodle lay dozing on a satin cushion, his tongue lolling; he had no intention of moving any more than had his mistress.

"I rather thought I would show Mr Darville the splendid statue of the Duke of Bedford at close quarters, ma'am," said Harriet innocently. "The sheep are very - realistic." She hoped Rupert would not catch her eye.

"Ah – I see – something agricultural. Very well Miss Larkhill, if you must," said Lady Elspeth who was rather looking forward to a Sunday afternoon nap without visitors. "Take care to keep out of the sun, stay under the trees. Susan will be happy to accompany you."

Miss Finch begged only to fetch her knitting, assuring them that a little breath of air was just what she desired. Harriet unlocked the gate in the iron railings which surrounded the large private garden. The enclosed square was deserted and after one turn about the tired grass, Miss Finch begged leave to settle herself on a bench and finish her stocking.

"Let us at least approach the Farmer Duke for form's sake," said Rupert. "I know you have some ulterior reason for bringing me out here, Harriet," he said leading her across the grass. "Yes, a most imposing statue; the sheep are almost as fat as the putti," he said giving the edifice a cursory glance. "Now what was it you wanted to say to me? Tell me quickly, is anything the matter? At home? They are all well in Larkhill?"

"Oh yes. Miss Humble writes regularly. It is just that I think I have had an adventure."

"Of course you have; it was only a matter of time. You have not caused any embarrassment to the McAllisters, I hope?"

"No!" said Harriet affronted. "But I may have helped to avert one."

"Come and sit down on this bench and tell me. We cannot stare at this lump of bronze all afternoon, sheep or no sheep."

"I need your analytical brain – or I think I do, but then I don't know what to think at all."

"What's the mystery?" he asked leading her to an empty bench out of earshot of Miss Finch.

"There was what Sir Hamish would call an 'incident' and it has left me a little puzzled. There is no one I can consult, except you, to give me a logical explanation."

She quickly recounted the theft of the Ravensburg Cross and its unexpected retrieval. "But you see, I cannot believe it was found so easily or returned so quickly. No one returns a valuable jewel they find in Oxford Street! The Reichsgrafin is innocent of any duplicity, I'm convinced. She is delightfully feather-headed and indiscreet, but there must be something else! Or am I imagining things?"

Rupert's every sense was alert. All his instincts told him that Harriet's experience was another extortion attempt, and a successful one. A stolen valuable, a mysterious note and an unexpected find. Harriet's story implied there was now a definite likelihood that Hinton's painting might be returned and he felt a spark of hope.

If the Ravensburg Cross had been restored to the owner undamaged, so might the Velasquez. Rupert hoped it would sweeten Will's bitter pill.

He looked down and gave Harriet a warm smile. "Coincidences do happen, you know," he said mildly. "Not everyone in London is a thief. The Reichsgraf was probably very generous in his reward to whoever returned the cross."

"No reward was advertised. The Count wanted the theft to be kept as quiet as possible. He said 'much could be achieved by discreet means'."

"Precisely. Perhaps it *was*, as the cross was returned so quickly. Are you sure you should have told me of it?"

"The Reichsgraf told Sir Hamish," said Harriet in justification. "I know *you* can be trusted to say nothing."

"There, you have your answer; diplomatic means *were* used. Sir Hamish has his people everywhere. Don't let it trouble you further. Accept that you are a heroine and have rescued yet another 'cousin of the queen'."

"No, no. How can you be so flippant! I mean the Reichsgraf told Sir Hamish about the loss *after* the cross had been returned! Sir Hamish had no hand in finding the reticule or getting the jewel back."

Rupert was now even more convinced that the Imperial Count had paid a substantial sum for the return of his property. "And you have told me everything? About the letter the Count received?"

"Yes. I have no idea what it was but he seemed quite shaken by its contents and wanted me gone as soon as politeness allowed."

Rupert knew that he would have to approach the Count directly if he wanted any more information. He was conscious that he needed to report to Hinton. And he wanted time to plan. Rupert stood up and held out his hand to help Harriet rise.

"Think no more of it. Do not make yourself uneasy. William McAllister has filled your head full of nonsense. You're not a child anymore and I know your practical common sense will bring you to see that to pursue the matter might cause embarrassment to Sir Hamish." Harriet looked disappointed. "You must excuse me if I take my leave." He consulted his fob watch. "I had quite forgot the time; Will Hinton expects me. Allow me to escort you and Miss Finch back to the house."

Her happy mood of the afternoon evaporated like dew. He looked at her frowning face and kept hold of her hand. "I recommend that you put the whole business out of your mind. Instead, I look forward to welcoming you and the Beaumonts to the Royal Observatory in a day or two – not quite as exciting as *The Rivals* or jewel robberies, but I'm sure you will learn something from your visit."

"Very well Mr Darville. I see I was mistaken in my anxieties and it would be improper to pursue the matter further," returned Harriet primly.

Harriet was disappointed at Rupert's lack of interest in her story. Perhaps she had been unwise to turn to him for advice; respectable young ladies did not have adventures in London. He had been kind but dismissive and she felt rather foolish.

That evening, Sir Hamish summoned Harriet to the study and bade her take a seat. He tucked two fingers into his fob pocket and looked at her across the desk appraisingly. She had become a remarkably fine looking young woman; a little town polish had worked wonders.

"Harriet, you will be pleased to hear that Mr Darville and I have been discussing your difficulties with regard to the trusteeship of Young Clem."

Harriet sat in obedient silence. She had a sudden anxiety that Rupert had told Sir Hamish about her use of the guineas in the chest.

"We have formed a plan that, when you return to Larkhill, I shall accompany you along with Mr Tamar, my man of business. I believe you have met him?"

"Yes, when Young Clem's adoption papers were drawn up."

"Quite so. He remembers *you*." He would expand no further. "Mr Darville and I consider it quite the best thing for everyone if I assume your uncle's duties as a trustee."

"He would never agree!" broke in Harriet.

"Oh but certainly he would, if the matter were put to him in the correct light," he said smoothly. "Do not alarm yourself Harriet. I understand that Sir John has become – difficult; alas a fate that threatens most of us in our advancing years – but I have had much experience of 'difficult' people over the course of my career. Have you ever *been* to France?"

"Sir John threw his chamber pot at Dunch once," said Harriet nervously.

"Then we will have to ensure that the receptacle is nowhere to hand when I visit. A simple signature or two and the business will be done, and by what Mr Darville tells me, your uncle will have forgotten within the hour that I was even at the manor."

She thought for a moment. "If Rupert agrees then I can see no reason to object. In fact," she started to smile, "it would be the very thing! I would be so relieved if you took over the responsibility for Young Clem, the child is as much a McAllister as a Larkhill."

Sir Hamish did not wish to be reminded of his late niece's supreme folly and moved smoothly on.

"Thank you Harriet. I knew I could rely on your good sense. It has been agreed that the trustees, that is Mr Darville and myself, should henceforth release a regular sum from the interest on the capital, into *your* care every month. Mr Tamar will arrange matters. Mr Darville suggested that you have your own bank account, but I'm not inclined to think that we need to go that far. The money is naturally to be used for Young Clem's upkeep until he goes to school, when other arrangements will be made – but you will not find us asking for monthly accounts."

Harriet professed her thanks as best she could. Sir Hamish took it as his due. When she had quite run out of breath he said: "Now I have some disappointing news and a little good news."

Harriet sat with an expectant look on her face.

"I took your jewels to Rundell and Bridge who inform me that there is a glut on the market just at this moment, because of the advent of so many foreign, and I can only fear impoverished, members of the nobility who are visiting London. Mr Bristow advises that you keep them by you for another year and when the market improves, we can reassess the situation."

Harriet's face fell.

"However, I took the liberty of asking for them to be cleaned and repaired."

"But I can't-"

"I will settle the bill. It always pays to keep your property in the best possible condition for the future, and I have Young Clem's interests in mind. Now for something more pleasant," he continued briskly. "Mr Bristow says he can certainly find a buyer for the topaz set. He has a particular client who has rather old-fashioned taste and has a liking for stones set in heavy silver. You have no special fondness for them have you?"

"I think them hideous – but they did look well on Aunt Betsy once."

"Then he offers you a hundred guineas for the necklace, earrings and the bracelet. Shall we close with him?"

"So much?" cried Harriet clasping her hands in delight. "Oh, yes, please, that would be such a help toward the new threshing machine or the cottages!"

Sir Hamish looked surprised. "Will you not use the money to defray some of your expenses while you are in London?"

Harriet hesitated. "Uncle John gave me twenty guineas, which is *more* than sufficient for my needs, and you and Lady McAllister are so generous to me. I have only a few weeks here, so I need very little pin money. No, the manor must come first."

Sir Hamish shrugged. "Very well. However, I think it best that when the money is paid and the refurbished jewels returned that I continue to keep them in my strong box until you return to Wiltshire."

Harriet almost danced out of the room and wanted only someone to share her happiness with. She must thank Rupert for his understanding about the trusteeship and he was certain to be interested in something as mechanical as a new threshing machine. She went up to bed once more in perfect amity with her old friend.

In the study, Sir Hamish wrote a bankers draft to 'cash' for one hundred guineas and made a mental note to abstract the topaz set from the cleaned collection before restoring the Larkhill heirlooms to Harriet.

******

The Reichsgraf turned the visiting card over in his fingers. 'Rupert Darville, Esq.', and on the back in black spider scrawl, the words 'regarding the Ravensburg Cross.'

"Show the gentleman in," said the Imperial Count reluctantly to the hovering valet. Adelaide had gone to mass at the embassy chapel with her maid and he had been looking forward to a quiet evening alone with his cigars.

The count assessed the tall dark man who bowed stiffly as he entered the hotel suite. He looked pale with eyes like a cat but was dressed soberly and had the manners of a gentleman. To his surprise, Rupert addressed him fluently in German, apologised for the intrusion and lack of introduction.

Recognising Rupert as the 'famed explorer and natural philosopher', the Reichsgraf relaxed a little and indicated a chair. They exchanged pleasantries.

"To what do I owe this pleasure, Herr Darville? Or should I address you as the Honourable Rupert?"

"The 'honourable' is a courtesy title only, not used in speech or on visiting cards," Rupert explained shortly.

"Ah, the etiquette of the English is very confusing. You were pointed out to me in the Travellers' Cub as a serious man of science. How can I be of assistance, sir?"

Rupert recounted the bald facts of the Velasquez theft and asked whether the Reichsgraf could throw any light on the matter. He gave no specific details. At first the Reichsgraf pretended to be baffled as to why Mr Darville should approach him at all. When Rupert pushed him further he denied all knowledge of any extortion regarding the Ravensburg Cross.

It was not until Sir Hamish McAllister and Miss Larkhill were mentioned, that the count admitted that there had been a little 'embarrassment' relating to the 'temporarily missing' gift for the king. He rang for coffee and offered Rupert a cigar from an ornate wooden box.

"Fine Turkish?" asked Rupert examining the pale golden leaf and taking the cigar cutter from the tray.

"I see you know your cigars, sir."

"I know a good Damascus when I smoke one," said Rupert drawing dryly on the yellow tobacco. "Which is very rarely, to my regret."

The count lit one for himself, dropping the taper in the empty hearth. For a few moments the men smoked in silence. The count was thinking hard.

Coffee was brought in and poured into little cups, thick and bitter. Rupert declined the sugar. The waiter handed round the cups, flipped his napkin and left.

Eventually Rupert asked: "Do you still have the extortion note, my lord?"

"What makes you think there was an extortion note?"

"Come, sir, do not prevaricate. The Ravensburg Cross was not 'found' without payment."

There was something about this man's demeanour that made the count trust him. "I destroyed it, as soon as the cross was returned to me."

"Can you remember what it said? Where were you instructed to send the money?"

The Reichsgraf took a long draw on his cigar. "To a John Smyth, a most unusual spelling, *poste restante*, Portsmouth. I could not go galloping off to your south coast to find this man, you will understand."

Rupert nodded. "It's the same *modus operandi*, I fear. We suspect a post office employee of being involved."

"Then where are the government's agents?" demanded the count, waving his cigar in the air. "I lost two thousands of your English sovereigns to this blackguard! I could not pursue the matter with your police; there would have been a diplomatic scandal. Sir Hamish said nothing of this other theft to me!"

"He knew nothing of it himself. Miss Larkhill kept your secret until your gift was safely with the king and then, when your wife sent her a message through Sir Hamish, saying that the reticule had been found in Oxford Street, Miss Larkhill felt at liberty to inform him of her part in assisting the Reichsgrafin. Only my friend's stolen property has prompted his involvement, not your missing cross, of which he had no knowledge."

The Reichsgraf calmed himself and took another sip of coffee. "Yes, of course, Neither my wife not Miss Larkhill were aware of the letter and its demands." Harriet's account of the note was the one thing that had brought Rupert to the Clarendon. "I was intent on keeping everything quiet you understand. Two thousand pounds," the count waved a dismissive hand. "Why, I could drop that in a night at the tables, but to be humiliated in front of the English court was unthinkable!"

"May I ask, my lord, how was the jewel returned to you?"

The count studied the ash on the end of his Damascus. "Two days after I sent my servant to the Post Office with the money, a street urchin delivered the cross to my suite. The packet passed through the hands of at least three other inn servants before my valet brought it to me. I have no idea who sent it and was more concerned to have the gift restored in time for the king's reception."

"Do you still have the wrapping, sir," asked Rupert urgently. "We may be able to ascertain some clues from it."

The Reichsgraf looked baffled. "My servant disposed of it." He stepped to the bell pull. "This was more than a week ago. I do not have any hopes of you finding the villain now. I would prefer not to pursue the matter." The Reichsgraf's pride was returning. "You will agree, two thousand pounds was a paltry price to pay to save my honour. It is all best forgotten."

The valet, a very correct personage, however, had not forgotten. He remembered a rough piece of Hessian tied with string, which he disposed of as soon as possible. "Did you remark anything untoward about the wrapping?" asked Rupert.

The valet paused and wrinkled his nose with distaste. "It smelt."

"Of what?"

"Pepper."

******

Sir Hamish was seldom at home for dinner; the demands of the coronation kept him at his desk until the late hours. In compensation, the family were delighted when Andrew announced: "I am relieved of my duties for two weeks. Lord Glynn says nothing can be done during the celebrations." He explained to Harriet: "This is the Company's slack period; we won't be despatching or expecting many cargoes now until September."

"Then perhaps you would care to join our party to visit the Royal Observatory, tomorrow? Madame de Lessups and Miss Beaumont will be there," suggested Harriet in her impulsive way.

"Mr Darville has arranged it all with the Astronomer Royal, Mr Pond. I'm sure you understand about clocks and mapping and navigation. *You* will know all about it being in shipping."

Andrew readily accepted, rather touched by Harriet's naïve enthusiasm. "I know a little about shipping of course, but cannot hope to rival Mr Darville in navigation – or in any other field of knowledge."

"Will Captain Valentine be one of the party?" asked Lady McAllister, spearing a strawberry with precision.

"I do not know," said Harriet. Andrew looked momentarily grim about the mouth. Harriet resolved to send word to Curzon Street to inform Madame de Lessups of Andrew's intention to join them. She would also send Annie with a note for Rupert at Lord Patrick's rooms in the Albany, informing him of the extra guest.

"I hope you don't expect *me* to come with you, Miss Larkhill," said William.

"Certainly not. You would be bored beyond reason."

"I regret I find I cannot accompany you tomorrow, Miss Larkhill. I have just been informed of an unexpected committee meeting of the Society for the Promotion of Christian Knowledge," Lady McAllister broke in. "It is most inconvenient, but they insist they cannot do without my presence. Susan, you need not attend. You may have the afternoon to visit your – lame duck."

"You would be very welcome to come with *us* to Greenwich," offered Harriet. "A drive out into the country would be so pleasant, away from smoky London."

Miss Finch declined with effusive protestations of thanks. As Lady McAllister had so generously given her this free time she would spend it as her employer had advised.

"Pinin' for the country already Miss Larkhill?" asked William.

"Not at all. Merely for some fresher air in this heat. But I should not complain. One can only hope this fine weather continues for the coronation. No, Mr McAllister, I have never been so happy as I have been here in London."

It was a sentiment she would revise within twenty-four hours.

The carriage drive took them across London Bridge, hurried through the smoking factories of Southwark and the slums of the Borough and made for the Dover Road south to New Cross. From here, Madame de Lessups's coachman found his way to the new villas of Blackheath. As they drove into the Royal Park at Greenwich, the Thames meandered on their left, dotted with busy wherries and hoys. Great ships swam up river hauled by tugs, white sails billowing like swans' wings.

Soon the carriage was climbing through the park. Philippa exclaimed at the cows cooling themselves under the trees. Below them, the white box of the Queen's House, flanked by two colonnaded wings formed part of the Royal Hospital Asylum for the children of naval seamen. As the carriage toiled up the hill Andrew made a heavy fourth, the sun glinting in his red hair like flame. Captain Valentine was not with them and the party was in high spirits.

Harriet's happy mood faltered when she saw Mrs Somerville and Miss Snoddie standing next to Rupert in the cobbled courtyard of Flamsteed House. She chided herself; this was just what the dowager countess intended. Nevertheless, Harriet had a sudden doubt. She did not want Rupert to be as unhappy in his second choice of life's partner as he had been in his first. Jacob rushed forward to open the carriage door and put down the steps.

Mrs Somerville was mildly embarrassed and said: "You will forgive us ma'am for intruding on your party but Mr Darville dined with us last night and I could not resist his kind invitation."

"Not at all, Mrs Somerville," soothed Madame de Lessups. "This is Mr Darville's expedition and we are gratified to have such a distinguished lady such as yourself among us – and Miss Snoddie of course."

Miss Snoddie stood silent by Rupert's side, the ferrule of her parasol grounded in the dust. Her spotted print dress was a little tight.

"How did you manage to swing this, Darville?" asked Andrew looking up at the white turrets and the dome of the Royal Observatory.

"John Pond and I are both old scholars of Trinity. He's twenty years my senior but we have been in correspondence periodically."

"You men of science move in a tight circle."

"But a world-wide one. Come, I'm glad you are with us, McAllister. Pond is waiting for us in the Octagon Room. Jacob, show Madame's coachman where to stable the carriage."

The visitors by-passed the four humble living rooms of the Astronomer Royal and his students. They climbed up to the Octagon room where the famous observations were made.

The high-ceilinged room streamed with light from several tall, small-paned windows. A brass telescope stood angled at one open window. One of the blue-coated assistants was taking measurement from the quadrant fixed to a window mullion.

"Mr Pond has made many improvements to the instrumentation since he became Astronomer Royal and has begun to employ the method of observation by reflection," said Rupert to an uncomprehending audience.

The Astronomer Royal modestly discounted his friend's praise and instead explained the importance of the navigational star charts, Tompion clocks and mentioned the ten-foot Troughton telescope. "I regret we cannot open the dome this morning, and we would see nothing of the stars on such a bright day."

Mrs Somerville asked pertinent questions about the constellations and the Earth's magnetism, deferring to Rupert when she could. Andrew spoke a little of shipping schedules and Miss Snoddie suddenly asked how frequently the information gathered at the observatory was made available.

"We are obliged to publish our findings every year and will always supply data to any serious student," replied the astronomer mildly. "Naturally we have many people including, Mr Darville, who supply information for celestial navigation."

"For the *Nautical Almanac*?" asked Andrew, pleased to be able to contribute.

"Quite so. We have recently increased the number of assistants to six, there is so much work to do. We have yet to determine true north for our telescopes and badly need some obelisk in north London to aid our calculations."

At that moment Mr Pond was called away and Rupert strolled over to speak to one of the young assistants. Andrew was demonstrating the telescope to Philippa. Miss Snoddie whispered. "Miss Beaumont must be far out of her depth in surroundings such as these, but gentlemen often succumb to a pretty face rather than a fine mind."

"One does not necessarily preclude the other," said Harriet mildly. She walked towards Rupert who was now gazing out of the window in a reverie. She put her hand on his sleeve to make him turn and said softly: "Forgive me for speaking here, but I must thank you for agreeing to let Sir Hamish take over Young Clem's trusteeship."

He was about to answer when Miss Snoddie swayed forward. "Mr Darville, do you not deplore domestic interruptions when one can command such intellectual marvels as we have here?"

"I regret that I command only my horse and my servant, madam. But I will always be at any *lady's* command." He paused and waited for her request. She coloured slightly and walked away.

"I don't think she *meant* to be rude," said Harriet untruthfully. "And I apologise if I disturbed you."

"Nonsense Harriet, you do not disturb me at all. And let me hear no more about the trusteeship. Sir Hamish and Mr Tamar are handling the business. I want no thanks; they have relieved me of a chore."

Harriet said no more. The thought that Rupert had regarded being Young Clem's trustee as an irksome duty started an unpleasant chain of reflection.

"When are we to go up on the roof? I wish to look at the view," Miss Snoddie announced to the room in general. She had dislodged Andrew and Philippa from their window and after a few unsuccessful attempts at focusing the telescope had abandoned it. She was bored.

"Should we not wait until Mr Pond, returns?" suggested Mrs Somerville. But Miss Snoddie was making for the door and the steep staircase to the roof.

"Mr McAllister, would you come with me? I do not wish to trip on the stairs," ordered Miss Snoddie.

Philippa looked affronted. Harriet hesitated, but Andrew, ever the gentleman, reluctantly followed Lavinia Snoddie from the room. Harriet made to follow when Philippa said: "Are you not afraid to go up on the roof?"

"No, not at all. I have often been on the leads at Larkhill Manor. The parapet looked high enough and the astronomers go up there every day, but if you don't wish to go, I will stay with you."

Madame de Lessups would not hear of it. Miss Larkhill must follow her friends and she herself would bear Miss Beaumont company in the sunny Octagon room. Harriet lifted up her skirts and began to climb. She found Rupert directly behind her. As they stepped out onto the roof of Flamsteed house, a light breeze lifted the wide brim of her straw hat. She had refurbished it with cream roses and tied it beneath her chin with a huge satin ribbon. Once on the roof, her dark eyes sparkled with pleasure.

White clouds scudded across the bright blue sky. Harriet breathed in the fresh air deeply enjoying the warm sun on her face. In the distance, London was a grey smear, its church spires poking through the haze of smoke like ships' masts. Below them the steam yacht *Hero* paddled its way to Margate. Rupert stood beside her, surveying the scene, his black curls ruffling in the wind.

Andrew was pointing to the Isle of Dogs on the other side of the river. Miss Snoddie listened with her mouth a little open.

"Across there are the East India Company docks, they were built on the sight of the old Brunswick dock. Can you see that tall building? That's the mast house and we do a lot of refitting and repairing there. It's the export dock now and behind is the import dock – eighteen acres of it!"

"I can see one or two ships," said Harriet. "But where are the warehouses? I cannot see any large buildings. Where are all the goods stored?"

"All our cargoes are unloaded here and taken by road in closed carts or by lighters to the legal quays up river and then onto our warehouses in Billiter street and Cutler street. We no longer berth our ships in the Pool of London, our merchantmen are too large and the Company dare not risk the losses from the appalling thievery in the port."

"I'm sure I could see much more if we use the telescope. You must show me how to direct it, Mr McAllister." Miss Snoddie walked briskly to the other side of the roof intent on commandeering the instrument for her own use.

"What is your impression of the view, Miss Larkhill," asked Rupert pointing to the cityscape.

"I am reminded that I must ask Miss Humble to have the chimneys swept while I'm away."

Rupert gave a crack of laughter. "No poetic inspiration? No sacred thoughts?"

"None. I am far more interested in what Mr McAllister's has to say about the great docks."

"Then look over to your left and you'll see the Royal Naval Dockyards at Deptford."

"If you wish it, I will be poetical and say it is a bristling forest of masts, sprouting in the service of His Majesty. That would please Mr Shawcross."

"Are you intent on pleasing that gentleman?"

At that moment the rest of the party appeared on the roof accompanied by a flurried Mr Pond. Andrew immediately came forward to assist the ladies. Philippa clung to his arm and had a determined look about her.

"Ah, here you all are, forgive me for abandoning you," said the Astronomer Royal. "What a lovely day it is, of course a little chilly at night-". He caught sight of Lavinia's hand on the large brass telescope. "Dear young lady, could I beg you not to touch the instrument? It is specifically calibrated to one particular sector of the heavens. My assistant takes nightly measurements and we would not wish to disturb his calculations, would we?" He laughed nervously. "Where would our data and tables for Mr Darville's predictive algorithms be?"

Miss Snoddie reluctantly dropped her hand and moved away saying: "Very well, but I can assure you I'm quite capable of restoring a telescope to its original setting."

Rupert squinted his eyes against the sun. "I had no idea the area to the east of London was so uninhabited, McAllister."

"There is traffic enough on the Commercial road these days and, as my father says, London is continually expanding. I suppose the riverside is pretty rural until Gravesend but there are a number of villages still existing, plus any number of derelict landing places with rotting wharves which have long silted up."

Rupert surveyed the busy Thames. "You should have come on the steamer. I believe there is now a service from London Bridge to Greenwich. You would have been here much sooner."

"I do not dispute it, but I was a last minute addition to the party. I would not disrupt Madame de Lessups' arrangements."

After they had all scrutinised the horizon and picked out St Paul's in the distant haze, there did not seem much more to say. A slight awkwardness had fallen on the party. By mutual consent they descended and make their thanks and adieus to the Astronomer Royal.

Rupert had bespoken a light luncheon in a respectable inn on the road back to town. Mrs Somerville and Miss Snoddie were included in Rupert's invitation. He had reserved a private room, wood panelled with open windows looking out onto a pretty orchard. Insects hummed across the grass. Harriet happened to take a seat next to Rupert but when he disappeared for a moment to speak to the landlord about the wine, Lavinia Snoddie took his place.

"I cannot bear to have my back to an open window," she said, fidgeting with the cutlery.

"We could always close it for you," replied Harriet.

"Oh, no. I would much rather have the view and talk to you and Mr Darville."

By now the others were seated and Rupert, on his return, was forced to take the empty chair on the other side of Miss Snoddie. In the event, she spoke to no one but him. Harriet was engaged by Mrs Somerville's lively talk and was only occasionally distracted by Miss Snoddie's speedy appetite.

Jacob helped to serve and, as he leaned over the table between the diners, Miss Snoddie scrutinised his head with interest. "I wish I had such a devoted page as your black boy, Mr Darville. Did you acquire him on your expedition?"

"Jacob is a native of the volcanic island of Ombay to the north-west of New Holland. I offered him certain inducements and he chose to come with me as my servant."

"What an interesting shaped head he has," she said staring at Jacob's woolly pate and the twisted topknot. "I would deem it a great service if you would allow me to perform a phrenological examination on him.""

Jacob, not quite understanding what was being proposed but aware that this lumpish lady was referring to him in predatory terms, looked alarmed until Harriet reassured him with a confident smile and shake of the head.

"I fear that Jacob would not understand the reasons for your 'examination' and may take any assault on his head very much amiss," returned Rupert.

"But you could explain it all to him Mr Darville, surely, in the name of science? I wish only to measure his skull with a pair of callipers and trace the indentations and cranial protuberances of his head. The topknot would have to come off, of course. To be able to compare the skull of a living savage to that of a sophisticated European would be fascinating!"

"Indeed it would be. I would not attempt to pre-empt your conclusions. However, I assume you will permit my servant to make a similar examination of *your* head Miss Snoddie?"

By now the whole table was listening and Harriet was gripping her hands in her lap.

"Good Heavens, no! How can you think I would allow -? How could he – an uneducated native -." She gathered her indignation about her. "I am surprised you should suggest such a thing Mr Darville. Apart from being wholly unversed in phrenology what interest could such a primitive have in examining *my* faculties?"

"Rather the head as a whole I think," mused Rupert. "In his native land Jacob is a head hunter. He already has several initiation scars of his tribe yet has acquired only one shrunken head. I can assure you he feels it keenly. A young warrior such as Jacob is judged by the number of skulls he takes as battle trophies. We would not wish to frighten such a savage into retribution by attempting an assault on his head."

Miss Snoddie did not respond to Mr Darville's dry delivery. Catching Harriet's scandalised glare Rupert modified his tone. "Come Miss Snoddie we will not argue over a servant." He raised his glass to her and said kindly: "Would you take wine with me?"

"As you wish," replied Lavinia, unbecomingly flushed but trapped by his seeming retreat. "A toast to what, Mr Darville?" asked the lady, reaching for her glass.

Harriet held her breath.

"To empirical science, what else Miss Snoddie?"

******

"You're very quiet Miss Larkhill. I trust the day has not been too much for you?" said Madame de Lessups as they made their way home through the villages. "We cannot have you 'burning the candle at both ends' as the young gentlemen would say. Isn't that right Mr McAllister?"

Andrew broke off from his tête a tête with Philippa. "Indeed ma'am a very pleasant day, but perhaps a trifle long for the ladies. I admit the fresh air does make one sleepy."

Harriet smiled at the thought of having too much fresh air, but nevertheless felt a little dejected.

"Have you been long acquainted with Miss Snoddie?" asked Madame de Lessups correctly divining the source of Harriet's gloom. "She seems a young woman of very decided opinions."

"Her father is a noted medical man in Edinburgh, her uncle is an Oxford don."

"Ah, an intellectual by remove."

"I don't think she is very intellectual," said Philippa suddenly. "She knows nothing of Mr Scott's books *or* poetry. I don't believe she reads at all!"

"She reads heads instead," said Harriet under her breath.

"For someone who claims to understand people's characters, I am surprised she does not know her own better! She is so rude and spiteful!"

The occupants of the carriage did not know how to respond to this unexpected pronouncement. Andrew looked embarrassed, Harriet disclaimed awkwardly and Madame de Lessups scolded Philippa for her outburst.

"My dear, a lady must never comment on anyone's character unfavourably in public, especially on so short an acquaintance – whatever one may happen to think in private."

******

Harriet had every intention of continuing her walks with Annie until expressly forbidden to do so. Today's prospect was St Paul's cathedral. By now Harriet knew well enough to take a cab from the rank on the corner of Russell Square. As the hackney drove smartly up Ludgate Hill, Harriet had a sudden association with Lud's long barrow at home and chided herself for her sentimental thoughts of Rupert. She was surprised out of her reverie by the sight of the cathedral.

The two young women stared at the west front with its Corinthian columns, imposing pediment and huge dome. Its twin turrets towered to the sky. Harriet craned her neck to take in the magnificent structure.

"Big, ain't it Miss? Though it be not as big as St. Peter's in Rome," Annie pronounced.

"Let's see if it's just as beautiful," said Harriet a little shaken. She often forgot that Annie had accompanied Sylvia in her scandalous flight across Europe.

They made their way round to the north entrance, climbed the steps and paid the fourpence entrance fee. Annie admitted she had never actually been inside St. Peter's as she had been too busy taking care of Miss Sylvia and then the baby. Harriet did not feel it right to question her further. The incident was closed. They were all different people now, with different lives.

"More steps!" moaned Annie as they were ushered towards a circular staircase. "I spend all day going up and down stairs!"

"You want to try the Whispering Gallery, surely? And the guidebook says it is the best place for viewing the paintings in the cupola."

For the next hour Harriet dutifully paid out for each of the curiosities on display, though Annie grumbled. They admired the monuments, the fluted pilasters painted and veined with gold, the black and white marble floor, the size of the cupola, the elegance and the grandeur.

A verger politely approached them, holding a prayer book in his hand. "Do you wish to stay for divine service Miss? The public are allowed in now. It is a quarter before ten."

"My goodness, the time! Lady McAllister will be downstairs in an hour." They stepped out into the swirling streets, momentarily dazzled by the sunlight. "We should not have stayed to admire the military flags or the royal pew. Come Annie we must find a cab, or I'll be in the suds!"

"Give the boy a penny Miss and get him to fetch you a cab."

As neither the boy nor a hackney appeared after ten minutes, and the nearest cab rank was empty, like most country-women they preferred to walk. Harriet studied the map in her guide book.

"If we walk down Newgate and then along Cheapside, past Lincoln's Inn then we can cut north to Russell Square. And we'll see a lot more of the City that way."

"If you say so, Miss," said Annie dubiously. The crowds were pressing even thicker now as the morning wore on. The City churches struck the hour and Harriet and Annie quickened their pace.

The road was full of waggons and town carriages, with clerks and water-carriers dodging between the hooves and wheels of the traffic. Hawkers crying their wares elbowed them off the pavements.

Harriet was tempted to stop and examine the contents of the print shops. "Goodness how shocking," she cried at some vulgar political cartoon but tore herself away and sped on. By the time they reached the top of Chancery Lane they paused for breath. Harriet consulted the map again. "I think we should turn north, up here, and that should bring us to High Holborn,"

But the way was blocked by an overturned cart and a struggling dray horse. A crowd had gathered and the heated argument mixed with the horse's pitiable whinnies made the girls move on.

"Let's walk down to the next turning, it shouldn't take us much out of our way. Surely we can cut through there? We can come to no harm if we walk smartly and stay together." Harriet pushed on through the crowds.

The next turning was a dark alley which they decided to avoid. A fair step further on they came to an unmarked street with perhaps a slightly shabbier class of shops but Harriet, conscious of the time, decided to chance the diversion.

Within a very few yards she realised she had made a mistake. The street led into a warren of courtyards and blind alleys. The slum was a honeycomb of the lowest lodging houses in London, inhabited by thieves and prostitutes. Wretched houses with broken windows patched with rags and paper crowded in on them. Wet clothes, strung on poles, sagged in the stagnant air. There was filth everywhere; an open sewer ran down the centre of the cobbles fed by the emptying of chamber pots from the nearest window. The stench was appalling. Pock-marked children with matted hair, bare feet and scanty clothes, ran and screamed and begged at the skirts of Harriet and her maid. From every doorway the inhabitants of the rookery turned to watch them.

"Let's get out of here, Miss," said Annie, clutching her basket tightly. "We've somehow got us into St Giles."

Harriet again consulted her map to no effect. There was no help for it, they were lost. Harriet turned the map upside down but the neatly drawn streets showed no similarity with the maze of dark alleys in which she and Annie found themselves.

"Time is getting on. I think we had better retrace our steps," she said decisively,

"Can I be of 'elp, young misses?" One of the loungers left his wall and swaggered towards them.

"No thank you," said Harriet closing the guide book with a snap. "Come Annie, the Strand is this way."

"Is it the Strand you'll be wantin'?" The man had an Irish accent. "To be sure, I can take you there in a trice. If yous just like to come with me, now." Another man joined him and began to follow.

The girls smartened their pace. Harriet made for a patch of blue sky and by luck hit on an open square where, outside a low tavern, a cluster of men slumped on rough wooden benches, coughed and spat. A great noise of argument and shouting erupted from the interior. Suddenly the door burst open and a figure in a blue coat of military cut was hurled to the cobbles. The burly landlord followed and tossed a bucket of slops over the sprawling figure.

"Gert up, yer great drunken lump! Swindle me of my money would yer?" The blue coat did not stir. Harriet and Annie clutched at each other, backing away. The onlookers jeered and pushed at the figure with their feet. The landlord, impatient for signs of life in his erstwhile customer, rolled the figure onto his back with a swing of his foot. He bent down, rifling his pockets for anything he could find. "Don't show yer ugly mug here agin or you'll I'll draw yer claret for good an' all! Rob me of my dues would yer!" He rose, pocketing a silk handkerchief, several coins and a leather pocket book. "Gan, yer not worth the taking. Not a decent bit of bobbery about yer!" And giving his victim a vindictive kick in the ribs he turned and disappeared into the tavern.

Harriet instinctively made a move forward. Only Annie's tight grip pulled her back into the doorway. "Don't be foolish, Miss, there's nothing we can do 'gainst all those rough men!"

"But did you see who it *is*, Annie? It's Captain Valentine! We cannot *leave* him like this. I cannot stand the man but poor Madame de Lessups would be distraught if anything happened to him and I would always blame myself."

"'Tis no business of ours, Miss. An' look at them drunken louts. We'd not be safe going past them."

Harriet hesitated. "You're right. The best thing would be to get out of this maze as soon as possible, and tell some gentleman about Captain Valentine's plight."

Harriet was relieved to see the recumbent figure stir and drag himself to his hands and knees. A lock of black hair fell over his eyes. A couple of the onlookers decided there was more to be gained now from assisting the gentleman than by molesting him and dragged themselves from their bench to help him to his feet.

The two girls backed away down a side alley and on further into the shambles that was Seven Dials.

On all sides they were confronted by scolding, drinking, smoking, squabbling and swearing low-life and still the two Irishmen stalked them. In vain Harriet looked for a landmark to guide them towards safety.

It was the dog that made them run. A great hairless hound with slavering teeth and a ferocious bark leapt out from a doorway and hurled himself towards them. Harriet flung the guide book into its face but that gained them only a moment's respite. The dog, now fully enraged, charged.

Harriet lost her nerve. "Run, Annie! Run!" She and Annie ran until their lungs were about to burst. They flung themselves round a corner and Harriet ran smack into a solid wall of flesh, clothed in a long grey driving coat. The obstruction immediately clamped one hand on her shoulder and spun her behind him. Taking two steps forward, the gentleman whipped a sword from his cane and commanded the dog to halt. The cur stopped, tongue lolling, saliva dripping onto the cobbles. It snarled threateningly but kept a bloodshot eye on the rapier point. Someone whistled from an alley and the hound at last bounded back into the warren of the slum.

The instant he turned, the great figure resolved itself into Lord Everard. Annie nervously appeared from her place of refuge behind some barrels.

"Miss Larkhill, my dear young woman! Whatever brings you to this dark place – with only your maid for protection I see?" He casually returned his sword to its sheath.

"Oh thank goodness! We are saved! It's you, Lord Everard." She tore her eyes from the sword-stick. "I feel very foolish to have got myself lost and in such a scrape. Thank heavens it's you. I own I was becoming - very alarmed. The dog, the dog, frightened me."

Everard took her hand, murmuring soothing nothings all the while. "Let me escort you back to Russell Square," he said, gallantly offering his other arm to Annie. "What on earth can have possessed such a gently-bred young female to wander the worst rookeries of London?"

"I was trying to find my way back to Russell Square and took a wrong turning. We have been to see St Paul's," gushed Harriet. She explained the dearth of hackney carriages.

"I normally do have a good sense of direction – at least in the country. What must you think of me! Pray do not tell Lady McAllister – or even Sir Hamish, in fact no one at all, if you please! What a country bumpkin I would seem."

His lugubrious face smiled down at her. "I would not dream of betraying a lady, however - misguided." He walked them purposefully through several dingy courts and alleys.

"But what luck you are here, sir." She noticed that people went about their business and the urchins melted back into doorways as they passed. Everard might be a gentleman but his bulk was imposing. "What brings *you* into these dreadful slums?"

"My family has an old servant who has fallen on hard times. I only recently learnt of her plight and her whereabouts and have this moment come from offering what help I could."

"How kind of you, sir. A true knight errant. Oh gracious, I almost forgot! We saw Captain Valentine, somewhat worse for wear, I fear, and he was being attacked, or not really attacked but thrown out of a tavern, but I do think someone ought to rescue him."

"I regret to say that such a circumstance is not new to Captain Valentine. He is well-known in this neighbourhood. He is quite used to being thrown out of taverns. No harm will come to him apart from a sore head." He steered her around a pile of dung.

Harriet looked dubious. "But what if he's murdered? He was barely conscious when we saw him, and there was a great crowd of ruffians around him."

"If you really are concerned for that gentleman, Miss Larkhill, then of course I will turn back and seek him out. But first allow me to put you and your maid into a carriage and see you safely on your way to Russell Square."

Harriet thanked him warmly. "He had just been ejected from the Blue Boar, if you can find it - I remarked the signboard," said Harriet waving an arm vaguely behind her. "And he seemed barely conscious. Madame de Lessups worries so about her nephew, and indeed I think she has grounds for her anxiety. Though I would not say a word to her about this incident."

"I see I do not have to explain the situation to you, but the lady knows the captain is well on the way to ruin himself before he returns to India," said Everard solemnly. "I fear he will stray into criminality, seeing some of the company he keeps. I hold no brief for the fashion of welcoming back the prodigal son, but Marguerite de Lessups has the kindest of natures. You, Miss Larkhill, would be wise to avoid his company."

"He is hardly likely to seek me out," said Harriet betrayed into indiscretion. "Financial considerations will shape that gentleman's affections," and then felt uncomfortable at her outspokenness.

Everard smiled. "You have guessed it Miss Larkhill. Only money can save Valentine now and as he has already lost a considerable sum at the tables, he must marry a fortune. But I will rescue him from this latest fracas, for your sake." He squeezed her arm looped in his.

"So chivalrous, Lord Everard," said Harriet, a little puzzled by such attention but pleased that something would be done. By this time he had led them unhesitatingly out of the slums and into Bloomsbury Square. Before her stood the high wall around Montagu House.

"Oh, the British Museum!" cried Harriet, thankfully. "I know where I am now, and we can be home directly. Thank you Lord Everard. Pray do not trouble yourself to find a hackney from here. It is but a few steps. My maid and I will walk."

"Then let me escort you."

"Good heavens, no, I thank you. How would I explain you to Lady McAllister? That won't be at all necessary; we shall be quite safe." She looked up at him pleadingly. "I would far rather you enquired after Captain Valentine's welfare."

He hesitated for a moment. "Very well, I will leave you on one condition, Miss Larkhill, that you do not noise my charity abroad. I would not have my reputation as a leader of high fashion destroyed by a tale of slumming in the alleys of Seven Dials, let alone the weakness of my good deeds. What would society think if they knew I had been less than selfish and demanding? I could never raise my lorgnette again."

"They would think the better of you. And you do yourself an injustice, sir."

"Nevertheless, Miss Larkhill, I trust you will be as discreet as I will be concerning our fortuitous meeting this morning?" He looked down at her smiling conspiratorially.

"Why, of course Lord Everard. Annie and I will say nothing of this adventure, though I am certain it would enhance your standing in the eyes of the world, even if it ruined mine. I will be silent, as long as we can reach Russell Square before eleven o'clock and do not encounter Lady McAllister."

Everard took out his fob watch. "Never fear, you have plenty of time. Lady McAllister will not be down, if I know her habits. You may avoid her *pince nez* yet."

******

Harriet was thankful to have a quiet afternoon before her second appearance at Almack's. Her adventure of the morning had shaken her and left her in a pensive mood. She sensed that this mishap was something she could not confess to Rupert; he had a streak of sobriety in him that would not countenance such behaviour and he had been dismissive of her last escapade.

Lady McAllister held out no great hopes for the attendance of the *ton* who, she predicted, would be saving their strength and their finery for the coronation or the Devonshires' Ball. She was right, Almack's was thin of company but the moment Harriet entered the room between the McAllisters, several people moved towards them. Shawcross as ever claimed Harriet for the first set leaving the McAllisters to greet their friends. The Hintons were absent.

Harriet was happy to see more of the ballroom and its dancers. The atmosphere was calmer than her first visit but just as elegant. Patriotic red, white and blue bunting decorated the musicians' gallery. The sight of Lord Everard talking with a bewhiskered Russian general in white, a great glittering star pinned to his chest, reassured her that nothing untoward had evolved from the morning's episode.

When Shawcross returned Harriet to the crowd of dowagers, one large lady in peach brocade and gold tassels fell on her with cries of delight. It was the Reichsgrafin. "My dear Miss! So pleased I am to see you!"

The ladies stared in amusement but no surprise at the Reichsgrafin's extravagant greeting; dear Adelaide was known for her emotional outbursts. "A little accident, in the street," she explained to her friends. "My arm was hurt. But Fraulein-" her memory failed her. "The niece of our dear Elspeth," she improvised. "Most helpful was to me."

Several lorgnettes rose as Harriet brushed aside the thanks, aware of Lady McAllister's stiffening back.

"I had no idea Miss Larkhill had been of service to you, Adelaide – or was walking abroad alone."

"One is forced to admire these English demoiselles – they have such *esprit*," smiled the gorgeously bedecked Comtesse de Metz-Colmar. "My daughters have never left the *hôtel* without their governess or a footman; they could not find their way about Paris alone." The implication being that no lady would ever consider doing so.

Seeing Lady McAllister's eyes begin to bulge in disapprobation, the Reichsgrafin led Harriet aside. "Sir Hamish has told you? You had my message?" she whispered. "The cross was found and my husband's honour was saved! All because of you!"

Harriet was more surprised at the Reichsgrafin's sudden command of English but was sorry for it. She felt that this was still a matter not to be noised abroad and begged the Reichsgrafin to say no more about the incident.

"Ach, of course not! My husband most angry with me was."

Harriet was rescued by William who had been dancing energetically with a spritely young woman. "Come and make up a set Harriet. We need another couple for the quadrille and you ain't bad at it you know. Cholmondley says he knows you from some outing of his mother's." Bertie Cholmondley came forward and Harriet, who mentally referred to him as the fox-hunting boy, gladly gave him her hand; she could see Mortimer Shawcross hovering with intent.

Rupert appeared an hour later, just as the young people were going down to supper. He looked agitated and on seeing Harriet made directly for her. They shook hands as the others disappeared.

"Is Sir Hamish here tonight? I need to speak to him urgently," he said scanning the ballroom. "Forgive me if I do not take you down, Miss Larkhill, but I have business that will not wait."

She took one look at his strained face and said: "Certainly, Sir Hamish is in the card room, I believe."

"You are a most accommodating woman," he said, giving her hand a squeeze.

Mortimer Shawcross appeared from behind a pillar like a plump little genie out of a bottle. He offered Harriet his arm to go down and partake of thin slices of bread and butter and plain cake. Harriet accepted with a sense of inevitability and heroically refused to turn around to stare after Rupert's disappearing figure.

She had no time to puzzle over Rupert's behaviour before Lord Everard paused behind her chair. "I am relieved to see you this evening, Miss Larkhill. Taking in the sights is such an exhausting pastime. But I am happy to inform you that more than one lost soul was rescued and sent safely home."

Harriet's eyes rounded in alarm. Surely, he of all people would not be so indiscreet as to mention the morning's escapade. "Thank you my lord. I take it you mean the military gentleman?"

"Indeed." He bowed and moved on, leaving the young people quizzing Harriet with lively curiosity.

Mortimer Shawcross had a sudden doubt about this unsophisticated country damsel. A lady who was mysteriously intimate with Stephen Everard may not be such a biddable spouse.

Rupert had come to Almack's specifically to find Sir Hamish. That morning he had watched Will Hinton put five hundred pounds in notes in a silk bag, wrap it in brown paper, string and sealing wax, and address it to 'John Smyth Esq, to be collected, Bristol Receiving Office'.

He had shadowed Hinton into the building but had seen nothing untoward. The two men had waited all day for some communication from the post office officials or a note from Sir Hamish. No word had come and Will Hinton was strung like a wire. When Rupert had called at Russell Square that evening, Figgis had informed him of the family's whereabouts.

In the card room, Rupert found Sir Hamish reading a scrap of paper with a frown on his face. He looked up. "Ah, Darville, just the man!" With an apology he threw down his cards and rose, taking Rupert to the wall. Sir Hamish handed him the note with some embarrassment.

"Freeling's failed to find the parcel or the thief. This note's just been sent on from White's," Sir Hamish apologised. "They bungled the affair by the sound of it – and they know it. Not one of my own men, I hasten to add. I left it to Freeling to alert his senior clerk. A mistake I fear. Come and have a drink – damn there's none to be had in this place."

Rupert's heart sank. He was angry at the incompetence of the Post Office and what he felt was his own mistake in relying on others. "Thank you sir, but no. I must inform Hinton of this at once."

"Hinton's Velasquez is it? I thought as much. No need to look so annoyed; I'll be discreet. You stick by your friends, I see."

Rupert damned himself for the slip of his tongue. The day's suspense had made him jumpy. Sir Hamish apologised and further offered his help.

"Thank you sir, but there's nothing more that can be done tonight." Rupert bade Sir Hamish an abrupt farewell. At least he could put Hinton out of his suspense. They must wait and hope that the Velasquez would be restored as was the Ravensburg jewel.

Escaping from her friends Harriet climbed the stairs to the ballroom to watch for Rupert. She confronted him as he strode out of the card salon. "What has occurred? Is the Countess well? Your sister-in-law? What has happened?"

"Not now Harriet." Harriet took a step backwards. "Ah, here is Mr Shawcross come in search of you – as always." Rupert turned quickly, swayed a little, squinted and regained his balance. Smiling, he placed Harriet's gloved hand in that of the Member of Parliament.

"I leave this lady to your care sir. She might be the only light at the end of the tunnel."

Harriet and Mr Shawcross stared in astonishment at Rupert's retreating back.

CHAPTER 6   CORONATION

The Great Day came. Sir Hamish marshalled his guests for a dawn breakfast and ferried them in convoy to their reserved seats in the pavilion opposite Westminster Hall. A hired cart followed with the servants and picnic hampers. It was as well to be early as the populace had been camping on the streets overnight. By six o'clock Charing Cross was jammed with carriages of the nobility, many of the guests forced to abandon their vehicles and make their way to Westminster Hall or the abbey on foot. Artillery fire could be heard in the parks and from a gun-boat on the river, alternating with the joyous peal of church bells.

The McAllister party took their seats, Miss Finch arranging cushions and rugs against the chill misty morning. The ladies wore their most splendid finery and the gentlemen their largest silver buttons. Captain Valentine looked hollow-eyed but dashing in his military uniform. However, they were all outshone by Ram Kumar, Beaumont's Indian servant, in a cream satin sherwani and scarlet turban with a glittering dagger tucked in his sash.

"Oh, do not mind Kumar," said Philippa, seeing Lady McAllister's alarm. "He has been with Papa since I was a baby. We could not go on without him."

Thus appeased, Lady McAllister thought that the towering warrior could only add consequence to their party. Neighbours waved and hallooed when sighting their friends; it was like being at the opera or the theatre.

Although the west doors of Westminster Abbey were out of sight around the corner, from their seats they could see the comings and goings into Westminster Hall where the king and court were gathering. Excitement rose at glimpses of the lavish costumes of the arriving dignitaries. Harriet did not expect to see the Earl and Dowager Countess of Morna who would not be part of the procession but only spectators in the abbey.

"What a pity we will not see dear Sophia and the earl," said Lady McAllister. "Sweet man, so unsophisticated. The dear dowager is very anxious about him; Lady Glynn says it is to be such a long ceremony in the abbey. I find the earl a refreshingly unaffected gentleman, *quite* a change from the usual frippery young man-about-town. I felt he was a trifle overwhelmed at my soirée, until I had quite put him at his ease," said Lady McAllister.

"Almost a natural, you might say," drawled Captain Valentine, "though he's sharp enough when it comes to horseflesh."

He bent down to retrieve Philippa's shawl and draped it around her shoulders. She smiled her thanks at him. Harriet looked on with a frown. Andrew inched his seat a little forward behind the ladies.

The processional walkway stretched from Westminster Hall to the abbey. It rose three feet in front of the spectators' pavilion and consisted of a platform of boards covered in blue fabric surmounted by a rolled cloth canopy in case of rain, but to everyone's relief the day promised to be fine. His Majesty's foot-guards in full dress uniform were stationed along the walkway at a lower level. There was ample space to walk between the pavilion and the processional way, now crowded with food hawkers and couples strolling arm in arm greeting acquaintances. William leapt over the wooden wall and went in search of mischief.

There was not much to do except wait and compare everyone's dress and speculate on the latest arrivals. Lady McAllister and Madame de Lessups began a gentle rivalry in identifying the illustrious personages. Every window of the surrounding houses was packed with spectators. Gaily decorated stands towered to the skies on the most precipitous of scaffolding. Harriet looked up, wondering where Rupert was. He had chosen to spend the day with his natural philosophy friends, but she did not know exactly where. Figgis passed among them with coffee and sweet rolls.

At eight-thirty all the roads were closed. At ten o'clock people began to take out their watches. Murmurs of 'he's late' ran around the stands. William reappeared with the news that the king had torn his robes while dressing. Lady McAllister looked horrified. "All that money wasted!" and then hushed herself, not wishing to appear vulgar.

"What's worse is that the queen has been hammering on the abbey door since six o'clock, demanding to be let in!"

"Good Lord!" said Sir Hamish, "I must get over there! I never thought the woman would really attempt anything! Where's Lord Liverpool?"

"What are the guards doing, allowing such a disgraceful scene!" blustered Shawcross.

William ignored him. "Don't worry, they didn't let her in. I swear they put a couple of prize-fighters in pages' costumes to manhandle her out of the way."

Sir Hamish relaxed a little but did not deny the prize-fighters. "Where is the queen now?"

"Gone. Crossed bayonets and a slammed door got the message across. I'm surprised you didn't hear the row!"

"Poor lady, how humiliating for her," said Harriet.

"Humiliating, nothing! Damned dangerous – I beg your pardon. The crowds didn't like it either. Londonderry was right; the mob has turned against her."

Nevertheless Sir Hamish excused himself and disappeared. Everyone fell to discussing the latest shocking turn of events. A heavy gun fired, startling everyone.

"Don't be alarmed! That's the signal to show that the king has arrived in the Hall. He spent the night in the Speakers house," said Shawcross. "There will be a great deal of ceremony now, with the presentation of the royal regalia to the king." He enjoyed being in a position to inform the ladies.

At last a second signal-gun fired and the coronation procession began. The anthem struck up and, to the sound of trumpets and beating of drums, the herb-women turned the corner by the Champion's Stables to great cheers. A bevy of handsome young women of good birth, dressed in cream gauze, strewed flowers to ward off the pestilence.

"What pretty Jacobean ruff collars. The king must have read *Kenilworth*. Lord Everard says the spectacle is to be quite historical in appearance, all of the king's devising," said an excited Philippa. "I *do* wish Lord Everard were here to explain it all to us."

"You will be able to wave to him in the procession," said Andrew stiffly as the band struck up.

Harriet scanned her programme. "All the participants are listed but how are we to know the significance of the costumes of the regalia?"

"I flatter myself I am acquainted with the nobility who frequent the House. I speak to them often in St Stephen's Hall," said Shawcross. "Even the Whigs, occasionally. Some of them are quite decent fellows." The solemnity of the day had put him in charity with the political opposition.

Mortimer Shawcross sported a red rose of England in his button hole and had chosen a red brocade waistcoat under a bright blue coat. "It behoves a man to show his patriotism on an occasion like this," he protested when teased by the younger members of the party.

There followed a stream of dignitaries from Westminster, the City, the law courts, senior clergy, various Knights of the Bath and Knights of the Garter, all wearing their gold chains and insignia. Harriet was delighted to see Lord Londonderry among them, walking alone carrying a soft hat of black velvet with an immense plume of white ostrich feathers.

"Why is the marquess on his own? Shouldn't he be with the other peers?" asked Philippa in concern.

"Londonderry is another Irish title, my dear," Shawcross leaned over. "He is not a peer of Great Britain." He sounded dismissive. Harriet gave a louder cheer, thinking the marquess looked dignified in his isolation.

Lady McAllister wondered aloud as to her dearest friend Emily's seat in the galleries of Westminster Hall. Her neighbours were too busy cheering to be impressed.

The costumes were stunning. White satin vied with crimson cloaks edged with gold. Slashed doublets in damask and hose of white silk contrasted with gold copes and frothing ostrich plumes. Every ensemble was edged with miniver or ermine and laced with gold and silver thread.

The figure of Stephen Everard could not be missed among the barons. His height and bulk marked him out. He was chatting easily to his neighbour and seemed unperturbed by his robe of crimson velvet and ermine cape. Philippa was disappointed that he did not once look into the crowds.

"You cannot deny that any man looks at his best in scarlet," said Valentine half to himself as he tugged the skirt of his uniform coat a little straighter.

Heralds trumpeted the arrival of the standards of Ireland, Scotland and England, Hanover and the Union, carried by lords and surrounded by viscounts.. Behind the earls came the marquesses and then the Lord Chamberlain of His Majesty's household bearing a cushion on which were placed the ruby ring and the sword to be donned by the king in the abbey.

"Don't say a word about rubies!" threatened Harriet as William opened his mouth. "Or sapphires! I will not have you spoil the occasion with tittle-tattle!"

When the Royal Standard passed, Mortimer Shawcross went into paroxysms of hurrahs. The dukes in their robes of estate came next, carrying coronets decorated with gold strawberry leaves. Lady McAllister lost her *pince nez* at the sight of the Duke of Wellington and had recourse to her smelling bottle. Harriet did not care who they were, the costumes were dazzling. The sun winked off Archbishops' golden copes and the gold purse carried by the sweating Lord High Chancellor in a full-bottomed wig.

"How hot they must be," cried Harriet beneath the strident band music. Madame de Lessups had long since discarded her shawl and was using her fan with vigour.

Privy Councillors, officers of the royal household, interspersed by the quartered tabards of the Pursuivants of Arms, followed hard behind. Harriet could not keep up with the relentless march of nobility toward the abbey.

"Can that be Prince Leopold? He's dressed as a Garter Knight!"

The women craned forward to see the widower of beloved Princess Charlotte, the king's only child tragically lost to puerperal fever four years earlier. As a foreign prince, Leopold of Saxe-Coburg Saalfeld was not allowed to wear any British robes of state. Today he wore the dark blue robe of the Order of the Garter and carried a Field Marshall's baton in his right hand. Mr Shawcross knew all the details.

"Poor man, he will never recover," fluttered Miss Finch, "such a tragedy, to lose one's spouse *and* the child!"

"And such a loss to the nation," commiserated Shawcross. "I can't see the king marrying again – even if he gets rid of the Brunswick. But one must get an heir, for the sake of the family name."

And then came the royal dukes: Gloucester, Cambridge, Clarence, Sussex and York. Behind them came the Lord High Constables. Mr Shawcross became solemn at the sight of more sacred regalia to be used in the ceremony, carried on velvet cushions by the highest in the land. The ladies marvelled at the medieval golden beauty of St. Edward's Crown.

"He won't be wearing that on the way out," said Beaumont. "He's spent six thousand pounds on the new one." But no one took any notice of such carping.

The crowd roared as the king came into view. A great swell surged through the spectators as everyone jumped to their feet. Here at last was His Majesty King George IV.

The king looked resplendent in a black Spanish hat surmounted by sprays of ostrich feathers and a heron's plume. His twenty-seven foot train was held wide by the sons of peers and Lord Francis Conyngham, Master of the Robes.

"I see he puts the son to good use as well as the mother," murmured William, as Harriet clapped frantically in approval.

The king's train was of crimson velvet, edged with gold and ermine and embroidered with gold stars. Harriet was not so sure of the carapace it made over his suit of cloth of silver, lavishly trimmed with gold lace and braid. To her surprise His Majesty walked with a firm tread and seemed the picture of happiness and good humour, bowing on all sides in return for the deafening shouts and applause from all quarters.

Lady McAllister was betrayed into sentiment. "To think that thirty years ago we regarded him as Prince Florizel. I maintain His Majesty is *still* the First Gentleman of Europe!" She waved her handkerchief madly.

As the king passed, Harriet could see brown ringlets curling from under his hat. "I think His Majesty looks very fine, but how hot he'll be in that wig."

The king's pace quickened so that those in the upper windows could see him and not have their vision obscured by the cloth-of-gold canopy carried by the barons of the Cinque Ports.

In a few moments the king was out of sight. The dregs of the cavalcade, the king's private equerries and ushers, pages and footmen strode past in full livery. The procession ended with a fine showing of the Yeomen of the Guard. It had taken half an hour for the procession to walk three hundred yards from Westminster Hall to Westminster Abbey.

A feeling of contentment seeped through the crowds. The spectators sat back in their seats, either exhausted by the emotion or eager to share impressions. People turned to smile at each other in satisfaction. If some of the gentlemen didn't quite fill a stocking as well as their ancestors or looked faintly ridiculous in their Tudor ruffs all was forgiven in the knowledge that this coronation beat the Emperor Napoleon's into a cocked hat!

Mortimer Shawcross was bursting with pride. "What wouldn't I give to be inside the abbey! Who would not be an Englishman today!" He dabbed his eyes with a florid handkerchief.

"I'd give anything to be inside Westminster Hall for the banquet!" said Captain Valentine. Harriet had to agree, her stomach was starting to rumble and Philippa looked rather limp.

"How can they seat three hundred or more?" observed Harriet. Like any woman, the logistics of mass catering fascinated her.

"I heard the remainder of the palace of Westminster is to be used, covers will be laid in all the state rooms. The banquet is going to be another theatrical performance, there will be an appearance by the king's champion on that white horse you admired so much at Astley's, Miss Beaumont."

"How ridiculous!" snorted the Nabob. "We live in the modern world. What's this medieval nonsense got to do with empire and trade!"

Madame de Lessups hushed him gently.

Sir Hamish returned, full of news about the queen's failed attempt to be part of the coronation.

"Lord Hood has done himself no good with the king, taking the queen's part as he did. He offered her his own ticket of entry, but she had the sense not to go in to the abbey without her ladies. Sir Robert Inglis persuaded her to leave; sound man. The mob was spoiling for a fight of course, setting about anyone who did not doff their caps at the queen's name. There's been a deal of rioting by youths and vagabonds. Grillons was attacked. Poor Londonderry has had all his windows broken, and so have many others. Where's the champagne, my dear? I need sustenance."

Elspeth had some qualms as to whether it would be sacrilegious to eat while the ceremony of anointing and crowning was taking place within earshot, but Sir Hamish assured his guests that it would be fitting to drink a loyal toast to His Majesty. Luckily this coincided with shouts of the Recognition from the abbey. The McAllisters and their friends gathered round – only Rupert was missing.

With "God Save King George the Fourth" ringing over the roof tops, Harriet raised her glass to her new sovereign.

******

The ceremony in the abbey went on for over four hours. Long before the twenty-one gun salute was heard from St James's Park, Lady McAllister ordered the picnic hampers to be brought out. Madame de Lessups had augmented the McAllisters' frugal fare with French pastries and iced punch. A party atmosphere permeated the luncheon, augmented by the arrival of the Cholmondleys and other strolling friends.

Sir Hamish had organised runners to report back on progress inside the abbey but apart from thrilling to the sound of the anthems, the young people grew restless.

"Look! Look! Up there in the sky!" someone shouted.

Above the stands floated a gas balloon bearing His Majesty's arms and the words 'George IV. Royal Coronation Balloon.' The gondolier carried the English flag and headed north on the light breeze.

"View Halloo! It's taken off from Hyde Park," said Bertie Cholmondley. "The fête's started! Tally ho! After it!"

"What a boon they would be on the battlefield," said Captain Valentine.

"I wonder how it stays up," said Philippa shading her eyes against the sun.

"Gas of some sort – hot air over Parliament most likely," said Bertie, to Shawcross's obvious irritation.

Rupert would know, thought Harriet.

Andrew and Captain Valentine offered to escort the young ladies to the park. Fingers were wiped, napkins shaken and promises made to return to their seats before His Majesty left the abbey to return to Westminster Hall. Mr Beaumont insisted that Ram Kumar accompany the party. This was enough to send the young people jostling with the rest of the crowd towards the sound of more lively revelry.

Shawcross, feeling his age and his dignity, thought it better stay with the ladies in Sir Hamish's stead. William had vanished with his father. As half the cabinet was inside the abbey it was left to Sir Hamish and other Home Office officials to manage any crisis or disturbance. Mr Shawcross considered the Nabob almost a foreigner and not the man to leave in charge, considering his obvious hostility to the event.

"Hold on to your purses, ladies," said Valentine, taking Philippa's arm in his. "The park will be a thieves' paradise. Half the rogues in London will be on the hunt – or burgling houses."

Harriet had never experienced such crowds and was heartily glad to have Andrew and Ram Kumar shepherd them through the myriad of pavilions and stands. Tableau vivants, wrestling matches, highland dancing, horse races, fortune tellers, fire-eaters, freak shows and Black Sal shies provided something for everybody. She suspected there were cock fights and dog races in discreet corners. The nobility rolled through the park in their carriages stopping only to admire the commons at play.

Bertie Cholmondley kept disappearing to bet on the dog racing. Anne Cholmondley, quite used to her brother's sporting obsessions, companionably linked arms with Harriet. The park reeked of hot pies, fried food and sugared cakes. By two o'clock, the beer stalls were running dry and some of the crowd was dispersing to return to the processional route.

They had missed the boat race on the Serpentine; in compensation Bertie Cholmondley suggested they all hire rowing boats and join the flotilla on the lake. Philippa shrunk back at the sight of the crowded waterway, when Ram Kumar suddenly exclaimed aloud in his own tongue.

"Elephants?" cried Philippa. "There cannot be elephants on the water!"

A huge raft, carrying two gorgeously caparisoned grey beasts appeared around a bend in the lake. Each elephant had a young woman dressed as an Eastern 'slave' seated on its back, pretending to guide the animal with an iron rod. The elephants, harnessed one behind the other, 'pulled' a triumphal chariot. The mammoth barge was towed by four boats manned by watermen in blue uniforms.

"By Jove, I wonder where they got those Indian elephants from," said Captain Valentine momentarily diverted from his pursuit of Miss Beaumont. He began to talk to Ram Kumar and discuss the finer point of elephant training as the barge slowly disappeared from sight.

"Now, why not take Miss Beaumont on the lake?" whispered Harriet to Andrew McAllister. "Miss Cholmondley and her brother are ahead of you. Most of the rowers have gone in pursuit of the barge, the water is not half so crowded now."

"Do you not want to go on the lake, yourself, Miss Larkhill?"

"Not at all. I would be seasick," prevaricated Harriet. "Now is your chance, while Captain Valentine is occupied."

Andrew acted promptly and within moments had persuaded Miss Beaumont that the air would be cooler on the lake and that Miss Larkhill would surely follow. He had adroitly handed Philippa into a small boat before Valentine noticed that his quarry had escaped him.

"Another neat diversionary tactic, Miss Larkhill," said the captain watching Andrew row his fair maiden out of harm's way. "And not the first time elephants have been used in this cunning manner. But I will come about I assure you."

"*I* did not arrange for the barge to distract your attention," said Harriet with wide-eyed innocence.

He gave her one of his wicked smiles and nodded to the receding figures of Andrew and Philippa. "Shall we follow them do you think? Do you trust yourself to me Miss Larkhill, landlubber that I am?"

"I do not trust you an inch Captain Valentine and would much rather have an ice and stay cool under those trees," replied Harriet heroically. She had never been in a boat and badly wanted to try the experience. However, she did not trust Valentine sober or tipsy, let alone on water.

"You are right, of course. There is no point in pursuit unless one knows capture is certain. We could hardly throw a grappling iron and board a rowing boat."

The captain left Harriet in the care of Ram Kumar and went off in search of ices. It gave him the opportunity to refresh himself from his hip flask and reconnoitre on his own.

After some reflective moments studying the crowd Harriet became aware of a group of people surrounded by romping children making their way to the landing stage, intent on taking to the water.

"Why, Miss Larkhill," exclaimed Mrs Somerville. "All alone? We were so hoping to see you. My husband was asking after the McAllisters but a few moments ago, and here you are like a good fairy."

Harriet rose, curtseyed gave garbled explanations and tried to keep her eyes from Rupert and Miss Snoddie. Rupert looked his usual pale, inscrutable self.

"Have the gentlemen abandoned you, Miss Larkhill?" asked Lavinia, her gloved hand firmly in Rupert's arm. "They will always desert the good and homely for something new and exotic."

"Just so. However, even I cannot hope to rival the appearance of an elephant."

Rupert unwrapped Miss Snoddie's arm quickly, saying: "Miss Larkhill, allow me to introduce you to some particular friends of mine: Mr and Mrs Babbage." He indicated a small-featured gentleman with a high-domed forehead who looked rather preoccupied.

"The Somervilles of course you know. The children, I'm afraid are a mystery known only to their respective parents."

After the laughter had subsided Harriet said "Mr Babbage, I am sorry to say I cannot understand how your 'difference engine' will work but Mr Darville assures me it will achieve something wonderful regarding calculation."

Mrs Babbage broke in. "No one can understand it Miss Larkhill, not even his own wife! I have forced him to bring us today to get away from his wretched drawings. And all the gentlemen did was to make predictions about the flight of the hot air balloon and where it would come down!"

"Miss Beaumont wished to know what keeps the balloon afloat."

"Coal gas," said Rupert promptly. "This is the first time it has been used to fuel a hot air balloon."

Harriet gave him a dazzling smile.

The children started to clamour for their boat ride and when all was settled between the parents, and the various offspring disposed of between three boats, Lavinia turned to Rupert demanding to be taken on the river.

Rupert took out his fob watch. "A thousand pardons ladies, I must meet my mother and brother. They are not invited to the royal banquet and surely the ceremony in the abbey must be over by now."

"Oh, no, we would hear the guns firing. The timetable is very behindhand," said Lavinia. "We have plenty of time for a row on the lake. Miss Larkhill will not mind if we leave her to rest, she has her Indian bodyguard to protect her."

Rupert suddenly dropped to the bench. "Forgive me ladies, I am not quite myself." He removed his hat and tugged at his cravat.

Harriet sat down beside him. "Look, here is Captain Valentine with a tray of ices. Just the thing to cool you down." Though Rupert looked grey rather than flushed.

Valentine took the situation in at once. He put down the tray of ices on the bench and offered Rupert his hip flask. "Darville? I didn't expect to see you here. A hair of the dog?"

Rupert glowered but took the hip flask gratefully. "A momentary indisposition only."

"Damned heat. And we've all been up far too early. Good God I haven't seen the dawn since I left Calcutta. Been at your books too hard? You don't want to get brain fever with all that studying. Or is it something you've picked up in the tropics?"

Rupert took a mouthful of brandy and straightened his shoulders. "Thank you captain, this should set me right. A moment's dizziness, that's all it was. There is no need to make a fuss. Do not alarm yourself, ladies, I am quite recovered."

"Where's Jacob?" asked Harriet. "You should go home Mr Darville! Only you'll never find a hackney in these crowds, all the roads are blocked or closed."

"Leave him to me Miss Larkhill. I'll take him back to his lodgings," said the captain.

"I assure you I am quite recovered, though perhaps not strong enough to essay rowing on the lake-"

"You must not dream of attempting it Mr Darville. I am quite used to rowing. My aunt in Lincolnshire has a great lake on which my sisters and I amuse ourselves every summer. Let me take you out on the cooler water and I'm sure you will recover in no time."

"Nonsense!" said the Valentine. "Miss Larkhill is right. Bed is what you need. We cannot have you staggering around frightening the horses! My friend Fitzmaurice – d'you know him? Old Mountshaft's son? He has his carriage waiting by the east gate. We'll take you home in that."

The captain was bored and looking for an excuse to escape. He had bumped into some cronies outside the boxing booth and more exciting diversions awaited if he could extricate himself from the McAllister party. He had given up his pursuit of Philippa for today and hoped she would be piqued by his absence when she returned from her boating trip with Andrew McAllister.

"You'll give my apologies to everyone, won't you Miss Larkhill. Say whatever is necessary to my aunt," he said putting a hand under Rupert's shoulder. "Miss Snoddie – you'll make things all right with your friends, I take it?"

Lavinia looked put out but nodded coolly. "If you think it is really necessary, don't let me detain you."

Rupert, looking dazed and a little angry, shook off Valentine's arm, stood up. "Forgive me ladies. I would not disrupt your party, but I am committed to my meet my brother." He made a sketchy bow, picked up his hat and followed Valentine's scarlet back into the crowds.

"Men are such weaklings, don't you find, Miss Larkhill?" said Lavinia helping herself to one of the ices. "Mr Darville has been perfectly well all day, I have been with him since dawn but ask any gentleman to do something he does not wish to and they become great babies."

Harriet was shocked by this *volte face*. "Mr Darville looked genuinely unwell to me – however momentarily. His departure had nothing to do with us; he was engaged to meet his family."

Lavinia continued to eat her ice. "I fear his organ of adhesiveness may be atrophied."

"Whatever do you mean?"

"Did he ever have a fall as a child? Causing some trauma to the head?"

"Not that I am aware. I know he was sickly as an infant, and perhaps neglected."

"I thought so. Mr Darville's faculty of attraction to others, or 'friendship' in the common parlance, is sadly underdeveloped."

"He is merely shy, and always has been – except with a special few," Harriet said defensively.

"There, you see! If he would but allow me to do a reading of his skull I could prove that his organ of adhesiveness is not sufficiently prominent. In fact I would not be surprised to find an indentation at the back of his skull." She put down her empty glass cup and picked up another ice.

"Ah, here come Mr McAllister and the heiress. He is making headway I assume. I hope she doesn't bore him to death before she gets him to the altar. Of course, I could be considered an heiress myself, you know."

"Indeed?" Did Rupert know? Was the Countess aware of this?

"My aunt has left her fortune – her considerable fortune - equally between myself and my younger sisters. She has no children of her own and cannot live long."

"I congratulate you."

"I could scoop the lot, if I wanted to," said Miss Snoddie casually licking the bowl of her spoon.

"Good God! Why would you? How could you think of refuting your aunt's wishes or depriving your sisters of their inheritance? What possible grounds could you have for contesting the will!"

Harriet's plain speaking rattled Miss Snoddie. "Well, I mean – er – if I were a man, as the eldest, then naturally I would inherit everything. If the world were fairer to women I would be entitled to it all."

"You have a poor grasp of the law, Miss Snoddie," said Harriet dryly but decided to say no more. Miss Snoddie's arrogance and attitude appalled her. The next time she saw Rupert, she would have find out exactly how things stood between him and Miss Snoddie.

******

All the fashionable world went to the Devonshires' Ball. Royalty was to attend later which meant that every man with an honour donned his decoration. The ballroom was a kaleidoscope of glittering diamond stars pinned to broad sashes swathing manly chests. Medals hung on gaudy ribbons and each uniform button was polished to perfection. The men outshone the women.

Harriet knew she looked well. Rupert's shot-silk had made up perfectly into the latest style of conical skirt, ruffles at the hem, plunging neckline, scooped back and ballooning short sleeves. There had been enough material left over to make a reticule. Lady Durrington's gift of white evening gloves and Aunt Amelia's garnets completed the ensemble. She had no need to be ashamed of her appearance.

Lady McAllister had included Harriet in the coiffeur's visit. Once Harriet had made it clear that she would not abandon her plaits – "For how else could I keep my hair tidy when I am at home in Wiltshire?" - she was more than happy to succumb to monsieur's attentions. Accordingly, her hair was washed, trimmed, oiled and styled in great loops. She sported three imposing peacock feathers and a red rose held in place by a shining mother-of-pearl comb – a present from Miss Beaumont.

Philippa's sweet nature delighted in Harriet's chance to go to the most prestigious ball of the season. She had no desire to attend the event herself, feeling it would be much too grand and overwhelming. She begged only to be told every detail at their next meeting. The gift of the comb surprised Harriet; she felt she did not stand on such close terms with Miss Beaumont to warrant such an expensive gift. The gift surprised Miss Beaumont even more, as the comb came from her father, who had been brusque to the point of sharpness when he ordered his daughter to put a card in with the shagreen leather box before sending it round to Russell Square.

The only note that threatened to spoil Harriet's evening was Lady McAllister's ruff. The little chiffon ruffle about her hostess's throat was undoubtedly in the latest style. Unfortunately it made that tall and angular lady look more like a heron than ever. My lady's maid had made some feeble attempts to dissuade her mistress from wearing it, but Elspeth was conscious of the growing lines about her long neck and thought to follow the king's historical theme. Her husband and sons seemed not to notice.

Devonshire House in Piccadilly was in the Palladian style, its regular flat façade concealing a sumptuous interior. The McAllisters joined the line of guests treading slowly up the exterior steps and into the lofty entrance hall. Great urns spilled over with hydrangeas and from above came the faint strains of the band of Coldstream Guards.

In the great crush of people Harriet made out Lord and Lady Glynn and was swept up into their circle to hear the details of the coronation ceremony in the abbey. Everyone had a tale to tell. Harriet drank it all in especially when someone recounted the evening festivities in Hyde Park, which sounded magical. Even the elephants and their barge had been lit up. The midnight boating on the river made her sigh with regret.

"Don't be disappointed Miss Larkhill," said Lord Glynn. "The entertainment wasn't a patch on the Peace celebrations of '14. Then, we had a naval review, a battle on the Serpentine-"

"Yes, but that was all foreigners," said Shawcross.

"The crowd was a touch raucous. The park was no place for a lady. You and Miss Beaumont were wise to stay at home in the evening."

After watching the king's triumphal return from the abbey at four o'clock, the McAllister party had fought their way home. The banquet in Westminster Hall would not start for another two hours and the party was exhausted. Elspeth took to her bed and Harriet was happy to accompany the Beaumonts to Curzon Street for a light super and to watch the fireworks from Mr Beaumont's attics. She had been invited to stay the night.

Now she could not help looking about the ballroom for Rupert and his family, but not even Lord Patrick's distinguished figure could be seen among the crowd. She told herself she was curious only to see the famous emeralds and hoped that the Countess would emerge from one of the card rooms. After a moment, Harriet mentally shook herself and, accepting Bertie's invitation to dance before Mortimer Shawcross could find her, allowed herself to be led onto the floor for the boulanger.

The next two hours were spent in a whirl of dancing, dresses and the latest *on-dits*. Refreshments were served at midnight. Just inside the supper room, Lady McAllister and Harriet spied Catherine Hinton, alone, looking as white as her lace with her handkerchief to her lips.

"My dear Mrs Hinton, are you quite well?" asked Lady McAllister.

"A trifle faint," gasped that lady. "If I could find somewhere quiet and perhaps a little cooler. I will be better directly."

"Of course, these rooms are becoming insufferably hot. I am surprised that so many invitations have been issued. I thought Devonshire had more discernment; this must be the biggest crush of the season."

Harriet opened a little door behind them to reveal a small salon, dimly lit and blessedly empty. The French windows onto a little balcony stood wide letting in the night air. Mrs Hinton allowed herself to be led to a sofa and sank down with a sigh,

"Thank you Lady McAllister. My husband has gone to procure me a glass of water – there is any amount of wine to be had but, I fear I cannot trust my digestion."

"I understand. I was just the same in your situation."

Harriet produced her smelling salts, a thoughtful gift from Miss Humble in preparation for her foray into the wild waters of the polite world. She had not dared produce them for Rupert.

"Use this Mrs Hinton, and I will find your husband for you."

Lady McAllister began to fan the sufferer, just a little too close to her face.

At that moment Will Hinton put his head around the door. "Ah, there you are my dear." He came in, clutching a tumbler of iced water. "Still not feeling quite the thing? Thank you ladies, I could not find Catherine in better hands." He watched his wife take a few sips and the pallor gradually leave her face. "There, you are better again, my dear. It was only the heat. Come and sample the stuffed widgeon and cream truffles. I have never seen such fare!"

Mrs Hinton looked distinctly bilious.

"I believe your wife would be better at home, sir, after she has recovered a little," said Lady McAllister.

"We cannot have another of our party cry off! What will our friends think of us? The Glossops have kept a place for you in the supper room. Darville has already pleaded fatigue and cut the ball."

Harriet looked up. "Is he ill too?"

"I shouldn't think so," said Hinton. "It's my belief that dancing and such jollities bore him; they always did. None of the Darvilles is here tonight, though we expected them. We are a sadly depleted party."

"Nevertheless," said Lady McAllister. "The exigencies of the past few days are bound to exhaust a lady in – of- a delicate constitution." She caught Catherine's eye and all at once subsided.

"If you say so, ma'am." Hinton turned to his wife. "What d'you think my dear? Do you really wish to go home? And miss a splendid supper and the arrival of His Majesty? You need not dance again if you are fatigued."

Catherine nodded carefully. "I had the honour of meeting the prince when he was Regent." It was an occasion she did not wish to repeat. She patted her damp top lip with her handkerchief. "He would not remember me, now. And I really could not swallow a morsel."

Hinton straightened up. "Very well, if you are certain. I cannot think it but a shame to miss such a fine repast. I will tell a footman to call our carriage. Perhaps Lady McAllister and Miss Larkhill would stay with you while I inform our friends of our departure."

When the Hintons finally left, the ladies returned to the supper room. The banquet was truly overwhelming. Tureens of soup, dressed lobsters, turbot, great chargers of sliced roast meats, daubed geese and braised capons, sauces and vegetables weighted the tables.

Pyramids of meringues and strawberries, pineapples, peaches and more hothouse fruits crammed the buffets. Creams, jellies, sweetmeats, pastries of all description, were laid out for three hundred guests, supervised by an army of waiters. Wine and champagne were unstinted.

"The Duke has surpassed himself; such opulence rivals the coronation banquet," said Lady McAllister with barely disguised disapproval. She had heard all about the feast from Lady Glynn who had nearly fainted with hunger waiting for the royal banquet to start. When the feast eventually began, Lord Glynn, like several others, had been forced to pass a chicken leg up to the balcony for his longsuffering wife.

"It's almost as impressive as the banquet for the Regent's Fête – when was it? 1811?" said a fair, undistinguished gentleman, partly to his wife and partly to the table. "All cooped up in that gothic conservatory. D'you remember my dear?"

"Certainly! How could one forget such a lavish display?" Lady Liverpool sighed. "Would you believe, fish swimming in a silver canal all down the table, ending in a cascade."

"Prinny always had damned expensive tastes," said her husband. "We should have taken warning. Much like this latest folly. The shires aren't going to want to pay more taxes to cover the king's play-acting."

"I heard the king hired most of the jewels in his new crown from Rundell & Bridge," said Lady McAllister in placatory tones.

"I doubt if they'll ever see them again. He's mistaken if he thinks parliament will pay for everything, with the economic situation as it is."

"My dear, pray do not talk politics tonight," begged his wife.

"For my part I think the coronation at a hundred thousand is well spent," murmured Sir Hamish. "And Carlton House will not be wrecked afterwards. To provide entertainment for the mob in the parks and open the public buildings was a masterly strategy, my lord."

"Bread and circuses," said the Prime Minister.

******

Returning satiated to the ballroom, Lady McAllister, who could not get out of the habit of treating Harriet as a paid companion when Miss Finch was absent, asked: "Would you look in the little salon, Harriet, I must have left my fan there before supper."

Harriet obliged, regretting the lost opportunity of another dance. She threaded her way through the crowds, past circulating footmen and lounging dandies.

The little salon was empty and lit only by a pair of guttering candles on the high mantel piece. In the moonlight shining through the open curtains, by the sheerest chance, she spied Lady McAllister's fan lying under the sofa and stepped quickly across the room. As she bent down to retrieve it a hand shot out and grasped her arm.

"It's the little watch-dog!" said Captain Valentine with a jovial slur. "Come to have some fun, eh?" he said with a leer, looking up from a high back wing chair. "Not on duty tonight? No heiress to protect? You can have a little flirtation yourself! My, you look tasty! Never been kissed and would like to try?"

"How dare you, sir!" she threw off Valentine's hot grasp and stood rigid with fury. She could not imagine how he had gained entry into this august gathering.

Valentine did not dislike Harriet and she looked very fetching in her ball gown but her look of contempt and the effects of the brandy made him turn ugly. He suddenly lunged, grabbing her wrist again, and said in an altogether different tone: "You'll regret your interference my girl. No one comes between me and my prize. Miss Beaumont is mine!"

Harriet suppressed an urge to strike him across the face with the fan and wrenched herself free. "Oh, don't be so gothick!" she said derisively. "Men like you are only fit to frighten children." With rapid strides she crossed the room and, not feeling half so brave as she pretended, fled. A string of expletives followed her.

"That's you told, Val," came a sleepy voice from another sofa on the other side of the room. "Always thought you were rather brutal in your treatment of women. You'll scare the filly away if you carry on like that." A yawn punctuated this observation. A young man raised his head above the back of a sofa and blinked owlishly.

"It wasn't the heiress – and how long have you been eavesdropping, Fitzmaurice?"

"Been asleep the best part of thirty minutes if that clock is right." The young lord peered at an ormolu monstrosity on the mantel piece. "God, Devonshire's brandy is vile. Why did we ever come to this damned noisy affair?"

Captain Valentine straightened his stock and reached for the flask in his coat pocket. "Vile, yes. That's why I bring my own."

He looked at his crony thoughtfully, considered threatening him with silence and discarded the idea. If Harriet's riposte got about then Valentine knew how to twist it into a moment of female pique by the 'plain friend'. He took a swig from the flask and promptly dismissed her from his thoughts.

Beyond the door, Harriet was so distracted that she went smack into a broad back encased in a beautifully tailored dark plum coat. Lord Everard turned like a whip and then recovering from his frozen stare, melted into smiles of recognition.

"Miss Larkhill, of course, who else could have such an original approach? I seemed destined to always run in to you like this, or is it you who runs into me? A delight, whatever. A thousand apologies, ma'am! Such clumsiness, how can you forgive me? I trust you are not hurt? Your costume not disarrayed?" He took her by the elbow and steered her away from the door of the little salon.

"No, no, not all my lord," protested Harriet, highly embarrassed. "Forgive me, I had not expected to find someone so close outside the door."

"Alas the smoke in the card room has forced me down to the supper room again. Let me procure you some refreshment in token of apology for being so maladroit."

Harriet was happy to agree. She sank down onto a gilded chair in order to regain her composure; she was not sure she could spar with Lord Everard just yet. She had a sudden longing to see Rupert's tall dark figure in the crowd and again wondered at his absence. She would have expected to see the Countess and the new Earl among the nobility, even if Rupert had cried off. Lord Patrick, she knew, would certainly have been invited.

By the time Lord Everard reappeared carrying two glasses of iced punch and a dish of meringues Harriet could meet his polite look with a cheerful smile. She had not expected such attention from one so lofty in his notions.

"May I say how delightful you are looking this evening, Miss Larkhill. Your usual quiet good taste has burst forth into a radiant peacock. The shot silk turns you into one of Mr Darville's birds of paradise. I applaud the feathers - a masterly touch! Such a bold colour, not many young ladies could carry it off. And how clever to realise that the shimmer of red in the silk will be picked out by the rubies around your lovely throat."

"Garnets," said Harriet. "I do not aspire to rubies. It is Miss Beaumont who has the rubies, or rather will have," her mind inevitably wandering to Philippa after Valentine's clumsy attack.

"Ah, I can only plead the candle-light for my error and that the glint of the gems shows what superb quality the stones are."

"Lord Everard, you are far too kind. If I did not know that you are a monstrous flatterer of every woman who comes across your path, I would think you are making mock of me."

Everard reared back as though in horror. "Dear lady! Can it be that you doubt my sincerity?"

"Whether you are sincere or not, tonight I will accept all that you say as truth. I can never hope to have better approbation than yours and whether real or imagined it is balm to my wounded pride."

"Have you been wounded tonight?"

"You are quick to take me up on my words, my lord. Let us say that not everyone of the duke's guests is a gentleman."

Everard shook his head in sorrowful agreement. "I assume you have learnt that polite society is not all it claims to be. I regret I am not a fighting man Miss Larkhill, or I should immediately arrange a meeting with anyone who has troubled you so."

"Oh, I was not troubled, or only for a few moments. I daresay the gentleman himself will have no recollection of it in the morning. And you would not have me be indiscreet, I know," she said, her lips twitching.

"If ever you *are* indiscreet, Miss Larkhill, I would take it as an honour to be the *first* recipient of your confidence."

His raillery made her laugh but she kept her own counsel and said. "Be content to rule every lady's wardrobe without wanting to know her secrets as well. You have quite restored me to equanimity." She raised her glass to the smiling gentleman in thanks.

"I am doubly gratified by your trust in my poor taste – but if you will allow me, just one hint, one gentle remonstrance, which I am certain your good sense will perceive is given from the kindest of motives-"

"Sir, you terrify me!" cried Harriet in mock alarm.

"The fan, Miss Larkhill, the fan. It really will not do!"

"This? It belongs to Lady McAllister."

"But *green,* Miss Larkhill!" He took it from her in wonder. "Elspeth had applied her usual thrift in her purchase I see." He sighed. "And the colour, Miss Larkhill, with peacock blue! I'm shocked that even Lady McAllister would think it suitable to be part of this magnificent *toilette."* He waved his hand expansively at her dress.

Harriet laughed. "The fan is *hers.* Lady McAllister left it in the little salon by mistake. I had merely retrieved it for her when I so clumsily encountered you."

"I am relieved to hear it." He laid his hand on his heart. "My opinion of Lady McAllister's taste remains unsullied, despite the fact that the fan is made only of painted cotton."

"But her opinion of *me* will be ruined if I do not return the fan to her at once. I have been gone at least these twenty minutes."

"We will say you could not find it immediately. Will she be placated or incensed, I wonder, if I accompany you?" He held out his arm.

"Oh, placated I'm certain. Lord Everard, may I beg a favour? You have such influence and have such a delicate way of advising ladies on their dress – would you be very kind and persuade Lady McAllister to abandon her ruff?"

Lord Everard looked wary. "The ruff is the very latest thing from Paris."

"It is of course most fashionable," Harriet hurried on, "But it does not suit her, as you will see and only someone as influential as yourself could persuade her to give it up." She found she did not want Elspeth to be made a laughing-stock.

"I have never refused to help a damsel in distress," said Everard, offering her his elbow.

Several people took notice of the pretty girl in shimmering blue on Everard's arm and wondered if this was his latest flirt. "Is that the heiress?" asked one gentleman, turning aside. "I hear Stephen is almost under the hatches; bad investments, unlucky dice. York won't save him, he hasn't got a groat himself!"

By now they had climbed the stairs to the ballroom and Lord Everard raised his lorgnette to scan the throng. At that moment the dancers broke apart in their figure and Elspeth McAllister could be seen quite clearly, head held forward, shoulders raised, ruff bristling like a ring of feathers on her long neck.

"Ah, I see what you mean, Miss McAllister. An unfortunate choice of accessory, I have to agree. Even without the *pince-nez* there is a regrettable resemblance to a bird."

"A heron?" said Harriet anxiously.

"You are no ornithologist, Miss Larkhill. A vulture to the life."

CHAPTER 7   SECRETS

The following afternoon, Harriet knocked boldly upon the door of Rupert's lodgings in Brook Street and asked the boot-boy if Lady Darville was at home.

"Oh Miss, the lady's gone away to Ireland and there's no one here but Mr Darville and the doctor," said the lad looking frightened.

Harriet frowned and was grateful when the landlady appeared from the back rooms. "Mrs Foster, is anything amiss? I am here to see Lady Darville."

The landlady twisted her hands in her apron with purpose. "Good thing you're here Miss. Mr Darville was took poorly yesterday and seems no better. I hope to gawd it ain't the cholera. He tol' me I had to send for Dr Yardley, but now you're here perhaps you can discover if it's anything infectious and whether the gen'lman can be moved?"

Harriet's lips tightened and, leaving Annie in the hall, mounted the stairs with determination. Jacob opened the door to Rupert's sitting room in beaming relief. "Come in Missarriet, massa very sick. Doctor come, say massa no good. Come in, come in."

The doctor was standing by the table his medical bag open. He looked round quickly and said without compunction: "That you should not, young lady, I cannot guarantee your safety against infection. Are you a relation of the gentleman?" He ceased to delve into his medical bag and looked at her with disapproval.

"I am his cousin," said Harriet promptly. "And in his mama's absence I know she would expect me to do all I can."

"Mmm. Cousin, you say. He did not mention you." The doctor frowned as if in puzzled recognition.

"Probably not. Have you informed Mr Darville's uncle?"

"Lord Patrick has ridden after them, to fetch the gentleman's mother," replied the doctor. "I have advised that she be sent for and trust she has not crossed into Ireland yet."

"Then until at least one member of the immediate family arrives you will have to make do with me." She smiled in what she hoped was a winning manner.

Doctor Yardley looked sceptical, stared into his bag and after a moment said: "It's against my better judgement, but as no other relation seems to be at hand I must accept your word. Mr Darville is gravely ill and someone in the family should care for him. Darville assures me there is no chance of infection, but I am not willing to take that responsibility. I would prefer not to allow a lady into the sickroom."

"But I am here as you see, so I may as well make myself useful." Harriet divested herself of her bonnet and coat and gave them to wide-eyed Jacob with a heartening smile.

Dr Yardley stared. "But I know you don't I? Where have we met?"

"I helped the German lady who had a fall in the street. And you are Doctor Yardley."

"Quite so, I knew I had seen you before." He seemed to relax a little.

"What is wrong with Mr Darville and when did this all begin? Mrs Foster fears the cholera – as we all do." Harriet sat down calmly to listen to what the doctor had to say.

"Mrs Foster knows nothing about such matters," said Dr Yardley with professional asperity. "According to her, Mr Darville came to see his mother and brother off to Ireland yesterday. I understand they have been staying in his rooms for the period of the coronation. Then he came back here for some papers and collapsed. Mrs Foster *says* Mr Darville would not let her send for medical help as he knew all about his own illness. But the black boy here got scared and insisted that I was sent for. In my opinion his mother should return and I took it upon myself to send a note to the uncle. Lord Patrick has this moment set off. With any luck her ladyship should return by this evening. Until she comes I can only suggest a hired nurse, but as they are in short supply this season – so many foreigners in London of course, getting themselves into difficulties - that I have little hopes of finding one."

"Jacob and I can manage the patient, if you tell me what to do."

The doctor frowned. "The lad is willing enough but he doesn't understand what I say and I need someone level-headed to take charge. I know you are resourceful, Miss – er- Darville?"

"Larkhill," she provided.

"Yes, you proved to be very level-headed regarding the Reichsgrafin. I have never encountered such hysteria on both the lady *and* gentleman's part-"

"But what of Mr Darville?" insisted Harriet. "He is our patient now. Do please give me your instructions."

"Very well Miss Larkhill, but will your friends allow you to stay with the gentleman?"

"Why ever not, Dr Yardley? I will have my maid with me. I am quite used to sickrooms, but by all means send a nurse if you can and we can share the duties. Now, pray tell me what's to be done."

The doctor gave a slight shrug and said. "If you insist, Miss Larkhill, as a member of the family I cannot prevent you. I have no doubt as to your competence. Mind, I take no responsibility for the outcome with regard to your own health, but if you will take advice from me, we might yet pull the young man around. I can assure you it is *not* cholera; Mr Darville insists it is a tropical ailment called malaria and I tend to concur with his diagnosis."

Dr Yardley deserved his reputation. He advocated measured doses of the fever-tree bark, powdered and mixed with wine, called quinine. "The French have made great strides in this matter," he said producing a brown bottle and a measuring glass from his bag. "Mr Darville tells me he used cinchonine during his travels in the south Americas to control such intermittent fevers. Give him one of these powders every four hours, mixed with a little watered canary wine to keep the fever down, it must not go to his brain. If he lapses into a coma we may lose him. You have an advantage in that he is convinced he will recover; that should carry him through, but I've seen sailors die of this, the heart gives out under the stress of fever – there is no certainty of anything."

Harriet promised to do everything she was bid and to take every precaution for her own welfare.

"Then I will inform Mr Darville that you are here to nurse him but I warn you he may object."

But Rupert did not object and the doctor returned to the sitting room shaking his head. "It seems Mr Darville regards you in something of the light of a sister. He welcomes your arrival. You have your patient, Miss Larkhill. I have already bled him, which seems to have reduced the fever a little. The next manifestation will be the ague, so keep him warm as much as you can. However, I will return this evening and see how you do." The doctor took his leave not entirely happy.

Miss Larkhill scribbled a note to Lady McAllister and sent Annie back to Russell Square with a list of necessaries she guessed would be absent from this bachelor household. "You do not have to return, Annie. Even though Mr Darville says this malaria is not infectious, we do not *know* that."

"Oh Miss Harriet! How can you think I'd desert you or Mr Darville? I've seen 'im through birth and death and when I thought he'd nearly go mad. What's a little bit o' fever to that? I'm not leaving you here alone with that useless Jacob!"

Harriet hugged her maid. She made her way to the bedroom where Jacob had retreated. "Massa got fever: cold cold hot hot. You give him drink now?" He was in secret terror lest his master die and he be cast on the world again.

Rupert had been put to bed, a fire made up and windows firmly shut against the miasma of the morning. By the afternoon Rupert had no energy except to shiver and ask for more blankets. He did not question Harriet's appearance except to grin weakly and fear "it would be a long haul this time."

"Then I will haul away with you. And Annie too. Dr Yardley has explained all about the quinine mixture and I am about to ask Mrs Foster to find you a hot brick." She had a suddenly longing for Aunt Betsy's sure hand in the sick room and spoke more bravely than she felt.

"You cannot mean to stay all day?" he said through chattering teeth. "Yardley says he will find me a nurse."

"I will stay until the nurse comes," she soothed him. "Your mama would never forgive me if I abandoned you. Dr Yardley assures me this malaria is not infectious. And if you're worried about the proprieties, Annie will stay too, the nurse is coming for the night shift, Mrs Foster is below. Jacob will do all that is necessary for you. I am here merely to pour out your medicine."

Rupert let out a weak laugh "I have not the strength to protest, but I would not allow you to remain if there was the slightest chance-"

"Hush, let us see if we can keep you warm," she said and pulled the blankets further over his shuddering figure. She was shocked at how ill Rupert looked; his cheekbones stood out like blades and she did not like the yellow tinge to his eyes. Annie prepared the stone hot water pigs and Harriet asked for bedding from the Countess's room only to find the second bedroom locked and the uncooperative landlady unwilling to look for the spare key. Instead Harriet piled Rupert's bed with his coats and cloak and added her own.

Ignoring Mrs Foster's hostility Harriet made a little bread and warm milk on the kitchen range but Rupert vomited up anything she tried to coax him with. Every muscle ached and soon he admitted to a blinding headache. Nothing they could do seemed to warm him, though she chaffed his hands and feet until he snatched them away from her in impatience.

To her relief, a nurse arrived, seemed slatternly and unconvinced by Dr Yardley's mixture. She looked suspiciously at Jacob. "Wouldn't be surprised if *he* was the cause of the young gentleman's trouble – coming from foreign places. I don't want him around my feet when I'm nursing."

"I suggest you will be only too glad to have him. My maid will be helping me during the day. Jacob is loyal to the death and will not be separated from Mr Darville. He is a strong and willing boy, if you will but speak slowly and kindly to him, you will find him an invaluable assistant for night nursing."

The nurse sniffed and said she would return in the evening. Before long Lady McAllister arrived, Cicero under her arm, demanding to know why Harriet felt it her duty to minister to the Darvilles. Harriet followed her hostess into the sitting room. She was acutely aware that only the most serious of actions on her part would have bestirred Elspeth McAllister into coming in person.

"Forgive me, Lady McAllister, for being so rude as to leave your house with no warning. But truly it was a crisis. I was so hoping you would give me your approval. Mr Darville is very ill, and I have promised the Countess to – to ensure her son's well-being."

"That's all very well, but I have a responsibility to you Miss Larkhill while you are under my roof. I cannot allow you to put yourself in danger of infection. What would people say? Nor can I allow you to bring infection back into my own family."

Harriet gathered her wits rapidly. "That would be unthinkable! I will return straight to Wiltshire as soon as the dowager countess returns." Her heart sank as she uttered these words. "But both Dr Yardley and Mr Darville believe the fever is not infectious. Mr Darville has suffered from it before and believes he contracted it from a mosquito bite in the Americas. I am in no danger."

"Danger or no danger, I must think of my family." Lady McAllister continued somewhat grudgingly: "However, I would be sorry to see you return home prematurely through your own impetuosity. Perhaps something can be arranged. Andrew could stay with the Glynns and William has his rooms in Inner Temple. My own safety of course is of no importance. It is Sir Hamish we must think of, and his value to the nation."

"Of course Lady McAllister. I regret I was thinking only of Mr Darville's welfare."

Lady McAllister's sense of propriety rose up. "This whole episode is most unfortunate. And much as it pains me to have to say; I cannot think it right that you should stay unchaperoned in a gentleman's residence." The *pince-nez* glinted.

"But no one need know and Annie will stay with me. The doctor attends daily and there will be a professional nurse with Mr Darville at night. The Countess is sure to return by tomorrow – or even this evening. But I cannot possibly leave Mr Darville entirely in the hands of strangers until then."

"If there is to be a night nurse, then there is no reason for you to stay here at all."

"But the infection, Lady McAllister? We dare not risk my bringing it back into Russell Square, now I have already been in the sickroom and ministered to Mr Darville."

Lady McAllister looked put out. "What about your engagements? Have you forgotten you are promised to the Hintons?"

"It had gone right out of my head. Pray do give Mrs Hinton my apologies – you could say a sudden indisposition. No one would query my absence for an evening."

Lady McAllister pursed her lips. "What Sir Hamish will say when he hears of this I dread to think. He is certain to be very shocked and may come and fetch you himself, whatever I advise. But as you are so determined to stay, for the moment, you may as well have the items you requested." She indicated a large basket standing in the hall. "I have added one or two of my own trifles: honey, a receipt for Scotch porridge, lavender water. You might find them useful." It would not do to be remiss in any little attention to an earl's brother as long as it involved no great expense and no danger to her sons.

For one wild moment Harriet considered asking Lady McAllister to stay and assist her with the nursing but her hostess was already rising to her feet. "Remember Miss Larkhill you are not to return until we know that you are clear of infection. However, if you require anything further, you may send your maid to the area steps."

"Thank you Lady McAllister. How thoughtful of you. I beg of you do not dream of risking yourself or dear Cicero to exposure by visiting again. I will keep you informed as to Mr Darville's progress."

Lady McAllister stiffened at sweetness in Harriet's tone and replied: "I will send Miss Finch to enquire after the patient tomorrow morning."

After seeing her visitor to the door, Harriet rushed back to her patient. Rupert had progressed from shuddering chills to a rising fever. He assured her that this was the normal progress of the ailment; he had suffered so on the voyage home and in Paris. She measured out the prescribed dose of Dr Yardley's medicine, in the hope Rupert would keep it down before the fever took its hold.

For the next four hours Rupert tossed and moaned and sweated into the sheets. Annie and Jacob held him up while Harriet forced the quinine into his mouth and followed it with all the seltzer water Rupert had in his rooms. Jacob was sent out for more and any ice he could find in the sweltering evening. The nurse did not reappear.

Through the long hot night the women took turns to tend their patient; neither of them slept. When Rupert at last slipped into a restless doze towards dawn, Harriet ordered Annie to the sofa in the sitting room. She herself curled up in the armchair by the dead embers of the bedroom fire still watching and thinking. The rumble of the night-soil carts leaving and then the water carts arriving kept her on the edge of wakefulness.

Dawn saw Rupert feverish and querulous again. As she coaxed him to drink some barley water, Harriet kept assuring him of his mother's imminent return.

"I do not need my mother," he said pettishly. "I want a dose of laudanum, I ache so damnably."

"You may have some if Dr Yardley agrees," she said equitably, "but until then the quinine mixture will have to suffice. When he comes, you may ask him."

Halfway through the morning another basket of delicacies arrived in the trembling care of Miss Finch, this time with a note from Sir Hamish: *"Dear Harriet, I see you will never choose discretion over valour. Have no fear, Rupert will survive. We look forward to your speedy return. Ever yr obedient -"*

The day was exhausting as Rupert continued to swing between teeth-chattering cold and raging fever. In desperation they soaked towels in cold water and wrapped them around Rupert's burning body to reduce his temperature. His heart was racing like a mouse on a wheel. He wasn't making much sense, but rambled about Sylvia and Clement and the expedition. Harriet took consolation in that Miss Snoddie's name never passed his lips.

Dr Yardley could only bleed Rupert once more in an attempt to abate the fever. His recommendation of leeches was violently spurned. "I had enough of the brutes in Montevideo," groaned his patient.

The doctor had no idea why the nurse had not appeared but to his regret could not promise to procure another. Still the dowager countess did not arrive.

The following day there were constant visitors. Mr Beaumont came with a vial of chlorine to disinfect any drinking water and brusquely endorsed Rupert's belief that malaria was not catching. At different times in the day both William and Andrew McAllister arrived on the doorstep to enquire after the patient. Harriet sent messages of thanks but conscientiously refused them admittance, mindful of their mother's wishes.

Will Hinton arrived and insisted on seeing his friend. When Rupert in a lucid moment agreed, Harriet gave in to his pleadings. "Only for a few moments, Mr Hinton, I beg. We have but just got the fever down and I cannot have Mr Darville fretted to flinders again."

"Oh, no certainly not! What I've got to tell him will cheer him no end! Our prayers are answered. I've got it back!" He clapped his hands on her shoulders with enthusiasm. "We found it in the stables this morning, would you believe! Wrapped in a piece of old sacking-"

He broke off, realising she did not understand a word of what he was saying. He dropped his arms to shake her hand vigorously saying: "Just let me put his mind at ease. I promise I won't stay long. He'll feel better with what I have to tell him. I'm having a crate of oranges sent from Covent Garden for you. We can't neglect the dear fellow."

Mr Hinton stayed considerably longer than a few moments but left equally enough when Harriet reappeared with a bowl of gruel. Harriet did not ask what Will's good news was, and Rupert did not enlighten her. She could see that his mind was calmer for the moment and did not want to pester him.

Mrs Foster was kept busy answering the door to members of the scientific community enquiring after Rupert's welfare. Dr Somerville came with good medical advice: "Believe me Miss Larkhill, as long as the fever does not return, Mr Darville will soon mend. He will be weak of course but with a diet of fruit and clean water, later followed by a little warm whey – avoid all coffee, tea and sugar at this stage – then all should be well. My wife sends her regrets at not being able to come in person but Miss Snoddie insisted on attending a lecture on the 'Physiognomy of the Criminal Classes'. Mr Darville was to take her but my wife and eldest son kindly offered to accompany her instead."

Harriet was touched by his friends' heartening predictions but in the afternoon Rupert became fretful again and tossed himself into another fever. Harriet kept an anxious ear open for carriages but if they stopped at their door it was only more visitors. Eventually she asked the landlady to tie up the knocker so as not to disturb the patient.

By evening Rupert became quieter, his breathing slowed and after she and Jacob had sponged him down and Annie bullied more fresh sheets out of Mrs Foster, Harriet had the relief of seeing Rupert sink into a peaceful sleep. Dr Yardley, on a fleeting visit, looked very pleased.

Annie appeared with a jug of beer and a tray of food. "Get this down you, Miss. You've not had a bite all day. Me and Jacob had a bit of dinner in the kitchen an hour ago. Not that Mrs Foster knows one end of a frying pan from another."

Harriet gratefully took the bread and ham, but it turned to paper in her mouth. She pushed the tray aside. "I believe we may be over the worst of it. If Mr Darville sleeps the night through, then I have great hopes."

"Let me watch now, Miss. When he wakes it'll be you he wants to see."

Harriet reluctantly agreed. "I'll try to sleep and you must wake me at midnight. If the nurse comes, you may send her away." She moved towards the sitting room. "I do wish the Countess and Lord Patrick would come – I cannot think what has happened to them."

"Don't you worry Miss, they'll be here as soon as you've got your shoes off. Jacob and I'll look after the master."

In the sitting room, Harriet opened the window. Miasma or no miasma she had to feel a blessed draft of air on her face. Church clocks chimed the hour as she looked across the skyline of the smoky city. Between the houses she caught a glimpse of a gas-lit square and heard the coaches of the *ton* rolling to their parties and dinners. After walking about the room to stretch her back a little she retired to the sofa and, in vain, tried to sleep.

Annie called her at midnight, reported that Mr Darville was still sleeping moderately well, but needed his next measure of medicine. That done and Rupert settled again, Annie departed for the sofa in the sitting room. Jacob curled up on a blanket on the floor at the foot of the bed and Harriet once more sought the armchair.

She lit a candle, shaded it from the bed and, staring into the dead embers of the fire, took stock of her situation. Her conclusions were not encouraging. After an hour of fruitless cogitation she fell into a fitful sleep ever alert for the wheels of a carriage.

Some while later, Harriet was aroused from her doze by the sound of steps on the staircase. The bustle of arrival was swiftly followed by the appearance of the dowager countess, looking shattered and demanding to see her son.

"Harriet, thank goodness you're here. How long has he been like this? We have been on the road since dawn. An accident with the hired chaise." She stripped off her gloves and placed a hand on her youngest son's forehead.

"He's been ill about three days, since the day you left, but he is much improved this evening. Dr Yardley thinks he may be over the worst and he will surely rally now he knows you are here." Harriet placed a chair next to the bed for Lady Darville and sent Jacob to find refreshment. "Mr Darville knows all about the condition. He says it is a recurrent fever caught in the tropics and he will have bouts of it all his life. He told us we had to keep the fever down at all costs."

"Yes, yes, I am well aware of the malady; it kills thousands." The dowager countess searched her son's features. At this point the patient's eyelids fluttered. Lady Darville leant over her son. "Rupert, Mama is here," she said softly, caressing his brow. "We'll soon have you well again."

"Mother, you here?" A frown appeared as a crease between his yellow cat's eyes. "You should be in Ireland with Gerald," he said faintly.

"Ssh, Gerald is well content, and cock-a-hoop now that he has a daughter, two daughters." The dowager countess waited a moment or two to let the information penetrate. "You are an uncle now Rupert, twice over. A true uncle."

Harriet felt herself stiffen and then decided to ignore the slight to Young Clem, if it was meant as one. Exhaustion made her sensitive. The dowager countess was only telling the truth after all.

Lord Patrick Darville appeared on the threshold wearing his travelling cloak. "Miss Larkhill, your servant, ma'am. Mrs Foster has informed me of your sterling service to my nephew. How does he?"

"Much better, certainly much improved today, but I am so glad you are here, he has been very ill," she whispered.

"Harriet?" came a croak from the bed. "Is that Harriet? Where is she?" Rupert made an effort to raise himself from the pillows but the dowager held him back.

"You will see Harriet tomorrow. The girl has been wearing herself out nursing you and must go to her bed this instant, it is past midnight."

"But ma'am, I assure you-" protested Harriet. "I have been here only two days. Annie and I-"

"I will watch over my son tonight. That is why I am here. We cannot impose on your good nature any more. Lady McAllister will be coming to cudgels with me if you catch the fever."

"But it's not catching-" began Harriet and then subsided. "Of course, Countess." Her practicality surfaced. "Dr Yardley says Mr Darville must have his special draught every four hours. He should be given the next one at four in the morning. The fever must not take a hold again. Jacob has been of great help. I will collect my things."

"Good heavens, Harriet, don't be foolish! I did not mean to turn you out of doors! What would Sir Hamish says if you arrived on his doorstep at this hour. Your maid may assist me," she said as a tousled Annie appeared in the doorway. "You may sleep in my bed tonight, Miss Larkhill and Lord Patrick will take you back to Russell Square in the morning. I take it you are staying here with us Patrick?"

"I will sleep in the sitting room, there's a couch there. Come Miss Larkhill you look quite exhausted and we must impose on you no longer."

Lord Patrick held out his hand and walked her to the door. "My sister-in-law's room is just across the passage; you will be on hand if you are needed," he said reassuringly. "But I think you are right, he has shaken off that skeletal look he had about him when I left. We cannot afford to lose another heir, especially when that dreadful woman has presented us with paltry girls."

Harriet did not have the strength to reply.

******

The Countess's room was now unlocked. It felt cooler than the stuffy sick room, the shutters were open and the curtains only half drawn at the window which had been opened an inch or two. The dowager's trunks stood undisturbed in a corner, her travelling bag unpacked by her maid who had retired to the attics. Harriet, feeling her way towards the bed, put the candle down on the tallboy next to it and crossed to the window to lever it up a little more. Not a breeze stirred the ash tree in the garden below. She found her way back to the bed, kicked off her slippers, untied her garters to remove her stockings and after a struggle, unlaced herself out of her stays. Climbing up the mattresses, she made herself comfortable on top of the bed and slid under the light satin counterpane.

She could not sleep; although she was growing more accustomed to them, the noises of the night were enough to keep her awake. Her overtired brain would not let her rest. Even though it was summer there was a tang of coal or coke dust in the air but she did not stir to close the window – any air, however polluted, was preferable to none. She compromised by half closing the curtains around the bed. The sound of movement in the room across the corridor indicated that the dowager countess seemed vigilant even after her arduous journey.

At three in the morning she woke to the sound of the church clocks striking and sensed someone in the room. She was conscious of a different dull light and thought some crisis had brought Jacob to rouse her. She squinted through the gap in the bed curtains and was about to call out to the youthful figure silhouetted against the window when with a shrinking stomach she realised it was not Jacob.

She lay back down, trying to flatten herself into the mattress. Her heart thumped so hard she was afraid the intruder would hear it and discover her. As her eyes accustomed themselves to the gloom she could see the intruder hunched and rummaging through the Countess's dressing table. Drawers squealed on their runners, metal chinked and paper rustled. Harriet rose slowly to her knees and reached for the brass candlestick beside her. She poked it between the half open curtains of the bed and levelled it at the intruder's back. She didn't quite know what to do next.

"Stop what you are doing at once or I will shoot you," she ordered slowly and clearly. The figure immediately turned, swept the dark lantern off the dressing table with a crash and made for the window. Harriet tore back the bed hangings and threw the candlestick as hard as she could. It thudded into a heavy oil painting on the wall, bringing it down with a crash to the floor.

The candlestick rolled noisily among the debris. In an instant the figure leapt to the open window and slithered through into the branches below.

Harriet, gasping for breath, sank down onto her haunches. After a moment, sounds of slamming doors and running feet came from the corridor. The bedroom door burst open.

"My God, what's happened here!" bawled Lord Patrick holding his candle high. He was in his shirt sleeves and bootless. "Miss Larkhill, what is the meaning of this?"

"Housebreakers, I fear, sir. If, if you send a servant into the garden you may still catch him or any accomplices. I, I have no idea if they were at all successful," Harriet gasped, quite dazed by her own action.

"The emeralds?" asked Lord Patrick sharply. "Did they steal the emeralds?"

"I have no notion. I saw him ransacking the Countess's dressing table but what he pocketed before I threw the candlestick at him I do not know. Do be careful of the painting sir. I fear the canvas is torn beyond repair and the frame quite smashed."

At that moment Lady Darville, swiftly followed by Annie, appeared in the doorway in high dudgeon: "What is all this commotion? I had just coaxed Rupert into sleep when he was most rudely awoken by a terrible noise. Has the ceiling fallen in?"

"I threw a candlestick at an intruder. He may still be in the garden."

"She may have saved us from burglars, Sophia. She surprised some villain who was trying to steal your jewels."

"Well done Harriet." The Countess stepped to the window. "There's a great claw of iron here, like an anchor, but the rope's dangling free. The devil's gone away!"

An outraged Mrs Foster appeared with an oil lamp. On the orders of Lord Patrick, she was dispatched to rouse the boot boy and search the garden. Harriet pushed herself back into the pillows and started to shake. Annie rushed forward to wrap the coverlet around her mistress and cluck in her west-country way. The dowager countess seemed more amused than anything.

"My dear Harriet! What a fright you gave us! What pluck! Are you hurt? Did you hit the rogue? Fetch the brandy, Patrick, the girl's had a shock. I could do with some myself."

"Thank you, there is no need, thank you. I am entirely unharmed. I would recommend that you search your jewel box to see what remains."

"How clever of you to frighten him off. I heard you shout," said the Countess as Lord Patrick went about the room lighting more candles with his own. "You are quite the heroine!"

"I saw only a shadow, of a boy I think. I mistook him for Jacob at first."

"Jacob is with me," came a shaky voice from the doorway.

"Rupert!" squeaked Harriet pulling the coverlet further round her state of undress.

Rupert Darville stood in his nightgown and bare feet, one arm around Jacob's shoulders, leaning heavily on the boy's squat form. Jacob darted nervous glances between the dowager countess and Lord Patrick.

"What have you been up to Harriet? And why the devil are you here?" Rupert looked at her in some puzzlement. A trickle of sweat ran down his white face.

"Go back to bed this instant," ordered his mother. "You'll catch your death. This is nothing for you to fuss about. Miss Larkhill has seen off a burglar," she said as if it were an everyday occurrence. "Jacob, take your master back to his room at once."

Rupert slumped into an armchair and gave the ghost of a laugh. "Of course Harriet has seen off a burglar. She steals golden guineas and rescues the queen's cousin. What is a mere house-breaker to her, no matter if it's someone else's house and the jewels are paste?"

"He's delirious, Sophia. Better send for Dr Yardley." Lord Patrick turned to Mrs Foster who had returned with a sorrowful shake of her head to report the garden was empty. It was evident that not much of a search had been made and the thief was long gone.

"You there, girl," ordered Lord Patrick, looking at Annie. "Help my nephew back to his room. Miss Larkhill can take the couch in the sitting room for what's left of the night. I'll sleep here."

"Should I send for the Night Patrol, my lord? We could have all be murdered in our beds!" panicked Mrs Foster, her curl papers bobbing under her nightcap.

"Don't be ridiculous, woman; there's never a constable within a mile when you need one," returned the dowager countess. "As it is they can do nothing until daylight and we want no more disturbances tonight."

Mrs Foster departed muttering something about the antics of the quality: "If it ain't cholera then it's house-breakers".

Lord Patrick bent down among the hairbrushes and hairpins to retrieve an old-fashioned chased-silver box. He held it loosely with its hinged lid swinging open.

"Sophia, some of your jewels may be among this mess," he gingerly brushed the debris with his stockinged foot, "but I suggest we wait until daylight to search properly. I regret, there's no sign of the emeralds, we would surely see the tiara."

The dowager countess, crossing to the dressing-table and taking the empty jewel box from his limp hold, said impatiently: "Don't fuss Patrick, The emeralds are quite safe."

"Safe? How? Where are they?" Lord Patrick looked about him in a huff.

The dowager countess turned to Harriet. "I hid them under the mattress before we left. Miss Larkhill's sitting on them."

******

In the sitting room the following morning Harriet faced the Inspector of police and told him what little she could. The incident was added to his list but as nothing was stolen, everyone was inclined to minimise the matter. He took the grappling iron and rope and went away.

According to the dowager countess, Rupert had passed a moderate remainder of the night and was sleeping peacefully at last. After breakfast Harriet boldly asked to see the Darville emeralds and the dowager had no reason to refuse.

"They are beautiful," breathed Harriet looking at the large diamond tiara set with five massive emeralds. Nestled among the green velvet boxes lay a pair of double drop earrings set in silver and an elaborate corsage ornament. She made no effort to touch them.

"Damned nuisance to wear," said the dowager shutting the box with a snap. "And now Patrick must return you to Russell Square."

"If they'll have me. Lady McAllister is afraid of infection. I suspect my boxes will already be packed and standing in the hall."

"Elspeth McAllister always had more education than sense. Am I to understand she means to bar you the house?"

"She did not object when I suggested going back to Wiltshire. But she did send several delicacies for Mr Darville," added Harriet conscientiously. "And we do not *know* if Mr Darville *is* correct in his assumptions about the fever."

"My son may be tiresome but I've never known him to be wrong about anything."

Harriet could not disagree.

"Has my son seen much of this Miss Snoddie?" the Countess asked abruptly. "I understand she has reasonable expectations from an aunt in Lincolnshire."

"He has met her in the company of the Somervilles several times, I believe," replied Harriet woodenly.

"Well, what did he say? What does he think of her?"

"As a gentleman, your son says nothing, but I am told that she does not make him laugh." Catherine Hinton had taken an instant dislike to Miss Snoddie.

"What's that to do with the business?" the dowager's face tightened. "However, that doesn't sound very hopeful. He'll never get her to the first fence if he carries on like this. Is there no one else that you think might be suitable? Perhaps we are on the wrong track. They say opposites attract. What about Miss Beaumont, the long wisp of a thing you go about with? D'you think she could be induced to have Rupert? Is the Nabob in the market for a title for his daughter? Or is he looking higher than an Honourable?"

"Lady Darville, your son is barely out of danger! Can we leave this subject until he is at least on his feet again?"

"I do not have the time to waste."

Harriet flushed. "Then I must withdraw from the obligation you have placed upon me. It was wrong of me to accept, and with all humility it was wrong of you to ask it of me. I called here three days ago specifically to tell you so. I dislike being used as a match-maker for your son, in fact I find it distasteful and somewhat improper. Mr Darville can find his own bride, if he wants one."

"It seems he doesn't want one. But he must, he has an obligation to the name."

"The new countess may have more children, a son, and there is Lord Ralph to inherit before Rupert," cried Harriet in disbelief. "The Darville name will not die out!"

"The countess was failing when I left her. Her accouchement did not go well. Twins are always a weakening business. And we cannot depend on Ralph." The dowager suddenly looked desperate.

"Nevertheless I regret I can no longer assist you in finding a wife for your son."

The dowager rose in agitation and began to pace around the table. "What milk-sops the younger generation are! Such 'nice' consciences! In my time marriages were arranged by the family and that was that! I was certainly never consulted in the matter. I rubbed along perfectly well with the third Earl – up to a point. Nothing by the back door and three male heirs in the cradle. Why can't young people ride to the bridle instead of all this talk about love and-"

"Mr Darville is over thirty, a world traveller, a scholar, and a gentleman of great discernment. He will choose his own mate," said Harriet angrily.

The Countess looked at Harriet with a sudden flash of fear. "I'll take my whip to him if he does." A spasm of pain crossed her face and she clutched at her side, sinking down into a chair with a barely suppressed groan.

"My dear ma'am! You are ill!" Harriet rushed to the dowager and knelt before her, taking her hand.

"Nothing, an old injury, broken ribs, it pains me from time to time. All that jouncing about on the road did me no good," but her blanched cheeks belied her dismissal of the symptoms.

Harriet poured some coffee and offered it saying: "You are in pain and obviously not well. Allow me to send for Dr Yardley."

"You will do nothing of the sort Harriet! I know well enough what ails me. Give me a moment and I will recover." She looked directly into Harriet's anxious brown eyes. "I'm not dead yet, and I'll thank you for mentioning this to no-one, and I mean no-one."

Harriet sat quietly watching the Countess pant a little and then straighten her back as though riding her favourite hunter. After a moment the pallor receded but her face looked as sharp as a hatchet.

At that moment Mrs Foster announced that Mr Beaumont had arrived to enquire after the invalid. The dowager countess grunted and said: "Show Mr Beaumont in. Don't go away Harriet. You can still be of use."

Mr Beaumont arrived with a huge bunch of flowers for the invalid. "My daughter sends these with her good wishes for your son's speedy recovery," he said thrusting the bouquet at the dowager. She at once passed them across to Harriet, asking her to find a vase.

Once the patient's progress had been spoken of, Mr Beaumont said: "I have seen this disease often in India and Darville himself knows its progress. There is no need to fear it spreading among your people."

"Your knowledge is invaluable, Mr Beaumont," said the dowager holding herself upright. "Unfortunately the McAllisters do fear it and will not welcome Miss Larkhill back until all possibility of infection has passed."

Mr Beaumont shrugged when informed of Harriet's predicament and said. "I had thought better of Sir Hamish, but he has his sons to consider. However, this suits my purpose admirably." He turned to the dowager and said bluntly: "I came to see if I could persuade Miss Larkhill to pay us a visit in Dulwich. My daughter begs me for a companion and the young ladies are always together when in town. And I assume Miss Larkhill cannot be needed in the sickroom while you are here?"

"You are to the point Mr Beaumont; Harriet and I were discussing the matter when you were announced. I assume you will speak to Sir Hamish, but Miss Larkhill is her own woman and she is in no way obligated to remain with us, especially now my son is over the worst. If Harriet wishes to go, she has my blessing."

Harriet seethed with indignation but turned a smiling face to the Nabob.

"What do you say Miss Larkhill? You read me a lecture on my little girl's susceptibility to any town buck not more than a week ago. Will you come and keep us company in Hibiscus Lodge and teach her how to go on?"

"I am flattered by your offer, Mr Beaumont, though I doubt if *I* could teach Miss Beaumont anything about being a lady, especially in the short time I have left in London. I had planned to return to Wiltshire in little under a s'ennight," said Harriet.

"It's not moral guidance that my daughter needs but how to be up to snuff in the world; you said so yourself. The nuns are not worldly women and she has no mother to advise her on company manners."

Harriet thought this was rather hard on Madame de Lessups but let him plead his case. Perhaps he wanted Marguerite to himself instead of having her dance attendance on his daughter.

"Could you not spare my daughter an extra week or two?" he continued. "I thought you were fond of her? Of course if you are needed back in Wiltshire, there is nothing I can say except we ourselves will be leaving for Nice in the middle of August. You must allow us to convey you back to your home whenever you wish it."

The thought of leaving Rupert disturbed her, but she knew she was no longer welcome in Brook Street or Russell Square. Even worse was the prospect of returning to Larkhill before the allotted date and surely they could spare her for another week or so.

"Then I will come Mr Beaumont, and thank you for it."

"Splendid! I like a woman who does not prevaricate. Then that's settled. My daughter said I was not to return without you but when would it suit you to come to us?"

"I must return to Russell Square for my things. If Lady Darville is certain I can be of no further use here?"

The dowager had visibly relaxed at Harriet acceptance. The harshness vanished from her voice. "My dear, you have been invaluable but if Mr Beaumont needs you it would be wrong to ask you to stay."

The women looked at each other in perfect understanding.

Mr Beaumont rose. "Then allow me fetch your luggage from Russell Square, Miss Larkhill, while you make your farewells here. I will explain the situation to Lady McAllister, then she need have no fear of you bringing malaria under her roof. Will you be ready to leave for Dulwich in a half an hour?"

"How clever of you Mr Beaumont, you couldn't have thought of a better plan," said the dowager briskly, ushering him to the door.

Taking her cue, Harriet rose and said: "Then I will say goodbye to R – Mr Darville – and Lord Patrick, and find my night bag."

Jacob opened the door to Rupert's room; his face split into a white grin. "Come in Missarriet. Massa want to know if you here. He ask all the time."

Harriet stepped in to see Rupert propped up on his pillows, sallow and drawn, weak as milk, but the feverish glitter gone from his eye.

"Harriet. How long have you been here? Jacob says from the very beginning. And what happened last night? Did I dream that you surprised a burglar?" He stretched out his hand in welcome and then dropped it to the coverlet when she seemed not to notice and went around the room collecting her belongings.

"Annie and I have been here barely a day or two, just until your Mama arrived from Ireland. But now that Dr Yardley says you are on the mend, I am going on a visit to the Beaumonts."

"Why? Why are you leaving? I thought you would stay until-" he tailed off. "However, you have your own engagements and I cannot expect you to spend your time waiting on a convalescent. Shall you be at Dulwich for long?"

"I cannot say. I am to be the official dragon to see off Miss Philippa's undesirable suitors," she said cheerily, picking up the despised green fan and her book.

"I see. A much more attractive proposition than being cooped up in a sick-room. I envy you the country air."

"Indeed it is." Harriet would not pander to Rupert's self-pity. "But as soon as you're able, why not convalesce at the coast? The sea air would do you good. Margate perhaps, or you have not yet seen His Majesty's oriental pavilion at Brighton?"

"Harriet-" he began. Their eyes met for an unfathomable second and then Harriet looked away.

Jacob stood in the doorway with a note for Miss Larkhill. "From Lady McAllister," said Harriet scanning the handwriting. "You'll forgive me if I open it now, it may be urgent."

She read the short note with rigid self-control and slipped the letter into her pocket. "Lady McAllister enquires after my return, but Mr Beaumont will have to disappoint her. I must take my leave of you." She came to the bed and held out her hand.

"You are going this instant?" he said in bewilderment, struggling to rise on an elbow.

"Mr Beaumont will collect my belongings from Russell Square and will return to fetch me. I am almost certain I heard his carriage in the street. I must not keep him waiting. Jacob will take care of you. "

"But you will not be away for long Harriet? You will come and see me soon?" He looked up into her smiling face, keeping hold of her warm fingers.

"Of course. But you must rest now and do what your Mama and Dr Yardley say."

And with that she left him.

A little while later Harriet emerged from the Countess's room in her bonnet and pelisse, her night bag in her hand. The dowager countess was closeted with the patient. Lord Patrick was hovering in the hallway and beckoned her into the sitting room. "Miss Larkhill? My sister-in-law tells me you are leaving with Mr Beaumont. Why so soon? Has anything occurred to drive you away?"

"Tongues, Lord Patrick," she said ruefully. "Lady McAllister fears she cannot keep the gossips quiet any longer. My being here unchaperoned with your nephew is deemed very shocking to various ladies of the *ton*. Though how they came to know about it I cannot say! I may have forfeited my entry to Almack's, or so she predicts in the note she sent round this morning."

"Stuff and nonsense! What a malicious bunch of old biddies! You are a distant cousin and we cannot thank you enough for all you have done for us. Sir Hamish will soon put a damper on this! I'll lay a pony he knows nothing of the matter! Sophia tells me that Lady McAllister is fearful of infection-"

"And we must respect that, Lord Patrick. She does not abandon me because of my morals; I believe she meant her note only as a kindly warning. Though what I can do about it I am not certain and, in truth, I am not much concerned."

"You're a sensible girl and Sophia must stop the gossips by taking you about with her! Show that we approve of you. That'll kill any nasty rumours."

Harriet gave him a sceptical look. "Do you honestly think that would serve, Lord Patrick?"

"Er – yes – well. My sister-in-law has always been – unconventional. Perhaps that's not quite the answer."

"Then it is better that I go to Dulwich with the Beaumonts. The London season will be over and this minor tittle-tattle forgotten in a few weeks. By which time I will be safely home in Wiltshire. Mr Beaumont's invitation is quite providential and he will explain it all to the McAllisters. He is most likely waiting for me now." She made a move to go.

Lord Patrick did not look happy, but took her hand. "Rupert, I know, believes he owes his life to you, for getting the fever down-"

Harriet brushed aside the thanks. "I merely followed Dr Yardley's good advice."

Lord Patrick still seemed uncomfortable, starting to speak and then stopping several times. "Please be seated for a moment Miss Larkhill. There is something I wish to say to you." He fingered his sideburns awkwardly and then clapped both hands behind his back in resolution. "I must come straight out with it. Miss Larkhill – Harriet. What my nephew said last night. About the emeralds." He did not know how to continue.

"About them being paste you mean?" said Harriet opening her big brown eyes.

"The very same."

"Oh I paid no heed to that! Poor Mr Darville was evidently in a high fever. One should never take account of what invalids say in their ramblings," she replied easily.

"Precisely."

"And the dowager countess was so kind as to show them to me this morning. Such beautiful stones, so - 'sparkling'. One could never mistake them for paste."

"Exactly so. Then I think we can say no more about the matter."

"Indeed not, Lord Patrick."

"Miss Larkhill, you are a jewel yourself. For taking care of my nephew, putting your reputation in jeopardy, and defending the Darville heirlooms. We will have to consider you one of the fa-"

Harriet cut him short by picking up her dressing bag and holding out her hand said briskly: "Goodbye Lord Patrick. Do apologise to Mr Darville for me, about his oil painting, and see if you can persuade him to convalesce at the seaside, though he knows his own mind best."

CHAPTER 8   HIBISCUS LODGE

Hibiscus Lodge stood in a sunny glade out of sight of the main London road. The façade was swathed in heavy pink blossoms, giving the lodge its name. Philippa waited in the window for her papa's arrival and ran down the steps to greet Harriet as she alighted from Mr Beaumont's town chaise.

Philippa tucked her arm in Harriet's. "I am so glad Papa has brought you, I have never begged for anything so hard in my life! What a squash to get everything in the carriage. I don't know what I would have done if you had not agreed." Her father was ordering the servants to bring in the luggage. Annie clutched Harriet's portmanteau.

Philippa said: "You have the room next to mine, such pretty paper, so different from the convent, and we will have *such* things to talk about! Was poor Mr Darville very ill?"

Harriet took off her bonnet and looked about her. Her first impression was of rich reds and cinnamon browns though the walls were a cooling shade of eau-de-nil. Persian rugs carpeted every room, brass lamps hung from the ceilings. On the mantle shelf in the drawing room, either side of a silver-framed looking glass, stood two wooden elephants carrying ornate silver howdahs. Through the open French windows she could see a perfectly scythed lawn bordered by gravel paths and trees and yet more pink and white hibiscus bushes.

She breathed a sigh of contentment, her bruised spirits lifted at the sight of such greenery and the pleasant thought that she was at least wanted as a companion if as nothing else.

Philippa's face took on an anxious air. "You will not mind not going to Almack's tonight? Papa said he would send you in the carriage if you so wished but who is to chaperone you? I do not-"

"No, no! My dear Miss Beaumont! I would not think of it! I would much rather stay here and have a quiet evening with you and your Papa. I will own to being a little tired." Philippa still looked anxious. "I assure you, I have been twice to Almack's and that is enough." She thought of Lady McAllister's note and then patted Philippa's arm. "The *ton* will certainly not miss me and I will not miss them. I wished only to write home about the experience – and find it is nothing to write home about at all!" She smiled at Philippa's troubled face. "A quiet evening with perhaps a little harp music will suit me far better."

Harriet's removal to Dulwich did not mean that her town life was over. She regretted the loss of her explorations with Annie but after recalling her promise regarding Young Clem, she had the reward of being taken to the Royal Menagerie in the Tower of London. Mr Beaumont offered to escort his daughter and her friend. He was curious about the tigers and Harriet was determined to send Young Clem a first-hand account of the wild beasts.

Madame de Lessups joined them on their arrival at the Beaumont's house in Curzon Street where they were to stay the night. Both girls were surprised not to see Captain Valentine in attendance. Philippa whispered "I thought Captain Valentine would be here to tell us about his tiger hunts. They sounded so exciting when he spoke of them at the McAllister's party."

"Your Papa I'm sure will have many thrilling tales to tell."

"Yes, but not to me. He never speaks to me. He will be exchanging reminiscences of Ranjipur with Madame and we'll have no gentleman to protect us."

"The creatures are behind bars; we'll be quite safe," said Harriet. She thought they would be safer without the captain and wondered if his absence was a diplomatic gesture after the scene at the Devonshires' ball.

"What are you whispering about, Philippa?" demanded Mr Beaumont. "Have you one of your headaches?"

"No-o, sir."

"Then do come along, Madame is waiting for us in the carriage."

Philippa need not have been apprehensive at the visit; the menagerie now contained but four lions, a panther, a leopard and a grizzly bear called Martin – a gift from the Hudson Bay Company. The animals were lethargic in the summer heat and the smell from the cages pungent. They did not stay long. Mr Beaumont and Harriet were sadly disappointed.

"Well, what a take-in," said Harriet. "How can one be thrillingly afraid of such a sad creature called Martin? But I will do the best I can to make him seem ferocious in my next letter home. Though I know Mr Darville's stories will entertain Young Clem far better than these poor creatures."

"Have you heard from Mr Darville? How is he recovering?" asked Madame de Lessups climbing up into the carriage.

"I do not know. I have not heard. Perhaps the family have taken him back to Ireland to recuperate." Harriet tried to sound unconcerned.

"Oh, no. He is still in London. Mr and Mrs Hinton said he was to dine with them this evening."

"Then Mr Darville must be considerably better."

"They hope to bring him to the concert in Hanover Square afterwards, if he feels strong enough. I told Mrs Hinton we would all be there."

"I doubt if he'll come," said Beaumont. "It takes more than a few weeks to recover from these bouts of fever."

"Rupert Darville appears to me as being a gentleman in the prime of his life and very determined," returned Madame de Lessups. "Mrs Hinton tells me he been making calls already."

Harriet was confused. She was surprised to find her peace of mind disturbed when she had been trying so hard not to think of Rupert. It was of no concern to her where he left his calling card.

While she was dressing for the concert, Philippa knocked shyly on her door.

"Come in! Oh I see you are ready before me. I won't be a moment." Harriet adjusted her earrings and dismissed Annie. She could see that Philippa wanted to talk.

"Do you think Captain Valentine will come to the concert this evening? We have not seen him since the coronation when he was so kind to me," asked Philippa plaintively. "He says he is a music lover."

"He is a popular gentleman with many calls on his time." Harriet waited with her hands in her lap for the inevitable lament.

"But he has been such a particular friend of ours since we have been in London. I do not understand why he appears and is so agreeable and then disappears for days." It was the cry of a bewildered child deprived of its toy.

"I am glad you have mentioned that gentleman's name. I feel that I can ask you - what is your opinion of Captain Valentine?"

"He is a hero," said Philippa. She was bursting to confide her youthful infatuation to a sympathetic ear.

"I felt sure he would be. Did he do something particularly brave in India?"

"He told me he led a charge against a marauding band of dacoits who were attacking a caravan and killed I don't know how many bandits."

"How commendable. Did he receive a medal?"

"I- I don't think so. He did not say. But he was given six month's furlough and that the Nawab of Nanda gave him a bag of gold as a reward."

Which had melted away on the gaming tables if Harriet had heard correctly. "He's a brave young man certainly but perhaps not the most 'steady' of gentlemen – as his unexplained absences prove."

Philippa looked troubled but did not argue; his air of recklessness was charismatic. She felt Captain Valentine was dangerous but when he told her of his wondrous adventures there was a caressing look in his eye which she had never received before.

"I do not understand why people do not like him; he has a good address and is so very entertaining but Papa refuses to invite him to Hibiscus Lodge. Madame de Lessups introduced him to us when I first came to London, but now even she has started to frown on him."

"They may wish to put you on your guard perhaps?"

"Whatever do you mean?"

Harriet paused. She could not believe Philippa could be so naïve. "I'm sure you know that you are an heiress, Miss Beaumont, and a temptation to any fortune hunter."

"Yes, no – I must be of course. But I cannot bear to think of Papa – passing away."

"Good heavens, no-one is thinking of your papa's demise. He will live for many years yet. But when you marry he is certain to see you comfortably established, with settlements and such things."

"Oh, do you think so?" said Philippa in faint surprise.

"Naturally! I assume you will have a substantial dowry when you marry. You must know this?"

Philippa turned her face away to the window. "Yes, I did wonder – but Papa has never spoken of it. He still regards me as a little girl. Papa would not discuss such things with me. I would be in the convent now if it were not for Madame de Lessups; it was she who persuaded him to bring me to London for the coronation."

"Has Madame de Lessups mentioned your financial prospects to you?" asked Harriet.

"No. Marguerite says it is bad form to discuss money."

Harriet, who knew the value of Larkhill Manor to the last blade of grass, suppressed a sigh. "Quite right, a lady must never mention such a sordid subject in public. But you will find that the whole world revolves around the acquisition and disposal of money, though no-one admits it." She reined herself in at the sight of Philippa's face.

"You are young, pretty and gently bred. In a year or two you can have any husband you choose." She knew it would be Mr Beaumont who would do the choosing, but pressed on with her homily. "Someone will value you for your true worth, in time. Meanwhile try not to be swayed by a handsome face and a smooth tongue."

"Do you mean Captain Valentine would marry me for my money?" Philippa asked. Such wicked things happened only in gothick novels and Captain Valentine was far from being the devilish tyrant who would carry her off. The gallant captain was a hero of her girlish fantasies. A romantic declaration of love was all she dreamt of; seduction or marriage was an unknown void.

"I would not blacken a man's character on the basis of hearsay, but I know from my own experience that his is an acquaintance not to be cultivated," said Harriet deliberately.

"How do you know? What did he do?"

"Well, nothing so very terrible," said Harriet caught between truth and the need to impress her message. "But it was all very unpleasant. A young and sensitive girl like you would be wise not to include the captain among her friends."

Philippa looked confused. "Am I to cut his acquaintance then?"

"That would be impossible, especially if Madame de Lessups is to be your step-mama. May I advise, if I may call myself your friend, that you avoid being alone with Captain Valentine and be aware that he is a gamester and has considerable debts – it is common knowledge, so I do not gossip."

Harriet decided to leave the matter there. She had given Philippa enough to mull over. She knew if she revealed too much there was a danger that her young friend might disbelieve her or see it as her mission to rescue the rake. His addiction to the bottle would show itself in time.

******

The concert in Hanover Square promised harp and piano recitals. Philippa had specifically wanted to go and, in the dwindling days of the season, Madame de Lessups saw no harm in indulging her charge.

Harriet could not prevent herself from searching the audience. Several faces were known to her and she received one or two stares of curiosity. To Harriet's dismay, Mortimer Shawcross was in attendance and indicated that he would be with them at the interval. At seats on the side, Harriet at last caught sight of the Hintons, but Rupert was not with them. She did not know whether to feel relieved or disappointed but schooled her expression under Philippa's curious gaze. Before she could speculate further the concert began.

Harriet heard not a note of the music. Her mind kept drifting to Rupert's state of health and their last parting, or rather the dowager countess's antagonism. She shook herself into a sensible mode when the interval brought Mortimer Shawcross and the Hintons to their side.

"My dear Miss Larkhill, how delightful to see you among us again. Are you quite well? I trust there were no deleterious effects after your errand of mercy?" Shawcross looked at her with perfect amiability but there was a hint of speculation in his eyes.

"I am in excellent health, thank you."

"I did not hear about your heroic efforts until it was all over or I would have sent my man round to assist."

"There was no need, I assure you," she smiled gently. "Mr Darville has many friends and the McAllisters supplied all that was necessary."

"Ah, yes, Elspeth McAllister. Did I hear that you had left Russell Square?" Shawcross asked with seeming innocence.

Beaumont turned suddenly, pinning Shawcross with his black-eyed stare. "Miss Larkhill has honoured my daughter with a visit. She is under my guardianship now."

Shawcross was a little taken aback at the Nabob's vehemence but years of experience on the raucous back benches in the House stood him in good stead. He needed to be clear regarding certain matters. "Of course, how natural to seek rural refreshment after being cooped up with an invalid for so long – and quite alone I understand?"

Harriet forced herself not to stiffen at the implication. "Good heavens no, I was never alone with the patient. Sir Hamish will tell you."

The mention of his old friend reassured him somewhat but Shawcross could not resist adding: "And how providential that the Darvilles returned so promptly."

"Wasn't it?"

"I heard that you saved the young man's life."

"She was a ministering angel day and night," said Philippa, unwittingly ruining Harriet's careful answers.

Harriet could bear no more. "You will excuse me Mr Shawcross, I know; I wish to speak to Mr Hinton on a domestic matter that would only bore you. We are neighbours in Wiltshire and have mutual concerns which must be attended to."

She smiled politely on her suitor who said "Of course Miss Larkhill, your wish is my command. If I may beg to be allowed to call on you before you leave the metropolis?"

Her heart sank. "But I am in Dulwich," she explained apologetically. "Such a way out of town."

"Is no distance when there is such an inducement to travel."

"You know we are to stay the night in town, Harriet, and not leave for Hibiscus Lodge until the afternoon," said Philippa.

"Then I will certainly call on you in Curzon Street tomorrow morning, Miss Larkhill," said Shawcross with a flourish.

Harried coloured slightly and held out her hand. Shawcross bowed low and effaced himself.

The Hintons exchanged knowing looks. Harriet plunged in with questions about Rupert's health. "What a pity Mr Darville did not accompany you this evening. I am most anxious to know if his recovery proceeds well."

"I believe so, Miss Larkhill. He did not eat above a morsel, though my wife produced a particularly delicate dinner for an invalid. But then Darville was never a great trencher man."

"He was exhausted, Miss Larkhill and indeed I did not press him to come with us even though I knew you would be here. I did not tell him that the Beaumonts would be coming to the concert. He had had enough company for one day." She sounded quite apologetic.

"He'd spent the morning with Humphrey Davey and the Somervilles, planning some book he wants to write. I keep telling him he needs a wife to look after him." Hinton looked down at his wife affectionately. "It would please us all if he could be induced to settle in Wiltshire. I would like to see Darville living near us of course. I know his mama wishes it. Tell me Miss Larkhill, old friend as you are of the Darvilles, what do you think of this Miss Snoddie?"

"Don't be foolish Will!" broke in Catherine hurriedly. "Lavinia Snoddie would not do for Mr Darville! They are both dry sticks and Miss Snoddie is something tedious. If you're fond of your friend then find him a wife who will make him less awkward in society. I've told you, Mr Darville needs someone who will bring some amusement into his life."

Hinton looked embarrassed and said "Yes, well –er – we should not be discussing such matters. We must return to our seats my dear; I see the musicians are reassembling. Your servant Miss Larkhill."

******

The morning after the concert Harriet received the expected visit in Curzon Street. Mr Beaumont was occupied with Lord Everard in his bookroom but the Member of Parliament assured the butler that it was the young ladies he wished to see. He was shown into the small morning room at the back of the house.

After some awkward talk of the concert, Shawcross begged for a few moments alone with Miss Larkhill. At a nod from Harriet, Philippa picked up her embroidery frame and left the room. Harriet saw no point in delaying the matter and sat quietly on the sofa until the gentleman, after a glance at the closing door, turned towards her. To her amazement Shawcross proceeded to sink slowly to his knees with an ominous creak of corsets.

"My dear Miss Larkhill, you cannot be unaware of my sentiments towards you. I esteem and adore you!" He put his hand to his breast. "These few weeks have touched my heart and one word from you would make me the happiest man in the world. Could you find it in your heart to take pity on a forlorn bachelor and become my wife?"

Harriet noticed the omission of his first family and was about to let him down gently when he continued with an account of his estate, his income and plans for remodelling the gardens at Grantham Grange. Only the pain in his knees made him stop.

"Mr Shawcross I am truly honoured at your proposal but I regret that I must refuse your kind offer. I esteem you greatly and a have spent many happy hours in your company, but my more tender affections are not engaged. I hope I have not led you to believe that I solicited anything more than your kind regard during these past weeks. Pray rise and we can talk more comfortably of this matter." She held out her arm which he was grateful to receive.

"Is it the suddenness of my proposal that has startled you, my dear?" Shawcross sat gasping a little as he gained the sofa. "We have known each other but a few weeks yet I wished to make my feelings clear before you left town. I see I have caught you unawares, but I thought you were not disinclined to consider an old but ever-ardent suitor." He looked hopeful but seeing Harriet's shake of the head continued: "You reject me now but you may wish to reconsider my offer when you have returned to Wiltshire, perhaps? I know young ladies usually beg for time to examine their feelings, and I am quite willing to wait – for a favourable answer." He looked even more hopeful.

Harriet had no wish to cause her suitor any pain and said quite prosaically: "Mr Shawcross, I see that Sir Hamish has not explained my circumstances sufficiently clearly to you. I am the sole mainstay of a crumbling manor - which I will *not* inherit - a dozen indigent tenants, my dying uncle, an ageing governess, my rowdy five-year-old nephew and several dependent servants. I am persuaded you would not wish to take on these responsibilities to add to your own." She knew all about the unhappy household in Grantham; William had been more than informative.

Her words gave Shawcross pause for thought but he rallied manfully. "Arrangements could be made for their support. There would be trusts and allowances; I am not an ungenerous man." He seemed a little puzzled. "Forgive me, but I understood that Sir Hamish was your uncle or guardian?"

"Neither," said Harriet with a sorrowful smile, "though he will take responsibility for my nephew - eventually."

Shawcross thought McAllister had been less than candid but he was fond of Harriet and found her good company. The more he thought about it the more he convinced himself that her confession proved that she was perfectly capable of managing his ramshackle house in Lincolnshire. He was about to speak again when she cut across him.

"Dear Mr Shawcross. It would not serve. I am certain you would prefer to stay in London for most of the season and for Parliament, of course. And I know you like to visit friends and entertain your sporting colleagues in Lincolnshire during the autumn and winter; you hunt do you not?"

He preened a little in confirmation. "I'm proud to call myself a Burton man."

Harriet continued: "And so you should, but that would not do for me at all you know. I do not hunt and I cannot leave Larkhill Manor, at least not for more than a few weeks; they could not go on without me." Harriet sent up silent apologies to Miss Humble.

Shawcross had a sudden qualm; perhaps the rumours he had heard about Harriet and Rupert Darville had some basis in truth after all. "Then we could hire a housekeeper to take care of your people," he said, not to be thwarted.

"Ah, but *I* couldn't be without Larkhill. Yet what a clever thought! Why couldn't *you* hire a housekeeper for Grantham Grange? Some respectable older woman who could be in permanent residence and welcome you home with everything to your liking whenever you cared to arrive? It is *so* much better to have a servant to do one's bidding than an unwilling wife or daughter. And then you need never be prey to recriminations when your parliamentary duties take you up to London, or away from Grantham."

She guessed Shawcross, despite all his good intentions now, would not willingly be shackled by a wife in town.

Shawcross absently delved in his pocket for his snuff box and looked confused. "But companionship, Miss Larkhill! What of companionship? A man of my age needs a pretty face and a kind heart at the other end of his table."

Harriet's eyes twinkled. "Of course you do. I'm sure a gentleman of your consequence and charm can conjure a dozen young ladies in Lincolnshire to grace his home. Someone who would have her own family near her while *you* are busy with your duties for the nation."

By now Shawcross was opening his snuff box and taking a pinch to settle himself. "A local girl you mean?" he said doubtfully.

"I would think that most suitable. They say absence makes the heart grow fonder. Imagine how delighted she would be every time you returned from London.

And if your new wife does not wish to be always parted from you, as I'm sure any lady of discernment would not, then you can occasionally show her off to your friends – to give her a little London assurance, like you have to me."

Shawcross stopped with a pinch of his favourite sort to his nose. "*Your* heart wouldn't grow fonder would it, Miss Larkhill?" he asked a little wistfully.

"I couldn't be fonder of you than I am now, Mr Shawcross," she replied with a tender smile, "but we will not marry." She paused. "Could we say no more about the matter and go on as before? We would not wish the gossips to make free with this."

Shawcross took his snuff, dabbed his nose with deliberation and returned his handkerchief to his sleeve. The activity gave him time to gather himself. "I will not give up. I will forever be your slave, Miss Larkhill," he said solemnly.

"I trust not Mr Shawcross when there are dozens of ladies who would be worthy of your adoration far better than I. What I do need, as a friend, is your advice about snuff."

Shawcross deflated but, in the face of Harriet's candid brown eyes and for the sake of his own pride, he offered her his services.

"Before I go home I wish to buy my uncle some snuff as a present. I have no idea what to buy and where to go; Sir Hamish does not partake. Sir John has taken the same mixture for thirty years but he complains he cannot smell it as he once did. I believe it is a problem of fading senses but he will not admit it. So I wish to buy him an extremely pungent sort in the hope that he will take some pleasure from it."

As a connoisseur, Shawcross's interest was caught.

"It's all in the keeping you know, Miss Larkhill. Snuff must be stored at an even temperature, not too dry and on no account must it be allowed to get damp. Where does he have it?"

"He has taken to keeping it in a wooden snuff shoe in his pocket, which of course means it spills everywhere. He cannot manage opening a snap lid. He is partly paralysed, one arm is useless."

Shawcross looked sympathetic; but felt perhaps he had had a lucky escape after all. However, she was a splendid girl and he had no wish to be on awkward terms with Hamish McAllister.

"If you have no objection Miss Larkhill, I would deem it an honour to accompany you on your shopping expedition? We will go to Jermyn Street and I will do my humble best to advise you on the best sort for your uncle."

They spoke a little more with a certain amount of awkwardness on both sides until Shawcross took his leave.

Philippa heard the front door close behind Mr Shawcross and immediately ran downstairs to the morning room.

"Well, dear Miss Larkhill, did the gentleman propose? Am I to wish you joy?" she asked breathlessly coming into the room.

"He did propose, and you may wish me joy – but only because I am *not* going to marry him," said Harriet.

Philippa clapped her hands in delight and then shamefacedly said. "I thought you *liked* Mr Shawcross!"

"I do, but not well enough to become his wife and he knows that, if he did but consult his heart. He has exactly the amount of desire to marry me as I have to marry him – which is not a shred."

"Oh, how cruel you are!" said Philippa sinking down onto the sofa. "Poor Mr Shawcross. He will go away and pine for his lost love."

"Not at all! We are the best of friends, and he is to escort us on our shopping expedition before I leave London," she said to Philippa's astonished face. "We have agreed to say no more about the matter and I depend on you to be discreet." Harriet looked serious. "Your Papa need know nothing of Mr Shawcross's visit this morning. We would not wish to embarrass the gentleman."

She looked at Philippa's crestfallen face. "Do not look so troubled. You saw yourself that it was no great romance; just a summer companionship, and not enough for me to alter my condition in life – however tempting."

"You mean the gentleman wasn't rich enough?"

"Good heavens, No! Whatever do you take me for? In fact Mr Shawcross is more comfortably endowed than I thought. But we do not love each other," she replied simply.

"Of course, even I could see that. But I did not think you believed in love at all and that it did not matter." Philippa sounded mournful.

"On the contrary it matters very much. I do not believe in romance. Heroes are the most uncomfortable of people; one is always waiting for them to fall off the pedestal. I'd far rather have a husband with his feet already on the ground."

"You mean a gentleman such as Mr McAllister?"

"Precisely," replied Harriet, pleased at Philippa's insight.

Miss Beaumont still looked puzzled; she did not know where Rupert Darville fitted into Miss Larkhill's philosophy.

******

The Beaumonts begged Harriet to extend her stay with them. She was due to return to Wiltshire in early August but by dint of Philippa's pleadings and Mr Beaumont's examination of shipping timetables, she agreed to extend her visit for a further ten days. The Beaumonts would take her home in their well-sprung travelling carriage, stay a day or two at the manor and then continue their journey to Southampton to catch a ship to France. She was more touched by Mr Beaumont's approval of the idea than his daughter's sentimental pleadings.

Harriet wrote another postponing letter to Miss Humble, feeling guilty and relieved at the same time.

It came as a shock to Harriet to discover that Miss Beaumont was carrying on a secret correspondence with Andrew McAllister. A walk to the village to post her own letters and few words from an indiscreet clerk put Andrew's missive to Philippa into her hands.

"I am surprised at you! You cannot be so foolish! Your Papa knows nothing of this I take it?" she said when confronting Philippa.

Philippa shook her head. "Please, please do not tell him. We are to return to France so soon and I'll never be able to see Mr McAllister again!" she said with brimming eyes.

"Certainly you will see him again! When you come out next Spring. If Mr McAllister feels as you do now – and I have no doubt he does, then he will wait for you to return."

"Oh, do you really think so?" asked Philippa doubtfully.

"Do not think badly of all men;" said Harriet, relenting a little. "I know I warned you against Captain Valentine but I did not mean to thrust you into Andrew McAllister's arms." She almost laughed at the situation.

"You said you approved of him! Do you think he is a fortune-hunter, too?" asked Philippa looking woebegone.

Harriet composed her face. "Not a whit! I believe Mr McAllister has a true regard for you, unlike the captain, though I *am* surprised he countenances this correspondence."

Philippa blushed. "It – it was my fault. I, I felt so very lonely until you came and Mr McAllister is so very kind to me. I wrote to thank him for a poetry book he lent me and to ask how I was to return it to him. There cannot be anything improper in that?"

Harriet suppressed a smile at this transparent excuse. Philippa hurried on. "I only told him when next I would be in London – and he answered, and we met at Lady Bixby's and I returned the book."

"Then he wrote back on some flimsy pretext and it continued from there," supplied Harriet understandingly.

"Your papa will be very angry at this, and servants talk. Look how easily Mr McAllister's letter fell into my hands."

"I will show you all the letters, Miss Larkhill, and copies of my own. There is nothing improper in my writing or in Mr McAllister's replies."

"I don't for one moment think there is. But what your Papa will do if he finds out, I dread to imagine. You would not wish to cause a breach with the McAllisters?"

"You wrote to Mr Darville," protested Philippa. "There was nothing objectionable in that!"

"I have known Mr Darville since I was in leading strings. He is a cousin by marriage. The matter was quite different. And my uncle and aunt were happy to encourage the correspondence when he was abroad."

Philippa shamefacedly handed Andrew's letter to Harriet.

"I will not read it, Philippa," she said, refusing to take it. "I know you are too good to write anything that you shouldn't. However, you must write one last time and say you will correspond no more unless with your father's permission. You must either return or burn any notes you have from Mr McAllister and ask him to do likewise with yours - otherwise I cannot answer for the consequences."

Philippa looked frightened. Harriet relented. "Andrew is a gentleman, he will understand and approve." She sat down beside her friend and took her hand. "Why not invite Mr McAllister and his mother openly to Curzon Street or Hibiscus Lodge?"

"Oh, I couldn't do that!" said Philippa aghast. "What would Mr McAllister think of me! So fast! So forward! I would not forfeit his good opinion!"

"Invite the whole family then. The weather is still fine; why not ask all the McAllisters to a picnic in your lovely garden. Your papa could not object to that."

"I would not know what to do! I have never entertained before. You would have to tell me how to manage. Would it be possible? Will Papa allow it? Do you think they would come?" Philippa stopped trembling at this novel idea.

"Without a doubt. One must always return calls and invitations and Lady McAllister has been your hostess more than once since you have been in town. And leave your papa to me."

It did not take long for Harriet to convince Philippa that it was her social duty to return Lady McAllister's kindnesses.

"Should I invite Mr Shawcross? He did include me in the party at Astley's, and he has called at Curzon Street very often of late. He is such a kind gentleman. Or would that be too painful for you, Miss Larkhill?"

"I believe he has gone out of town," said Harriet quickly. "But you must ask Madame de Lessups, she had given up her summer to be your chaperone."

"But not Captain Valentine?" asked Philippa.

"But not Captain Valentine," agreed Harriet.

"And we could invite Mr Darville," said Philippa becoming more enamoured with the plan.

"Whatever for?" said Harriet caught off guard.

"I – I –thought you enjoyed his company, that you were old friends. I would invite him for you."

"Mr Darville may be too tired after his illness for an excursion to the country and this picnic is for your benefit, Miss Beaumont, not mine." Her words made Philippa shrink back into her shell and Harriet realised her mistake. "But of course, you must invite him, if you want," she said calmly. "This is to be your party and you can arrange it exactly how you wish."

Later, Harriet cornered Mr Beaumont in his study and, using his own arguments against him, suggested that Philippa should organise her first social event. "Nothing so grand as a dinner and not an insipid ladies tea party, but a luncheon and then tea somewhere in your grounds – nothing in public, just a few friends *al fresco*."

"A picnic? I haven't been on a picnic since I was in Ranjipur," said Beaumont, considering. "Only the McAllisters you say, and Madame?"

"The perfect company for Miss Beaumont to practise on – all such close friends who won't mind if anything goes awry. Not that I think for one moment anything *will* go wrong – a picnic is such an informal affair and I will be on hand to assist or advise. We would of course be delighted at your attendance."

"Andrew McAllister is to be invited I take it?" he asked with resignation.

"We cannot avoid it, and indeed should not. Miss Beaumont must become accustomed to entertaining gentlemen. One would not wish to offend Sir Hamish. Mr Andrew is a perfectly unobjectionable young man."

"Unlike Richard Valentine, you mean?" He gave her one of his hard stares.

Harriet looked innocent. "The captain is a charming distraction - to all the young ladies - you will agree. But we will not invite him."

Beaumont gave a brief nod of satisfaction.

"Unless you think we will offend Madame de Lessups by omitting him?"

"His aunt knows perfectly well my feelings on the matter. You need not ask the captain."

******

Lady McAllister was inclined to take umbrage at Harriet being whisked off to the Beaumonts so quickly. Under her husband's silent disapproval she had come to repent her actions and now would have grudgingly accepted Harriet's return. She also missed her presence in Russell Square. Sir Hamish, recognising his wife's dilemma, pointed out that after a suitable interval she could pay a duty call on the family when they next came to Curzon Street. Lady McAllister promptly sat down to write a pretty note assuring Miss Larkhill of a welcome in Russell Square when she had had a chance to recuperate from her nursing duties. No mention was made of the risk of infection.

To Lady McAllister's surprise, a few days later, enclosed in a bread-and-butter letter from Harriet, a note came from Miss Beaumont, inviting the family to a day at Hibiscus Lodge. Sir Hamish was forced to decline because of another crisis in Whitehall but Lady McAllister and her sons accepted. Though William voted a picnic 'a dull affair' he was determined to see the Nabob's Indian bodyguard again.

On meeting Beaumont near the Royal Exchange, Sir Hamish had learned that Madame de Lessups and Mr Darville were to make up the picnic party. He suggested that the McAllister carriage collect them.

"A conciliatory gesture my dear," Sir Hamish said to his wife. "Lord Patrick tells me that Rupert Darville, for some paltry reason, refuses to leave town to convalesce. He's still very peaky, I gather. Perhaps a day in the country will do him good, or we can but hope that Harriet will talk some sense into him."

The unusual spell of warmth continued and promised to make the day at Dulwich a pleasure, but as the McAllister carriage turned into Curzon Street, Lady McAllister's face took on a look of chagrin. Captain Valentine was waiting for them. Andrew held himself and his mount in check as the captain's horse caracoled up to the McAllister carriage.

"What a day for a gallop, eh, McAllister?" said the captain looking devilishly handsome on his mount. "When my aunt told me of this jaunt, I knew it was just the thing to give old Creon his exercise."

Andrew looked stony-faced while William wondered where Valentine had bought his spirited grey.

"I trust there will be no galloping on the road," said Lady McAllister coldly. "There will be enough dust as it is. We have Mr Darville with us who is recovering from a serious illness."

Rupert indeed looked hollow-eyed and was cursing himself for not yet having the strength to sit a horse, but he had a specific reason for visiting Hibiscus Lodge.

At that moment Marguerite de Lessups came out of the house, with a jaunty hat and veil pinned over her dark waves. She was helped into the carriage to sit next to Lady McAllister saying evenly: "Richard insisted on coming; he adores Indian Treasures and Mr Beaumont's are almost as fine as Mr Hinton's *chinoiserie*. Mr Darville, how happy I am to see you out and about. I trust the journey in this heat will not tire you."

"I am used to the conditions of the tropics, madam. English sun does not affect me," he responded ungraciously.

"I too am also inured to heat after my years in Ranjipur," she replied calmly. "But I do like to keep the sun off my face," she said opening her parasol to obscure the sight of her nephew.

Rupert was far more disturbed by Cicero lying panting across his feet and Miss Finch's paper sunshade which threatened to put out his eye.

In deference to the ladies and the dust, the gentlemen rode behind the carriage. The two brothers had instinctively drawn together but Andrew felt he should enquire about the captain's life in Bengal. Valentine spoke only about his successes at polo and parties and the military exploits of the East India Company in which he naturally figured. Rupert closed his eyes against the low tones of feminine trivia filling the carriage.

Marguerite de Lessups was uneasy. She had hoped to keep this invitation from her nephew but when he arrived unexpectedly in Curzon Street that morning and found his aunt making ready for her excursion he promptly decided to tag along. She made it quite clear that he was not wanted. She had even tried to bribe him with a generous bank draft to stay away; she guessed he had come for money to pay his gambling debts. Despite Marguerite's efforts, and wishing to discomfort his rival as well as press his suit with the heiress, the captain would not be fobbed off. He felt he had lost ground to make up.

"What's the problem, Aunt? I thought you wanted me to indulge in a little flirtation with Miss Beaumont, that it would be good for her."

"You have gone too far Richard. I hear such tales of your behaviour that bring me to the blush. I know your debts – at least I hope I do, but the company you keep and the women you frequent! If you go on this way, soon every drawing room in London will be shut against you. You are already something of a laughing stock."

"All the more reason to go to Dulwich then," he said, strolling to the sideboard and helping himself to a sherry. "You want me to marry money don't you? And then I'll be off your hands for good. Or rather we'll all play Happy Families together when you reel in old Beaumont." He raised his glass in mock salute. "By the way have you set a date yet? Don't leave it too long or he'll slip the hook." He tossed back his glass.

Madame de Lessups paled with anger. "I do not want you to marry Miss Beaumont or upset her or her father in any way. And put my decanter down this instant!" she said prizing the cut glass from his fingers.

"Come, Aunt that's hardly fair! It was you who introduced me to the Beaumonts in the first place!"

"That was before I knew what a disgrace you are! Your poor mother would weep to see you now. If only you would stop drinking, Richard! You will kill yourself before you return to India!"

"Marriage to the heiress would sober me immediately," he said wickedly. "And there would be no need for me to return to my regiment at all."

"Her father would never allow it!"

"We could always elope. She has a weakness for the big bad wolf." He ran a finger across his moustache.

Marguerite looked desperate. "You are not invited! We will go without you!"

"Philippa will be delighted to see me – I'm such a change from those boring McAllisters. You can say I have come to make up the numbers."

******

Philippa met her guests on the steps of Hibiscus Lodge, making a pretty picture beneath the arched pink blossoms. Behind her stood the Indian warrior, Ram Kumar.

Captain Valentine dismounted and came forward unabashed. "Miss Beaumont, your devoted servant. I could not keep away when my aunt told me of this delicious picnic of yours. You will forgive me I know," he said bowing over her hand, "and find a crumb for a poor soldier in that generous heart of yours."

"The man's repeatin' himself; a sure sign of boredom," muttered William.

Andrew tightened his lips and handed his horse to a groom.

Philippa looked at Madame de Lessups, uncertain what to do about this unexpected guest. Her father appeared behind her. His button-black eyes darted to Valentine and then to Madame de Lessups. There was a plea in Marguerite's eyes that the gentleman could not ignore even if he ignored the presence of her nephew. Good manners dictated that nothing more be said.

"Forgive me, a matter of business I had to attend to," said Beaumont. "Lord Everard has recently left us. He could not stay, some appointment at Oatlands. Philippa, see to our guests. They will be in need of refreshment after their journey."

His daughter, more flustered by her father's coldness than the arrival of her visitors, led everyone into the Lodge.

Harriet was waiting for them in the drawing room and rose quietly as the party entered. She looked very well in cream muslin sprigged with turquoise, with a turquoise ribbon threaded through her hair. Her outward composure hid some anxiety. Lady McAllister embraced her awkwardly but Harriet had eyes only for Rupert. She was shocked at the purple smudges beneath his eyes and the hollowness of his cheeks. He bowed over her hand with a face like a sphinx. It was a moment before she realised that Captain Valentine had gate-crashed the party.

William, after shaking hands heartily with Harriet, whispered. "No wonder we didn't meet Everard on the London Road. Goin' to the Duke of York's, eh? Andrew will have to bestir himself. It looks as though my lord is sniffing around the heiress now, let alone Valentine."

"Why is Captain Valentine here? Miss Beaumont did not invite him. Mr Beaumont will be furious – with somebody!" Harriet felt indignant.

William pulled a face. "It's my guess the widow couldn't put him off. I think she's realised the brave captain is more of a liability than an asset. And now Stephen Everard's in the running?"

"Don't be so foolish, Mr McAllister. You heard Mr Beaumont say that Lord Everard's visit was a matter of business. Miss Beaumont and I did not see him at all, this time."

William looked knowing. "This time? So there have been other visits? Business my eye! Any business would be conducted in Curzon Street or in the City. No, Everard's after the daughter and her money and Beaumont wouldn't say no to a title in the family, I'll be bound."

Harriet gave him a look of disapproval and turned to the others. "Mr Darville. I am so glad to see you. I had some notion that you had gone out of town to convalesce. Are you well?"

"Some trifling matter keeps me here at the moment but I have plans for a sea voyage in the near future."

"How wise. Sea air is just the thing to brace one after an illness." Harriet had no idea what she was talking about but the platitude covered the alarming thought that Rupert was planning another long expedition abroad.

Philippa gave her guests a tour of the Lodge where everything was admired and remarked on. Eventually she led them into the dining room.

"A light luncheon before we adjourn to the gardens," she explained. Because of the fear of thunderstorms the picnic idea had evolved into a sedate luncheon party followed by tea in the maze if the weather proved kind.

"Please be seated, everyone," said Philippa indicating the polished cedarwood table laden with a bounty of meats, savouries and hothouse fruits.

Lady McAllister was relieved not to be faced with a curry dish. Ram Kumar circulated with wine and lemonade. Mr Beaumont reappeared and took his place at the centre of the table with the married ladies either side. Harriet sat between Rupert and Captain Valentine who was studiously ignored by everyone. Conversation flowed steadily. The shocking sudden death of Queen Caroline had led to wild speculation. More than one pamphlet had hinted at skulduggery and the populace had swung in her favour once more.

"It's my notion she was poisoned," said William taking a slice of capon. This was greeted with protest from everyone, his mother being particularly severe.

"Don't be absurd, William! You know Her Majesty's physicians thought there was an 'intestinal obstruction'. Forgive me Mr Beaumont, one should not discuss such matters at the table, or at all, but my husband has been much occupied with arranging the funeral procession; hence his absence today. I am only thankful we do not have to go into black gloves."

The king was all but ready to dance on his wife's grave; only his being in Ireland saved him from the anger of the mob.

Captain Valentine ignored the conversation and applied himself to the wine. He was wise enough not to make Philippa the object of his attentions. Once sober, he had practically forgotten about his scene with Harriet at the Devonshires' ball; only a faint notion that he had upset her in some way remained. His friends laughed slyly whenever Miss Larkhill's name was mentioned - there *was* that rumour about her setting her cap at Darville of course. Not that he cared, except he knew it would be better to keep on the right side of Philippa's friend now she was installed in the house.

At the end of the meal, strong coffee was served at the table and Ram Kumar appeared with a salver of honeyed sweetmeats.

"Are these dusted with what I think they are?" whispered William, examining the dainty confectionery.

Madame de Lessups confirmed his guess. "Silver is very often used for garnishing Indian sweets. It is tasteless and causes no harm, I assure you. Mr Darville will correct me if I'm wrong."

Mr Darville did no such thing.

"We are very privileged," she smiled at Philippa. "Miss Beaumont is treating us as *very* honoured guests today." She picked one up and put it whole into her mouth.

"You'll have no trouble including these on a reducing regime, Mama!" said William.

"I have never been on a reducing regime in my life," replied Lady McAllister, picking up another doughy ball sprinkled with rose water and silver dust. She had no quarrel with a man who was the architect of his own fortune but she would not be overawed by Mr Beaumont's display of wealth. She fell to describing the great confectionery centrepieces of the tables of her friends, which led to a discussion of the coronation banquet and recollections of other royal feastings. Lady McAllister spoke of the Regent's Fête as though she had been there herself.

"I'm afraid we cannot supply live fish at the table madam, but my daughter will show you a very pretty stream in the grounds, after luncheon," replied Beaumont.

Under this authoritative discourse Harriet turned to Rupert. "Cannot we tempt you, Mr Darville?" Rupert had eaten very little during the meal. "Mr Beaumont's native cook is very proud of his sweetmeats."

"I regret I have not a sweet tooth. Coffee is sufficient." He hoped it would clear his muzzy head. The whole point of his coming was to quiz Harriet on something that he hoped would lead to the recovery of Will Hinton's ransom money. He was surprised at how glad he was to see her and puzzled as to why she was somewhat subdued. He put it down to his own lethargy.

"You must eat something, Mr Darville. It is most important to recover your strength. I'm sure Dr Yardley would agree," she whispered.

"You sound like my mother," he said with a grimace.

Harriet kept her countenance. "Is the Countess well? Has she gone back to Ireland?"

"Some days ago. My brother's needs and that of his children – or future children, are of more pressing concern." He could not disguise a hint of bitterness in in his words. "She knows I will be my old self within a week."

"Quite so, and to that end may I urge you to try this pastry. You would not wish to offend your host I'm sure, and his cook went to so much trouble."

"I would rather have an opportunity to speak to you alone, Miss Larkhill," he bent his head towards her.

Harriet paused in the act of placing a pistachio-filled filo on his plate. She did not think it wise to be alone with Rupert but could not think of an excuse to refuse.

"Why, certainly Mr Darville, you will not wish to walk around the gardens in this heat so soon after your illness. Mr Beaumont would quite understand if you rested on the sofa in the drawing room after luncheon. I trust there is nothing wrong?"

"No, not at all. I merely wish to discover some information – which has slipped my mind."

She looked surprised.

"I can only plead my recent indisposition."

"Then I will make some excuse to return to the house when I can. Would that answer?"

"Perfectly Miss Larkhill," and satisfied, he popped the pistachio sweetmeat into his mouth.

While Harriet talked stiffly to her other neighbour in an effort to distract him from his glass, Rupert looked carefully about the room. He stopped at an illustrated scroll on the wall. "Moghul, I believe, sir?" he said, catching Beaumont's eye.

"Of no great merit. Fifteenth century I'm told. From the reign of Emperor Shah Jahan."

"Indeed, one can see the Persian influence in the calligraphy."

"Sir Hamish and I saw a painting exactly like that in His Majesty's pavilion at Brighton," said Lady McAllister. She had been on a public tour but hoped the others believed she had been a guest there with Sir Hamish. "Mr Darville. You must go to Brighton, it is the perfect place for invalids, such bracing air."

"Are you not afraid of housebreakers, sir, with all these valuable possessions in so isolated a place?" said William, dusting his fingers.

"There is little in Hibiscus Lodge that would attract thieves. My best pieces are still in Paris and they are well guarded. My daughter does not care for oriental art."

"Not even Indian jewellery, sir? I've seen some wonderful pieces in gold and turquoise in the bazaars which would suit Miss Beaumont admirably," said the captain with tantalising look at Philippa. Silence descended like a blade.

"My daughter has no need of jewellery in the convent. *Next* year she may choose whatever stones she wishes, from Asprey's" replied Beaumont coldly.

Philippa looked uncomfortable and Andrew was about to leap to her rescue when the captain, having replenished his glass yet again, plunged on: "Talking of precious stones, sir. May we beg a sight of the famous Rajah's rubies?"

"I regret the Rajah's rubies do not exist," Beaumont replied putting down his coffee cup with care. "I deplore this banbury tale put about by ignorant persons and mischief makers. I would not put my people in danger by bringing such stones to England, let alone keep them here in Dulwich. My daughter's welfare is of paramount importance."

Philippa looked even more embarrassed at her father's words.

"How true! 'For who can find a virtuous woman? For her price is far above rubies'. *Proverbs, 10',*" said Miss Finch out of nowhere and then retired into confusion as all eyes turned to her in astonishment.

At that moment Cicero leapt up on Miss Finch's lap, and then onto the dining table, claws slipping on the polished surface and sending the sweetmeat salver crashing to the floor. Coffee and pastries spilled across the Persian carpet. Miss Finch screamed. Philippa flinched and leapt to her feet. William choked. Captain Valentine laughed and the elder ladies exclaimed in horror. Mr Beaumont rose and pulled the bell rope as Cicero jumped from the table and squeezed under the sideboard after his sweet reward, tail wagging in triumph. Rupert bent down and ruthlessly dragged the dog out by its collar. "There's rather a mess on your carpet I'm afraid, sir."

Harriet groaned inwardly at Rupert's lack of tact.

"The servants will see to it. It is of no matter. Ladies, do not distress yourselves." Mr Beaumont's voice was testy. "Philippa, take your guests into the garden!"

"Perhaps Cicero would be happier in the stables," said Harriet looking up at Rupert who was virtually choking the life out of the poodle. "Or one of the servants could take him for a run?" She looked at Lady McAllister for permission.

"Of course, of course! Susan, what were you thinking to bring Cicero into the house?" She turned to the Nabob. "I assure you, Cicero is normally so well-behaved; we have *never* had a problem with him in Russell Square, but in a strange place you know-. There will be no serious harm done to your carpet, Mr Beaumont. However, I must apologise-"

"Think nothing of it Lady McAllister," soothed Marguerite. "A brush and a damp cloth will put all to rights, if the servants move quickly." She looked expectantly at Philippa.

"Ladies, if you would care to come upstairs for a moment and then we will join the gentlemen on the terrace. Perhaps you would all be interested in the shell cavern?" said Philippa taking her cue and waving to the French windows. "It is so pretty by the stream, so peaceful. And then perhaps you might like to see the gardens before we have our tea? If everyone is quite agreeable I thought we would have our picnic in the maze," she said hurriedly.

There were nods of agreement and a general move. Rupert begged the company's indulgence to be allowed to join them later when the sun had dissipated a little. All was concern and understanding. Attention was diverted from the chaos in the dining room. Curtains were closed, cool drinks brought for the invalid whom they left with his feet up on one of the sofas in the drawing room, a handkerchief placed strategically beneath his boots. Lady McAllister envied the gentleman's opportunity to have a short repose after such a warm drive and lavish luncheon.

The rest of the party eventually met on the terrace and wandered across the lawn and along a winding path through the hibiscus bushes. Mr Beaumont excused himself, saying this was his daughter's party and he had some urgent letters to write. He promised to join them later and did not feel he should quite abandon Mr Darville. After five minutes Harriet returned to the Lodge with the plea that she had forgotten her parasol, and made her way to the drawing room.

Rupert swung his legs to the floor when she appeared from behind the curtains.

"Good girl, I knew you'd come."

"How can I help you? You really should rest. Is it about the Reichsgraf's cross? There is no need to concern yourself with my stupid mishaps; I promise you I have thought no more about it."

"Harriet, can you remember anything particular about the evening at the opera – anything unusual?"

"No, only that I enjoyed it very much."

"Harriet, do at least think a little! You said something to me that might have a bearing on a – certain matter I have in hand. Only my fever has made me forgetful." He looked embarrassed. "Did you say anything concerning the theft of the Ravensburg jewel?"

"Ah, so it *is* connected with my adventure! But I could not have mentioned the theft to you that night; I did not know *then* that the cross had been returned, so did not feel free to mention the incident to anyone."

"Nevertheless I am convinced that you said something, saw someone that sparked an observation, which may be important to my – problem."

"If you told me what is troubling you then I may be able to remember what I said that is so important!"

"I cannot. The business is not mine; I am acting for another – who does not know that I am doing this. And I certainly will not involve a third party - again." He was determined to find the culprits and retrieve Will Hinton's money after the debacle at the General Post Office.

"You are being very mysterious! Will you please tell me why my adventure is *now* so important to you?"

"I've told you it is not."

"Oh."

"At least only indirectly. I want you to cast your mind back to the evening of the opera."

Harriet looked blindly into the middle distance and thought hard of something quite different. "Is your problem something to do with Mr Hinton?"

"What do you know, Harriet?" Rupert said sharply.

"You may not remember, but Mr Hinton visited you when you were – very ill. He said he had to speak to you urgently and seemed *very* excited about something which had been 'returned'. Quite unexpectedly found, he implied, and that you would be very happy with the news. Which sounds very like what happened to the Ravensburg Cross, don't you agree?" She looked at Rupert with a lift of the eyebrows.

He said nothing and she continued. "Had he lost something? One of his treasures? Is that why you are so concerned? He came to Brook Street especially to tell you that he had found it!"

"I cannot say anything – it is not my secret to tell."

"Nor was the Ravensburg Cross mine," said Harriet. "But I told *you*."

Rupert did not want to involve anyone in his quest for Hinton's ransom, and certainly not Harriet, but the longer he took the less chance he had of finding the thief or Will's money. Too much time had already gone by since the painting had been returned. He looked at Harriet's intelligent, inquisitive face and in a moment of weakness he confirmed the theft of the Velasquez and the extortion letter.

"And you think the same thing happened with the Reichsgraf's jewel?" she asked breathlessly when he had finished.

"Yes, but the count has given up all hope of tracing his money and had nothing of note to help. The Ravensburgs left England yesterday."

Harriet sat with a puzzled frown on her face. The Darville emeralds crossed her mind, but it was an incident she wanted to forget. "So *that* is what Mr Hinton meant, when he insisted on seeing you," she said at last. "His Velasquez had been returned."

"Will was very agitated and none too discreet," said Rupert remembering his friend's blurred and exhausting visit. "He had to pay a substantial sum for the painting's return and I mean to recover the money for him if I can."

"Why? Why should *you* feel responsible?

"I advised him to pay up and put my trust in – another."

"Who?"

"No matter," he waved a dismissive hand. "I should have handled the affair myself. Hinton came to *me* for help and I failed him. And you must tell him nothing – in case I should fail again."

"Nonsense! I have no patience with such nice notions of honour. Mr Hinton is a grown man and perfectly capable of managing his own affairs – why should he rely on *you*? And if he *did* ask for your help you are still not fully restored to health in no *condition* to render him assistance. *He* would not expect you to recover the ransom."

"Thank you for your faith in my abilities," said Rupert dryly. He ran his hands through his hair. "Nevertheless I feel it incumbent on me to at least make some effort to retrieve his money."

Harriet felt dismay. She did not entirely believe her own words but did not want Rupert to worry himself into a relapse. He was hardly recovered from his malaria and lacked subtlety in his approach at the best of times. But she knew that appealing to common sense above honour was fruitless. Gentlemen were nonsensical about these things.

"Then let me help you," she said, breaking a dozen promises to herself.

"I am best alone. I cannot involve anyone, not even Will – and certainly not a lady. Who knows what criminal avenues I may have to pursue?"

Harriet snorted. "*I* have no intention of pursuing criminal avenues and neither should you! Why not ask William McAllister to help us there – if we have to? He seems to take a pride in frequenting some dubious areas of London. If one can believe half of what he boasts."

"I have already approached him, but he has discovered nothing."

Unbidden, the image of Lord Everard leapt into her mind. She dismissed an unsettling thought before it formed into words and continued: "And what is this thing I have to remember about the evening at the opera?"

He gave a soft laugh. "Dear Harriet, if I could tell you, my problem would be solved."

Harriet put her chin on her hand and reviewed their night at the King's Theatre. Between them they recalled who said what in general terms and then Harriet suddenly said: "I know! It was Lady Bixby's diamonds!" She turned to Rupert with sparkling eyes. "Don't you remember? We saw the Bixbys in the corridor. I was so pleased to see the diamonds – though they were in a poor state. And Lady Bixby had not worn them to Almack's the night before – which I thought odd, even though Lord Everard said I had no sense of colour-"

"Everard? What has he to do with the matter?"

"Nothing at all!" she said hurriedly. "But you *must* know he's the arbiter of taste and suggests what every woman should wear on every occasion! Goodness, no female of fashion stirs forth without his approbation. Lady McAllister is quite in awe of him. You should have heard him talk about the coronation! He has told Philippa and I all about the costumes and the regalia. And as for jewels; he advised the Reichsgrafin on where to have the cross mended and-" She stopped but Rupert only blinked, and then she added hurriedly: "Do you think Lady Bixby had her diamonds stolen too?"

"Possibly, or it could be a coincidence. There could be a dozen good reasons why she did not wear them to Almack's but did to the opera. However, I agree; Lady Bixby's wayward diamonds *were* at the back of my mind. Thank you, Harriet, your account confirms what I could not analyse in my befuddled state during my illness."

"What will you do now?"

"Pay her a visit and see if she will admit to being the victim of an extortion plot and hope she has some evidence or clue as to the perpetrators. It's a long shot but we have nothing to go on so far but one demand note from the Velasquez. The note and sacking in which the Ravensburg Cross was returned has long gone."

"Then I must come with you. You cannot turn up in her drawing room and start questioning her; she hardly knows you. We must talk to her alone; if the diamonds *were* stolen she may feel to blame and not have told her husband about it."

"What if their absence and reappearance is perfectly innocent, or she denies they were stolen?" He looked at her with troubled eyes.

Harriet was startled at his moment of self-doubt. All her life he had always considered himself to be in the right.

"Then we must say it is nothing but a silly rumour of which we felt duty bound to inform her and we will do all we can to refute such gossip."

Rupert brooded. "And if it's true? What if she has nothing to show us?"

"Then we must make her remember all she can. As you did me. But she's the type of woman who delights in keeping letters – tied up in blue ribbon most likely."

Rupert gave a weak smile.

Harriet pondered for a moment. "I have it! Meet me tomorrow at eleven o'clock at the Cholmondleys. Anne has just become engaged, you know. No one will remark if I call to offer my good wishes. You know her brother, I believe – Bertram, the sporting young man?"

"My mother has hunted with him. I've shot against him at Manton's occasionally. He sent me a copy of *The Sporting Magazine* to while away my convalescence." He did not sound grateful.

"What a charming thought! And it gives you the perfect excuse to call and thank him. Then we will contrive to leave together. You can escort me to the Bixbys – but we will not tell them that."

Rupert looked at her with admiration. "You are very devious Harriet."

"Nonsense! Just practical. Mr Beaumont will bring me up to town as I know he's going into the City tomorrow. And you *must* tell the Hintons of your plans. They're entitled to know what you're undertaking on their behalf. Mr Hinton is an old friend who should *agree* to you pursuing this ma- matter."

"Mad scheme, you mean," he said wryly.

She sighed. "I know you won't rest until you've made some efforts to help Mr Hinton. I promise not to interfere but at least allow me to give you an introduction to Lady Bixby. After that I will leave it to you gentlemen to do what you think best."

He felt a sudden gratitude for her clear-sightedness. No further arguments or explanations were necessary in his weary state; she had grasped all the implications and provided the next step. He was surprised to find that sharing the burden, even with Harriet, made him feel more hopeful. And perhaps she was right in encouraging him to include Will.

A footstep in the hall made Harriet jump up. "I have to fetch my parasol and go back to the others," she whispered. "And you must get some rest – I can see this has been a great worry to you."

"Harriet – I must- thank you-"

"Hush now, Mr Beaumont is coming. It would never do if I were discovered in here with you."

She slipped out of the French windows and round to the servants' entrance and up to her room to fetch her parasol. She did not know whether to be relieved or disappointed that his interest was stirred only by the theft of Hinton's property. He had said nothing of her nursing him or his mother's antagonism, but then he had not mentioned Miss Snoddie either.

A little while later, Harriet found the others admiring the grotto. A stroll down an incline of ferns led to a sunny spot where an artfully contrived cave had induced some earlier generation of ladies to stud the interior with sea shells. A curved stone bench had been placed in the entrance to the grotto.

"What an idyllic spot, don't you agree Madame de Lessups?" said Lady McAllister appropriating half the bench. "The sound of the spring is so soothing as it falls into the pool. I would ask your papa to erect a statue of a naiad, just here, Miss Beaumont. I feel it would enhance the classical symmetry of the grotto."

Philippa made some inarticulate answer and continued. "It is said if one attempts to count all the shells in the grotto, once can never arrive at the same number twice."

Miss Finch pulled a reluctant Cicero into the little cave and became absorbed in counting.

"I sit and read here every afternoon," said Philippa with her first genuine smile of the afternoon.

"I expect she reads poetry here," hissed William half kicking pebbles into the runnel of water.

"She does and I'm sure I would to – if I had the time," said Harriet.

"Would you?" said William in evident surprise.

"I am not *entirely* devoid of feeling, Mr McAllister, and I like poetry very much. I think this place is charming, but to my mind it has something of Coleridge about it; I find all these bushes a little sinister." A barrier of dark laurels grew thickly over the bank above them. "Though I daresay that is because I am used to the more open country of Wiltshire."

"What do you do when Miss Beaumont is reading her poetry?"

"I practise at the piano," said Harriet virtuously. "The Beaumont's instrument has a particularly fine tone."

Captain Valentine was looking about him, evidently bored and, seeing his quarry in the enemy's hands, decided to transfer his attentions to Harriet. The wine had made him impervious to the hostile undercurrents swirling about him. There were often disconcerting gaps in his memory these days and Harriet's civility at the table made him think he hadn't behaved so very badly at the ball after all.

"Do you refer to *Kublai Khan*, Miss Larkhill? 'A cavern measureless to Man' and all that? I certainly wouldn't consider counting all those shells. What patience you ladies possess." He stepped inside the grotto almost treading on the dog. "It's pretty dark back here. By Jove there's a huge clam and some sea urchins that could only have come from the Indian Ocean. Come and look Miss Larkhill."

Harriet disliked dark enclosed spaces. "No thank you Captain. Someone will count them one day but Mr McAllister and I intend to contemplate this pretty pool." They walked a few yards beyond the grotto to a reedy basin which marked the end of the stream.

"I will say he holds his liquor very well. Are we meant to throw a coin in it, d'you think?" asked William, swishing his cane among the tall grasses.

"And make a wish? There are already a lot of pretty pebbles at the bottom, but no coins. Perhaps Miss Beaumont has everything she could wish for."

"I doubt if she *knows* what to wish for," muttered William. "I've never seen a girl who is so contrary in her feelings. One minute she is hanging' on to Andrew like a doll, the next minute she is all a-blush for the captain."

"She is very young and has not yet learned to school her emotions. I think she craves a kind word from a gentleman, any gentleman, even you."

"That Pa of hers is a hard nut. No wonder she's such a mouse. I don't know what Andrew sees in her – apart from the money of course."

"I don't think he sees the money at all," said Harriet looking towards the young couple standing where the waterfall splashed noisily into the stream.

After Madame de Lessups and Lady McAllister had admired the cave, Philippa and Andrew led the way back to the Lodge. Miss Finch followed behind Harriet and William, holding on gamely to a frisky Cicero. The gardener was waiting for them on the step, very bucked to have a captive audience.

"Do forgive me if I leave you now. I must speak to the servants about arrangements for our picnic," said Philippa. It had been decided between the young ladies that Philippa was to have the management of her first tea party and that Harriet was to be called upon only in a crisis.

"Will you not come round the gardens with us and be our guide through the maze, Miss Beaumont?" asked Andrew.

"No, indeed," she flushed prettily. "I know the way to the centre too well and would take you straight to Cupid's bower," and then blushed even more as Andrew heroically closed his lips. "We thought it would be a cunning diversion after the gardener has shown you the flower beds and the shrubbery."

"With an extra éclair for the person who reaches the middle first," chortled William. He bent to whisper to Harriet. "It seems we must work for our reward."

"A new experience for you, sir," said Harriet.

"A pretty conceit my dear," agreed Lady McAllister, determined to be amenable to the heiress. "The Minotaur's labyrinth. But what if we get lost? Who will rescue us? We will have no Ariadne's thread to guide us." She attempted to be jocular. "Perhaps Miss Larkhill knows the way?"

Harriet demurred although she recognised the lady's olive branch. "You will have to excuse me ma'am; I do not trust my sense of direction beyond Larkhill."

Philippa clasped her hands. "One can always see the statue of Cupid at the centre and you only have to call and one of the maids will guide you to us. But I assure you, Lady McAllister, it is the simplest of paths with only a few misleading turnings, just for amusement you know."

Lady McAllister turned to Madame de Lessups. "I assume you know this maze sufficiently well to guide us, Marguerite?"

William's ears pricked up.

"No, not at all. I regret I have not had the pleasure of being a regular visitor to Hibiscus Lodge," she replied evenly. "But I have every faith in Mr Beaumont's provision for our entertainment and Philippa's hospitality."

"Cicero will guide us, Mama. He craves cream cakes even more than Andrew," said William in a spirit of mischief.

After the parterre and knot garden had been admired, the clipped yews and lavender beds discussed, the gardener gave them directions to the maze. He was pleased to see the back of the dog who had scratched the gravel into dirt.

"Where is Captain Valentine?" whispered Harriet, walking in front with Andrew.

"I don't know," replied Andrew uneasily. "He disappeared half an hour ago. Sleeping off luncheon somewhere. I trust Beaumont has locked up his brandy."

"Do come along you two," interrupted William. "Let's find this mysterious maze. I've had enough of botany, I want my tea." He looked back at the older ladies in despair. "Why are women incapable of walking and talking at the same time? Mama and Madame de Lessups have found another bench! And Cousin Susan can never control Cicero." They watched the little companion fluttering after the dog who had found his freedom in the shrubbery.

"We should go on ahead," suggested Andrew. "Miss Beaumont will be wondering what has happened to us. We've been a while in the gardens."

"I have been taken inside it only once," said Harriet as they entered the maze. "I depend on you gentlemen to find the centre."

William led the way. After several minutes of taking wrong turnings, some acid comments on Andrew's part and some teasing from Harriet, William begged a leg up from his brother to peer over the thick hornbeam hedges. Andrew complied.

"You cheat, Mr McAllister," laughed Harriet, but she too wanted her tea. The afternoon was very hot. "Once you know the way you must go back for your mama and Madame de Lessups. They cannot rely on Cicero, he's no pointer."

"What can you see, Billy-boy? Dammit you're heavy. I've not given you a stirrup since we were boys."

William came crashing down in a shower of leaves. "You're in prime twig! All that sparrin' at Jackson's has given you the muscles of a bull! I can see the top of a statue with a bow and arrow. It must be Cupid, but no sign of Miss Beaumont."

"But which way are we to go?" asked Andrew, with some impatience.

"First right, walk all the way round to the other side of the maze, turn left as soon as we see the statue," said William promptly. "I knew that was the route all along."

"Then go and fetch Mama while I escort Miss Larkhill. We'll save you a pastry," responded Andrew, straightening his coat before striding off.

It took only a few more minutes to reach the centre of the maze. Harriet's triumph and Andrew's impatience died at the sight of a struggling Philippa and an obviously foxed and amorous Captain Valentine.

"Miss Beaumont," said Harriet instantly. "Forgive us for being so late. Madame de Lessups and Lady McAllister were distracted by your charming garden, but they are directly behind us. What a tempting table you have prepared."

A pink-faced Philippa wrenched herself from the captain's grasp and straightened her fichu. "Miss Larkhill! Mr McAllister! What must you think- Yes, thank you. Please, take a seat". She looked as much embarrassed as alarmed and started to aimlessly rearrange the delicate china and napkins on the embroidered tablecloth.

Harriet shot a warning look at Andrew whose gaze was riveted on Valentine. That gentleman had casually seated himself on a wrought-iron bench and flung an arm along the back.

"Have you been here long, Valentine?" Andrew's large shoulders seemed to swell.

"Long enough," said the captain with just a hint of slur in his voice.

"Philippa, I'm sure Lady McAllister would not object if you pour us all some tea at once. Here let me help you with that urn." Harriet stepped forward and gently pushed a shaken Philippa into a wicker chair behind her. "Where is Kumar? The maids?" she whispered.

"I sent them back to the house for more chairs," said the girl close to tears.

"Splendid," said Andrew, galvanised into action. "Miss Beaumont, may I suggest that Miss Larkhill assist you to find some more chairs at the house, and you could see what has happened to the rest of the party."

Harriet immediately turned to help Philippa rise. The girl looked bewildered. "Thank you. Of course, the chairs, I will go at once, thank you Miss Larkhill, Mr McAllister," she said obediently. "But?" She darted a nervous look at Valentine who was observing the scene with a lazy smile on his lips.

"Captain Valentine and I will find plenty to - occupy ourselves with until the others arrive," replied Andrew unconsciously clenching his fists.

Valentine gave a derisive snort and smoothed his hair back from his forehead.

Harriet hesitated a moment and then hurried her friend out of the bower. "Say nothing Philippa, until we are alone. Do not refine upon the matter here".

Philippa looked on the verge of tears. "But he tried to kiss me! And tore my muslin! I thought he was a gentleman!"

"Yes, how very disagreeable. Men do that sort of thing, even curates when in their cups," said Harriet delving into her reticule for a handkerchief. "Dry your eyes and put up your chin; what will your Papa think? He'd send you back to the convent tomorrow if he had any idea of this scrape. I did try to warn you. How came you to be alone with that dreadful man?"

"He followed me into the maze, and was so helpful in arranging all the tea-things. And then he said we had not enough chairs and cushions for us all –," she broke into sobs again and then sniffed bravely.

Harriet groaned inwardly and hoped that Andrew McAllister would have enough sense not to make a scene. She dare not predict how this gentle giant would react when roused. "You told me there was another way out? The others must not find you like this!"

Philippa clutched her friend's arm. "The gentlemen will not fight will they?" she asked in horror.

"I sincerely hope not, for the sake of your china."

"But a duel?" Philippa almost screeched.

"Good heavens No! If they came to fisticuffs that might settle the matter, but nothing will happen on your father's property. Now quickly, show me the back entrance to this maze and we can escape to the house."

******

Without a word Andrew unbuttoned his coat and threw it over one of the wicker chairs. "Someone needs to teach you a lesson about how to treat unprotected young women!"

The captain rose leisurely to his feet, swaying a little. "And you think you're the one to teach me?" he said derisively. "Mind your own business,

McAllister. Miss Beaumont would come to me tomorrow; I only have to crook my finger. You've got no standing in the matter. Her father don't seem to mind me being here."

Andrew moved away from the table, his face like granite. "You'll take those words back or I'll ram your teeth down your throat!"

Valentine shrugged and removed his coat. "If you insist on this farce then I suppose I'll have to flatten you, though you won't do yourself any favours with the Nabob or the heiress."

McAllister squared up like a true boxer but, seeing Valentine unsteady on his legs, dropped his stance. "I cannot fight you in your condition; you're drunk!" he said in disgust. "Go home, man! You're no fit company for ladies. I'll make your excuses for you. We'll meet again when you're sober. I presume you have friends?"

"On the contrary, a little liquor always makes me a more formidable opponent!" said the captain with a glint in his eye. He raised his fists. "Or are you afraid? Gentlemanly sparrings aren't quite the same thing are a bare-knuckle fight. Come on and let me see what you're made of!" He crouched ready to spring.

It was a messy scrap. Andrew lashed out in anger, Valentine dodged the blow and caught Andrew sharply in the ribs. Shaken, Andrew stood back and took stock of his opponent.

Valentine laughed. "Give it up, McAllister, I can beat you drunk or sober."

But Andrew's normally placid nature was on fire. Without a word he presented himself face on to Valentine who, over-confidently this time, aimed for the young giant's chin. Andrew parried the blow and punched Valentine in the solar plexus which sent the captain sprawling to the gravel.

"Do you give up?" asked Andrew panting a little. He stood over the supine, dishevelled figure. "Will you leave now?"

"Dammed if I will," said Valentine scrambling to his feet. "My boots slipped on the gravel. If you were any kind of a sportsman you'd admit that."

"Take your boots off then," returned Andrew.

Valentine ignored the offer. He bent double in an effort to regain his wind. Andrew waited like a rock until the other man was ready.

"Let's get this over with before the women return," said Valentine. He felt a little sick after Andrew's blow.

After another quick punch and parry the two men clung to each other in a wrestler's hold. At last, Andrew's superior weight told and he threw the captain across one knee and hurled him away with a violent heave.

Valentine fell awkwardly to one knee stumbling backward ignominiously into the hedge. With commendable speed he leapt to his feet only to meet a cracking blow to the jaw. This time he stayed down.

Andrew stepped back sucking his knuckles. "Take your coat and get out of here," he ordered, throwing the red uniform over Valentine's heaving body. "And if you're going to cast up your accounts, do it in a field further off."

******

It took sometime before Harriet could persuade Philippa to return to the garden. Harriet assured her that Captain Valentine would be gone or of no further trouble. "Mr McAllister will ensure you are not bothered again. Now wash your face. We *must* return or your father will demand an explanation. You cannot abandon your guests; what would Lady McAllister think?"

When the girls returned, the rest of the party was already settled around the tea table. Captain Valentine had vanished. Harriet noticed a suspicious skinning on Andrew's knuckles, but he only shook his head when she raised an enquiring eyebrow. Philippa, paler than before, jumped whenever a sugar lump landed in the cup and gave monosyllabic answers. Harriet chattered to Madame de Lessups about the gardens in Ranjipur, gamely supported by Andrew who tried to draw a subdued Philippa into the conversation. Lady McAllister talked of the grounds at Repton and her friends' great houses. No one commented on Captain Valentine's absence.

"But where is my nephew?" asked Marguerite at last. "I have not seen him this hour. We did not lose him in the little wilderness, surely?"

Andrew explained calmly that Captain Valentine had been unexpectedly called back to London on urgent regimental business. Madame de Lessups hid her disbelief under a veneer of good manners. His absence was a relief to her as well as the others but she knew his disappearance looked bad. William drank his tea with relish and waited for further explanations.

The moment passed, when the voices of Mr Beaumont and Rupert were heard. They were discussing the difference between the unicursal labyrinth and Jerusalem mazes as they appeared in the entrance to Cupid's bower.

"I fear I must contradict you -" Rupert could be heard saying but Beaumont cut across him at the sight of his guests.

"I see you are all here, apart from Captain Valentine. Some sudden toothache, he said. Had to rush back to town. Darville and I met him on the lawn."

Valentine's bruised and swollen face had fooled neither of the two men and Beaumont was very angry to think that there had been a brawl in his grounds. He was pleased by the captain's departure but not the manner of it. Andrew too was now definitely in the Nabob's bad graces. Philipp Beaumont could not bring himself to look at Marguerite, his feelings were in such turmoil.

Before Lady McAllister could question the reason for the captain's absence, Mr Beaumont said: "Philippa, pour Mr Darville some tea. He led us straight here without hesitation," he added rather grudgingly.

"Then you should have the extra éclair, Darville, before Cicero snatches it from the table," said William in a misplaced effort to lighten the mood. At the sound of his name the poodle got to its feet expectantly.

"Oh, Mr William, dear Cicero would not be so ill-mannered as to-" fluttered Miss Finch tugging in vain at the leash.

Rupert broke in: "Thank you but the tea is sufficient. A good Assam I presume?" He stared Cicero into submission. "Perhaps I may offer the last pastry to one of the ladies?" said Rupert looking up from the now obedient dog.

Lady McAllister and Marguerite declined. Philippa shook her head with downcast eyes.

"Then Miss Larkhill? It must be you."

"I'm obliged, Mr Darville. I will share the cake with you," said Harriet, determined he should eat something and aware that Rupert knew of her country appetite. "I'm certain you will divide it with precision."

CHAPTER 9   ANOTHER PROPOSAL

A long reflective night led Harriet to regret her impetuous promise to help Rupert. In fact she regretted her suggestion of the whole event and cringed at the distress it had caused. She resolved to never concern herself in anyone else's affairs again and wished herself at home. However, she was committed to her appointment and was in some part pleased to get away from Hibiscus Lodge. There was unspoken gloom that the previous day had not been a success and the fine weather had now given way to heavy drizzle. Bedraggled blossoms drooped from the hibiscus bushes, scenting the air and littering the paths with curling petals.

Philippa succumbed to a migraine after the previous day's stresses and pleaded for a quiet morning in bed. She was dismayed at Harriet's intention to leave her. When the headache subsided she wanted more than anything to discuss yesterday's events and have a shoulder to cry on. Harriet's lame excuses for her desertion made her cross with her friend.

At breakfast Harriet begged leave to accompany Mr Beaumont to town to do some personal errands. She would take Annie and be in the company of the McAllisters' friends all day.

Mr Beaumont eyed Harriet suspiciously but agreed to put her down at the Cholmondley's door and collect her at Madame de Lessups house in Curzon Street in the afternoon. "I expect you there promptly at four Miss Larkhill," he said beating the shell of his boiled egg with irritation. Harriet whisked away to get ready.

Despite the rain, Mr Beaumont refused to let Annie ride inside. Once in the town carriage and on the road to London, Mr Beaumont spoke bluntly. "Now that we're on our own, Miss Larkhill, I wish to have an explanation of yesterday's 'meeting' between Valentine and young McAllister."

Harriet truthfully disclaimed all knowledge of any meeting.

"McAllister landed the man a facer! Don't tell me otherwise! And don't pretend you don't know what I mean! Darville and I saw him skulking off, though Darville was too much of a gentleman to remark upon it."

Harriet thought Rupert had probably been too abstracted to notice.

"Had Valentine been molesting my daughter?"

There was no use prevaricating. Harriet met his gaze boldly. "Trying to steal a kiss if he could, sir. Nothing more. Your excellent canary may have been stronger than he thought. Mr McAllister and I arrived before any harm was done."

Beaumont stared out of the window, his beady eyes darting back and forwards with anger. "The drunken libertine! I should never have allowed him near her!"

Harriet looked at him sympathetically. She knew his loyalties were torn between his affection for Marguerite and love of his daughter. She felt doubly saddened at the failure of the day.

"No one is to blame sir, except Captain Valentine himself and I think you will not be seeing anything of him again."

"No, by God, I'll make sure of that! The sooner he returns to Bengal the better. The man is nothing but a leech. We'll *all* be well rid of him."

Beaumont looked Harriet full in the face. "My daughter was not frightened? You swear you and she saw nothing of the fight?"

"Nothing sir – if there was one."

"I'm not a fool Miss Larkhill and neither are you. I saw the fellow nursing a broken jaw before he fled the place. McAllister acted on the best principles, I'm sure, and I'm indebted to him for my daughter's sake - but to start a brawl in a man's grounds! I need to be certain there will be no repercussions. No bandying about of my daughter's good name!"

"I had taken Miss Beaumont up to her room long before then, sir. Mr McAllister will say nothing of the incident, to anyone. He is a sensitive young man of the highest morals. He *is* secretary to Lord Glynn and must of necessity be discreet."

"But Valentine might cause trouble. I must speak to his aunt."

He broke off abruptly and stared blindly at the raindrops trickling down the carriage window. Harriet got not another word out of him for the rest of the journey.

******

The Cholmondleys gave Harriet their usual boisterous welcome. That morning their rooms were full of callers offering good wishes to their newly-engaged daughter and her fiancé. Anne displayed her sparkling ring with blushing pride. Harriet added her genuine felicitations and then sat anxiously waiting for Rupert.

"I must say Darville, you're looking a deal brighter than when I saw you last," said Bertram when Rupert entered. Harriet thought so too. She envied him; he looked as though he had had a decent night's sleep at last. After the regulation twenty-minute visit, Harriet and Rupert left together, Mr Darville offering to escort his young relative to Curzon Street.

Bertie Cholmondley stood by the window and moved the curtain a fraction. He looked down at them walking closely together along the pavement under an umbrella. He glanced back at his sister and her fiancé, surrounded by her admiring friends, and was hopeful that he would win his bet after all.

By happy chance Lady Bixby was alone when two visiting cards were brought to her on a silver salver. She abandoned her letters and bade the butler show her callers up immediately. She had no idea why these two should wish to see her. Was something amiss or could the rumours about Rupert Darville and the country cousin be true? Her sentimental heart was intrigued. Had they come to her to assist them in their doomed romance? An elopement perhaps? What an odd pair they would make and what would dear, straight-laced Elspeth think of all this?

She welcomed them both with an enquiring face. They did not look like a couple in love, but somehow they fitted together. After the usual enquiries about Lord Bixby's gout and compliments on Mr Darville's recovery there was an awkward silence.

Harriet was a little hesitant. "Lady Bixby, forgive us, but we have called to see if you would do us an immense favour. We do not wish to intrude on your privacy and realise the impertinence of our request but could you possibly tell us if, if any of your jewellery has gone missing recently?"

Lady Bixby's hand flew to her bosom. "Gone missing? Whatever do you mean? What are you suggesting Miss Larkhill?" Her polite smile faded.

Rupert shifted in annoyance.

Harriet twisted her gloves in her hand. "We have a friend, two friends in fact, who both lost something precious recently, and paid substantial sums to have them restored." She looked directly at her hostess. "We have reason to think the same unfortunate occurrence has had happened to you."

Barbara Bixby blustered. "Good heavens! Whatever gave you that idea? I've never heard of anything so ridiculous! What motive can you possibly have for embroiling me in this ludicrous supposition? I have no idea what you mean by it!"

Harriet revealed her suspicions about the missing diamonds, which sounded remarkably thin even to her ears. She fully expected Lady Bixby to ring for her butler to show them the door.

Lady Bixby paled. She had told no-one, not even her husband, of the theft. She had persuaded her tetchy lord to find two thousand pounds in cash, supposedly to pay her scattered gambling debts, and hoped the matter would rest there. But if this country nobody and this dry stick had stumbled upon her calamity, who else might know?

"I can assure you the diamonds have never been out of my possession! I had them cleaned a few weeks ago ready for the coronation which may account for my not wearing them to Almack's that night but I can assure you Miss Larkhill they are safely in my possession now! I cannot think why you have embroiled me in this sordid episode – such gross impertinence - And if for one moment this absurd idea held a grain of truth, what is it to you?""

Rupert said baldly: "There is a chance we could recover the ransom money if we had more information. However, I would need to see the extortion note and any wrapping that came with the returned necklace."

Lady Bixby paused. Rupert's almond eyes looked at her with penetration for an endless minute.

"And if there were any truth to this fabrication, it was more than three weeks ago. The money will be long spirited away by now!" She turned pink with embarrassment at her own revelation and sat clutching her bosom. She made no more efforts at denial.

"Not necessarily. I have information implying that there has been no surge of cash or rash spending among the criminal fraternity. I suspect it's been stashed away somewhere. If we trace these rogues then we may *all* get our money back."

"All? Were *you* a victim, Mr Darville?" If someone reputedly as clever as Rupert Darville had been duped then she need not feel so guilty.

"Not Mr Darville, Lady Bixby," said Harriet. "But a close friend, a noted art connoisseur who had a famous painting stolen and subsequently returned."

Lady Bixby felt she was in good company and began to breathe more slowly.

"And a most successful foreign diplomat, an imperial count, was also a victim," added Harriet, correctly reading the lady's mind.

"Why are *you* involved Mr Darville, if you were not taken in by these people?"

"I persuaded my friend to pay the extortion demand and now feel I must do all I can to retrieve the ransom."

"Oh, how honourable. Just like a gentleman to help a friend. And you Miss Larkhill? This is not a matter for a young lady to concern herself with. The McAllisters would not allow it."

"I was on the spot when one of the 'treasures' was stolen and saw what misery it caused, let alone the wickedness of crime. Sir Hamish knows about my involvement in the incident, but I would be obliged if you would not worry Lady McAllister with this matter."

Lady Bixby felt even more relieved. "Yes, indeed, discretion is all." If Sir Hamish knew of these thefts then the retrieval of the money was a distinct possibility. She had always been slightly in awe of the cool Sir Hamish. She also wanted to put all right with her husband again and she had no intention of discussing her folly with anyone, let alone the censorious Elspeth. She had one more reservation.

"What about the police?" she asked, looking from one to the other. "Have they been told of your friends' troubles?"

"They drew a blank in one matter, if they bothered to investigate at all. They were not informed of the second," said Rupert, "And never will be if we keep this matter strictly between ourselves. Now, do you still have the ransom note and anything that might lead us to the thieves?"

Lady Bixby at last got up, pulled a tiny key on a thin gold chain out of her bodice and went to her escritoire. She turned suddenly. "And my husband? I will not have him told, or involved in anyway. He is a sick man." The terrible row over her supposed gambling debts still soured their encounters.

"I can assure you, you may safely leave the matter in the hands of Mr Darville to make enquiries," said Harriet. "No one but ourselves need know anything."

"I cannot guarantee to return your money," said Darville. "And I take it you would not want a prosecution if the thieves were caught?"

Barbara shook her head. She felt remorseful enough about the loss of her diamonds. Throwing them over a chandelier and telling everyone now seemed the height of foolishness. Much as she would like to see the villains transported she could not bear the further censure of her husband or the ridicule of her friends if this were ever to come to court.

"This cannot be made public," she said adamantly. "It would cause irreparable damage – to everyone."

"Quite so ma'am," said Rupert. "The other victims feel the same, which is just what the thieves rely on. And now, if we could just peruse the evidence you have?"

Lady Bixby unlocked her desk, clicked a snib on a secret draw and drew out a folded piece of paper and some rough cloth. "I don't know why I kept them. As some justification for my actions I suppose," she said sadly.

The demand note was similar to the others, except the money was to be posted to the Truro Post Office.

Rupert turned the frayed sacking over in his hands. "I would guess it's torn from some bale of spice." He held it to his nose and passed it to Harriet.

"Nutmeg," she confirmed. "But that doesn't get us much further."

Lady Bixby looked bewildered and disappointed.

Rupert held the hessian up to the light from the window. "I think there may be some kind of faint mark on this," he said. "May I keep it Lady Bixby?"

"Certainly. Take the horrid thing out of my sight! I never want to see it again!"

Annie was waiting for them below and walked three paces behind as they made their way towards Park Street. Harriet had persuaded Rupert to sink his pride and inform Will Hinton of his quest. They were welcomed with delight by the Hintons.

"You're in time to help us celebrate," said Will, expansively. "I've sold the Velasquez! For not quite as much as I'd hoped but a decent enough price. I've just got Wilson to crack open a bottle of Veuve cliquot. You'll stay to luncheon? Catherine, make them stay!"

Mrs Hinton added her entreaties. "Of course they'll stay. Where would we be without our Wiltshire friends? If it weren't for Mr Darville we wouldn't be celebrating like this."

Her husband frowned but Rupert said: "Miss Larkhill knows everything, she usually does." He took a champagne flute and raised his glass to her silently.

Will was disconcerted by Rupert's indiscretion but waited until the butler had left the room before saying "You know of our little mishap then, Miss Larkhill?"

"There have been possibly three 'mishaps', to my knowledge. I'm sure Mr Darville will explain it all."

"This is your story, Miss Larkhill. I concede the floor to you."

Luncheon was lively. Harriet gave a carefully edited account of the other two incidents. Catherine was inclined to be inquisitive but in her turn, did not want their own theft to become common knowledge. She was rather surprised at Harriet's astuteness.

"What an exciting time you have had, Miss Larkhill, but thank heavens we can put the whole unpleasantness behind us now."

"You may have sold your painting Will, but you are still down on the deal," said Rupert coming into the conversation at last. "I intend to get the ransom back for you."

An explosion of protests and refusal followed. Hinton would not hear of Rupert being to blame in any way for the debacle at the Post Office.

"Dear fellow, you did your best when *I* didn't know where to turn. It's not your fault these miserable functionaries don't know how to guard their own!

I won't hear of you taking any more trouble in this affair. It's a lost cause and most likely dangerous. The police weren't interested and we've no way of finding the thieves or the money."

Rupert took Lady Bixby's piece of sacking from his pocket and spread it out on the dining room table among the silverware. "This was wrapped around one of the pieces of jewellery that was returned. There's a mark on it which we may be able to identify. I believe the Velasquez was returned in something similar?"

Hinton looked uncertain and leaned back in his chair.

"You won't remember," said Harriet to Hinton. "But when you came to see Mr Darville when he was ill, you mentioned that 'it', I mean the Velasquez – though I didn't know you were referring to the painting at the time - had been found in a piece of old sacking in the stables. So if you still have it, we will have two pieces of baling cloth to scrutinise for clues."

"Of course, yes, yes, my groom brought the painting to me. He knew what it was at once. But I cannot say where the stuff is now. Burnt most like."

"Could we look for it?" asked Rupert evenly.

"Of course, dear fellow, if you think it will be of any use."

They rose from the table and, while the gentlemen walked around to the mews, Catherine took Harriet upstairs to her boudoir.

"What a mystery it all is, Miss Larkhill. But I think you really should persuade Mr Darville to let the matter rest. He cannot be fully recovered and such exertions can only be injurious to his health. We will be returning to Hinton Parva very soon. Perhaps I should invite Mr Darville to Hinton Hall to recuperate in the country? We owe him that. What a pity Quennell House is not yet vacated. My husband cannot quite start the drainage scheme this year but Will misses his horses so and the Bath races will be on. We would love to have Mr Darville's company. Perhaps the suggestion would come better from you?" Catherine tilted her pretty head on one side like a bird.

"Mr Darville is not the type of gentleman who is easily persuaded."

"No. No. I suppose not," replied Catherine thoughtfully. "But he's looking very much better than when he last came to dinner with us. Did he enjoy Miss Beaumont's picnic? The air must be so much healthier in Dulwich. I do enjoy our visits to London but I *am* looking forward to going home. I hope we will improve our acquaintance when we are all together in Wiltshire."

She looked coyly at Harriet and burst out: "Mr Hinton and I are expecting a happy event at Christmas."

Harriet leapt up from the spoon-backed chair and gave her congratulations. There followed a certain amount of discussion on diets and names and maternal anxieties. Harriet beamed. "Juliana Durrington was safely delivered of a girl on coronation day. They have named her Georgiana in honour of the king. I am to be godmother, so I must be home in time for the christening."

Their feminine talk was interrupted by a stentorian summons to the dining room from Mr Hinton.

"Would you believe, we've found it! Darville spotted it among the feed bags."

Rupert was busy spreading the two pieces of hessian out on the damask tablecloth. "Unfortunately they're of different colours and different weaves. I was hoping for a match."

"Does that mean they are from different warehouses?"

"Possibly, but more likely from different suppliers abroad. We need to find some kind of shipping mark. Once we know the shipping company and the wharf for which it was destined then we will have something to go on."

The hessian which had held the Bixby diamonds showed nothing but a faint circle of tar. Hinton's much larger remnant showed a long straight streak and something which might have been a triangle.

"What an odd smell," said Catherine. "It reminds me of Christmas pudding." But there was still a hint of the stables about the room.

Rupert stood back. "We'd have to search every warehouse on the dock front to find where these rags came from. And that isn't enough to lead us to the culprits. I cannot make anything out from these tar markings."

"Perhaps Andrew McAllister could help?" suggested Harriet. "He spends much of his time inspecting East India Company goods. He might recognise the marks."

"The Company hasn't had a monopoly on the spice trade since 1813," replied Rupert. "These could be from bales stored anywhere between the Port and Gravesend. We'd have to question every wharfinger on the river."

Harriet closed her lips. Rupert gave her a long look. "I suppose it will do no harm. I have already involved-"

"Who else?" asked Will sharply. "We agreed we mustn't let this get about, dear fellow."

Rupert folded up the pieces of sacking and put them in his pocket. "I asked William McAllister to keep his ears open among his criminal contacts. I mentioned no names. Unfortunately he discovered nothing, though that was some time ago."

"At least you kept your enquiries within the family. But I think we're on a fool's errand." Will slapped Rupert on the back and walked him away from the table. "Give it up Darville. Come home with us to Hinton and forget the matter. No harm's been done. Forget it! I learnt a good lesson from my foolishness and am only a few hundred down. Now come to the small salon and give me your opinion on some satsuma ware I have just bought."

Rupert, his face inscrutable, allowed himself to be led away.

******

Wilson procured a hackney as St George's Church chimed a quarter to four.

"Would you put me down in Curzon Street," asked Harriet, settling herself opposite Rupert. "Mr Beaumont is to fetch me from there."

"Aren't you coming with me to the McAllisters?" Rupert asked in surprise.

"No, I cannot be late. Mr Beaumont is very strict in these matters."

"I thought you wanted me to speak to Andrew McAllister. Or do you think, like Hinton, that I'm wasting my time?" He sounded put out.

"I said I would put you in the way of speaking to Lady Bixby's and then I would do whatever you gentlemen thought best. It is plain that Mr Hinton wishes you to drop the matter."

"But we have raised Lady Bixby's hopes, and have the two pieces of sacking as some sort of lead. We must continue," he protested.

"Then continue if you must. But I am going home to Larkhill in a week and am far too busy to help you any further."

"As you wish, Miss Larkhill." He was shaken by her sudden abandonment. He leaned his head out of the window and gave the jarvey the order for Curzon Street.

When the hackney pulled up outside Madame de Lessup's house, the Beaumont's town chaise was already waiting outside. Rupert escorted Harriet to the door which was quickly opened by a flunkey. Beaumont was standing in the hall, his cloak on, speaking to Marguerite. She turned to her new callers. "Come in, Come in, Miss Larkhill! Mr Beaumont has just promised to stay for a dish of tea. I can easily send a servant to Dulwich with a note to reassure dear Philippa."

Rupert, shook his umbrella and backed away.

"No, no Mr Darville. Come in out of the rain. You must stay too!" Madame de Lessups came forward with hands outstretched.

"You promised you would sample my chef's Parisian cuisine one day. It may not be dinner but I can promise you pastries every bit as good as you would find in Montmartre. Do not disappoint me." She drew him into the circle.

Rupert demurred but Marguerite insisted. "Viscount Frodingham is here and I know you and he are good friends. We will have such a stimulating party despite the dismal day. Mr Shawcross of course has honoured us and several other people you know. You have never been to one of my Thursday afternoons before."

Harriet looked at the lady's glowing eyes and then at Beaumont's unexpectedly amiable expression. Her cheeks creased in sympathy, happy that the Nabob and his intended bride had made up their differences. Whatever fate had in store for Captain Valentine, Philippa would still gain a beloved step-mama.

The next moment she felt uncomfortable at the thought of Mortimer Shawcross and Rupert in the same room, but nothing now would dislodge Mr Beaumont. He threw off his cloak and Marguerite ushered them into her pretty French drawing room. Harriet admired the dove grey wall paper and the romantic rococo furnishings.

Viscount Frodingham, a tall gangly man of forty with passion for fossils, swept Rupert to one side with exhaustive enquiries about his health.

Mortimer Shawcross greeted Harriet with only the faintest of hesitations. He had been to Tunbridge Wells for the waters and felt much purged from the treatment, he said. Harriet hoped this applied to his sentiments as well as his digestion. They talked a little self-consciously of the restorative properties of the Bath spa and the varied reports of the Cheltenham Pump Room, and when Shawcross drew out his enamelled snuff box, Harriet reminded him of his promise. Arrangements were made to meet in the next few days to buy Sir John's snuff. Shawcross was happy to take charge of the expedition.

"Who's the pretty brunette?" asked Lord Frodingham over Rupert's shoulder. "Talking to Shawcross. She's new to town, surely? I haven't seen her before this season, but then I have been dancing attendance on my father in Yorkshire for the past month."

"How *is* your father?"

"Still alive," said Frodingham gloomily. "Not that I wish to step into the old boy's shoes, but it's deuced hard on my mother. We thought it really was the end, this time; water on the lungs. Nothing else would have made me leave town during the coronation. But he rallied, he always does, more's the pity."

Frodingham grinned suddenly. "But then I have the reward of finding a new face over the tea cups at the widow's. Who *is* the little Nut Brown Maid?"

Rupert surprised out of his observation said: "She is my late wife's cousin." But felt somehow this was not quite right. "Miss Harriet Larkhill. She stayed with the McAllisters for the coronation and is now visiting the Beaumonts in Dulwich."

"Ah-ha! So that is the formidable young lady I have heard so much about."

Rupert stiffened. "You mean the house-breaker business while I was ill? Harriet would certainly have no compunction in confronting a burglar." Rupert turned to look at her again; he was suddenly aware that Shawcross was being very attentive.

"A house-breaker? Good God! No, you don't say so? But you must enlighten me, Darville! The young lady is heroine enough with her rebuff of Captain Valentine, so I have been informed. You look surprised! Have you not heard? My dear man, how remiss of you. You must not hide yourself away in the Traveller's."

A crease appeared between Rupert's brows and Frodingham thought it best to explain. "Word has it that Miss Larkhill has prised the little Beaumont from Valentine's ignoble clutches *several* times and that gentleman threatened to throttle her if she interfered again." The incident had lost nothing in the repetition.

Rupert shifted uncomfortably. He had been aware of none of this. "The man was drunk, I take it?"

"I have no doubt of it, though he usually holds it well. But I have this all from Everard. He says he overheard the quarrel at the Devonshire's ball; I swear the man has the longest ears in Christendom. Miss Larkhill is gaining quite a reputation."

Rupert frowned. "Stephen Everard is a popinjay and Valentine an arrogant puppy; one cannot take him seriously."

"Which is exactly what Miss Larkhill said – to his face. Called him 'gothick' and gave him a smart set-down. And now you tell me she has tackled a burglar! You have redoubtable women in your family Darville."

"She is not in my family," said Rupert, his mind uneasy.

"Then don't you think she should be? But there is *some* connection, surely, and you may dismiss the captain for a blusterer but you are so out of the world that you may not know that he is now considered a regular bad lot. He has designs on the heiress of course. Marguerite has had to bail him out more than once. And there's talk of opium dens down at the docks and a suspicious quantity of thieves cant."

Frodingham raised his eyebrows suggestively. "He's not here, I notice."

"For a man who has been out of town for a month, you are remarkably well informed," said Darville shortly.

Sensing the men's scrutiny, Harriet turned from Mr Shawcross and smiled over her shoulder. Rupert left Lord Frodingham standing and went straight across to her. The thought of her walking into danger without his knowledge had alarmed him. Harriet must not get into a scrape. He pulled her from her elderly admirer. "Harriet, what's this I hear about Captain Valentine threatening you?"

Harriet made a brief apology to her companion and turned to Rupert frowning. "Hush, that's old history. Such a little thing! And I did so particularly *not* want it spoken of. How did you discover it?"

"Never mind who told me. What were you thinking of, exchanging insults with such a blackguard! And what exactly did happen in the maze yesterday?"

"Nothing of consequence," she said lightly. "And nothing to do with me – or you."

"You are getting yourself talked about!" he hissed.

"Good Lord! I'm not some school-room Miss that has to be protected at every turn. If you are referring to the incident at the Devonshires' ball, Captain Valentine deserved a set down for – for rather boorish behaviour. That is all." She shrugged it off. "What can he do? He can hardly call me out."

"He can ruin your good name."

"I rather thought I had ruined his. As I will be here only another week, what does it matter?" She looked pointedly at her arm and he released his grip. Shawcross stepped across and protectively drew her away. Rupert looked after them with annoyance.

Their farewells were lost among the general departure. Mr Beaumont was anxious to outrun the rain and reach Dulwich before the dinner hour.

Frodingham pressed Rupert to dine with him, promising a nice little beefsteak followed by plum pudding. "And then a game of billiards? I must talk to you about the shooting. I take it you are coming down to Winestead after the twelfth like you used to in the old days? We missed your crack-shot aim while you were away. My gamekeeper tells me we'll have a bumper year for grouse."

"Look for me a little later, Froddy. I've a small matter of business to attend to which keeps me in London for a week or two longer."

******

Despite the rain Rupert walked to Russell Square lost in thought. If he followed Harriet's advice and turned to Andrew McAllister for information, how far should he involve Harriet herself? She had made it clear that she wished to withdraw, which of itself was unexpected. Harriet's return to Larkhill the following week would remove her from the scene entirely. He felt oddly deserted.

Figgis informed him that Mr Andrew was still at his office and was not expected home for dinner. Rupert turned his steps to Leadenhall Street and the extended classical frontage of the East India Company's headquarters. A minion led him through the marble halls of commerce where a warren of busy scribbling writers helped to fill the coffers of the most successful trading empire in the world.

He found Andrew McAllister in a private office of decent size and comfortable furnishings. Maps of India and the South China Seas decorated the walls. Above the mantelpiece hung a portrait of Elizabeth I. The door to Lord Glynn's adjoining office was ajar but the great man was absent. Andrew put down his papers and dismissed his clerk, rising from the desk with hand outstretched.

"Darville, to what do I owe the pleasure? Come in – you're very wet but I thought it too early to have a fire lit. Let me take your hat. Would you care for a hot grog to warm you through? It won't do overtire yourself so soon after your fever." McAllister went to the tantalus. "You're lucky to catch me here. I don't officially return to my duties until next week but I thought I'd come in to prepare for Lord Glynn's return. I get the rum from Jamaica, you'll like it."

Rupert shed his wet coat and sat down "I haven't had rum since I was aboard the *Neptune*," he said. "I shipped my own supply. It's not something the French have taken to."

While Andrew busied himself with lemons, water and a spirit stove, Rupert broached the subject of his visit. He once more gave a brief account of the theft of Hinton's property and the other two extortion plots. He spoke openly of the Velasquez but mentioned no other names and Andrew, as a discreet private secretary, did not press for more details.

Rupert produced the two pieces of sacking from his pocket. "Can you make anything out from the marks on these? I need a clue as to the shipper or the warehouse of destination. All the ransom notes had a smell of spice about them and these rags certainly smell as if they come from a spice importer."

Andrew looked at them carefully, putting them side by side and then changing their position several times. He took them to the darkening window.

"I would have to see them in daylight, but I can make little of these marks now. The material looks old; you can tell by how easily it frays." He shredded the edge of one remnant between his fingers. "They've been stencilled in tar. It looks as if they're from the outer covering before the bales went into the ship. A wooden chest would have a brand mark – much simpler to identify."

"I cannot go searching every spice warehouse on the docks – can't you tell me anything at all?"

Andrew lit candles and spread the sacking pieces out on his desk. He shook his head. "Nothing, except they are not from the Company's warehouses."

"I agree; the East India Company's *chop* cannot be mistaken. I thought at first this triangle may be part of the 4 – which of course isn't a 'four' but the 'Sign of Four' based on an ancient symbol adopted by Christianity, standing for the first two letters of Christus in Greek." Rupert stopped in the face of Andrew's disapproving stare. "Forgive me. I am not quite myself. I have much on my mind."

Andrew opened his desk drawer and took out two pieces of paper. "Draw the marks as you see them, Darville, and I'll study them and ask around my colleagues, to see if they can make any sense of them."

Rupert did as he was bid and handed the sketches to McAllister. "I intend to go to Lloyd's and see if they have a list of shipping lines that may use these marks. God knows but these devils might still be fleecing some poor innocent even now, and people are too afraid to speak out."

"Your intention to help Mr Hinton retrieve his money is commendable – but is it wise? Why not leave it in the hands of the authorities? Or my father?"

"Your father has done his best and is busy with far weightier matters. Time is passing; if I hadn't been ill I could have done far more sooner." He broke off and then said more positively: "I'm relying on your brother to alert me to any untoward activity in the criminal fraternity."

Andrew looked unhappy; he had no faith in his brother's wild claims. He took a breath and said: "I'll help you all I can, but, before I do, I must know whether Miss Larkhill is implicated in this search."

"What makes you ask that?"

Unconsciously Andrew always coupled Darville and Harriet in his mind. He chose his words slowly. "Stephen Everard was talking about the Ravensburg Cross at White's one night - he prides himself on being a connoisseur of stones - and how pleased His Majesty had been with the gift.

He also mentioned that the presentation almost didn't happen. Do I guess correctly that this was one of the other items that was stolen – and obviously returned? Miss Larkhill's name was connected in some peripheral capacity, if I remember."

Harriet's name had arisen because of the Reichsgrafin's compulsion to talk. When Everard had enquired as to the repairs of the Ravensburg Cross, Adelaide had spilled the whole story of the theft to him, implicitly reproaching Everard for not accompanying her to the jeweller that day. She exaggerated Harriet's role in order to emphasise his own neglect.

Everard was more amused than put out and recounted the drama as a trivial story against himself over the faro table. This incident had drawn attention to Miss Larkhill who had garnered further interest by the courtship of Mortimer Shawcross and her confrontation of the burglar. The scene with Captain Valentine and her scandalous nursing of Rupert Darville had made her notorious.

Rupert said grudgingly: "Yes, it's true. Harriet was there when the Ravensburg Cross was stolen, but she has had the good sense to withdraw and leave everything else to me – which I must confess is most unlike her."

"I am relieved. As a member of the family I cannot think my mother was wise to permit Miss Larkhill to leave our protection." Andrew stopped, not wanting to blame Darville for Harriet's predicament. His own mind was preoccupied with the softer emotions and he believed all women were frail vessels to be protected. He could not ignore the rumours about Harriet and had almost threatened to knock a man down for his insinuations, but his common sense had prevailed and instead he had gone to his father who had advised silence.

"Matters will sort themselves out in the end," Sir Hamish had said languidly. "Darville is a gentleman; he will not let any harm come to Harriet."

Andrew looked speculatively at his guest and saw a strong-faced, serious man with inscrutable eyes. He wondered if Darville, with his head full of higher matters and mixing only on the fringes of society was aware of the talk. He seemed obsessed with this idea of recovering his friend's money, to the exclusion of all else.

Andrew admired Rupert, who had an intellect he did not aspire to and was said to be a bruising rider and an excellent shot. Sweet Philippa thought he was a paragon of learning and rectitude. Andrew had not dreamt of disillusioning her with stories of Rupert's elopement and failed marriage.

His own thoughts, leaning towards the matrimonial, preferred Rupert to Mortimer Shawcross as a connection and, following this line of logic, he realised that Darville, as the widower of their dead cousin Sylvia, was more closely related to the McAllisters than was Harriet. The question was: what would Rupert do if he became aware that his name was being linked with Miss Larkhill's in a most unsavoury way? Did the man have a right to know? Did Andrew have the duty of a relative – in whatever degree - to tell him?

Andrew thought that he did.

******

Harriet looked up from her book, an uncertain smile breaking over her face as she saw Rupert's tall dark figure approaching slowly along the path. She rose to greet him. There was a slight chill in the damp air and the grotto behind her looked grey and dull.

"Good morning Mr Darville. To what do we owe this courtesy? Have you discovered something about Mr Hinton's ransom? Was Andrew of any help?" She looked from his pale face to his spattered riding boots. "I did not expect to see you so soon. I trust the ride to Dulwich has not tired you?"

"Not in the least. Please resume your seat, Harriet; I have something I wish to say to you."

Harriet sat down again on the stone bench, feeling slightly anxious, Rupert looked so very solemn. "Is there anything the matter? Your mama? Have you had bad news from Ireland?"

"All my family are well, I thank you. It is of you I wish to speak." He took a place beside her and clasped his hands between his knees, staring at the rushy waterfall. He had ridden here reluctantly, feeling tired in mind as well as body. He was glad to rest after his journey but now he was here he did not know how to begin.

"Harriet," he said not looking at her. "I have never properly thanked you for your kindness to me during my illness - no, do not interrupt; I know what I wish to say. I owe you my life; even Dr Yardley says so."

"You are my oldest friend-" she said lightly.

"Exactly! We have known each other so long and are so – comfortable together, why should we not consider ourselves as something *more* than friends?"

She looked at him with a wary withdrawal of her head.

"Harriet, have you ever considered becoming my wife?" He turned to look at her.

She was bereft of words.

"I see the suggestion does not please you," he said quietly, turning his head away again.

"It has startled me, to be sure. But I think you cannot mean what you say. I am honoured, of course, by your proposal, but you are still recovering from your fever, and I think not quite yourself, Mr Darville. There is some confusion of mind-"

"I told you, I am perfectly well. But that does not give me an answer."

"Your – family would not approve."

"I do not marry to please my family."

"But you might marry *someone* to put an end to their insistence."

"I see my mother has been speaking to you," he said grimly, and then shifted a little. "I am fond of you Harriet and I assumed you would be pleased to have the protection of my name. I believe you came to London in search of a husband, did you not, to solve all your financial problems? Forgive my plain speaking."

"Plain speaking!" She bridled. "You are mistaken in your assumption, sir. If such had been the case, I would have accepted Mr Shawcross's generous offer a week ago." Rupert looked surprised as Harriet continued: "Yours is not the first offer of marriage I have received, Mr Darville, and I trust not the last."

She knew very well what had prompted this proposal. "You have heard some ridiculous rumours, from Lady McAllister I suspect, and feel you must 'behave like a gentleman'. I thought you had more sense - or at least had learnt your lesson." He had married her cousin from mistaken notions of chivalry; she would not have him repeat the same catastrophe with her.

"If you are referring to my marriage to Sylvia, then-". He waved a hand as if to ward off the memory. Harriet felt a mixture of fury and shame and said nothing more.

Rupert continued in a controlled voice. "I thought a marriage would suit us both. You understand my work, my aspirations. We have been friends since childhood and I believed that you were not entirely averse to me. I hoped to be of service to you and all my friends at the manor. I see I was mistaken."

"But we are not children any more, I have discovered that. We are different people from - from what we once were."

"People marry who have barely an acquaintance! And my uncle quite holds you as one of the family already. Are we not cousins – of a sort?"

When Harriet said nothing Rupert continued: "You are being talked about in the clubs, Harriet. Bets have been laid."

It was cruel of him to have revealed this and the moment it was said he regretted it.

Harriet felt as if she had been slapped, and paled a little. "So this marriage is indeed to suit your notions of respectability? And am I to marry you out of gratitude because society deems I have been lax in my honour? Or have you wagered money on my accepting you?" She had the satisfaction of seeing him flinch. "Do not disturb yourself, I will be gone from here soon and you can continue your philosophical career untainted by my association, though perhaps a little lighter in the pocket."

"For God's sake Harriet! This is not like you, to take such a pet. I never thought you could stoop to such vulgarity of mind! You've never been averse to the truth and I have done you the courtesy of making my motivation clear. Such marriages are commonplace. Now will you be my wife or not?"

"No, Mr Darville, I will not. I do not wish for a commonplace marriage with you or anyone else! I thank you for your offer but suggest you approach Miss Snoddie who will support you in your work far better than I and will inherit a fortune, which will be far more acceptable to your mother."

"I do not wish to marry Miss Snoddie," he said rising abruptly. "And I think less of you for bringing that lady's name into this conversation, and for maligning my mother."

"I beg your pardon, my tongue runs away with me," muttered Harriet. She stared blindly down at her book. Her wretched, wretched tongue! She didn't know when she had first longed for Rupert to propose to her – but not like this, never like this! A marriage of convenience, to save her name and make his life comfortable, with no word of love. He would regret within the year as he had done with Sylvia. She shut the book abruptly and took a deep breath.

"I apologise, Mr Darville, if I impugned your motives – about the, the betting in the clubs, I mean. I do not perfectly understand the matter. What exactly are these despicable people saying?" She looked up at him with anxious brown eyes. "I have a right to know."

Rupert towered above her blotting out the sun and said with distaste: "They are betting on the likelihood of our marriage." He would not disclose the far cruder phrasing or the inclusion of Shawcross as another candidate.

"And that has prompted your suit," she said hollowly.

"Not entirely."

Harriet said as levelly as she could: "I am so sorry to disappoint whoever these 'romantic' gentlemen are but they are destined to lose their money. I would rather we remain friends, as we have always been –" But as she said it, she knew their former easy relations had been irrevocably damaged. She could not assuage him as easily as she had Mortimer Shawcross.

Rupert bowed stiffly. "Of course Miss Larkhill. We will say no more on the matter if the subject is so distasteful to you. May I escort you back to the house? Or would you rather compose yourself here a little?"

"I will stay awhile thank you but will be in shortly if Mr Beaumont asks after me."

Rupert lingered awkwardly as Harriet resolutely opened her book and stared blindly down at the page. He felt bewildered and affronted at Harriet's attitude, and his guilt over his ungentlemanly betrayal made him blame *her* even more for this debacle. He did not know how to put it right. As he walked away along the path to the Lodge he felt a great raw wound in his chest and realised he did not know what to do now that Harriet had refused him.

CHAPTER 10   ABDUCTION

A few days later, the Beaumonts and Harriet went up to town in the big travelling coach. Mr Beaumont, in a better mood, allowed Annie to ride inside. Ram Kumar took up the seat next to the coachman and blew loudly on a horn whenever they approached a toll-gate.

The coach deposited them in Jermyn Street where crowds thronged around the bow-fronted windows. Ram Kumar cleared away the street vendors and pickpockets with a bark of Bengali, his hand on the hilt of his dagger. Mr Beaumont showed no sign of leaving his daughter to make her purchases unattended. Harriet caught sight of Mortimer Shawcross's rubicund face.

"How kind of you to do me this favour," she said, shaking hands with him. "Mr Beaumont has shown an interest in our expedition and has come with us."

Beaumont ordered his coachman to walk the horses. The pleasantries once over, Mr Shawcross ushered them into Pain's the tobacconists.

"Do you take snuff, Mr Beaumont?" asked Shawcross, somewhat on the defensive. The Nabob's appearance made his own presence superfluous.

"I smoke the occasional cheroot. You do not patronise Fribourg and Treyer?" asked Beaumont.

Shawcross, who thought Miss Larkhill's purse may not run to the prices charged by the foremost tobacco purveyors in the country, gave a depreciating cough. If he had known the Nabob was to be of the party he would have certainly suggested meeting them in the Haymarket.

"I'm sure Mr Pain's shop will be most accommodating and it is very convenient for Floris." Harriet nodded to the famous perfumery a little way along the street. "Philippa and I would not wish to keep you from your business in the City any longer than is necessary, Mr Beaumont."

The shop smelled of dark tobacco and other pungent scents. Rows of round-bodied jars climbed to the ceiling labelled with strange and exotic names. A selection of exquisite snuff boxes in cloisonné and silver sat under the glass counters. Delicate chatelaines of snuff accoutrements tempted the connoisseur who preferred to blend his own sort. On the other side of the shop a crowd of young gentleman were choosing cigars from boxes and drawers decorated with foreign labels. Smoking was becoming fashionable again among the upper classes.

"Plain snuff on this wall, Miss Larkhill and mixed on the other," said Shawcross waving his arms like a conjurer. Philippa wrinkled her nose and took a seat as a shopman bustled forward offering assistance to the gentlemen.

"The young lady is looking for a snuff suitable for an elderly relative," said Shawcross.

Harriet explained her requirements, and the shopman, quite used to ladies of quality - though usually married ladies - ordering their own special blends, set to with a will. Producing a small spoon he deposited a pinch of mixed snuff on a square of paper and offered it to Harriet. After trying a series of samples doused mainly with attar of roses, Harriet was driven to say: "My uncle has taken the Strasbourg violet mixture for many years, but I think would appreciate something - different." She personally found the smell cloying.

"Ah yes, Miss. Strasbourg violet, a great favourite with Her late Majesty Queen Charlotte. The subtlety of the ambergris and bitter almonds perhaps might escape the nose of an older gentleman. Should you like to try a plain sort? Something with a more rugged odour?"

He brought down yet another jar, this time labelled 'Brazil'.

"Ugh! That smells rather unpleasantly of cheese." Harriet sneezed. Mr Beaumont came across from the cigar counter where he had just purchased a box of the best Havanas.

Shawcross looked mortified. "Try a plain simple Virginia, Miss Larkhill. It's good quality tobacco. Most gentlemen will appreciate that."

The shopman, recognising the voice of a true noseologist, climbed up his step-ladder and brought down another pot-bellied jar.

"You're right Mr Shawcross," said Harriet taking her nose out of the sample. "There is an unmistakable smell of the card room, but I'm afraid my uncle never liked to gamble."

"Then why don't you mix it with something," suggested Mr Beaumont, breaking in with a touch of impatience.

"Of course! Could this be blended with – with apple, my uncle's favourite fruit?"

Shawcross and Beaumont rolled their eyes at this adulteration, but the shopman knew his clientele and their tastes.

"Certainly Miss, we can do that for you. Shall we say a pound of the Virginia apple mix and a new Denby jar to keep it in? Very pretty Miss, with a hand-painted scene of the Abbey, only a few shillings extra. It would be a crime to have the new blend mixing with the Strasbourg violet."

Mortimer Shawcross nodded in agreement.

Harriet looked dubious and then said. "Yes, I'll take it – such a perfect souvenir of my London visit."

"Thank you Miss. We can have it ready for you by the end of the week. Will you collect or shall we send it?"

The shopman named a price which startled her but as she was taking out her purse, Mr Beaumont reached over, giving the shopman his card. "Send it to this address. I'll pay now as we will be leaving the country shortly."

Harriet had the sense not to object in public but felt her gift to her uncle being taken out of her hands. She burned inwardly as she watched Mr Beaumont produce a bank note from his pocket book and accept the receipt. To cover her confusion she thanked Shawcross profusely for his assistance only to find that the gentleman had no intention of taking his leave.

"It is my pleasure to accompany you Floris, Miss Larkhill. I have promised my daughters some scented soap. I dare not return to Grantham without it."

Trailing the gentlemen behind them the ladies moved on to Floris, perfumier to the nobility. Immediately they entered the shop they were met by the mingled aroma of flowers and essential oils. Candlelight glistened on flasks of perfume stacked in rows around the shop. The shelves and counters displayed combs, hair preparations and cologne for gentlemen. Floris was full, mainly of foreign visitors doing their shopping before leaving London.

Harriet was determined to buy nothing but Miss Humble's favourite lavender water; the Floris label would make the gift special. Her guineas were running low despite her assurances to Sir Hamish.

Philippa sighed with envy and stared with longing at the shimmering perfumes. "It is just like Paris," she said. "But Papa says I am too young for perfume and of course I cannot wear it in the convent."

"You use a toilette water. I see no harm in you wearing lily-of-the-valley or violet on special evenings. The fragrance is light and would suit a young girl perfectly well," returned Harriet.

"Oh, do you really think so?"

"I think we should have asked Madame de Lessups to come with us. She would be able to soften your father. Oh!"

She came face to face with Miss Snoddie hanging onto Rupert's arm. Harriet could not see a chaperone anywhere. Rupert tipped his hat, did not smile and with murmured apologies broke from Miss Snoddie to speak to Mr Beaumont. Shawcross inched forward to stand by Harriet's shoulder.

"Mr Darville has agreed to escort me while I make my purchases," said Miss Snoddie airily. She made no effort to explain the whereabouts of Mrs Somerville. "I'm buying combs for my mother and cologne for my papa. I hear that the king buys his hair combs here."

"Yes, I believe Floris has a royal patent now," said Mr Shawcross, forever in the know.

"Do you return to Edinburgh, Miss Snoddie?" asked Harriet hopefully.

"Oh, no. I intend to remain in London for some weeks yet. So many distinguished people have shown such interest in phrenology that there is talk of starting a society in London. My papa has agreed that my advice would be invaluable in that case and will join me here soon."

Harriet's heart sank. There was something about Miss Snoddie's claims that could never quite be refuted. She was conscious of Rupert talking earnestly to Mr Beaumont.

"I assume you're going back to – where is it – in Wiltshire?" asked Miss Snoddie.

"Larkhill."

"I'm sure you must be missing your farm. Mr Darville tells me you know all manner of interesting things about sheep."

Rupert had said nothing of the sort. Tired of listening to Miss Snoddie's pretentious claims for her pseudo-scientific obsession, in a weak moment he had praised Harriet's practical knowledge and experience.

Harriet felt Philippa's anxious gaze, and pulled herself together. "If you will forgive me, Miss Snoddie, I see an opening in the crowd. Miss Beaumont and I have so many errands to run." She dropped a curtsey and turned to the crush by the counter. Mr Shawcross was tempted by some new hair pomade and left the ladies to their perfume shopping.

"I'll come with you Miss Larkhill," said Lavinia. "I have been waiting this age for service." She jostled a smartly dressed matron in front who turned, gave her a cutting look and blocked her way.

"Such manners," tutted Miss Snoddie falling back. "But what can you expect from some provincial nobody come to town only for the coronation?"

Harriet almost laughed but waited patiently by the counter idly examining a pyramid display of little boxes of perfume. Each box contained two miniature bottles, one of attar of roses and one of jasmine.

"Philippa, do look! This is just the present for Lady Durrington and Juliana. I have no idea who would prefer what fragrance, but they can each choose which one they like best."

Lavinia Snoddie picked up a box and examined its contents. "Rose is my favourite. I have no need of jasmine."

Harriet watched in disbelief as Miss Snoddie calmly opened another of the small boxes and exchanged the miniature bottle of jasmine for one of rose. Lavinia closed the box now containing the two jasmine flasks and returned it to the pile without a blink.

Philippa looked frightened and Harriet was saved from having to protest by the assistant taking her attention. Purchases accomplished, Harriet had the pleasure of receiving her scanty change on a little cushion. Floris deemed it vulgar to handle money directly. Smiling with delight Harriet deposited her parcels into Annie's basket and turned away from the counter. She took Philippa's elbow to hurry her away. A little further along the counter Miss Snoddie was buying the box containing two flasks of attar of roses from the unsuspecting shop assistant.

Mr Shawcross, carrying his soap and pomade in a neatly wrapped parcel, reappeared to usher them out of the shop.

"She stole that scent!" hissed Philippa looking behind at Lavinia's stalking figure.

"Not at all," whispered Harriet. "Miss Snoddie paid the correct price for two bottles of perfume. The fact that she changed one for another means she cheated a little – no more."

"But, that's dishonest! You cannot approve! Think of the poor customer who might buy the box with two jasmine bottles in it, instead of one of each. What a disappointment they would feel! Should we tell Mr Darville?"

"I *don't* approve," said Harriet flatly. "But what can anyone do? *Caveat emptor* - and Mr Darville is quite capable of assessing Miss Snoddie's morals without our help."

Philippa was silenced by her friend's cynicism. Harriet's mind churned with a maelstrom of conflicting emotions. She wished to be away from this appalling encounter as soon as possible. She felt she should have protested. Had Rupert any notion of this woman's character? Her temporary pleasure in the change-giving quite vanished.

Rupert waited on the pavement talking to Beaumont by the open carriage door. The ladies turned to make farewells; insincere compliments were exchanged and Miss Snoddie moved towards Rupert with a proprietary air.

Mortimer Shawcross was still hovering, an inane smile on his face. Harriet turned to Philippa and said with feigned heartiness: "We shall have a busy afternoon. I have to buy Lieutenant George a new London guide book and Sir Charles something naval. And of course there's Young Clem to think of."

Rupert broke off his conversation with Beaumont and said quickly: "You must allow me, Miss Larkhill, to find your nephew something suitable. I consider myself an expert in amusements for little boys."

"I would not hear of it Mr Darville. Do not alter your plans for my sake; Miss Snoddie is waiting for you." She tried to sound polite.

"I *am* the boy's guardian, and may not see him again for some time. It would be my pleasure to escort you to a remarkably good toy warehouse-"

"And I must buy something for my little sisters," interrupted Miss Snoddie. "We can all go together."

Beaumont put an end to the exchange. "We're committed to Madame de Lessups in Curzon Street. Get in, Philippa, I do not wish to be behindhand. Then I must be off to the City. Shawcross, may we drop you somewhere?"

Mortimer Shawcross declined effusively. He wanted to toddle down Piccadilly and take a comfortable lunch at his club. Several people would be interested to know of this morning's meeting. Until Miss Larkhill left town there was a lot of money riding on Rupert Darville being brought up to the mark by the favourite, and now here was the Snoddie filly coming up fast on the rails. He made an extravagant farewell to the ladies with many heavy hints and promises of future meetings. Harriet answered with composure, uncharitably wishing him away.

The ladies completed their shopping and returned to Curzon Street in the afternoon to rest and dress before spending the evening with the McAllisters. Mr Beaumont was to meet them in Russell Square where Harriet would make her farewells to her original hosts at what Sir Hamish was pleased to call a 'family' dinner party.

"Am I to invite Mortimer Shawcross?" asked Lady McAllister. With Harriet no longer under her gaze she could not keep track of that young lady's romantic progress.

"I think not my dear. Shawcross spoke to me in confidence before he left for Tunbridge Wells. He was not successful in his suit."

Lady McAllister made a *moue*. "I'm very surprised. Mortimer has been in want of a capable wife for years. I would have thought a young woman in Miss Larkhill's position would have been pleased to accept such a respectable offer."

"Fond as I am of Mortimer Shawcross, I'm in no hurry to welcome him into the clan."

Lady McAllister's eyes bulged behind her pince-nez. "I am at a loss, Sir Hamish, as to why you insist on referring to Miss Larkhill as one of the family!"

"Because she is, indirectly."

"I like the girl well enough but here is only the most tenuous connection with the McAllisters," argued his wife. "Despite the fact that she alludes to us as her uncle and aunt to all and sundry."

"Unfair my dear," said Sir Hamish languidly. "A matter of mistranslation she assured me; some difficulty with her High German. However I would not be too hasty to write Harriet off. Andrew is a long way from marrying the heiress and William shows no signs of settling down."

"What has that got to do with Miss Larkhill?" said his wife removing her pince-nez.

"Think who Harriet *might* marry," he said as he left the room.

After his interview with Andrew, Sir Hamish had taken steps to have the wager quietly removed from White's betting book. The young gentlemen concerned were brought to see the error of their assumptions and the error of their ways by parents who did not wish their sons' careers blighted or social standing diminished. Sadly, Sir Hamish could not stop the unofficial betting which surrounded Harriet's matrimonial prospects. He was glad for her sake that she would be leaving London in a few days.

Everyone sat down to Harriet's farewell dinner in harmony. There had been an affecting little ceremony beforehand in the drawing room when the family had pressed various presents into her reluctant hands. Even Miss Finch had come forward shyly with a pretty handkerchief sachet, made by her own hand and embroidered with Harriet's initials.

"But I have nothing for you all!" Harriet burst out in embarrassment.

"Then Sir Hamish must bring back plenty of fresh eggs and poultry when he returns from his visit to Larkhill," said Lady McAllister with an eye to her larder. She had given Harriet three pairs of the finest silk stockings in atonement for her earlier coolness.

The soup had barely been served when Figgis returned with a wooden face, bent and whispered in his master's ear.

"Beaumont. I believe there is a messenger from Dulwich just arrived. Some matter of urgency it seems," said Sir Hamish.

Beaumont looked up in surprise, threw his napkin on the table and turned to Lady McAllister. "Your pardon, ma'am. You will forgive me if I attend to this."

At a nod from Beaumont, Sir Hamish rose and the two gentlemen left the room. Lady McAllister called Figgis back and demanded to be told what was happening.

Figgis at once became more dignified. "I wouldn't like to say, m'lady."

"Nonsense! You must tell me at once!"

Figgis turned to the table and knew a receptive audience when he saw one. "I gained the unfortunate impression that Mr Beaumont's residence in the country has been robbed."

The table erupted with cries of distress and demands for details. Miss Finch dropped her soup spoon with a clatter.

William said "I told you so!"

Lady McAllister told Figgis to hold the fish course and dismissed him. The next fifteen minutes were rife with supposition and alarm. Madame de Lessups made soothing noises until Sir Hamish returned.

"Ah, I see Figgis has been before me with the news. I'm sorry to say there has been a break-in at Hibiscus Lodge." Everyone groaned. "Luckily, the servant thinks only a few items have been stolen but there seems to have been an unnecessary amount of damage done to the house: broken windows and torn cupboards and so on. Mr Beaumont has returned there now to supervise the restoration."

"Will he be safe?" Philippa looked terrified.

"Of course, my dear. Your Indian manservant is with him and the thieves are long gone."

"The young ladies must stay with me tonight," said Madame de Lessups with decision.

"Exactly so, Madame. Mr Beaumont suggested just this arrangement before he left. He will send for the young ladies when Hibiscus Lodge is habitable."

"And I will escort you to Curzon Street, Madame. And if you will allow me, I will sleep on a sofa in your drawing room," offered Andrew. "To assuage any fears the young ladies may have."

"Thank you, sir, but there is no need," demurred Madame de Lessups. "My servants will be extra vigilant tonight."

******

Two days later William sent a note round to Brook Street asking Mr Darville to dine as he had some 'interesting' news. Rupert arrived at William's chambers promptly.

"Have you heard?" said William, greeting Rupert at the inner door. "Hibiscus Lodge was broken into on Saturday!"

"Hibiscus Lodge?" Rupert frowned and handed his hat and to the servant. "Are the ladies safe? Was anything taken?"

"The ladies were safe enough with us in Russell Square," said William ushering his guest to an armchair and shooing the servant out. "Or safe enough shoppin' in the afternoon when it all happened."

William drew another armchair closer to the fire. "There was nothin' much stolen, only a few of the Nabob's pieces and Miss Larkhill's trinkets. Miss Beaumont had no jewellery of value in the house I gather. But there was a lot of damage done. It sounds like the villains made a thorough search of the place. It's my guess they were after the Rajah's rubies."

Rupert dismissed this. "What about the servants? That native servant, Ram Kumar? He would frighten the devil in daylight. Did no one see anything?"

"Ram Kumar was in London with the family. The servants in Dulwich are local. They'd all sloped off to the fair on the green. A messenger arrived to tell the Nabob when we were at dinner and he went chargin' off to the scene of the crime."

He reached for the jug of porter, satisfied he had caused a stir.

"So this is your news," said Rupert flatly.

"Of course – isn't it enough?"

"I was hoping you'd heard something about the proceeds from the Hinton extortion."

"Not a whisper. I have put the word about as far as I can. My contacts tell me there've been a lot of new faces around the stews, because of the coronation – easy pickings you see. The jails are full. But no one's been sportin' their blunt more than is to be expected or they're taking it back to foreign parts with 'em. I'm going to be inundated with clients on King's Bench when term starts in September," he said with satisfaction.

Rupert realised he was going to get nothing out of William and cutting his losses reverted to the original conversation.

"I take it you know all the details about the burglary first hand?"

"Most certainly – no hearsay in this case. The girls stayed with Madame de Lessups overnight and Andrew and I escorted the three ladies down to Dulwich on Sunday afternoon. I must say, money talks, the place don't look half bad, but you could still see where the floor boards had been ripped and walls hammered. Most of the damage was downstairs in the study."

"Naturally Beaumont informed the police?"

"Oh yes, it's not one of your hush-hush extortion cases. Beaumont is storming about like a scalded ferret, trying to get the parish to take some action. There's not much hope because I swear it's a London gang and local constables won't cooperate with the London charlies. And it ain't as if anything valuable was stolen."

At that moment the servant returned, balancing two metal canteens full of hot steak and kidney pie from a cook shop in Fleet Street. The gravy slopped dangerously out of the rims.

While the servant set the food out on the rickety gate-leg table the conversation drifted to the funeral procession of Queen Caroline which had caused much unrest. When the servant left, William got up to pour a full-bodied burgundy into the wine glasses and invited Rupert to come to the table.

"Harriet should come back to us," said William following his own train of thought. "M'mother should not have let her go to strangers in the first place."

"I'm sure Miss Larkhill has too good a heart to abandon Miss Beaumont at this distressing time," said Rupert. "And she will be returning home to Wiltshire shortly."

"The burglary's put their plans back a few days. Beaumont has to settle with the landlord and reorganise the carriers and storage."

Rupert appeared unmoved. "You said Miss Larkhill's jewellery was taken?"

"Yes, all gone. I understand that she kept her gew-gaws in a drawer of a dressing table there. They're of no great value but Miss Larkhill was very upset to lose them. Beaumont broke it to her while we were there. I didn't think Harriet was so sentimental."

"I believe Miss Larkhill has a great deal of delicate feeling under that – happy exterior." Rupert was at his most pedantic. He picked up his knife and fork and stared at his steak and kidney pie with faint distaste.

"What a capital thing my father kept the Larkhill heirlooms in Russell Square," said William tucking in. "She'd have been in Queer Street if *those* had been stolen."

Rupert looked up. "I didn't know there were any. Why did she bring them to London? I never noticed her wearing them."

"You ain't the noticin' sort, Darville." William raised his wine glass, watching Rupert's face over the rim. "Harriet was going to sell them. She needed the money – and still does. Yet I swear she'd swop the lot to have her own jewellery back again. Miss Beaumont told Andrew that Harriet had *cried* over their loss."

He was right. Harriet had been a good companion when Philippa was anxious about her father and the problems the burglary would cause. Madame de Lessups kindly tried to divert the girl's anxieties, but when alone Harriet allowed Miss Beaumont to pour her heart out, and then talked her usual good sense. When Mr Beaumont told Harriet that her modest jewellery box had been taken, her friend's genuine grief had stopped Philippa's childish dramatics in their tracks.

Philippa found Harriet in the grotto sobbing into her hands. She was shocked when Harriet raised a tear-stained face and said: "I have lost everything, everything."

Philippa rushed to put her arm around Harriet's shoulder. "Don't cry, dearest Harriet! Papa will buy you anything you want. We can replace every piece of it before we leave London. Or he'll buy you better things in Paris!"

"You don't understand," sniffed Harriet. "I have lost everything that reminds me of anyone I ever cared for. They're irreplaceable." Her big brown eyes brimmed with tears; she wept for more than the loss of her jewellery.

Philippa was too inexperienced to know what to say in comfort. "Was your jewellery so very precious to you?" Being a modest girl herself she had not given Harriet's adornments much thought.

As if fixing them permanently in her memory Harriet began: "There was my cousin Jemima's pearl pendant; Aunt Betsy gave that to me when I was twelve. And Aunt Amelia's garnets. The locket with my parent's silhouettes; I have nothing else to remind me of them. And Rupert's earrings from Montevideo." She twisted her handkerchief in her hands and gave Philippa a watery smile. "And of course that beautiful mother-of-pearl comb that *you* gave me for the Devonshires' ball. I have nothing now to remind me of you and Mr Beaumont's kindness."

"Papa will buy you a dozen combs and you will not need reminding of us at all because we will write and visit constantly!"

Harriet laughed weakly but Philippa's concern was sufficient to make her straighten her shoulders and wipe her eyes. "I should go back to the house and tell Annie to start on my packing, this will never do," she said. "And you must do your harp practise before the carriers comes to crate it up. Do not fret about me."

By the time they had reached the Lodge, Harriet had regained her outward composure and Philippa felt she had achieved something adult for the first time in her life.

Unfortunately Philippa could not resist recounting this lachrymose episode to Andrew when they were alone. She had been taken aback by her friend's outburst. Andrew repeated a much more sober version to his brother in support of his belief that Harriet should never have been allowed to leave Russell Square. William now dropped the incident casually into the conversation with Rupert, like a match to a damp fuse.

"Will you be seeing Miss Larkhill before the Beaumonts take her home?" asked William, giving the fuse a tweak.

"No," said the academic, his eyes narrow with controlled indifference.

He had no intention of seeing Harriet again while she was in London, his humiliation was too raw. Her refusal to allow him to choose a gift for Young Clem had been the last straw. He had merely been trying to mend fences, but she had snubbed him and allowed that old fool Shawcross to act the *gallant*.

Nevertheless as he walked under the Inn's medieval gateway into Fleet Street, he pictured her laughing, teasing eyes, her good-natured inquisitive face. He had seen her angry, anxious, caring and prosaic. But he had never seen Harriet in tears and he found that the thought disturbed him.

******

The following afternoon Mr Beaumont arrived home from the City unexpectedly. "Where is my daughter?" he demanded. "I wish to see her immediately, in my study." He threw his gloves into his hat and thrust them at Kumar.

Harriet who had just that instant returned from posting a letter informing Miss Humble of the burglary and yet another delayed departure, said: "I left Miss Beaumont reading in the garden, sir."

Mr Beaumont gave her a penetrating stare and then nodded to one of the footmen. "Find Miss Beaumont. I wish to see her at once. Kumar, bring me some coffee. Miss Larkhill, you will oblige me by granting me an interview in my study after I have spoken to my daughter."

Harriet dropped an obedient curtsey. He turned on his heel and shut his study door with an odd look. She wondered at her host's sudden formality and hoped he had not discovered his daughter's correspondence with Andrew.

The footman scurried off and Harriet went back out to search the garden. Mr Beaumont's serious visage brooked no delay. A muted rumble could be heard in the distance and Harriet, who did not like thunderstorms, retreated through the French doors into the drawing room and waited for Philippa to reappear.

Great splashes of rain marked the steps of the terrace when she at last saw Philippa, huddled in her cloak, her hood up against the sudden summer downpour, hurrying across the lawn followed by the footman. Harriet beckoned her into the drawing room as the footman made a dash for the servants' quarters.

"Oh, just in time! Thank goodness! Are you very wet? Didn't you hear the storm coming?"

"I was reading, and dreaming, I must confess. I didn't realise the time. I wanted to be away from the removal men. I went to the grotto." Philippa threw her damp cloak across a chair and looked upset. Harriet thought it best not to scold. Her young friend was sad enough to leave London and her beau.

"Your papa wishes to see you in his study. Quick, upstairs and change your shoes and stockings, and put a comb through your hair."

"Why does he want to see me?" Philippa looked alarmed.

"I haven't the slightest idea but gentlemen hate being kept waiting."

"But my book! I've forgotten Mr McAllister's book! It will be ruined in the rain! I left it on the stone bench in the grotto when James came to fetch me. I must send him back for it at once."

"*I'll* get it for you. It would take too long to ring for a servant. You go to your father and I will rescue Andrew's book." Harriet did not relish another visit to the grotto but she knew the book was Andrew's parting gift to Miss Beaumont.

"You are so good, Harriet! What will I do when I have not got you near me?" said Philippa impulsively kissing her on the cheek. "You will get so wet!"

"I'll take your cloak, and look; I'm already wearing my walking shoes. I've just come back from the village. Now go and make yourself presentable for your papa. I'll be waiting for you in your room, with the book, when you've seen him, and you can tell me what it was all about. Don't look so anxious, I daresay it is nothing more than a surprise invitation." Thus appeased, Philippa allowed herself to be gently pushed out of the room.

Harriet pulled Philippa's cloak around her shoulders, flipped the hood over her head, gritted her teeth and pushed forward into the gathering gloom of the garden. Head bent she ran across the open expanse of grass as the rain pelted down. Gasping for breath at the edge of the woodland she flinched as a crack of lightning lit up the sky and a hostile growl of thunder rolled above the house. She dithered about going back or staying sheltered among the trees, but Philippa would be upset at the loss of her precious book. She may as well continue, wet and nervous as she was. It was only a summer squall, she told herself. However, she resolved to wait inside the cave until the storm had passed before retracing her steps to the Lodge.

Holding her hood tightly about her to protect her face from the brambles she took the shortest route. By pushing her way through the undergrowth she could quickly reach the way to the grotto.

Her wet skirts about her ankles impeded her progress but at last she found the ferny path by the stream. The sky was lifting a little but the rain forced her to keep her head down as she splashed towards the grotto. The noise of the little waterfall, swollen with the rain, drowned out all other sounds. When she reached the cave she hurried inside and immediately spied the book blown from the stone bench, pages sprawled in a puddle.

The next moment a thick wad of material was rammed over her nose and mouth and the hood of the cloak drawn even more tightly around her face. She was tipped backward, her flailing arms gripped by hard hands that whipped a thin cord around her wrists making her cry out in pain.

"Stow yer noise or I'll cosh yer 'ard." But her one scream had already subsided into gasps and a sensation of suffocation that terrified her.

Harriet struggled in vain. Coarse hands dragged a sack over her head and upper body. It smelt of nutmeg. Harriet's insides shrivelled in panic. She knew exactly what was happening. Clawing frantically at the loose weave she could do nothing to escape the suffocating cocoon.

"Get 'er legs. Bind 'em tight, this one's a kicker." In a moment she was trussed like a chicken and slung over a strong man's shoulder.

After some minutes of bouncing and choking she realised they had reached the lane beyond the park where she was unceremoniously thrown into the back of a cart. Providentially someone had scattered a few sheaves of straw over the hard boards.

"Go easy with her! The Captin says we weren't to damage the goods," a young voice said.

"Mind yer mouth! Just get 'er covered up and watch 'her! I'll drive the nag."

Her vision was obscured even more as she heard a canvas cover being pulled over the top of the cart. Her heart sank; however much she struggled, no one would spot her now. The young voice disappeared onto the seat with the driver. The cart jolted to a start and was soon making a cracking pace. She felt sick; her head throbbed where it had hit the floorboards. She couldn't breathe let alone cry out. Before long, Harriet faded into darkness.

******

Rupert found himself once more on the road to Dulwich. Madame de Lessups had been quite right to raise her eyebrows at his ill-manners to the Beaumonts, let alone his young friend. He told himself that it would be uncivil to allow Miss Larkhill to return to Wiltshire without making his formal farewells. He found he could not rid himself of the thought of Harriet in tears.

Rupert arrived at Hibiscus Lodge to discover Miss Larkhill absent, Miss Beaumont denied, and the maid who answered the door quaking in fear. Annie appeared from the back stairs and rushed towards him but at the sound of a visitor's voice Philipp Beaumont strode into the hallway and brusquely bade Rupert to join him in the study. He found Ram Kumar standing rigidly to attention as though awaiting a firing squad. Beaumont thrust a grubby piece of paper into Rupert's hand.

"Thank God you've come! Read this! It was meant to be my daughter of course but they've taken Miss Larkhill instead. No one seems to know anything about it." He cast an accusatory glance at his Indian servant. "First the break-in and now this!"

As Rupert read the clumsily scrawled capitals, Beaumont paced the room. "I must send a message to Sir Hamish, but thank God at least *you* are here, you stand for her brother. The servants saw no one, my daughter does nothing but cry that it was all her fault-"

"Miss Larkhill? Abducted? When did this happen? How did they take her?" Rupert broke in sharply.

"According to my daughter, from the grotto, an hour ago-"

Rupert turned on his heel and headed for the front door. Beaumont followed. "I have sent for the constables but these rogues could be anywhere by now. It took us a full thirty minutes to realise Miss Larkhill was missing and then another half an hour in fruitless search of the garden. Then this note came, by some urchin from the village.

He waved the piece of paper in rage. "I am to mail the ransom to John Smyth, Esq. *poste restante*, Liverpool. There must be an accomplice in the North. I cannot hope to put a watch on Liverpool post office day and night. I might have been able to do something in London – but Liverpool! I do have shipping connections there but -"

Rupert scarcely broke his stride across the lawn. "Calm yourself. I have good reason to believe this Liverpool idea is a wild-goose chase. This is not the first ransom note I've seen, though they appear to be trying to draw you further away."

"Explain yourself!" Beaumont demanded pulling Rupert by the sleeve. Rupert stopped with reluctance.

"This is the fourth extortion plot to my knowledge by this so-called 'John Smyth Esquire' and his gang." He snatched the note from Beaumont's grasp and raised it to his nose. "Nutmeg. *You* can help by listing all the shipping lines you know that have, or have had, spice warehouses in London, excluding the East India Company."

"Why?" Beaumont looked bewildered. "What good would that do?"

"I have reason to believe these villains use a warehouse, possibly an abandoned one, as their meeting place or hide-out."

"How do you know?"

Rupert pulled his arm from Beaumont's grasp. "There's not time to explain now. I must search the grotto." He strode off, his coat billowing out behind him. Beaumont followed.

"It's money they're after," continued Beaumont, twitching the note from Rupert's unresisting hand. "Twenty thousand pounds for my daughter's life. What will they do when they discover they have the wrong woman?"

"Kill her," said Rupert and started to run.

Beaumont arrived panting in the grotto. Rupert was already searching the ground. He looked up from the disturbed gravel by the stone bench. "They abducted her from here, right enough. I would hazard by the scuff marks that Miss Larkhill put up a fight." He caught sight of Beaumont's face. "Take heart, the other treasures were returned unharmed. Let us hope the same will apply to Miss Larkhill. Allow me attend to this, Harriet is my responsibility."

Rupert followed the signs of struggle and broken bushes up the bank to the park wall. He bent down, picked something from the spiky bushes and silently pocketed it. A little way along the wall stood a wooden door, temptingly ajar. The chain on the door was broken.

"There's been a cart standing here," said Rupert, examining the ruts in the muddy road. He looked up and down the lane. "A single horse and a two-wheeled cart, facing in the direction of the London Road, naturally." He examined the mud again. "I'd say there were two men involved. I would think there would have to be to subdue Miss Larkhill."

"There've been a good many carts about the place this last day or two - and removal men. I'm storing most of our goods in the Curzon Street house."

Rupert turned to Beaumont. "Where's the boy who brought the note?"

"In my kitchen but he knows nothing. He said a rough type in homespuns gave him a sixpence to bring the note to Hibiscus Lodge. He claims he saw the cart in the inn yard, with a tarpaulin cover. He assumed it was one of the carriers from London."

"Damnation! Then we must question the innkeeper at once. At least we might find out which direction they took after they joined the London Road. I could have passed them on my way here." Rupert turned back and headed towards the stables.

"I'll pay anything, Darville. Miss Larkhill may not be my daughter but she *is* my niece,"

Rupert stopped in his tracks, his eyes widening in disbelief. "Good God man, what are you saying!"

"She knows nothing of it, or if she did she never spoke of it. I was about to tell Philippa and then her this very afternoon. Harriet''s my sister Emily's child right enough. She looks nothing like the Beaumonts and I daresay she never gave it a thought. Andrew McAllister let it slip to my daughter – about Miss Larkhill's mother. I made enquiries and today received documentary proof from Ceylon-"

"Never mind that now! We have to find her! *Someone* must have seen them on the road."

But the innkeeper was unable to help; he was inside at the time seeing to the midday rush of customers and, as no horses needed changing, the ostlers were indifferent to Rupert's enquiries about a common cart.

"That means the horse was fresh and could have come from no more than twenty miles away." He turned to Beaumont. "You get back to the Lodge and speak to the justices and the constables – if you think fit. I'll see what I can find out on the road to town. The turnpikes should have news if they went in that direction."

"Send word to Russell Square or Curzon Street when you find her. I must inform Sir Hamish as soon as possible and start raising the money. I'll pay anything they ask, anything. Good luck Darville – bring her back safely."

Rupert silently swung himself into the saddle and spurred his horse back onto the highway in the direction of London.

******

Harriet did not know how long she drifted in and out of consciousness, trying not to choke on the gag. When she heard the cries of the gulls and caught the stench of the water she knew they had arrived at the river. Dear God, she was not going to be transported was she? But there was no frenzied bustle of loading and unloading, no shouting voices, no creaking of rigging, in fact nothing to show they were in any place of habitation. She began to feel very frightened.

At last, after splashing through deep ruts and pot holes, the cart came to a halt. The boy jumped down and spoke to the driver in some argot she could not catch. The canvas cover was pulled back and hands groped at her body. Harriet continued to slump and allowed herself to be carried awkwardly inside a building and up several flights of wooden stairs.

She was dropped onto a straw paillasse and the sack torn from her body. One of the men roughly pulled her hood back and at last a hairy hand ripped the suffocating wad from her mouth. She moaned pitifully and gagged, but just to breathe properly was a godsend. Harriet's eyelids fluttered and closed again as she collapsed back onto the straw, but not before she had seen her abductors.

"She may be a flash mort but she don't look much to me," said the youth.

"As long as she brings in the rhino, what's it to you? Get the blindfold on 'er or she'll have us all at the cheat's end!"

Harriet felt her head being lifted from the straw. Half propping her shoulders against his knees, the youth tied a filthy bandana awkwardly round Harriet's eyes and then laid her back on the mattress. She gave a moan, twisted her head and had the satisfaction of being able to see a fraction of her surroundings beneath the blindfold.

"Water," she croaked. "I must drink."

"She ain't dead then," said the youth.

"It makes no odd if she was. The Nabob don't know that and won't take no chances."

"We ain't gonna *top* 'her?" cried the boy in a fierce whisper. "The Captin said just a few days and then we let 'er go! I ain't in this for no killing."

The older man threw something on the table with a clatter. "Get her a drink. We don't want 'er pegging out before His Nibbs 'as seen her. Watch 'er – and watch yer mouth. I'll get rid of the wheels. An' keep this door locked!"

Harriet heard a lock being turned, the thud of feet going down an open staircase and the scrape of a wooden door being opened and closed somewhere in the depths below. A scratch of a tinder box showed the youth lighting a yellow candle and pouring something from a stone jug into a tankard. In front of him lay a heavy pistol, the small flame from the cheap tallow glinting off its silver facings.

Harriet didn't waste time asking obvious questions; she concentrated on gulping down the small beer that the youth held to her lips.

"Thank you," she gasped and turning her face towards him asked: "How long do you intend to keep me here?"

"Until we get the money. We've kidnapped you," he said with bravado.

"I gathered that," she gasped. "How much ransom did you ask for me?"

"Twenty thousand pounds." There was a touch of awe in the boy's tone.

"*You* won't see much of that," Harriet said faintly.

"It's still a tidy sum between three," the boy protested.

So there were three of them and one of them was a captain. She could not believe what she was hearing but she knew she had to make her move before the others returned.

Her voice cracked a little. "I doubt if *you'll* see any of the ransom. No one can raise that amount at such short notice. And your 'friends', I suspect, would divide any proceeds they do get neatly between them. I don't set much store by *you* getting any money out of this – and beware for your life."

"If there's no money, then it won't be *my* life that's in danger!" The boy pulled the tankard away.

"Let me go now and when the others are taken - as they will be - you can turn King's Evidence against them and get off or receive a much lighter sentence. Don't let this go any further than kidnapping or you'll hang!"

"Shut your noise or I'll gag you again!" He sounded scared.

Harriet licked her lips and nodded. "How long did you give – my father – to raise the money?"

"A coupla days," said the youth sulkily. He went to lower her onto the straw.

"Don't lay me down again. I feel sick. I want to sit up." It was imperative she kept her wits about her. Harriet's head ached abominably yet she was determined not to swoon again. There was a faint odour of spices in the air. The youth propped her against the wooden wall and drew the grey cloak, the treacherous grey cloak, around her.

"Won't you untie me?" she pleaded. "I can't feel my fingers. There's no danger of me escaping with you here. I'll put in a good word for you – my, my cousin is a lawyer."

"No, Miss. It's more than my life's worth to cut them cords. You just rest easy until the others gets back."

Resting easy was impossible. The hard wooden planks of the wall behind her were damp with rot as well as rough with splinters. Somewhere below she heard water slapping against wooden piles. She ached all over from her jolting in the cart and her wrists and ankles chaffed and burned every time she tried to ease them from the cords.

Her mind raced with the thought that this whole plot was the machination of Captain Valentine, bent on acquiring Philippa's money, either through ransom or a forced marriage.

She couldn't see how he was involved with the extortion plots, but supposed that in her befuddled state, she was not making the right connections. Surely he wouldn't harm her, just because she was not Philippa? Oh God, why had she antagonised him? What would he do when he discovered the wrong woman had been kidnapped!

"I'm cold. I can feel a terrible draught," she complained.

"There's a window pane broken," came the grumpy reply. "You can 'ave a blanket."

"Yes, please, anything, I'm so cold. Perhaps you could block the broken pane with something, some rag?" she suggested hopefully as a rough and smelly blanket landed on her legs.

"I 'aint got nuffink to block it with," said the boy.

"Take my stockings; they're no good to me now, they must be in ribbons."

"I don't like to."

"Don't be such an idiot. It's hardly to time for modesty. You must be as cold as I am with that wind from the river whistling through here."

He did not contradict her and after a moment's hesitation she sensed him kneel at her feet. "Gi' us your trotters then," he ordered. Her stockings were around her ankles, her garters loose. He yanked off her shoes and tugged her stockings from her feet. She yelped as he squeezed her bruised flesh, but without the stockings there was a little more leeway in the cords.

She heard the boy busy himself about the window behind her and a little to her left. "There now stop your moaning. I 'aint doing nuffink else for you." He stomped back to his seat.

"You're supposed to take care of me, so the captain said."

"What d'you know of the Captin?"

"More than you think. He's not a very reliable person. So you'd better let me go now – and come with me if you have any sense."

"No fear! I aint doing nuffink until the others get here. I want my share of that money!"

She heard the pistol being taken up and subsided to think.

A little while later Harriet said: "I need to use a chamber pot."

"There's a bucket." The boy sounded embarrassed.

"Then you'd better untie me."

"I daresn't! You'll have to wait."

"Don't be a fool! I presume the bucket is meant for the purpose? At least untie my ankles."

There was a movement and the boy knelt down again to fumble with the cord around her legs. Harriet leaned forward to rub her bruised and numbed feet with her corded hands. "Help me up. I cannot stand alone. I cannot see a thing with this blindfold on. You will have to lead me."

The boy did so. She slumped against him, finding he was no bigger than Jacob. Something told her he was the burglar she had surprised in Brook Street.

He led her slowly across the rough boards, her steps very uncertain. She sensed they had reached a corner. Her bare toes knocked painfully against a wooden pail. She held her wrists out to the lad. "Undo my hands. I cannot manage like this."

"No, Miss. You'll have to do the best you can." He dropped his hold on her arm and stepped away from her.

"Then turn your back," she ordered.

She had no way of knowing whether he did or not but trusted to the remnants of decency he had already shown. Under cover of fumbling with her dress, Harriet adjusted the blindfold to give herself a little more vision. She was in a small room with partition walls, open to the roof of a vast warehouse. A few forgotten file boxes on an otherwise empty bookcase and a spike of dusty dockets showed it had once been a makeshift office. A chequerboard of paler squares revealed twilight through some of the broken window panes. Two of them had been stuffed with her stockings. By the light of a smoking candle she could see a key poking out from the door-lock. The boy was sitting by the desk pointing the pistol at her. It took all her restraint not to jump.

"Lead me back to my mattress," she ordered, holding out her tied wrists. She could see the boy put down the pistol and come forward to steer her by both arms.

In a second Harriet gave him a powerful shove, kicked the bucket over, and saw the boy jump away with a cry of disgust. She flung herself across to the desk to pick up the gun between her roped hands.

The boy, hopping and cursing made a lunge at her. "You f--- doxy! I'll slit yer nose for that! You dirty bitch!"

Harriet yanked her blindfold down to her throat. "Stay where you are," she cried, blinking in the half-light. "Or I will shoot you!" She backed away to the door, both hands gripping the pistol, her fingers working to cock back the hammer. And realised she could not unlock the door and hold the gun steady at the same time.

The boy inched forward muttering curses and threats. They circled each other. Harriet moved away from the door and using the pistol gestured to the boy to come closer.

"Unlock the door!" she ordered.

"Not likely," he said with a wary eye on the gun. "You'll never get away from 'ere. I'd find you in a minute."

"Not if you were dead! If you don't open this door I'll shoot you!"

He leapt and snatched up the vicious looking spike from the desk to lunge at her. The candle toppled and they were in darkness.

Harriet squeezed the trigger, was nearly deafened by the report, and in the flash of powder saw the boy stagger and cry out. Throwing down the gun she turned to the door to wrestle with the key. Panic lent her strength as the key turned in the wards.

Like a deer in flight she ran headlong into the darkness, not knowing how to escape except that instinct drove her as far away from her jailer as possible. She stumbled, fell, was suddenly aware of the darker shadows of bales and boxes left scattered and abandoned. She threw herself behind a crate of forgotten goods.

A good deal of cursing and crying was coming from the far corner of the warehouse. Her own breath came in great nervous sobs.

She risked a peek from behind the crate to get her bearings when her eye caught a patch of grey on the floor at the far end of the floor. It was a moment before she realised it must be the light from an open trap door.

Escape! She limped towards it, the light from the storey below becoming brighter. She saw wooden rungs leading down to freedom and was about to drop to her knees when she stumbled over a heap of sacking. With her hands bound she was unable to save herself and, with a terrified cry, Harriet tumbled headlong through the trap door.

******

Rupert reached Russell Square after dark. Elspeth and Miss Finch surged into the hall at his arrival but one look at his face caused their words of enquiry to die on their lips. Sir Hamish led Darville into the study where his sons and Mr Beaumont had risen, looking towards the door in a tableau of expectation. Haggard and exhausted Rupert willingly took the proffered brandy but declined the arm chair. With his back to the modest fire he turned to face his inquisitors.

He held his hand up to quiet the babble of demands. "I lost them, God forgive me. There were too many carts on the streets to be certain which way they went after they got over London Bridge. I spent hours making enquiries round the docks and the legal quays, but security is tight there. High walls, guards on every entrance, stringent checks on all visitors. I don't know why the East India Company worried about thefts, McAllister; one couldn't get a flea in or out of London docks without someone knowing."

"Maybe, but ten years ago that wasn't the case. And most thieving is done by the watermen themselves on the river, not strangers."

Rupert took a gulp of his brandy. "I know. I went to the Marine Police Office. The Superintendent offered to keep an eye open for anything unusual during their patrols but there's so much movement, so much river traffic, it's impossible. And of course I couldn't take him entirely into my confidence. I searched for as long as I could. Wapping is a warren of sheds, manufactories, customs offices, doss houses. It's impossible to find your way after dark even if one knows the ground."

"Why are you so certain that Miss Larkhill is hidden in some warehouse?" asked Beaumont. He had been told everything that the McAllisters knew but would not be satisfied without proof.

"I'm not, but the smell of spice from the sacking and a few discrete marks is all we've got to go on. What we need is the logo of the shipping line which *may* indicate which wharves the company uses and where Miss Larkhill is being held." Rupert put his brandy glass down on the mantelpiece and drew another fragment of hessian from his pocket. "Have you got those sketches, McAllister?" he said to Andrew. "This might make things clearer. I found it snagged on the bushes near the grotto, going up to the park wall."

Andrew pulled the two sketches from an inner pocket and laid them on his father's desk. Rupert added the third scrap of material. The men jostled for position trying to make some pattern from the pieces in the flickering candle-light.

"Is that a tail? Or an arrow?" asked William, squinting. "What are those figures?"

"Bale numbers," said Beaumont knowledgeably. "They're not important. This daub here may be part of a manufacturer's mark; something of little use in our situation."

Sir Hamish brought a lamp over to the desk and took Rupert's sketches in his hands. "This wavy line - could it be the edge of a wing? A bird perhaps? Of course we don't even know if the shippers were English." He returned the papers to the desk. "The Dutch had the monopoly of the spice trade from the Moluccas for many years but I don't recognise anything of theirs, do you Andrew."

"There's not enough to go on, father." He spoke gently. The men looked disheartened.

"Lloyd's supplied me with the logos of all the shipping companies currently on their books. I could make out nothing for certain.

I daren't think how long it would take us to trace every shipping line that's used the Thames in the past ten years. I've spent a week knocking on the doors of shipping agents as it is and got nowhere."

Rupert left the hearth to pace the room, sounding angry. "I should have begun my search earlier; I should have found Hinton's money for him days ago and may have identified the thieves, then this never would have happened!"

"Don't blame yourself, my boy," soothed Sir Hamish. "You've done half the work without us. We can safely eliminate most of the waterfront already. And you look exhausted. You'll stay the night here, so we can make an early start?"

"No, Sir Hamish; I must go back to Brook Street, to collect a few things." Every man there mentally checked his gun cabinet.

"I don't see what else we can do, except wait," said William flatly. "I take it you want this whole business kept mum, for Harriet's sake?"

"Of course!" said Beaumont and Sir Hamish almost in unison.

"I notified the constables in Dulwich," admitted Beaumont. "But they won't venture beyond their jurisdiction for the next day or two; they're too busy riding about their own parish. You said the trail went cold after London Bridge?"

Rupert nodded confirmation. "It was by the purest luck I traced the cart to Wapping. I lost them after that."

"When we have Harriet home we can easily hush the matter up. People are too engrossed with the queen's death to nose out a private scandal," said Beaumont. "I'll take Harriet to Nice with us – that should suffice."

Sir Hamish did not wish to puncture Beaumont's optimism and merely said. "Then we should plan our campaign for tomorrow, gentlemen."

"We must look further afield," said Rupert. "What about the abandoned jetties and quays further downstream? It's logical that they would keep her somewhere empty and deserted." He looked enquiringly at Andrew.

Andrew nodded slowly. "It's possible. Dozens of small wharves went bankrupt when the London docks were built, yet the sheds and warehouses are still there."

"Where better to go to ground or hide a hostage?"

"By Jove, he's right you know!" said William. "You said the sacking was old."

Andrew's soft voice punctured the moment. "You may well be right, Darville but it would take days to search them all."

"Between us we can at least make a start." Rupert looked exasperated.

"I'm game," said William. "If you think it'll do any good."

"And if it doesn't?" asked Andrew seriously.

Rupert was rigid in his response. "Then we rely on Mr Beaumont to pay the ransom and trust Miss Larkhill is returned to us."

"I need another day to gather all the money together," said Beaumont. "I've got half of the demand – perhaps they'll be satisfied with that in cash."

"Can't you supply the rest in kind?" cried William. "Why not offer them one of your Rajah's rubies in part payment!"

"William, get a grip on yourself," demanded his father.

"The money's all promised," Beaumont said quickly, "But no man can produce twenty thousand pounds at the drop of a hat. The kidnappers have given me until Friday."

"We cannot leave things so long," snapped Rupert. "Think of Harriet in the hands of those vile monsters! One night is bad enough!"

Sir Hamish held up his hand for peace. "A delay is all to the good; it will give us more time for our search and a day to put my own arrangements in place regarding the General Post Office."

"Will Francis Freeing cooperate again? Can we depend on him? He was singularly inept last time," said Andrew.

"We will take it that his agreement still stands but we need not bother such a busy gentleman. Instead I will speak directly to the Chief Clerk, myself."

"Won't someone talk if they see you visiting Lombard Street?" asked William. "Freeling may have aroused suspicions last time."

Rupert broke in with impatience. "The fact that the gang are willing to employ the same methods, even for abduction, means they think the Post Office is still a safe avenue to use."

"And what could be more natural than a Senior Home Office official inviting the Chief Clerk of the General Post Office to luncheon? I hardly think he will refuse. Now gentlemen, if we can get down to the fine details I have hopes that everything will be in place by Friday, after which we will see Harriet safely restored to us and the villains dealt with."

******

Harriet was roused by the sound of angry voices. She had not the strength to open her eyes let alone beg whoever these inconsiderate men were to be quiet; her head hurt so.

She shivered with cold and moaned involuntarily. Someone waved a candle in front of her face but she refused to open her eyelids. She testily told whoever was holding the candle to go away.

It was a while before the fog in her brain started to clear and she sensed she was back in the partitioned room. Her hands and feet were securely tied and totally numb. Her hair had tumbled down and she was lying uncomfortably on her plait. She felt nauseous, chill and terribly thirsty again. The voices were coming from beyond the door.

"Goddammit, it's the wrong one! Can I trust you with nothing!"

Harriet could not place the new voice, educated though it was.

"Honest to gawd Captin, you said the gentry-mort in the grey cloak and the grey cloak it is. It ain't my fault if-"

The protestation was broken off by a scuffle and someone being slammed against the timbers and choked.

"You numbskull! You've lifted the other one, the friend, the companion. We won't get half what we asked, for *her* – if anything at all!"

"Then let's do her in quick and get out o' here!"

"You're a bloody fool! Get downstairs and keep a look out. You've made a real pig's ear of the business between you!"

She heard the heavy man scuttle away and the door open. Someone new came in, wearing shiny boots.

The boy started up with whining excuses. "I'm sorry Captin. She took me by surprise-"

"Can't you even guard a slip of a girl? God you stink! Keep away from me. No wonder she shot you!"

There was a burst of garbled explanations from the boy, cut short by the newcomer. "Give me that candle. And stop bleeding over the desk; we want no evidence left here."

Harriet sensed a figure crouch down beside the straw paillasse. A faint whiff of hair wax almost made her retch. The candle flame wavered in front of her face, providing a momentary warmth.

"Open your eyes Miss Larkhill. I can tell you're awake. You know too much about us to save yourself by keeping your eyes closed." The man spoke very gently.

"Take the candle away," she said pettishly. She was obeyed and Harriet opened her eyes to see a fair young man wearing a bright red swallow-tail coat. His features swam before her eyes; she could not focus properly, but she was shocked to find it was *not* Captain Valentine although there was something faintly familiar about his innocuous face. Her last hope faded.

"Dear, dear. You are not the rubies, or the daughter. What *are* we going to do with you?" asked the young man amicably.

"I don't know. My head hurts. I cannot see properly. I feel sick. You could release me?"

"After all the trouble you've caused? That would never do. Be reasonable, Miss Larkhill, we must have *some* recompense. You came a nasty cropper on the stairs in your foolish attempt to escape. I suspect you have concussion. My – colleague - and I found you. I would advise against you trying to escape again, it could prove fatal."

"Mr Beaumont will pay a ransom for me," she whispered hoarsely. She didn't know whether she was in more danger from the ruffians or this stranger.

"Yes, but how much? Exactly how much do you think you're worth Miss Larkhill?"

Two great tears rolled from beneath Harriet's squeezed lashes. "I don't know." All the fight had gone out of her. She was one mass of pain and was shuddering with shock and terror.

"Not as much as for his daughter, but we won't quibble. However," he said rising agilely to his feet. "I have a feeling that time is of the essence. You don't look at all well Miss Larkhill, so I think we should hurry your friends into paying for your release. You!" The man snapped his fingers in the direction of the boy who came forward, holding his wounded elbow now wrapped in his bandanna. "Give me your knife."

"You're not gonna untie her are you?"

"Far from it," said the man holding out his hand and snapping his fingers again. The boy looked apprehensive and slowly put his hand to his belt. Harriet's eyes widened with fear.

"You cannot kill me!" she gasped trying to push herself into the wall. "They'll hang you! Hang all of you! Sir Hamish will pay! Or Mr Beaumont – just give them time - please!"

"Ah, but that is just what we haven't got." He snatched the knife from the boy's unwilling hand and turned back to her. "I promise - this won't hurt a bit..."

Harriet screamed.

CHAPTER 11   RUPERT TO THE RESCUE

Sir Hamish's plans were exploded by Philipp Beaumont beating on the McAllisters' front door at dawn. Figgis, wig askew, ushered the grim-faced caller into the study. Beaumont refused to relinquish his coat and demanded coffee. Sir Hamish appeared in his dressing gown, a rare crease between his brows.

"What's happened? We were to meet at eight-"

"Ram Kumar found this on the doorstep of Curzon Street." Beaumont handed Sir Hamish a dirty lump of sacking, loosely tied with string.

Sir Hamish opened the wrapping with care. A long brown silky plait tumbled to the desk.

"There's no time to waste," said Beaumont urgently. "There was another note with it. Here, read this!"

Sir Hamish scanned the paper with compressed lips. "I see. We have less than twelve hours to find her." He looked at Beaumont. "That means they're afraid. There's a possibility that they've got wind of Darville's enquiries and intend to make a quick getaway."

"And if they're afraid then they'll panic."

"Which is exactly what we must *not* do." Sir Hamish put down the note with decision.

Figgis re-entered with a tray of coffee, followed by William and Andrew, both in various states of undress.

"Send round to Mr Darville at once, Figgis," ordered Sir Hamish. "Ask him to come to the house immediately, and armed."

The young men examined the note with its ill-scrawled capitals. "He's only asking for five thousand this time," said William. "They know they've got the wrong girl and that insisting on the whole sum, or even half of it, would delay matters. You've raised the five thousand already haven't you, sir?"

Beaumont nodded. He had sunk into an armchair by the dead hearth and was gulping a much-needed coffee. "I've raised double that. I can take it round to Lombard Street this morning. But will you have your man in place by then, Sir Hamish?"

"If you can delay sending the ransom until the last possible moment, say until five-thirty this evening, that will allow me to put more than one agent in place. Meanwhile the young men can continue with their searches. We must make every minute count."

At that moment the door to the study burst open and Rupert stood on the threshold, like an avenging angel.

"What is it? Beaumont – you're here? Forgive me; I couldn't wait until our appointment so I came early, only to meet one of your footmen on the steps with your message."

Figgis effaced himself, full of the latest development for below stairs, grateful that he did not have to deal with an hysterical Annie who was in Curzon Street.

Sir Hamish held out the second ransom note. "Beaumont's man found this on the doorstep this morning."

Rupert, white faced with lack of sleep, took it from Sir Hamish's outstretched hand. He glanced towards the desk, saw the sacking and lunged forward. He stopped at the sight of the braid of hair, as if afraid to touch it: "Dear God, I'll slaughter anyone who's harmed her," he whispered.

"At least we know she's alive!" said William.

"We know no such thing," said Rupert bitingly. "We know only that they had her, or her body, a few hours ago."

"They're watching my house," said Beaumont. "They know every move we make."

"Of course they are! Where else but London would you come to raise the money and to inform Sir Hamish?" Rupert swung away his mind working furiously. He indicated the note. "They say nothing about where and how Miss Larkhill will be returned."

Beaumont looked up suddenly. "You don't think-? They would not-? This is not India after all."

"I think they will be as ruthless as any of your dacoits," said Rupert.

"Then we must keep this from my daughter. She is with Madame de Lessups in Curzon Street and Kumar stands guard."

"It is not Miss Beaumont who is in danger but Harriet!" Rupert said savagely.

"The victim was meant to be Phi- Miss Beaumont. Of course her father is concerned for her safety!" said Andrew leaping to Beaumont's defence.

William looked alarmed at the escalation of hostilities. Catching sight of the young lawyer's face Beaumont said tartly. "Too much like the *Hue and Cry* for your taste, is it my boy?"

"Gentlemen! Gentlemen! Calm yourselves. This squabbling will not help my niece."

"Where are my wits?" said Rupert returning to the desk. Without ceremony he shook the plait from the sacking and held the hessian to his nose. "Nutmeg! Exactly as the first ransom demand. We can but hope that they haven't moved her. And look! Look at this! There's a clear mark."

Andrew crowded Rupert's shoulder as he held up the dirty sacking to the brightening window. A motif of two webbed wings and an open-mouthed beast could be discerned from the dusty open weave.

"Let me try the sketches with it. Of course they may not all be to the same scale but, here, I'll lay them out."

After some shuffling of the papers and the cloth by Andrew, the others came forward.

"A bird of sorts? The phoenix? Is there a shipping line by that name?" ventured Sir Hamish. "If there isn't, there should be."

"Wait! I believe we have the angles wrong." Rupert moved the drawing of an arrow head to the other side of the sacking.

"A triangle above a circle?" queried Andrew. "It's not some variation on your Sign of the Four, is it Darville?"

"No, it is some symbolic animal, I'm certain of it. Look at the beast's head – and if we put this piece of paper there – surely that is a claw?"

"A lion rampant? But then what is this, its tail?" queried William.

"The head looks dragon-like, but of none that I recognise," said Beaumont puzzled. "It's not Chinese or even Burmese."

"No," said Rupert standing back with confidence. "It's Welsh. It's the Celtic red dragon."

"It's not red at all!" protested William.

"Don't be a bigger fool than you can help," said Andrew. He turned to the others. "I believe Darville is right. The more you look at it the more it *does* look like a crude Welsh dragon."

"Now," said Rupert. "What do you know of shipping lines owned by a patriotic Welshman?"

Andrew shrugged his big shoulders. "Nothing. The only Welshman I know is a respectable river pilot by the name of Jenkins. If the line went into receivership more than ten years ago, well, I was still at school. If we at least knew the *name* we might be able to trace its records through old shipping lists but we have no time! And the company – whatever it's called - might have shipped to any of a dozen wharves on the Thames."

Beaumont was staring thoughtfully at the cold ashes in the hearth. "Wait. It may be nothing,but there was a pair of brothers, from Swansea, a set of rogues if ever there was, but damned good sailors. They had to be, with the rotting hulks they put on the water. They'd ship their grandmother for a profit. I only used them once, some years ago, never again-"

"For God's sake, what was the name of the line?" demanded Rupert.

"I'm damned if I can remember! Certainly not the Red Dragon or anything with 'Welsh' in the name. I had fourteen tons of silk ruined because of their careless handling. I cannot remember the wharf."

"Were they spice shippers?"

"They'd ship anything, but spice wasn't my trade. I left all the details to my factor in Canton. I suspect that once John Company's monopoly with India was abandoned they overstretched themselves and went bankrupt, like so many small shipping lines."

Rupert turned to Andrew with determination. "A river pilot you said?"

Andrew jumped. "Yes, Jenkins, but how can he help us?"

"He'll be familiar with all the riverside buildings from Gravesend to the Pool, surely?"

"You're badly out there. Our pilots operate only from Deptford to Greenwich. You're grasping at straws, Darville." Andrew addressed the others. "I think it is about time we called in the police."

There was a general stir of reluctance.

"How long would it take you to bring this Jenkins here?" Sir Hamish asked his son.

"If he's downriver or off duty, I cannot say. It might take all day to find him. If he is at the East India dock, at least two hours," replied Andrew dubiously.

"Send for him, wherever he is. We must dress. I shall put matters in hand regarding the General Post Office. Mr Beaumont will see to the ransom. And you gentlemen can portion out the riverside between you, ready for the search, in case this Mr Jenkins proves less than helpful."

In the event, Mr Jenkins proved more than helpful. Apprehensive at first to be called from his duties at the East India docks, he was only too pleased to do young Mr McAllister's bidding. He was overawed by the Russell Square surroundings but at least it was not the great offices of the Company in Leadenhall Street.

Andrew assured him this was a private matter even though there were four other gentlemen in the room. Sir Hamish's languid demeanour did not fool him; something serious was afoot but the chink of sovereigns and the memory of Harriet's pleasant face soothed his misgivings. He received no reply to his enquiries after Miss Larkhill and, thinking he had been presumptuous, confined his curiosity to the task in hand.

He looked at the sacking and the drawings, tapping the arrangement with his rolled up cap. "Oh, yes, indeed sir. I remember the old Cymru line well."

There was a grunt of recognition from Beaumont.

The river pilot continued: "They had no more than three ships at any one time – real sieves they were - they didn't last long as a company o' course."

"Where did they berth?" asked Rupert.

"Bowen's Wharf. Derelict now, it is."

"Did they use any other wharves?"

"No-o." The pilot sounded amused. "Bowen's Wharf was owned by some relation of theirs. They never used any other. We Welsh tend to stick together, see."

"Can you tell us where this Bowen's Wharf is?" said Sir Hamish, rising from his desk. "I have a map of the river here. Kindly point out its location as near as you can."

The pilot, well used to maps instantly pointed to a settlement a little more than a mile downstream from the East India Docks. A tiny cluster of buildings, unnamed, lay at the river's edge. "Here sir. Course there's not much left of it now but a rotting jetty and some old sheds. The warehouse is still standing though. I pass it every day. I haven't given it a thought for years."

The men exchanged significant looks. Andrew was about to usher the pilot out with a suitable reward when Mr Jenkins said: "You'll pardon me gentlemen, but were you thinking of visiting the place?"

"That's really is no concern of yours, Mr Jenkins," said Sir Hamish at his most urbane.

"Well," said Jenkins, looking anxiously at Andrew. "I only ask, 'cos if you *were,* then I'd advise going by river. You'll get there much quicker, see."

******

Andrew and Rupert rowed with energy. They had hired a boat at Temple Stairs and the two men had thrown their heart into their task. Andrew's brute strength gave them speed but he was surprised at Darville's proficiency until he remembered that Rupert had rowed at Cambridge. They shot under London Bridge into the Pool with its flock of tall-masted ships, jockeying for a berth. Mr Jenkins steered the boat between the gigantic clippers and smoking steam launches thronging the water. There was little time to admire the majestic buildings on the bank or be awestruck by the walls of the London docks. They were too busy dodging the ferries and lighters all working the tide. The flotsam and jetsam impeded their passage and the stink of the river was appalling. Round the great loop of the Thames they rowed, passing the heavily guarded naval dockyard at Deptford.

"Easy sir, steady on the stroke, we got a way to go yet. The tide's still in our favour but you don't want to exhaust yourself before we get there." Mr Jenkins steered them expertly round a buoy.

It had been arranged that William would join them at Bowen's Wharf in his tilbury. No one had dared to voice the reason it might be needed. If Beaumont heard nothing of the rescue attempt, he was to wait until five-thirty before taking the parcel of money to Lombard Street, accompanied by Ram Kumar as body guard. Sir Hamish disappeared, arranging to meet the Nabob in a coffee house opposite the General Post Office as soon as the ransom had been delivered.

It was midday by the time the river traffic thinned and the wide grey water was edged with nothing but willows and scrubby fields. Cows came down to drink and stared as the small craft pulled steadily downstream. Every now and then a broken jetty protruded from the muddy bank. Clusters of tumbledown sheds housed rotting boats. Swans rose honking from the reeds. They met two or three coal barges tacking up river, but most shipping preferred to wait downstream for the change of tide.

"Now then gents. Bowen's Wharf – or what's left of it – is around this next bend. There's a jetty and I'll tie the boat up there and wait for you," said Jenkins. Sir Hamish had made it clear that he was merely a useful accessory. Much as he liked Mr Andrew McAllister, the river pilot had no desire to be involved in the mysterious, and probably dangerous, doings of the quality.

The men rested on their oars for a moment. "Let me go in first McAllister," said Rupert, wiping the sweat from his forehead. They had stripped off their coats and cravats.

"What if they've posted a look-out? I'd be happier to do this in the dark." Andrew's shirt was sticking to his broad shoulders.

"So would I, but we have no choice. Time is against us. If they *are* expecting a search party, they'll hardly think we'll come by river. I trust William won't be fool enough to blunder in and scare them into doing anything – stupid."

They were about to take up their oars again when Mr Jenkins advised: "Let the tide take you, gently now, just the occasional stroke. If I'd known what was afoot I'd have brought my fishing rod. No one suspects three gentlemen fishing, now do they?"

Mr Jenkins put his finger to his lips as the boat rose and fell. The tide took them inevitably downstream. The sounds of the riverbank were soothing but nothing could prevent Rupert twisting round to see Bowen's wharf appearing from beyond the bend.

A derelict three-storey building rose between poplar trees. Each storey had a wooden double door flanked by small-paned windows.

A crane pulley was pinioned to the apex of the building. A cluster of low sheds littered the yard around it. There was no sign of life. The place looked deserted.

A few silent strokes brought the boat under the shelter of the jetty.

"What if she's not here?" whispered Andrew as Mr Jenkins tied the painter to a ring in one of the piles.

"She must be. There's no logical reason to think she isn't." Rupert searched among their coats at the bottom of the boat and pulled out his pistol. "Arm yourself, and get to the other side of the warehouse. I'll try to take them unawares from this side, but I may need back up."

Andrew put his hand on his friend's arm. "You don't know how many there are! We've no idea where they've hidden her! You're not a well man. How do you expect to break in?"

Rupert inched his head out from under the jetty and eyed the building. "With the maximum of surprise I hope." He pulled himself agilely out of the boat to climb the slimy bank and made a sprint for the undergrowth. Andrew followed, his time at Jackson's sparring saloon making him light on his feet for a big man. Mr Jenkins watched them go with mixed envy and apprehension.

Rupert crouched in the brambles under the trees, surveying the scene. "If I can get on the roof then I can swing myself down to the top storey, break in and take them unawares," he whispered. His cat's eyes darted about, appraising their surroundings and the opportunities they offered.

"Are you mad! You've not got the weight to break through those wooden doors, and they're certain to be barred from the inside."

"I know. I have other plans." Rupert looked into Andrew's appalled face. "It's perfectly feasible I assure you. I'll use the pulley. I've worked out all the angles."

"Angles be damned! How do you know Harriet's even *in* there. She could be anywhere in the building or even in the outhouses."

"On the balance of probabilities they'll hide her somewhere she can't easily escape from, most likely the top storey of the warehouse. It's instinctive to hide a captive as far away from the track to the road as possible. If it was night we might have the chance of seeing a candle glow. But in lieu of that I'll wager those are Harriet's stockings, or what's left of them, blowing in the breeze."

"Stockings?" Andrew jerked his head up to examine the windows. "You can't possibly tell from this distance, they could just be rags."

"Very white and clean ones, which shows *someone* has been in residence recently, and I believe is still in there." Rupert sounded buoyant. "I know she's there, Andrew."

"And if you're right - what about the climb! You can't get up on the roof, you'll fall! I don't want two dead bodies on my hands!"

"Don't disturb yourself; my time on the *Neptune* rid me of any vertigo. I did all my astronomical measurements from the rigging or the crow's nest. Height holds no fears for me. I only pray I can climb it without being heard. Surprise is of the essence." He looked at the patchy roof tiles of the warehouse. "If I dislodge anything, let's hope they think it's birds. Now, let me go. Follow me in when I give you a signal."

"I'll get round to the other side and have a nose about. I'll wait until you're on the roof," said Andrew. "Once I see you safely up there, I'll try to get inside, quietly. Though I still think it's madness. Why can't we rush them together?"

"You yourself said we don't know how many there are. The main door is probably locked and may be guarded. I can't risk them harming Harriet before we rescue her. Dead she can't identify them and they may well have a good escape route planned."

"We should wait for William," said Andrew.

"There's no time. We should be able to trap them between us; *you* can take on at least two yourself! Imagine if it were Miss Beaumont inside there."

Andrew cocked his pistol and patted Rupert on the shoulder. "You're right, let's go." He was heartened to feel his friend's powerful muscles under the fine lawn.

Rupert ran softly to the row of barrels lined up against a flat shed and pulled out a coil of rope he had spotted earlier. He pulled off his boots and stockings. Hefting the rope over one shoulder he jumped onto the barrels and climbed onto the shed roof adjacent to the sheer side of the tall warehouse.

He paused for breath, struggling to make a lasso from the stiff tarred rope. His hands were shaking. And then began the long job of throwing the rope up over the roof of the warehouse to loop around an elaborate rusting pole which once held a lantern at the yard end of the building. Every time the loop missed and fell back noisily Rupert flattened his ear to the wall to pick up the sound of anyone inside. Sweat trickled from his armpits.

At the fifth attempt the rope caught and held. Rupert tested it with his weight, felt doubtful but decided there was no time to waste. He climbed like a cat from broken brick to missing plank, part walking up the wall, part pulling himself up by his arms and feet twisted round the rope. He was weaker than he thought and had done no physical activity like this for more than a year. The rowing had already tired him; his muscles started to smart in protest. All the time he prayed that no one would hear him.

At the second storey he reached a small window on the side of the warehouse. For a blessed moment he rested his weight on the sill and peered in. He could see nothing of the dark interior but decided he could not risk being heard. For the last twenty feet he pulled himself up by the rope alone not daring to use his feet on the walls. By the time he reached the eaves he was soaked with perspiration and his shoulders burnt with the effort.

He clutched the guttering with relief only to nearly cry aloud when it came away in his hands. He dangled over the outbuildings below for what seemed like an eternity. Lunging for the rope again, inch by inch he crawled up the angle of the roof to the ridge, waiting for a slate to slip and crash to the ground. The pistol hampered him; he pulled it out and tucked it in his belt behind him. After an age he found himself clinging to the curved roof ridge. He lay gasping for breath.

Below, he caught sight of Andrew's red hair. He was creeping across the yard to a clump of rotting bales, on top of which lay the figure of a young lad, one arm awkwardly twisted. The boy had been set to watch outside. Exhausted by fear, pain and loss of blood, he had fallen asleep in the noonday sun. Church clocks chimed faintly through the haze over the City.

Rupert watched Andrew drag the boy off the bales, clamp a hand over his mouth and put a pistol to his head. Andrew looked up at the warehouse roof, saw Rupert and jerked his head in the direction of the boat. Rupert nodded and pointed to himself and then to the river end of the roof. He was committed. Very gingerly, he levered himself to his knees and then stood upright. He judged it would be too noisy to crawl along the roof ridge. He swayed precariously in the breeze. His wet shirt clung to him. With arms outstretched he began to walk along the curved ridge. Andrew averted his gaze, glad to concentrate on getting the boy to the boat as quickly as possible.

Rupert was tempted to run, as his shipmates had run along the yardarms, but there were no sheets or shrouds to hold on to here and he was out of practise. Yet he daren't risk being seen by any passing boat. He forced himself to take his time, putting one foot carefully in front of the other. His feet were tender after more than a year in shoes and his toes no longer accustomed to gripping narrow surfaces. His jaw muscles ached in concentration. He knew better than to look directly down and instead stared at the river, brown and choppy and mercifully empty – but for how long? A mile or so to his right he could imagine the bristle of masts in the East India docks. To his left, yet another bend in the widening Thames. The breeze cooled his sweating body but was dangerously fickle.

With legs like quicksand he reached the gable end, dropped to his knees and slid forward on his stomach. The warmth of the roof slates gave his aching body momentary comfort. He peered over the edge. Beneath the jetty Jenkins had brought the boat to the bank and was bundling the boy under the thwarts. Andrew was busy gagging him with his neckcloth.

Rupert dare not waste time. Before long the tide would be on the turn downriver bringing a billow of sails around the bend and he would be in full sight. He squinted down at the crane riveted to the brickwork below him. The hinges were rusted, the rope of the pulley frayed. If he hung from the ironwork his body would be parallel with the wooden cargo doors. He would have to swing himself to one side to reach the window and, to keep the element of surprise, make the whole manoeuvre in one fell swoop.

Andrew scampered up the bank and disappeared round the front of the warehouse. Rupert sat up, dried his sweating hands on his thighs and swung his legs off the roof. With a prayer he let himself drop, twisted to his right and gripped the protruding arm of the crane. For a precarious few seconds he hung there like a monkey on stick while the iron took his weight. It had supported far heavier cargoes than a man, but it did not move from its ninety degree angle.

He began to swing himself backwards and forwards, his arms straining in their sockets. He could feel the hinge moving under the momentum, the red iron filings flaking around his head. If only the creaking and groaning did not alert the occupants of the top storey, he might just do it.

With a supreme effort he moved his hands further out along the arm of the crane until he reached the pulley. If he could position the crane arm thirty degrees or so closer to the wall, the block and tackle would bring him directly opposite the window. The hinge at the wall seemed to be moving more freely now. He needed to lower himself onto the pulley and trust the old ropes would hold. There was only one way to find out.

With his last effort he dropped onto the block and tackle with a forward momentum. The hinge swung free, the ropes unravelled above his head. For a moment he looked like a corpse hanging in the wind until with a twist he jerked his body forward and arrowed his feet in the direction of the window.

Rupert crashed through the panes in a shower of splintered glass and rotten woodwork. He fell awkwardly and rolled, winded, among the shards. A figure swayed up from the desk with a roar of rage and groped for the pistol lying among a welter of gin bottles. Rupert rose to one knee, narrowed his eyes against the gloom and pulled his pistol from behind him.

The lumbering figure swore and aimed. Someone screamed. Rupert instinctively twisted sideways as the ball whistled overhead to embed itself in the woodwork behind him. The man tossed his pistol aside and whipped a wicked-looking blade from his belt. He charged. Rupert fired. The man stopped in his tracks with a look of surprise, swore, groaned and dropped to his knees, a great red stain spreading across his chest. After a heart-stopping silence Rupert got up and slowly walked toward the kneeling kidnapper. He casually pushed the brute to the ground with his foot.

Andrew came pounding up the open stairs and raced across the top storey. He crashed in through the flimsy door. "Darville! Are you killed? Is Harriet here? I never thought you'd do it! God what a mess! I heard the window go when I was trying to break down the main door. In the end I had to lift it off its hinges."

Rupert became conscious of a huddled figure curled on a mattress to his right. He threw down his pistol and sank to his knees by the paillasse.

"Harriet! Dear God, Harriet!"

"I'm so glad you've come," she wept, groping at his shirt. "Please, please take me home!"

He stared at her tied hands and feet. "McAllister, give me a knife, quick – there on the floor behind you."

Andrew drew one from his belt. "Use this one; I took it off the boy."

While Rupert cut the cords and rocked Harriet in his arms, Andrew surveyed the scene. He went over to the body. "This one's dead, more's the pity. We've only got the boy and he's not the ring leader. I hope my father and Beaumont have caught the real culprit."

"Let's get Harriet out of here." Rupert wrapped her in the grey cloak. As he struggled to lift her, a searing pain shot through his ribs. He stifled a groan and shifted her more comfortably in his arms.

"Let me, dear fellow," said Andrew. "You're bleeding and look about done in. You've cut your feet to ribbons on that glass."

"No, I have her now," said Rupert not to be deprived of his prize.

Getting Harriet down the open staircase was difficult. She was too weak and confused to climb down alone and Andrew's bulk precluded manoeuvring her between them. In the end Rupert put her over his shoulder and, with Andrew guarding her head, they at last reached the open air and sunshine.

It was difficult to know who looked worse: Rupert, white with exhaustion and smeared with blood and iron or Harriet, concussed and bruised and shorn. Rupert laid her on the warm bales recently occupied by the boy.

Mr Jenkins appeared with a belaying pin in his hand. "I heard all the noise and thought you might need me to lend a hand? *Yesu Crist!* Is that the young lady I met in the Burlington arcade? Your cousin, is it, Mr McAllister? What's happened to her?"

Harriet closed her eyes against the sun and drifted off into unconsciousness. Andrew and Rupert were reluctant to speak.

"With the German lady, she was. *Very* helpful. Looks a bit poorly now, isn't it?"

"Indeed Mr Jenkins, I'm wondering if it would be quicker and easier for the young lady if we took her back in your boat. I feel we should get her to a doctor at once," said Andrew, wondering what was keeping William and the tilbury.

Rupert pulled Andrew to one side. "We have to deal with the – remains." He jerked his head towards the warehouse.

"Surely we must inform the police? Abduction is a serious matter, Darville."

"I thought the families wanted this whole business kept quiet," hissed Rupert. He had a terrifying feeling of *déjà vu*. Everything seemed hysterically unreal in the cruel daylight.

Andrew hesitated. "What about the boy?"

"He saw nothing, he knows nothing. Your father can deal with him." He looked at Mr Jenkins who was leaning over Harriet solicitously and chaffing her hands. "I don't think we'll have any trouble from Mr Jenkins."

"What do you suggest we do?" asked Andrew.

"You go back in the boat with Harriet and the boy. It's quicker and smoother than by road. The tide will be with you soon. Take her to Russell Square and get word to your father. I'll wait for William and – clear up here."

Andrew was torn. Now the adventure was over, the seriousness of the consequences hit him with force. He was a law-abiding young man yet he did not want to taint a promising career with scandal and he held the family honour in high esteem. Rupert Darville, after all, seemed a bit of a wild card. Lacking any other ideas he was forced to acquiesce. After a few words with Mr Jenkins, Andrew scooped up Harriet and followed the pilot to the river bank.

Rupert steeled himself not to go with them. Instead he put his head in his hands, jerked upright with a sudden spasm and proceeded to walk about the place to plan his next move. Twenty minutes later William came bowling into the yard in his tilbury, with Jacob at his side.

"Darville! Good cheer! Thank God I've found the wretched place at last. I got misdirected by some old biddy. No one seems to have heard of the place. Have I missed it all? Where's that brother of mine?" He threw the reins to Jacob and jumped down from the vehicle. "Your boy insisted on coming with me. He and Harriet's maid have been haunting Russell Square all morning. Did you find her? Where *is* Harriet?"

"Gone back to London by boat with Andrew and Mr Jenkins."

"All taken care of? No harm done, then?" asked William looking about him.

Rupert snorted. "Harriet's been through the mill, I've broken a rib and we have a dead body on our hands." He jerked his head towards the warehouse.

William stared. "Whose?"

"One of the kidnappers. The other was a gutter rat Andrew caught about the place. He's taking him to your father."

"*You* shot the one inside I suppose?"

"Naturally."

"Damme, you're cool Darville, I'll give you that. Not that I blame you!" he added hastily, "but it puts us in a devil of a fix."

"Not if you do what I say." He took William to one side. "Let Jacob water and tend your horses, there's no need to involve him. You and I will see there's no evidence left in the warehouse."

Inside, Rupert led the way to the top floor and across the scatter of boxes and detritus of the trade. "Be careful not to trip," he warned.

"It *does* smell of spice in here," said William. "You were quite right in your guesswork."

"It wasn't a guess. I knew she'd be here. It was only a question of deduction."

William held his peace. He did gasp when he saw the mayhem in the partitioned office. The room was flooded with sunlight now the window lay in fragments. Rupert picked up his pistol and stuck it in his waist.

"We'll leave the rogue's pistol there, to show he fired it."

"Where's your coat and boots?" asked William, averting his gaze from the oozing corpse on the floor. He had never seen a dead body before and didn't want to see one now.

"My boots are hidden between some barrels at the side of the warehouse. I must retrieve them. My coat is in the boat with Andrew. I hope he had the sense to use it as a pillow for Miss Larkhill."

"Oh, never fear, my brother is a very knight errant with the ladies. I bet he don't like this result at all! Mind your feet, Darville, they're bleeding already and there's a deuced lot of glass about. How did it happen?"

Rupert cautiously picked up two torn white streamers from the debris and put them in his trouser pocket. "Can you see anything more of Harriet's belongings here? We must find her shoes."

William looked around, stepped fastidiously over the blood pooling on the floor and rescued them from the bookshelf. He stuffed one in each coat pocket.

"What do we do with the body?" he asked anxiously.

"Nothing."

"*Nothing?*"

"I'm in no condition to dig a grave, shallow or otherwise."

William had no desire to volunteer. "We could hide him in one of the sheds, no one would find him."

"Why move him at all? From the map, the nearest habitation is over a mile away which means the shots would not have been heard – especially as they were fired inside. No one has come to investigate and even if they do, we'll bar the main door behind us when we leave, if your brother hasn't destroyed it entirely. Someone might go poking round the sheds one day but they won't investigate a warehouse securely locked and barred."

"Could we dump the body in the river?"

"If we dropped it from the end of the jetty it would float back in on the next tide. A fisherman would find it and report it to the river police."

"We could weigh the body down."

"Think man! We have no boat to drop it in the middle of the estuary. Besides I want as little to do with it as possible. The more we complicate matters, the more chance there is of being caught."

"We could burn the place! Destroy the body!"

"Certainly, if you wish to attract the maximum attention. There's saltpetre in some of the barrels but even *I* don't know how to make explosives in twenty minutes."

William still looked anxious. "I feel we should do *something*!"

Rupert led William back outside.

"We'll have our hands full repairing the main door. Then I'll bar it from the inside and get out – the way I got in."

"Are you sure it wouldn't be better to report this to the authorities? As a member of the Bar and a Member of Parliament it is my duty-"

Rupert stopped at the foot of the wooden stairs and turned to face William. "Lost your nerve McAllister? I believe Beaumont was right about you." He stopped himself and then went on encouragingly. "You don't know your father very well do you? Believe me, he'll be the first person to go along with my plan. Would you drive him into his grave with the scandal?

Think what it would do to your mother and the rest of the family – let alone Harriet."

William still looked confused, all his bravado punctured.

Rupert felt deathly tired but tried a different tack. "Where's your sense of adventure? Your Scottish blood? You're not averse to wallowing in the gory details of the underworld – now you've had a brush with the real thing. Believe me, that man would have slit Harriet's throat! We'll leave the body to the elements and the birds."

William look embarrassed. "But murder, Darville-"

"If your conscience is bothering you, I shot the brute in self-defence and no jury would convict on the evidence we have."

William was still uneasy but could see no way out of the impasse without implicating himself. "Very well, but I don't like it."

"Neither do I, but needs must. Now get Jacob over here and don't say a word in front of him."

Between the three of them they lifted the heavy wooden door back on its hinges. Rupert bit his lip against the stabbing in his ribs. He turned the key in the lock on the inside and found the heavy cross bar to slot into place. The effort made him double over with pain. Slowly he once more climbed the open ladders to the top storey, dreading what lay ahead.

He took a last look about the place and made for the window opening. The block and tackle hung directly opposite the aperture like a gallows. With great care he balanced himself on the window rim, gripping the sides with white-knuckled hands. He jumped, hit the pulley with his chest and threw his arms around it. The rope rattled through the grooves, unravelling under his weight as he plummeted to the ground. Six feet above the wharf the rope snapped, sending Rupert crashing to the boards.

The impact brought William and Jacob tearing round to the riverside of the building.

"God Almighty! Did you jump?"

Rupert squinted up through his almond eyes at their frightened faces. "Not quite," he croaked. "But you're going to have to do the rest."

Under Rupert's direction, Jacob yanked the slip knot to release the lasso tied around the lantern pole. They threw the rope back among the barrels and retrieved Rupert's boots. William hurled the warehouse key into the river from the end of the jetty. The broken pulley and frayed ropes were left where they had fallen, seeming casualties of time and nature.

Jacob bound his master's ribs with his own neckcloth and William drove sedately back to London. He left Rupert in Brook Street without a second's thought; wanting only to get away and discover if his father had caught the instigator of the plot.

******

Andrew returned to Russell Square with his motley crew. At Temple Stairs they claimed that Miss Larkhill was seasick after her boat ride and lifted her fainting into a hackney carriage. Mr Jenkins kept Andrew's pistol trained on the boy though he was as injured as Harriet. At Russell Square Harriet was carried upstairs to be cared for by Lady McAllister and Annie who burst into tears at the sight of her young mistress.

McAllister marched the youth into the study. Andrew gave his father a brief resume of events in French, which startled his father and terrified the boy even more. Mr Jenkins was left kicking his heels in the hall until Figgis invited him into his private pantry to partake of some blue ruin in return for information.

The boy, one Martin Straw of unknown age and no known parentage, confessed to everything at once. He named a Nicholas Byrd as the instigator of the extortion scheme. "It's the Captin you want. I didn'ave no choice gov'ner. Bruiser Jack made me do it. He said he'd cut me. I ain't done nuffink like this before. The lady said she'd put in a good word for me! I didn 'urt her none!"

A sceptical Sir Hamish had hardly dipped his pen before it all came tumbling out: the Bixby diamonds, the German Cross, Hinton's Velasquez, the Darville emeralds. There may have been more but Sir Hamish held up a hand to stem the torrent of words. He looked at the clock.

"Andrew, go round to Curzon Street immediately and tell Beaumont to deliver the ransom in an hour. We have a name now. My men will observe and follow. We need to catch the villain red-handed with the proceeds."

"And then shall I join you?"

"No, I want you to stay with the Beaumont ladies. We have your career to consider and by the look of your clothes you have done enough already. Well done, sir."

Andrew disappeared, much to the relief of the boy. Big men frightened him. Better the devil of Bruiser Jack than the unknown swell who talked foreign. The women of the quality were bad enough. His elbow hurt something chronic. He felt faint again now that he had told all he knew, and the old gent was ignoring him.

"You may sit, before you fall down," said Sir Hamish scratching away with his pen. The boy sat tentatively on the edge of a chair, ostentatiously wiping his nose and his eyes on the back of his hand. "Keep silent until I have finished." After a few moments, Sir Hamish rang for Edward and charged him to deliver a note to the Chief Clerk, Lombard Street General Post Office.

That done, Sir Hamish steepled his fingers and looked balefully at the snivelling youth.

"And how exactly did 'the Captain' come to know about all these - opportunities?"

The boy looked surprised. "The Captin knows all about the gentry, he's a toff."

"And where does this 'toff' live?"

"Dunno. Bruiser Jack allus met him at the Blue Boar."

"As I daresay you did yourself. Did you receive any money from this man Nicholas Byrd?"

"No, sir! I ain't no receiver!"

"I mean, what happened to the proceeds of your extortion – your thieving?"

"The Captin said it was too dangerous to spend all that money at once. He'd keep it safe until the 'eat was off then we'd share it all between us and take ship for 'Merica."

"How trusting," said Sir Hamish laconically. "Did Bruiser Jack make no objection to this plan?"

"No, sir. He gave me a coin or two to be going on with, but it was a *good* plan. This was the last job, 'e said and we was to be paid off at the end of the week. Bruiser Jack said if ever the Captin looked like he'd double-cross us he'd cut out 'is lights."

Sir Hamish rang the bell. James appeared. "Take this urchin to the coal cellar and lock him in. Make sure he can't escape. When the doctor arrives to attend Miss Harriet, send him to me first before you take him up to the ladies."

"Very good, sir." The footman took the boy's collar gingerly between finger and thumb and propelled him to the door.

"By the by," said Sir Hamish turning to the boy. "Why is Mr Byrd called 'Captain'?"

The lad looked nonplussed. "Dunno, sir. He was summink in the navy, I 'eard tell."

An hour later, Sir Hamish entered Sam's coffee house and, peering through a haze of tobacco smoke, took his seat next to the Nabob in the bow window.

"Ah, Beaumont, I see your invaluable servant has kept a table free for us," he said acknowledging Ram Kumar. "Not the most inconspicuous of bodyguards, but his presence has served to convince any watcher that you kept your part of the bargain. I take it you dispatched the parcel safely?"

"Half an hour ago. I am awash with coffee and have read *The Morning Post* three times over. What happens now?" His button eyes darted across the street to the busy General Post Office.

Sir Hamish signalled to a waiter and ordered a pot of lapsang souchong. Newspapers and pamphlets were scattered across the table. Everyone was talking, scribbling, disputing. They would not be overheard in the smoky jangling din.

"I'm afraid we have to wait until six o'clock when our 'friend' finishes his shift. We know exactly who is the culprit and I have sent a note to that effect to the Chief Clerk who will point him out to my man on the inside. The Chief Clerk has kindly supplied us with the reprobate's address."

"How did you get your man in?"

"Who takes any notice of a sweeper?"

Beaumont acknowledged this with an approving grunt. "And then?"

"When my man sees the villain take, secrete, pass on, or do whatever he does with the parcel to get it out of the building, he will alert a second of my men to follow him."

"Then why are *we* here? I should get back to my daughter, I have left her in Madame de Lessups house. And my niece? How is *she*? No prevarication - your son tried to delude my womenfolk but I know Harriet couldn't have escaped totally unharmed."

"Shaken, bruised, still a little concussed but the doctor agrees, not materially injured. We thought it better to say that she had a fall down the stairs. She is upset about her hair of course." Sir Hamish peeled off his gloves and laid them with his beaver hat on the table, "but that will grow."

"Thank God! When this is all over, she must come and live with my daughter and myself. I will not allow my niece to live unprotected. I want her back under my roof."

Sir Hamish recognised this rudeness as genuine anxiety and diplomatically replied: "I agree entirely my dear sir, but what Harriet will have to say to the matter I cannot think. She will be as much surprised – and charmed no doubt – to learn of your family connection as I was. However, I would not advise springing your delightful news on her just yet; leave her to the ministrations of the ladies."

Sir Hamish took a sip from his tea and took out his watch. "We have just enough time for me to tell you about what I learnt from the young shaver in the crew. And to discuss exactly how we are to hush the matter up."

Twenty minutes later a shabby song seller pushed through the crowds thronging the pavement, tapped on the window of the coffee house and held a dirty ballad sheet up to the bottle-glass pane.

Sir Hamish nodded, tossed a coin from his waistcoat onto the wooden table and picked up his hat and gloves.

"If you want to be in at the kill, Beaumont, and I suspect you do, then you will join me in my carriage round the corner. Mr Byrd is on his way to his lodgings with your five thousand pounds in his pocket."

The McAllister town carriage crept along the edge of the pavement, following the pedlar more by his lusty singing than his appearance. The crowds heaved and swayed but somewhere ahead a fair-haired young man in the red uniform of the post office strode purposefully on towards Aldgate, a canvas knapsack slung across his shoulder.

The crowd gradually thinned and the pedlar fell back to warn Sir Hamish to halt at the end of the street of respectable lodging houses. With a nod of apology to the occupants the pedlar dumped his bag of ballads on the floor of the carriage.

"Give us a minute or so, sirs, then follow us to Number 42. We should have him nicely trussed for you." He stripped off his long coat, squashed his hat into a different shape and pulled down the brim. In a moment he had resumed his stroll behind the young man. A few paces after came a tall well-built footman, seemingly on some errand for his master.

Sir Hamish took out his watch. The Nabob muttered something about wishing he had brought his pistols.

"Your man is well armed," commented Sir Hamish looking at Kumar's dagger.

"This is not the neighbourhood where I would expect such a thief to be living," said Beaumont impatient to be active. He scanned the row of terraced houses with pretensions to gentility. "Are you certain the address is correct?"

"I told you, Nicholas Byrd is a respectable man – outwardly. He holds a position as a supervisor in the Sorting Office, hence his authority to commandeer any parcel he wishes. He is well-spoken, moderately educated - so the Chief Clerk informs me; I'd say not bad progress for a Coram's Field child."

"Blood will out," muttered the Nabob. "There's something rotten there."

"My wife would agree with you," said Sir Hamish not the least bit surprised at such snobbery from a self-made entrepreneur. He pulled out his watch. "I judge we have given my men enough time." He knocked on the roof of the carriage and called out. "Round the corner, Pole. 42 Whitechapel High Street, quick as you can."

The house door was open and swinging drunkenly on its hinges. The balladeer and the footman held a fair, dishevelled-looking young man in a red coat on the well-scrubbed doorstep.

His arms were tightly pinioned behind him. He was protesting vehemently. At the sight of Beaumont and Sir Hamish he fell silent.

"No trouble sir." The agent handed over a knife and a smart looking pistol. "We jumped him smooth enough, but the missus is in hysterics."

"Mrs? Is there a wife?" asked Sir Hamish in dismay.

"No sir; his landlady. Carrying on something awful, she is."

"Have you got the money? The parcel?" demanded Beaumont.

"Yessir. Looks like he was stashing it away behind the fireplace. Didn't have no time to do a proper search-"

"Leave that to us. Put him in the carriage. The Indian gentlemen will take care of him. That will be all. Report to me tomorrow. Well done." And with a few coins Sir Hamish dismissed his men.

Inside the house he found the landlady looking indignant and frightened at the same time, the maid-of-all-work supporting her nobly. She was overwhelmed by the lawyer's sudden appearance.

"Who are *you*? Wot you doing with my lodger? 'Es the most respectable young man I've ever 'ad. Never a bit o' trouble wiv the rent and clean as a whistle!"

Sir Hamish reassured the lady in his smoothest tones that the young gentleman was needed only for questioning by the authorities. He would doubtless be returned to her shortly.

"Like a son, 'e is to me! Wot's 'e supposed to 'ave done?"

Sir Hamish could hear Beaumont moving about upstairs. "Perhaps been a little light-fingered shall we say?" He pulled out his pocket book and ostentatiously laid three crisp bank notes on the table.

"For you madam. In compensation for any disturbance, damage, loss of rent and in the complete confidence that you would never wish this house to be associated with anything so heinous as criminal activity."

The landlady, at least grasping the sense of Sir Hamish's words, cried: "This is a respectable 'ouse, this is! We ain't no criminals 'ere!"

"Of course not, dear lady. And God forbid that anyone would ever accuse you of using the premises for the receipt of stolen goods."

At that moment Beaumont appeared in the doorway the canvas bag in one hand and a soot-smeared sack in the other. "Got it, McAllister, and a lot more besides. There was a loose brick in the chimney breast and I levered the rest out with a poker."

The landlady collapsed onto a wooden chair. The maid-of-all-work looked terrified.

"Wot's that? I ain't never seen it before! Take the dirty thing outa 'ere! Wot's he been doing to my upstairs front?"

"If you mean Mr Byrd, hiding his loot in it. I wonder if a judge would believe you were in ignorance – being that Mr Byrd was 'like a son to you'," mused Sir Hamish.

The landlady burst into tears. "A thief! I never want to see 'im again! Such a charmer he was. Wot about my good name?"

Sir Hamish, content that he had frightened the good woman into perpetual silence, added another banknote to the pile.

In the carriage, Ram Kumar held his dagger to Byrd's ribs. It was agreed that Byrd should be kept as far away from Harriet and the ladies as possible. Philippa was with Madame de Lessups. There was little talk on the journey to Beaumont's house.

"Do you admit you are an extortioner and a kidnapper?" demanded Beaumont unable to contain himself any longer. He leaned forward, kicking the sack at his foot. "We have the proof."

"You won't get any confession out of me, and you won't dare bring a prosecution," returned the young man sullenly. "And tell this clown to put his knife away. If I don't make contact with my men tonight, they'll kill Miss Larkhill."

Kumar jabbed the knife towards Byrd's ribs. Beaumont shook his head.

"Miss Larkhill is safe and well. She was discovered this afternoon and is returned to her friends."

"I don't believe you!"

"She was rescued from Bowen's Wharf," Sir Hamish elucidated. "Your boy, Straw, is in custody, and Bruiser Jack has – disappeared. Though happily not before telling us everything about you and your schemes."

Byrd stared out of the window obviously thinking hard. The carriage turned into Curzon Street. In the scramble to descend he wrenched himself out of Kumar's grasp and knocking Beaumont to the ground with his bound fists, made a break for it. Within yards of the carriage the Bengali warrior threw himself on Byrd, bringing him down with a crash on the cobbles and beating him into submission. With his arms tied, Byrd was unable to resist and was manhandled into the house and once more thrown to the ground. Only Beaumont's curt order stopped his servant from slitting Byrd's throat.

Beaumont excused himself to find his valet and begged Sir Hamish to make use of his book room. Kumar, his former negligence redeemed, tied Byrd securely to a chair. Sir Hamish dismissed him and eyed his captive over a welcome glass of madeira.

"It's no use threatening me with the law," said Byrd, licking the trickle of blood from his mouth. "Kidnapping is only a misdemeanour not a felony. I may not even be imprisoned. The only person to suffer will be Miss Larkhill herself and your family. You may as well let me go now."

"Ah the benefits of an education," said Sir Hamish, somewhat surprised at his captive's legal knowledge. "You have an admirable grasp of the situation as regards abduction, young man. But you seem to have forgotten all about the robberies and the extortion. You will certainly be imprisoned, if not transported for life for those crimes. Let alone theft from His Majesty's mail service, which will be dealt with very harshly, I can assure you."

"No one will bring charges against me." Byrd looked slyly under his lids.

"You seem very confident of that."

Byrd said nothing and Sir Hamish continued. "Even if you're right and I am forced to release you, what guarantee do I have that you'll cease your criminal activities and disappear into the woodwork?"

"Give me five thousand pounds and I'll take passage to America."

"*I* have not got five thousand pounds," said Sir Hamish, steepling his fingers.

"The Nabob has. Give me back the ransom he paid for the companion and I swear I'll leave the country within the week."

"You are, of course, a man of your word. However, I must consult with Mr Beaumont first. But I feel I should remind you that you were easy enough to track this time and will be so again. I am a powerful man with influential friends."

"And that's why you'll let me go," sneered Byrd.

Sir Hamish pondered theatrically. "Perhaps I should just lay information against you with the local magistrate, a very good friend incidentally. You would be in Newgate within the hour. Not a very pleasant prospect to a man of your 'refinement', I assure you. Or have you had experience of His Majesty's jails before? Unfortunately our current justice system is so very *slow*. Being a legal adviser to the Home Office, I am sadly aware of this. I *could* expedite the case, or I could not. I would only have to mention the words 'state security' and the case would be heard *in camera*; there'd be no publicity at all and you would be incarcerated for – ooh – a *very* long time."

Byrd shifted uncomfortably on his seat. He seemed to come to some conclusion.

"It'll be the worse for you and your family if you don't give me the money and let me go."

"In what way?" asked Sir Hamish sweetly.

Byrd told him.

With reluctance, Sir Hamish brokered a deal.

******

When Sir Hamish returned the bulk of the Velasquez ransom, Hinton immediately enquired after Rupert's whereabouts.

Sir Hamish looked sorrowful. "A recurrence of the malaria, I fear. He is being well-cared for and I think it would be wisest to leave him to recover in his own time. Visitors can be so exhausting."

"But it *is* Darville I have to thank for the return of the money?"

"Undoubtedly. Others were involved but, without his persistence, no one's money would have been recovered. You were not the only dupe of this gang. However, I am confident I can count on your discretion. Nothing would be gained by noising any of this abroad. You are leaving for Hinton Parva shortly I understand?"

"Yes, but I must see Darville first – to find out exactly what happened – to thank him!"

"I advise against it. He would not thank you for visiting him until he is fully himself again. I expect he will go down to Larkhill in a week or two to get his strength back, and you may convey your appreciation then. He particularly does not want any of the ladies to be told of this latest recurrence of fever – you know how they fuss."

When Sir Hamish had taken his leave, Will showed Catherine the parcel of bank notes. "They're the same numbers – bar a handful of missing notes. Darville's exhausted himself in this business but that damned lawyer has warned me off! He had the temerity to suggest I should not see Rupert or make any enquiries at all! He tried to fob me off with some excuse that the ladies would be upset if they knew Rupert was ailing. There's something else afoot, I'm certain!"

"Oh Will, we're going home in two days! We've had enough mysteries! Think of my condition!" She clung to his arm. "If Sir Hamish choses to be secretive then he must have a good reason. You must remember, we were not the only people to be robbed. Great Names might be involved. He is obviously trying to be discreet. The McAllisters will take care of Rupert – they are related. They most likely don't want Miss Larkhill informed in case she rushes off to nurse him again."

"Miss Larkhill? Harriet knows nothing about it; she's taken a bad toss and fallen down the stairs, tripped on her gown or something. She's back in Russell Square."

"Goodness! I must go and see her at once!"

"Splendid! And see what you can find out about Rupert."

******

Sir Hamish sat at Harriet's bedside. The narrow white room was cheerful with flowers, a fire burned in the grate; the warm spell of weather had given way to a grey tail end of summer. Harriet was propped on her pillows, a ruched bed-jacket around her shoulders, her shorn hair covered by a French muslin cap adorned with cherry ribbons. Her beloved trinkets lay scattered across the counterpane. She stroked them gently, her hands soft and white after six weeks' of idleness. The rope burns on her wrists were bandaged.

Sir Hamish took one hand in his. "So you see my dear, the matter is all settled. Byrd is paid off and will be out of the country in a fortnight. Mr Beaumont has him under his eye until then and has arranged an 'escort' for the voyage. The boy Straw has been sent down to Castle Elrick; my son Angus will make a decent man of him. And Bruiser Jack has disappeared off the face of the Earth."

Harriet still looked troubled.

"You have only to turn your mind to your recovery. Mr Beaumont will take you home whenever you are ready. I have informed Sir John and Miss Humble of your – accident. They will not look for you for a while yet."

"Indeed I cannot return home with a face full of bruises. Could you think of nothing better than to have me fall downstairs? I feel such a fool." She sounded half amused half sorrowful.

"If one has to tell a lie then it is best to make it as near the truth as possible. Now tell me, when will you allow Andrew and William to visit you? They are most anxious to see for themselves how you fare."

"Lady McAllister regulates my visitors," said Harriet. So far no gentleman had been allowed in. Harriet was grateful but could have done with a change from Miss Finch weeping copiously over her pillow.

"Quite right. You must not tire yourself. I fear I have indulged myself too long, you are looking quite pale," he said giving her hand a pat before rising.

"I wish I was!" smiled Harriet wanly. She had made Annie give her a hand mirror that morning and had been horrified by the reflection of purple bruises and grazed cheeks.

When news got about that Miss Larkhill had caught her heel on her dress and fallen headlong down stairs – no one knew precisely whose stairs were to blame – a surprising amount of callers came to enquire after her recovery.

Mortimer Shawcross sent perfume pastilles for the sickroom. Lord Everard arrived with an elaborate peacock-blue fan to cool the invalid, if she were to develop a fever, he said.

Lady McAllister was tempted to allow him into the sickroom but propriety won the day and she wanted him in her drawing room as long as possible. Instead Harriet was amused by his implied abhorrence of the cheap green cotton fan in the note accompanying his gift.

Young friends came with bonbons and magazines. Mrs Somerville and Miss Snoddie called with puzzles from the newspaper to entertain her, but Harriet's head was still too sore and her concentration too weak to appreciate them. Even Viscount Frodingham sent a basket of peaches. Philippa and Madame de Lessups called every day with fresh flowers or a picture book for her amusement. She heard nothing from Rupert.

After a few days, Harriet felt ready to come downstairs for a little while. She was making progress, though she had lost weight and suffered badly from nightmares. Her head no longer pained her but her mind exhausted itself with thinking alone in her room. Andrew escorted her down on his arm, Annie hovering solicitously behind.

Alone with Andrew for a few moments, Harriet asked quickly. "How is Mr Darville? I would like to thank him for his part in my rescue."

Not wishing to worry the still fragile Harriet, Andrew said precisely the wrong thing. "Oh, never worry your head about Darville, he's in fine fettle. He's busy with all his natural philosopher friends, or he's gone up to Cambridge to search out some papers. I hear he's planning on going on another expedition."

This was old news, but to have someone as reliable as Andrew confirm it made the prediction more certain. Harriet would have been horrified to know that Rupert was confined to his rooms nursing three broken ribs, multiple cuts to his body and a chronic malarial weakness. The McAllisters had agreed to keep this from her.

"Has that man Byrd left the country?" she asked, resolutely turning her mind away from Rupert.

Andrew flushed. "In a week he'll never trouble us again. And Captain Valentine will go too, back to Calcutta on the same ship," said Andrew, anxious to change the subject. "So we shall all be at peace."

She smiled up at him, as he tucked a cushion behind her. "Have you spoken to Philippa yet?"

Andrew flushed again. "No. I did not think the moment right. So much more of greater importance has been happening." He bent over to bring a little table to the sofa.

"Nothing is more important than your happiness!"

Andrew stood straight. "I would have things done correctly. I was never more relieved than when Miss Beaumont ended our foolish – but quite innocent – correspondence. I would not wish to deceive her father in any way. Her exquisite sensitivity in realising my dilemma and returning my letters, proves what an angel she is."

Harriet smiled. "I'm sure you will gain your reward in time. And be assured you will always have an ally in me."

"Miss Larkhill, Harriet – for you are truly one of the family now-"

At that moment Lady Elspeth returned, Cicero under her arm. "Ah, how good to see you comfortably settled my dear. Look who has called on us! Mrs Hinton!"

Catherine Hinton swept in, glowing with good health and all concern for her dear friend.

"I came as soon as I heard! Sir Hamish called this morning with something for my husband and Will has only just thought to give me the news of your accident. If it is not dogs or horses, husbands barely speak over the breakfast table. Gentlemen have no notion of what is important How came you to fall down stairs?"

She sat down in a flurry of silks and fashionable flounces. Harriet's anxious face relaxed at the knowledge that this worldly young matron was not in the secret of her abduction.

Catherine looked at Harriet's lacy cap. "Did you cut your head badly? Your hair will soon grow, but then you'll make short hair all the rage again; just think of Lady Caroline Lamb and her curls!"

"Harriet is too young to know to whom you refer," said Lady McAllister stiffly. "A woman of scandalous morals and indifferent literary talent."

It was hard to know which was the worst crime in Lady McAllister's eyes. Her condemnation made Harriet smile for the first time in a week.

Realising this was a most unfortunate topic, Catherine hurried on. "We're leaving for Wiltshire tomorrow. There's such a lot to do. You will forgive me if I do not stay above ten minutes, Miss Larkhill – and I would not wish to tire you. You must be inundated with visitors."

"Lord Everard called yesterday and stayed quite half-an-hour," said Lady McAllister.

"What an honour! Have you heard? He has miraculously come about again! He has won a huge sum on the lottery and can pay off all his debts, though my husband says he'll never be able to live within his means."

Lady McAllister sniffed. She would brook no criticism of her favourite but felt the public lottery was a 'low' form of gambling. "My son William informed us of Lord Everard's good fortune."

"To my shame I have come empty handed but you must allow me to take messages home to Larkhill for you," said Catherine turning to the invalid. "I'll make Mr Hinton drive me over himself to see Sir John."

"Thank you, yes. If you could assure my old governess, Miss Humble, that I may *look* unsightly but there is no major harm done and I hope to be able to travel in a week."

Catherine doubted this but after a few more minutes of talk said: "Well, what are we to make of all the Larkhill people coming to grief in London? Perhaps we should cleave to a quiet life in the country. The sooner we are all home the better!"

"I trust *you* have not come to grief while you have been in town, Mrs Hinton?" asked Lady McAllister peering over her embroidery.

"Why, no – I only meant – my husband did not make such a handsome profit on the Velasquez as we had hoped." She looked a little embarrassed.

"Who else has come to grief?" asked Harriet warily.

"Er – I referred only to Mr Darville and his attack of malarial fever."

"But he is quite recovered now."

"Indeed." It seemed Miss Larkhill too had been kept in the dark as to Rupert's relapse. Harriet looked so frail that she did not wonder at it.

Lady McAllister stirred restlessly and rose. "We cannot have Miss Larkhill developing a fever. This is her first day out of her room and we must take every care of her."

Catherine took the hint and, with further good wishes for Harriet's speedy recovery, departed.

Harriet fell into a reverie. She accepted that Catherine could not talk of the Velasquez extortion plot in front of Lady McAllister, and she seemed to have no knowledge of the abduction, but her reluctance to mention Rupert was odd. It could only be that Mrs Hinton had heard of the shameful bets laid in Whites and was politely avoiding the topic. Harriet could not blame Rupert for leaving town. A tinge of red slowly suffused Harriet's cheeks, highlighting her mottled bruises.

"My dear, are you well?" asked Lady McAllister, for once noticing someone apart from herself. "Susan, fetch Miss Larkhill a glass of water, she looks very hot." Before Harriet could prevent her, Lady McAllister had laid a hand on her bruised forehead. "There, I predicted a fever, I am always right. How thoughtful of Lord Everard to bring you a fan."

******

A few days later Harriet made her way to Sir Hamish's study unaided. Conversation died as she opened the door. Harriet caught sight of Rupert, stopped as if stricken and then tried to withdraw. "I beg your pardon gentlemen, I was not aware there was anyone in here."

William rose hesitantly to welcome her. "Harriet, please. Do come and join us." The others looked embarrassed. "We need your thoughts on this matter, a woman's eye to settle things. I hope *you* can convince Darville here that now the villains are caught we can all rest easy in our beds."

Andrew frowned at his brother. "We do not wish to distress Miss Larkhill any further by recalling unpleasant episodes which she would rather forget. May I escort you to your room, ma'am?"

"I came only to find a book, but I will help you if I can, though my mind is far from clear. I find. Dr Yardley's mixture makes my head swim."

"Is my mother not bearing you company?" asked Andrew. "You should not be left alone. You'll forgive me if I say that you look far from well."

Harriet was momentarily conscious of her lace cap and thin frame but she replied evenly: "Your mother has been called to Miss Finch who is somewhat agitated today."

Harriet sat down among the men. Rupert, silent, did not take his eyes from her. He looked as pale as she did.

"I am glad to see you, Mr Darville. I thought you were in Cambridge. I am so pleased you have recovered from your – exertions. I will not embarrass you by offering you my heartfelt thanks, even among such friends. I hope you know how I truly feel."

"To see you safe and recovered is all the thanks I need."

William was anxious to fill the awkward silence. "This kidnappin' has affected the whole household but if there are to be no prosecutions then there will be no trial and no fuss. Why are we all on the fidget? Father will keep it quiet. Beaumont will cover anyone's losses – if there are any. He won't want a scandal around his daughter. I'll be hanged why we're still worryin' at it like a terrier."

Harriet looked from one man to the other and said slowly: "So you think there is something- unfinished - about the business?"

"Darville's got a bee in his bonnet that there's another party involved. We've been rehearsing the events for this past hour. Even *his* brain cannot connect all the pieces. He's convinced we are missin' somethin' or someone. A fresh eye such as yours must prove he is wrong. You were involved as much as anyone."

Harriet cast a wan smile towards Rupert. "What exactly troubles you about the affair? It seems to be a matter of extortion for money, plain and simple. And in my case, merely mistaken identity."

"How did Byrd know which houses to break into?" Rupert asked suddenly. "*That* is what will provide the key to who is really responsible for these crimes. We have to assume some degree of inside knowledge.

Someone must have supplied Byrd with the information and may even have been the instigator of the robberies. Who knew the whereabouts of the items that were stolen? We cannot find a common factor among our suspects."

"Miss Larkhill should be in her bed or have Miss Beaumont for company," persisted Andrew. "We must not tease her with this."

"Miss Larkhill was the most affected," said Rupert bluntly. "Let her decide if we should pursue the matter or let sleeping dogs lie."

"I suppose you mean Captain Valentine to be under suspicion," she said with a slight smile at Andrew.

"Naturally!" jumped in William, unable to resist playing devil's advocate. "He was here when Maria Bixby spoke about her diamonds, he saw Hinton's Velasquez on its easel, let alone the other knick-knacks in Hinton's collection. He was in want of money – we all know that! But then he's come up trumps by offering to escort Byrd to India."

"He could still be the informant," said Rupert. "And now we have put one criminal in charge of another! Both men could have been implicated."

Harriet gently shook her head. "No, no, you are mistaken. Captain Valentine could be tied to two of the incidents, but certainly not all. Have you considered the emeralds? *Anyone* watching Brook Street or questioning the servants might have easily discovered that Lady Darville and your brother had unexpectedly returned to Ireland – providing a perfect opportunity to rob the house. They expected your rooms to be empty. Captain Valentine did not have a particular knowledge of your family's movements."

There were nods of agreement from the brothers.

"He was also not aware of the Ravensburg Cross, at least I do not think so; nothing that we know of connects him to it. And he was firmly told by Mr Beaumont that the Rajah's rubies were a myth. Why burgle a house for a fairy tale? And I doubt if he was aware that Hibiscus Lodge would be unoccupied that afternoon. No, Captain Valentine is not your ringleader - or informer. He might have been loose-tongued in his cups and, even if he was, I believe there was no mischief intended."

She paused for a moment before adding: "As Captain Valentine has sailed for his regiment in Bengal, there is no point in pursuing this avenue further."

"There, Miss Larkhill confirms everything that we thought," said William in triumph.

"What about the abduction?" said Rupert, Harriet's smile left her face but Rupert continued relentlessly. "Byrd and his accomplices admit that

Miss Beaumont was their intended victim. Valentine is the obvious candidate to want to blackmail her into marriage."

"Too obvious, and too horrible, I would think. A kidnapping for money yes, but a forced marriage is no marriage at all. And Andrew would have made Miss Beaumont a widow within the day, am I not right?"

Andrew smacked a fist into his palm. "Within the hour! I almost wish the blackguard *were* involved. I would have squeezed the life out of him for his villainy! Knocking him down was too easy! It sticks in my throat that we are dependent on him for seeing Byrd safely away."

"Mr Beaumont is very clever, I think," said Harriet. "Two birds with one stone? If you'll forgive the pun. Captain Valentine will never let Byrd get the better of him."

Andrew shrugged. "Perhaps. But Harriet is right; even you Darville must see that he would never be allowed to get away with such a travesty."

Rupert's said dryly: "Your brain seems remarkably clear today, Miss Larkhill." She inclined her head in acknowledgment.

"What if it were – not for marriage at all – but seduction," persisted William.

Andrew jumped to his feet. "William, for God's sake, leave it!"

Harriet looked up. "You mean rape, Mr McAllister? I do not think Richard Valentine would risk the death penalty for money – yes William I do listen to you when you talk legal sense. He had easier ways to come by it." She stated her case. "Captain Valentine was conceited enough to believe Miss Beaumont had a decided partiality for him. He only had to work a little harder on her affections; despite her friends' efforts to warn her of the dangers. Abduction would not be necessary – an elopement would be enough. She's such an innocent that she *might* have succumbed to his blandishments, in the absence of a more desirable suitor. But happily she did not. Besides, at no point did the kidnappers mention a fourth party."

Rupert shifted in his chair, the bandages on his ribs tightening. Andrew swung away to the mantle shelf and turned his back on the room. The men were silent for a few moments.

Rupert said: "And what of Lord Everard, Miss Larkhill. What are your views on that pink of the *ton*?"

She sighed. "Ah, the despised Lord Everard. I guessed he would be another of your suspects."

Rupert thought for a moment and, ticking each item off on his strong fingers, said: "One: It was Lord Everard's idea for Lady Bixby to hide her diamonds in the chandelier. Two: He knew the Ravensburg Cross needed to be taken for repair – you told me so yourself Miss Larkhill."

She nodded in confirmation.

Darville continued: "Three: he had seen Will Hinton's treasures with his own eyes. And fourthly, I daresay like everyone else he had heard the stories about Mr Beaumont's rubies. The attempt on the emeralds I cannot account for, but he knows enough about jewels to estimate their value."

Harriet gave Rupert a cool stare. "A point in his favour I would have thought."

"You *cannot* believe that Everard was in league with the thieves?" asked William ignoring this interchange. "He is far too *nice* in his connections."

"According to you he was a desperate man on the edge of ruin – why not him as well as any other?" said Rupert.

Harriet said mildly: "I admit that even *I* thought it might be possible, for a little while. My maid and I met Lord Everard in the most insalubrious area of London." Here she went a little pink.

"Good Lord, how did that come about?" demanded William.

"I got lost," she admitted. "We had just had the unfortunate experience of seeing Captain Valentine ejected from a public house in St Giles and Lord Everard providentially rescued us. It was only a little while later that I wondered if he himself could have been in the area for nefarious purposes. The reasons he gave me for being there were most plausible - and honourable - but he did not wish me to mention our encounter to anyone. Later, I wondered if he had been visiting a 'fence'."

Andrew turned round from the fireplace. "Miss Larkhill! Where did you learn such a term!"

"From your brother," replied Harriet innocently. "Why? Is it not correct?"

Rupert laughed.

"But then I considered that he would have sent one of his accomplices into the rookeries to dispose of the 'loot'," she continued. "I must say I am so pleased that he has won a fortune on the lottery and has come about again. For only a quarter of a ticket! I fear he will forever be a speculator." She hoped that would be the end of it.

"And the abduction, Miss Larkhill?" persisted William. "As a lawyer, I am duty bound to ask you the same question of our second subject as I did of our first. Let's nail this now. Why could Everard not have wanted to kidnap Miss Beaumont? You must admit that he was deuced attentive."

"Yes, but in the most avuncular way. I saw them together several times in Hibiscus Lodge and in Curzon Street. I believe his kindness to Philippa was meant to ingratiate himself with her father. It was Mr Beaumont's ability to lend Lord Everard substantial sums that attracted him to the family." She also suspected that was his motivation for his kindness to herself.

"Also, I have not been able to ascertain if he was aware of Miss Beaumont's movements – I mean her habit of solitary reading in the afternoon in the grotto. Be that as it may," she said on a note of finality. "I do not believe that Lord Everard is the type of gentleman that will ever be married. Mr Beaumont recognised this even if Philippa did not; he did not suggest that Philippa invite Lord Everard to any social event, which he would have done if he hoped Everard might eventually become his son-in-law."

Stunned silence held the room in thrall until Andrew said flatly. "Then we have run out of suspects. You had better abandon your theory, Darville."

"I agree, Mr McAllister," said Harriet. "It is common sense to conclude that there is no other party involved. The boy told me himself there were only three members of the gang. I understand that all the houses were watched by Byrd and his two accomplices. Therefore all the information on the jewels and their owners could have been easily obtained by observation, reading the Court columns, or by listening to servants' gossip."

The brothers loudly endorsed her reasoning, but Rupert was not convinced. "I beg your pardon, Miss Larkhill, and it pains me to insist, McAllister," said Rupert firmly, "but I still say there is a connection to this house."

"Fiddlesticks!" said Harriet with something of her old spirit. "If that were so there is only one person who was involved in *some* way or other with *all* these thefts."

"Who," said Rupert sharply.

"Me," said Harriet.

Rupert's eyes narrowed to slits.

"My dear Miss Larkhill!" expostulated Andrew.

"By George she's right y'know!" said William, ready for the argument.

"Harriet, this is not a game," warned Rupert.

"I'm well aware of that Mr Darville; my own peace of mind rests on putting an end to such speculation. I wish to sleep at nights."

Rupert looked embarrassed.

William steepled his fingers in front of him in his father's unconscious pose. "You're not confessin' to bein' an accomplice of this crew, are you Miss Larkhill? I cannot for the life of me think why you would be."

Harriet shrugged. "I have been chronically in want of money for years, Mr Darville will testify to that. Why should I not pass information along to the thieves in return for a 'cut of the swag'?"

Andrew groaned and put his head in his hands. "How long are we to continue with this farce?"

Harriet looked kindly on him. "Mr McAllister, I propose myself as a culprit only to prove to Mr Darville how ridiculous and dangerous is this idea of there being anyone else involved." She looked from one man to the next. "I fear I cannot help you any further. Now if you will excuse me-"

"What are you saying Harriet?" asked Rupert. "It is plain you have thought about this puzzle as much as we have."

Harriet resolutely closed her lips.

"You know who it is don't you?" There was an edge to his voice.

"No. I know nothing at all," she replied with strict accuracy.

"But you suspect there is *someone* in Russell Square connected with this business."

"You think the servants are involved?" William exclaimed in downright disbelief. "But they have not been privy to half that has been happening, and certainly to nothing beyond the house."

Harriet rose. "Forgive me gentlemen, I feel a little tired. Such mental exertions have brought on my headache again. I will leave you to your fruitless cogitations and advise you to accept that you have captured all possible culprits."

Andrew leapt to his feet. "Forgive *us,* Miss Larkhill. It was unpardonable of us to distress you so. Shall I ring for your maid?"

"No, no. I will go to my room and lie down for a little. I shall be quite recovered for dinner. Will we have the pleasure of your company Mr Darville?

"I regret I am engaged elsewhere, Miss Larkhill."

Harriet gave a deep curtsey as the men rose from their seats, and left the room.

"Well, there we are, Darville" said William, reaching for the decanter. "We should follow a woman's instinct and give up looking for anyone else. I said so all along."

"I'll concede that Miss Larkhill is correct in thinking that Byrd was the main instigator of the robberies. Your father said the man admitted to every extortion attempt. He'd be quick enough to fix the blame on someone else if there were an absent ringleader. But I still hold that he had inside information."

Andrew bristled. "I resent that Darville! Are you insinuating that William or I -?"

"Of course not!" said Rupert impatiently. "There's something we've missed, and Harriet knows what it is. I cannot understand her reticence – it is not like her. She cannot be protecting anyone!"

"The young woman has suffered a great shock to her nerves and wishes to put the whole matter to rest. I think we must respect her wishes. If you insist on taking the matter any further then I suggest that you speak to my father." With that Andrew left the room with a sharp slam of the door.

"He don't get his dander up often, my brother, but you've certainly ruffled his feathers there," said William to an entirely unmoved Rupert. "My father has hushed the matter up very nicely. What *is* the point of probin' any further? *Harriet* don't want you to."

Rupert, still cogitating, at last said reluctantly: "Someone once told me that we should always listen to Harriet. Perhaps he was right."

CHAPTER 12   LARKHILL MANOR

The Beaumonts took Harriet home a few days later. The McAllisters were genuinely sorry to lose her; even Lady McAllister behaved well at Harriet's departure.

"My dear Miss Larkhill, Harriet. You must visit us again whenever you wish – if you can bear to sleep under this roof after your shocking ordeal."

"My 'shocking ordeal' will soon be forgotten," soothed Harriet. "I see Russell Square as a place of refuge and could not have wished for kinder nursing."

"There will always be a home for you here. You have become quite like a daughter to me. Susan, give Miss Larkhill your salts; she may have need of them on the journey."

Miss Finch, cowering at the back of the group scurried forward, fumbling in her reticule. She pressed the bottle into Harriet's hand saying. "Anything, Miss Larkhill! Anything I can do for you! I would never have- if I'd only known-" and dissolved into incoherent tears. Lady McAllister swept the companion aside, removed her *pince nez* and pecked Harriet on both cheeks like a nodding stork.

Neither Harriet nor Lady McAllister had been told of the Nabob's relationship to Harriet; Sir Hamish wished the girl to recover before such news was sprung on her and did not trust to his wife's discretion. Sir Hamish reconciled himself with the thought that he would be seeing Harriet in a week or two, after the Beaumonts had given her the good news and sailed for Nice.

The Beaumont travelling coach was well-sprung and had every convenience. The servants and baggage followed behind. Cocooned in cushions and rugs Harriet dozed most of the journey away until their arrival at the Castle Inn in Marlborough where the Nabob had commandeered the best rooms.

Her welcome at Larkhill Manor was a tearful affair. Miss Humble produced the best linen and silverware and had spruced the place up for visitors. Dinner was simple, wholesome food directly from the farm, served on the best Spode. The Nabob didn't complain, saying such dishes reminded him of his nursery days and surprisingly began to reminisce about his childhood in Kent. The claret, as ever, was good.

Young Clem behaved beautifully, being allowed to join the adults for dessert. Which was more than could be said of Captain Blood, who frightened Philippa into fits whenever she went to the nursery.

The following day, Philippa explored the house and grounds glorying in the elaborately carved minstrel gallery and the gothic arches of the priory ruins. "How romantic. Just like *Ivanhoe*. How could you ever bear to leave this place," she sighed in raptures.

Harriet laughed. "I don't think I ever could, but for entirely different reasons, I assure you."

The young ladies walked into Larkhill and were greeted by curious friends and neighbours, all wanting to witness Miss Larkhill's recovery and be introduced to her wealthy friend. At least a dozen times Miss Beaumont regretted that she and her papa were taking ship for Nice within a few days. And no, Miss Larkhill was not going to accompany them, despite all their persuasion.

Mr Beaumont spent the afternoon with Sir John, leaving that old gentleman confused but somehow brighter. Harriet went up the Grand Staircase for her prescribed afternoon nap while Mr Beaumont took his daughter for a long walk in the fading rose garden.

When Harriet awoke she found Philippa sitting on her bed, looking very excited.

"Harriet, thank goodness you're awake! I thought you would sleep forever."

"It's Doctor Yardley's mixture. I believe I must stop taking it now I'm home. Fresh air is good enough to put me to sleep. What is it? You look as though you're going to burst." Harriet had already relapsed into Young Clem's vulgarity.

"I have something wonderful to tell you," said Philippa, clasping her hands. "We are *cousins!*"

Harriet's brow furrowed. "What *do* you mean? You haven't secretly married Andrew have you?" she asked looking confused.

"No, no, you don't understand! Papa told me this afternoon, in the rose garden. He has confirmed it with your uncle's papers – he had some of his own of course from Ceylon, but this settles the matter – though I daresay there'll have to be lawyers and affidavits and things, but Sir Hamish can do all that for you can't he? He's your uncle too. What a lot of uncles you have!"

"Philippa, Philippa! I beg of you, stop!" Harriet pulled herself to a sitting position and took her friend's hands between her own. "Start from the beginning and tell me what your papa said."

Philippa took a deep breath. "He said he had proof that your mama was Emily Beaumont, his sister who died in Trincomalee from the cholera."

Harriet looked thoughtful. "Well, my mama certainly was Emily Beaumont and did die of cholera in Ceylon, but how does it make her your Papa's sister?"

Philippa talked of registers and enquiry agents and correspondence with the Baptist Missionary Society. "Everything Papa knows or has found out matches what your Uncle John has. There is a box in your library, Papa said, with all kinds of old letters and proofs that Henry Larkhill, M.A. Oxon. married Emily Beaumont of Wisdon Park, Kent. Wisdon Park is where Papa was born, and he had a sister Emily. All the dates match!"

Harriet went very quiet, and then striving to get up said: "I must go to my uncle at once."

Philippa stood back, concerned that Harriet had not gone into ecstasies at the news. "Papa is in the library."

"I mean my Uncle John," said Harriet brusquely. "He will be upset, confused. I must go to him."

She found her uncle hazy on the facts, but not the least concerned by the matter. A thin gentleman had arrived claiming to be Emily's brother – he was not certain which Emily the gentleman referred to. Was Henry married? He had not seen him in such a long while. The thin gentleman implied that there was no need to worry about the upkeep of the manor or Harriet's future – not that he was worrying at all, damned impertinence, there was always plenty of money in the chest.

Harriet was at least thankful that Sir John had not been distressed by the news. How she felt herself, she did not know. In a daze she went in search of Mr Beaumont.

Beaumont was his usual terse self. Completely without emotion he explained his search and conclusions in a business-like way, and Harriet was grateful. He intended to provide her with a generous annual income, a dowry and promised her something in his will.

She spread her hands in speechless thanks. "And this is all because of something Andrew said? I did not know, I really did not expect - cannot accept such generosity."

"It's what I would do for any member of my family. Unfortunately I have only my daughter – and now a niece." He closed a ledger. "Sir Hamish will explain how the settlements will work when he comes down. He is already fully in my confidence. I understand you have been used to rely on him in the past."

Harriet nodded, her head whirling. Was she the last to know of her good fortune? Did Rupert know? She dare not ask.

"It will be such a relief not to have to worry about the estate – for Young Clem's sake," she said mechanically.

"I do this for you, Miss Larkhill – Harriet - not for your cousin's boy."

"Yes, of course – but there really is no need to do *anything* for me. I have no claim on you – I had no *idea* that we were related in any way!"

"No, you have no claim upon me, but I held your mother in great affection and now I find my daughter professes the same sentiments towards you, her cousin. It suits my purpose to see you comfortably provided for."

Harriet said no more; she needed time to absorb everything that had been said.

Mr Beaumont continued. "By the look of your books, you have kept the accounts very well, but the farms need investment. I know nothing about farming but one must keep up with the times or go under."

"Those are private ledgers, sir!"

"Ah, I forget, you are used to running the place directly. I gather you have no steward? I will find you a trustworthy man, or rather McAllister will find one for you."

"Thank you sir, but I prefer to choose my own employees."

"You are my niece and until you marry, it is more suitable to allow me to order your affairs."

"I do not wish to appear ungrateful, sir, and indeed I cannot thank you enough for your generosity of intent, but I am of age and well able to undertake my own responsibilities."

She realised she wanted this watchful man to show her some sign of affection, to tell her something of her mother. She repressed a desire to ask how much he had paid for her ransom. Did he care for her at all or was this gift what he thought he owed to his name?

Swallowing her pride she continued: "I will of course consult you on all matters of importance and always use Sir Hamish as my legal adviser."

He looked at her face. "Very well. I can see that this has been a great surprise to you. It will take some time for you to grow used to the idea of being a young woman of fortune and while I would wish you to live under my own roof, I concede that this for the meantime is your home. Nevertheless when I myself undertake matrimony and set up a permanent establishment in London, I expect you to live under my roof."

The interval between the Beaumonts' departure for Southampton and the arrival of Mr Tamar and Sir Hamish was not long. September was full upon them when Sir Hamish's hired coach crunched up the gravel drive. Mr Tamar chose to stay at the Three Crowns; he did not wish to be forever under his client's eye and found he discovered useful information in the public bar.

Much of the visit to the manor was concerned with financial business. Sir Hamish brought with him a sheaf of complicated documents which needed to be read and signed, all witnessed by Sir Charles Durrington and Miss Humble.

Sir Charles once more regretted the loss of Harriet as his daughter-in-law. Twenty thousand in the Funds was not to be sneezed at and there was handsome capital investment set aside for the estate.

"Someone will snap her up before the year is out, mark my words," he said to his wife.

"Harriet has more sense than to fall for a fortune hunter. I had hopes of her finding a beau in London but Juliana tells me Harriet has been very tight-lipped on the subject. Except for a Mr Shawcross who had some hand in helping her buy perfume, or was it snuff? I must say, the gentleman shows remarkably good taste," she said, dabbing the jasmine scent on her wrist. "Now, my dear, you've just time to go up to the nursery to kiss Georgiana goodnight before the dinner gong."

******

Sitting in the oak parlour one evening, Sir Hamish twirled the stem of his rummer between his long fingers. Mr Tamar had departed looking more cheerful after studying Sir John's Grand Junction Canal share certificates, The squire had been settled for the night and Miss Humble was reading to Young Clem.

"And you are quite well, Harriet? Lady McAllister particularly charged me with making enquiries about your health."

"Perfectly well, sir."

"No more nightmares? No sudden starts and fears?"

"None to speak of. Why do you ask?" She automatically pulled her cuffs down to cover her still-scarred wrists.

He thought she still looked a little drawn, the pretty mob cap hiding her short dark hair making her seem older than her years. The bruises had faded but so had the sparkle from her eyes.

"There has been a 'development' in that – unfortunate business."

He had been in two minds whether to tell her but something William had let slip led him to believe that Harriet was already aware of what he was about to say.

"I thought the matter was all resolved," she replied. "But if is there is more, then it is only right that I should know of it."

Sir Hamish thought that discretion should be rewarded.

"Miss Finch packed her bags and left the house the day before Byrd took passage for Calcutta. She had been instrumental in providing his gang of thieves with information."

Harriet understood where William got his taste for dramatic delivery. Her face did not change.

"I see this revelation has not surprised you in the least. Did you know about this?"

"I *knew* nothing. I suspected *something* when Miss Finch wept all over my pillow and blamed herself for nothing I could understand. I was in no condition to try to puzzle it out – then. It was only gradually that I came to wonder if she were involved in the thefts in some way. But I could not believe I had been so mistaken in her nature."

She looked directly at Sir Hamish. "Byrd is her son isn't he? The name reveals all. Her charity protégé was her son."

"Yes, what my wife called her 'lame-duck' and the polite world a 'bye-blow', the result of an unfortunate liaison in her youth," he said casually. "Byrd told me from the moment he was taken, and I told my sons. We tried to keep Lady McAllister and everyone else in ignorance, but Miss Finch picked up a careless word. She collapsed as soon as she heard the name of your abductor."

Harriet plucked at her skirt. "I was shocked and angry at first but, when I thought about it, I feel sympathy for the poor woman; how she must have suffered when she discovered her son was a criminal!"

Sir Hamish was surprised at Harriet's tolerance but she had had weeks to order her thoughts and emotions on the matter. Her feelings of outrage had faded with her bruises.

"I have to tell you that Byrd used his parentage as blackmail against the family." He sounded very severe and then reverted to his usual lawyerly tone. "Nevertheless, your Uncle Beaumont and I had no intention of bringing a prosecution, and doubly so when Byrd announced his connection with Cousin Susan."

He mused for a moment. "I should have considered an inside informer, but things were hectic at the Home Office at the time, the queen's death you know, and Darville did not choose to take me into his confidence over all the robberies."

Harriet ignored the reference to Rupert. "Poor Miss Finch, I pity her having to give her baby up to the Foundling Hospital and never be able to acknowledge him. I *know* she was an innocent tool. You'll never persuade me that she had a hand in the planning of all those thefts."

"No, she was an entirely innocent dupe. I gather she was inconsolable when she discovered her foolishness had led to the extortion plots. I had some plan of banishing her to the family estates in Scotland when the affair had died down. But she pre-empted them all."

"Good God she hasn't killed herself has she?"

"No, no! Not that I know of! It seems that Cousin Susan would not be parted from Byrd and is half way to India by now. She left no note and I had the task of breaking the dreadful news to Lady McAllister myself."

There was a moment of silence as Sir Hamish recollected the terrible scene, made even worse when Elspeth discovered that everyone else in the family had known about Miss Finch's 'treachery' for weeks.

"Andrew spotted Cousin Susan on the dockside at Gravesend, waiting for the jolly boat which was to put them aboard the *Andromeda*. He and Valentine had escorted Byrd down in our own coach. Andrew said she was the firmest he had ever known when he confronted her – quite defiant even. But you have the right of it; she'd meet Byrd secretly and entertain him with all the society news, never dreaming what use he would make of the information."

"Poor Miss Finch was such a nonentity as to be forgotten. But she was always there you know, in the background."

Sir Hamish wondered if there was a lesson to be learnt. Perhaps he should recruit more women as his agents.

Harriet frowned a little. "Tell me, why did Byrd try to steal the Darville emeralds? I have been trying to puzzle it out. He must have been mad to send the boy on such an attempt. Miss Finch *knew* I was in Brook Street with Annie and Jacob and that there were constant visitors to see Mr Darville. Did she not tell him the rooms were occupied?"

"There were no visitors at night. And Miss Finch was too discreet to mention to *anyone* that you were in residence; she has a genuine fondness for you Harriet and, considering her past, was a stickler for the proprieties. I gather she was trying to protect your reputation. As far as Byrd knew, the earl and his mother had been called urgently back to Ireland and Rupert was drugged with laudanum in the front bedroom, attended only by his black servant."

Harriet nodded. "But why did they break in at all? If they knew the Countess had gone, why did they think the emeralds would still be in Brook Street?"

"Lady Darville does not *live* at Castle Morna. I presume they saw her hurried departure with nothing but hand luggage. And I happen to know the emeralds are usually kept in the safety of Drummond's vaults."

"Yes, there would have been no time to deposit them in the bank before she went. From Byrd's point of view it was a risk worth taking, I suppose."

Harriet shook herself. "Lady McAllister must be distraught. Pray do not tell her I guessed anything about Miss Finch. I held my tongue for the best of reasons."

"My dear, the less we refer to the matter in Lady McAllister's hearing the better."

"I said nothing of my suspicions while I was in Russell Square as I had no proof and no good would come of them. I thought I was imagining things, being so nervous and stupid." She put her hand up to her temple. "I thought you would dismiss Miss Finch instantly which would have started tongues wagging. And I knew the perils of that." A faint pink tinged her cheek.

"Credit it me with more diplomacy than that, Harriet," Sir Hamish replied taking another sip of sherry.

"I wonder what drove Byrd to it?"

Sir Hamish contemplated his glass. "I believe Miss Finch had unwittingly given her son an inflated view of his own position in society, and he felt robbed of it. She'd managed to pay for a half-decent education for him. He wanted money to live like a gentleman."

"Ah, the 'Esq.' on the ransom demand, and even the spelling of Smyth and Byrd - not quite in the common way. Mr Darville was right in his suppositions."

"It grieves me to say so, but yes. Byrd served as a clerk for the Cymru shipping line when he was younger and then went to sea for some years. Hence his ability to climb and his familiarity with Bowen's Wharf."

"Hence 'the captain', as my jailers called him."

"Andrew says Miss Finch swore she knew nothing of the plot to kidnap Miss Beaumont. He tackled her on that. She was horrified that you had fallen victim and it was then that she began to realise her careless tongue may have prompted the earlier crimes."

"But what of the Ravensburg Cross? No one in Russell Square knew anything of the jewel until after it was stolen. How could Miss Finch have been indiscreet about that?"

"The missing piece of the puzzle? Young Martin Straw was an occasional pot boy at the Clarendon. *He* knew about the Ravensburg Cross needing repair - the dear Reichsgrafin was none too discreet in front of the servants. Martin Straw told Byrd; it was as simple as that. There's no way the crime could be put down to Miss Finch. And your appearance was purely coincidental – and fortuitous."

"Do you think we have heard the last of the dreadful business now?"

"Valentine has promised to send word to Beaumont from each port. The Nabob paid Byrd off handsomely, there's no reason for him to return."

"And Miss Finch?"

"She made her choice, many years ago. I fear she may hang around her son's neck like Mr Coleridge's albatross, which may be his punishment."

******

Harriet found she had to inure herself to Sir Hamish's references to Rupert Darville, of necessity frequent when discussing Young Clem's future. Rupert had become an accepted member of the McAllister family; danger and misfortune had brought them all closer together. Harriet had also risen in Elspeth's estimation since she had become a wealthy woman and she occasionally referred to Miss Larkhill as her 'niece in the country'.

One day, busy in the orchard, talking to Sir Hamish who was sitting in the arbour, Harriet recalled the time when she had fallen from a tree and broken a wrist. "I was such a tomboy!"

Sir Hamish was betrayed into lamenting Rupert's broken ribs and lacerated body. "He is almost healed," he said, "though I fear the malarial lethargy will always be with him. Dr Somerville thinks he is mad to attempt another tropical expedition."

Harriet put down her basket of apples and demanded an explanation.

Sir Hamish, surprised, realised they had protected Harriet from the details of her rescue. He was hesitant now – there was always the matter of Bruiser Jack's body to be got over. But she insisted on being informed and, making light of the matter, he repeated what Andrew had told him of Rupert's daring climb and rooftop walk.

"How did Mr Darville get *into* the warehouse?"

"He swung down on the pulley and smashed through the window; I believe it was rotten at the time. Don't you remember?"

Harriet furrowed her brow. "Yes, he was nearly shot by someone. I was so glad to see him. I have some recollection of being carried down those terrible wooden steps but that's all I remember until I was in the boat with Andrew and Mr Jenkins."

"Rupert for some reason went back inside and barred the door."

"How did he get out again?"

"The same way he got in, I understand. Or perhaps he lowered himself out of the window on the block and tackle?" Sir Hamish raised his eyebrows in speculation. There was a pause.

"What happened to Bruiser Jack?"

"He escaped," lied Sir Hamish.

"Why did no one tell me of all this?"

"We did not want to alarm you my dear, you were very fragile for many days after the rescue. And Darville himself went into 'hibernation' to lick his wounds."

"But I spoke to him in your study! I attempted to distract him from searching for another culprit."

Sir Hamish sighed. "That was unfortunate. I was busy organising the transport of Her Majesty's cortège to Brunswick and the young men thought you confined to your room. However, Andrew and William said your rebuttals convinced Darville to let the matter rest, for which we are very grateful." He shook his head. "Of course the truth came out in the end; it usually does, more's the pity."

Harriet was speechless, and angry that no one had told her of Rupert's heroism and injuries. She felt bewildered and betrayed. She had protected their good name but they had kept her in the dark about Rupert. She had tried to put the kidnap at the back of her mind, actively distracting herself from terrifying pictures of guns and knives and forcing herself to walk alone in the course of her normal duties. Erasing Rupert from her consciousness had been even harder and now she felt worse knowing he had suffered for her.

Common sense told her she could not blame the McAllisters for Rupert's absence; her ungracious rejection of his marriage proposal, her indecorous reputation and her ridicule of his justified suspicions meant that he must hold her in aversion. The fact that he had visited Russell Square but had made no attempt to see her and had behaved so coldly during the interview only confirmed his contempt.

"Put it all behind you Harriet," advised Sir Hamish endeavouring to interpret her expression. "No one knows of your 'mishap' down here. You're safe and, if you wish to, can afford to hire any number of stout fellows to keep watch if you still feel afraid."

"Does Mr Darville know that Mr Beaumont is my uncle?"

"My, how your mind does leap about so! But yes, when the first ransom note came, Beaumont said he'd pay anything for your release as you were his niece. Darville was certainly there and quite struck by the news. He told me so himself. Though to do him justice he has never mentioned the fact again in my hearing. I would imagine the whole world knows you're a rich woman by now."

That was the final blow.

******

Madame de Lessups was having a party. Town was rather empty of company, many families having gone into the country for the shooting season. However, as Marguerite's friends were predominantly urban and sedentary she had no problem in filling her rooms. Her French chef was not to be scorned.

She was leaving to join the Beaumonts in Paris. The Curzon Street house would be given up, she assured her guests. She hoped to be in England for the Christmas festivities and take up her marital duties at the head of Mr Beaumont's table, wherever that might be.

"A wedding in Paris," sighed Lady Bixby. "How romantic. What a pity it could not be a summer wedding. We would have all come over to throw rose petals."

"I hope the weather will be kind to us; the Embassy has the prettiest garden in the city and I have many friends in Paris."

"Oh dear, everyone is leaving town. Lord Everard is with the Duke of York, Elspeth will shortly be leaving for Scotland, even Mr Darville is sailing for exotic shores. And I cannot persuade Lord Bixby to go anywhere but Doncaster for the races."

A group of gentlemen were standing in the window idly watching the lamplighter go about his business. The nights were drawing in.

"It's a miracle that Shawcross ain't here tonight. I've never known him turn down one of the widow's feasts if he can help it," said William with deceptive innocence. "He must have better fish to fry."

Rupert sipped his canary wine seemingly unmoved. "He's probably gone home to Grantham."

"I hear a young friend of yours is to be married," said William watching Rupert's face. The betting book at White's contained a new wager.

Rupert's unconcern did not waver. "I'm sure you will enlighten me as to the favoured individual."

Thwarted of his fun William said: "Favoured be damned! I don't know who's to be the most pitied, Shawcross or his bride!"

Rupert flushed and was about to walk away when Sir Hamish joined the conversation.

"Ignore my son, sir. Mortimer Shawcross is a long way from being married. We should believe nothing until we see an announcement in *The Times*."

William's wicked voice trailed away at his father's cold stare. "I beg pardon. But there is so much talk of marriage in the air. What with Andrew mooning over Miss Beaumont and the widow about to tie the knot, one cannot escape the orange blossom."

"Not everyone wishes to escape it," said Sir Hamish. "The married state is to be highly recommended, ask your mother."

William retreated.

"I am always amazed that any woman would wish to shackle herself in marriage," said Rupert suddenly.

"Shackle? Good heavens, my boy! It's usually the gentleman who considers himself shackled. What radical idea is this?"

Rupert continued stubbornly. "A woman loses her financial independence and is forever at the beck and call of her husband. She must follow him everywhere, to her own detriment."

"A woman is in much the same position when she is a daughter or a sister. Wedlock has its compensations for a wife: companionship, status, protection, children."

"If a lady is rich enough to support herself and her family in comfort, she has no need of marriage. A female of truly independent spirit would spurn those things."

"A woman of common sense would not." Sir Hamish knew exactly where Rupert's thoughts lay. He moved away, hoping he had said enough. Lady McAllister and the card table called him.

Sir Hamish would have been gratified to learn that he had an ally in Madame de Lessups. As her own nuptials approached, she hoped to see all those about her happy and regretted whatever had gone wrong between her Larkhill friends. Like all who were privy to the kidnap and dramatic rescue she had expected an engagement to be announced shortly afterwards and was disappointed when Rupert held aloof.

Madame de Lessups turned from a group of ladies and went to where Rupert was standing alone in the window. "A penny for your thoughts, Mr Darville."

"I'm afraid there are more than pennies involved, Madame," said Rupert, for once caught unawares.

"I take it you mean Miss Larkhill's fortune? For a student of mathematics you seem to have overlooked the most powerful factor in the equation."

Rupert stiffened with a mixture of shock and outrage.

Marguerite pressed on. "Forgive me, but do you love Miss Larkhill and does she return your regard?"

The boldness of her attack left him speechless. Having few social skills he was forced back on the truth.

"I have not the felicity of knowing the lady's current feelings. But she has refused my offer."

"Ah, it was made before her sad adventure, I assume?"

"Quite so."

"And pride forbids you to pursue your suit now she is a wealthy woman."

Rupert looked mulish.

"As pride forbade her to accept your, no doubt, chivalrous proposal." Marguerite knew all about the slighting rumours and the betting books.

"Fie on you Mr Darville!" She took him by the arm and let him to a small sofa. "Monsieur de Lessups made more than adequate provision for my future. I loved him dearly and have happy memories of our lives together. Hence my willingness to trust to Mr Beaumont's affections and enter the married state once more. I assure you, I am an independent woman of means, Mr Beaumont's fortune does not come into it. I would marry him even if he were a fish porter in Billingsgate, not 'The Nabob'." She looked smilingly into his face.

"If you forgive me ma'am, the situation is not quite the same; my first marriage was not - as it should have been." He broke off and then said: "The financial inequality bestowed by Miss Larkhill's recent good fortune is anathema to any gentleman of sensibility," began Rupert.

"Harriet would not think so and neither would most of the people in this room! I cannot think of a more practical girl; Harriet has few romantic notions. Your rank will give her standing and freedom, and her money will ease the way for both of you. It would be the perfect match."

Rupert looked woodenly into the distance. He suddenly realised he would welcome a few 'romantic notions' from Harriet; her refusal had sorely dented his ego.

Marguerite pressed on. "Mr Beaumont has given her not such a *great* sum and she will insist on spending it all on that crumbling manor house of hers, if you allow her. Surely your mama wished you to marry a woman of substance? Then why not Miss Larkhill?"

"You forget, Harriet has refused me."

"Do you give up so easily on your experiments? Do you cease to explore the unknown after one setback? The situation has changed and so might the outcome. I was given to understand you were a man of loyalty to his friends and determination in his pursuits, not so easily diverted from his course."

Rupert looked at her with a tinge of respect. After a moment he said: "Miss Larkhill has sent me a letter."

"There! Courtesy alone demands that you reply, or pay her a visit before you embark for Bogota. You intend to see that young ward of yours I hope?"

"Duty demands that I must."

******

Harriet got dressed slowly. Her mood was subdued as she caressed the peacock-blue shot silk, trying to brush aside the memories it evoked. To any casual acquaintance Harriet had almost regained her health and looks since her return from London. Some even considered that she had gained a dignity which was put down as London polish. But those who knew Harriet well could see that the unfortunate 'accident' had weakened her confidence and hoped that time and loving friends would restore her lively spirits. Mr Beaumont's generosity had relieved her of her money worries, but no one guessed her true heartache.

Annie worked wonders with the curling tongs on her short hair. "There Miss. You look like a real lady of fashion tonight."

"I miss my braids," sighed Harriet, tweaking the ringlets at the side of her face. "They were so easy to manage."

"Your hair will grow again Miss. Now what's it to be tonight? Your locket or the garnets?"

"The locket, I think." Harriet felt a wave of loneliness, she wanted her family about her and although it warmed her o know that she had Rupert to thank for her life, she was even more bereft by his silence.

Harriet had put her anger and confusion to good use. After fuming at the idiocy of well-meaning people to protect her and feeling very low in spirits at its result, she decided to take matters in hand and clear the air between herself and Rupert. The letter took several days to write and emerged as a modest note of enquiry as to his welfare with the hope that he could spare the time to see Young Clem before he left for foreign parts. There had been no reply.

Sir John had retired early and Young Clem was already asleep after an afternoon romping at Home Farm. Only her good manners and the fear of causing talk forced her to go to the ball. She had missed Larkhill's Summer Assembly and could not cut the Carter's farewell dance.

The Durringtons welcomed her into their coach. Juliana, still nursing her baby, had declined to attend and Lieutenant George had done his duty by offering to bear his wife company at home.

The white block of Quennell House rose into the moonlight, clustered around with the carriages and horses of the gentry. The Durringtons and Harriet were announced on the threshold of the black and white marble entrance hall. The room glittered with chandeliers and thick wax candles. At the head of the marble staircase Darville portraits stared down on a popular orchestra from Salisbury.

The lower salons had been converted into supper, card and retiring rooms and were already full. The neighbourhood was out in force.

Harriet felt conspicuous in her shimmering blue dress and new coiffeur. The Carters welcomed her warmly and she found herself being introduced to a tanned and lively-looking gentleman. Their son Stanley was home from Canada at last.

"Miss Larkhill, delighted. I cannot flatter myself that you will remember me but the last time I saw you, you were in short skirts trying to fly a kite by the river Bourne on some disastrous picnic my mother had arranged."

"You are very unkind to your mother, sir, who organises all such events beautifully. No one can be held responsible for the English weather. But I remember you very well," said Harriet. "We in fact met once more, in the church yard one Sunday – but my cousin Sylvia was not present, so I can quite see how the occasion slipped your memory," she said teasingly.

"You put me to shame Miss Larkhill. I admit that Miss McAllister was the shining attraction of that summer." He seemed about to ask something and then was interrupted by the arrival of new guests. Harriet was swept away by the Durringtons.

The small orchestra struck up a country dance and Harriet wondered if she were to be a wallflower when the Reverent Cusworth appeared at her elbow and tremulously solicited her hand. Out of the corner of her eye she saw Eliza and Jane Carter giggling at the spectacle. They were both pretty, vivacious girls, who felt superior to their neighbours in the knowledge that they were soon to escape provincial life for the delights of the metropolis.

Harriet was kind and made the young curate a happy man for half an hour, despite his tongue-tied shyness. At the end of two dances she moved purposefully towards the Carter girls, trailing the curate in her wake and said: "Dear Eliza, you dance the cotillion so much better than I and the Reverend Cusworth is looking for a dainty partner for the next set. You are old friends soon to part, I know," she cajoled. "So I have brought the gentleman over to be saved from dancing with any of the *older* guests." She leaned towards Eliza conspiratorially. "Your Mama, I'm sure would approve." And with an encouraging tap of her peacock fan on the young man's arm, she went in search of Lady Durrington.

On the threshold of the supper room she found herself face to face with the Wests. Tonight Horace West wore an orange silk waistcoat heavily embroidered in a virulent green.

"Ah, Miss Larkhill. Out and about at last, I see. Not one to pamper yourself over trifles, I imagine."

"Thank you, sir, I am quite well, though perhaps not as stout as I would like to be. I'm sure Mrs West understands the exhaustion of a convalescent," she said smiling sympathetically at his silent spouse.

"Don't encourage her, Miss Larkhill. I could barely persuade her to come tonight. Another headache, she says, and her usual rheumatism and pains." Mrs West's lips thinned in suppressed rage as she stared into the middle distance.

"Then I would fortify yourself ma'am with Mrs Carter's excellent supper. And then a quiet game of whist?" She curtseyed and passed on

"What an odious man!" said Harriet, sitting down at the supper table next to Lady Durrington. "How his poor wife puts up with him I cannot imagine. He is positively cruel to her." She looked balefully across the room to where Mr West was holding forth.

Lady Durrington followed her gaze. "Not a gentleman, my dear, for all his high-bred relations. Mr Carter has better address and certainly treats his wife with more civility. I suspect Mrs West will murder her husband one day," she said calmly addressing the smoked salmon.

Harriet laughed. "Lady Durrington, for such a *nice* woman you have remarkably wicked thoughts."

"But my dear, gentlemen can be very difficult. I have yet to meet a married woman who has *not* wished to murder her husband at one time or another."

"But you have been married twice!"

"And very happily. A successful marriage relies much on compromise, I find. I tell Juliana so every day. But you are older and more sensible, Harriet, and must know that most gentlemen are far from being heroes out of epic poems. Unless of course you met someone very dashing in Russell Square?"

Harriet had come to accept that Rupert had always been her flawed hero and she was well aware that he was not her lone rescuer. But Rupert's tenacity and courage had given her hope that he cared for her and this had been cruelly dashed by his subsequent abandonment. His continued silence confirmed her belief that he regretted his ill-considered marriage proposal.

If Lady Durrington was hoping to prompt Harriet into a confession about what exactly had happened during her visit, then she failed miserably.

"I am sorry to disappoint you, Lady Durrington, but I met no-one very dashing in London. The men were either fops or politicians - well perhaps not all," she said, mindful of dear Andrew.

"And the inventors and natural philosophers? Gentlemen with such experience of the wider world and advanced ideas must be fascinating companions," said Lady Durrington blatantly fishing. This was the closest she dared come to mentioning Rupert Darville by name.

"On the contrary, I found them argumentative masters of arcane detail, with no time for love," said Harriet bitterly.

Lady Durrington was dismayed. She looked at Harriet and feared it would have to be the Reverend Cusworth after all.

After supper, a murmur of interest ran round the marble hall, heads turned at the bustle of a late arrival. Harriet politely kept her attention on the Reverend Butterworth, when that gentleman broke off in wonder. "Good Heavens! It's Mr Darville."

Harriet's heart gave a lurch and she allowed herself to peep around the clergyman's substantial bulk. Rupert, in his usual black coat and silk knee breeches, was striding across the floor towards them.

"What nice condescension to make an appearance at his tenant's farewell dance," continued Reverend Butterworth approvingly. "I cannot agree with those who find Mr Darville cold and unapproachable. He was so kind as to send me an example of the Amazonian blue butterfly for my collection – such a prize, such a magnificent colour! Very much like your dress, Miss Larkhill." This jocular comment was cut off as the crowd parted before them and there was Rupert staring straight at Harriet and bowing stiffly.

"Miss Larkhill, your servant ma'am. Would you grant me the honour of the next dance?"

Being so blatantly ignored, the Reverend Butterworth modified his opinion of his patron until his wife whispered: "You must make allowance for a man struggling under a strong emotion, my love. It is plain to see that Mr Darville has eyes for no one in the room but Miss Larkhill."

"An affair of the heart, do you mean?" asked the Rector in surprise. "I had not the slightest notion. You led me to believe Algernon Cusworth had an interest there!"

Mrs Butterworth suppressed a sigh. "I fear the acne will tell against him."

The Rector thought for a moment. "The Countess will not approve," he said, and then gathering his courage: "But I for one would think it a splendid match. I trust that *this* time I will be allowed to officiate at the ceremony at St Saviour's."

While commending her husband's strength of mind Mrs Butterworth cautioned him to be discreet.

All eyes watched as Rupert swept Harriet into his arms for the waltz. He was not the smoothest of dancers and only after an awkward and silent few moments, Rupert managed to start some conversation.

"You are well, I trust?" he said, searching her face. "Now that you are home among friends? Your letter spoke of nothing about yourself."

"Tolerably well, sir. And you? Have the after-effects of your injuries quite disappeared?"

"Quite disappeared, I thank you. I have come down to see my ward before I leave, as you requested."

Harriet felt her heart sink but bravely soldiered on. "And the McAllisters, they are well?"

"Yes, I believe so." Feeling something more was required, he added stiffly: "I met Sir Hamish in Regent Street. He seemed well."

"And the Beaumonts? Have they returned to Paris? Miss Beaumont found Nice too hot at this time of year. Philippa is normally such a faithful correspondent but I have not heard from her these two weeks."

"Confound it, Harriet! I have not come all this way to talk about your London friends!"

"Are they not *your* friends also?"

"Yes, but – I thought you would want to hear news regarding Nicholas Byrd."

"Certainly not! He is the last person I wish to hear *anything* about. I hoped he had vanished on the tide."

Rupert looked nonplussed.

Harriet continued in a business-like tone. "You said you came down to visit Young Clem. He will be so very pleased if you have brought Jacob with you."

Rupert's hand gripped hers more tightly at this veiled slight. "I have indeed brought Jacob. We are putting up at the Three Crowns. It was Sir Hamish's suggestion that I relay the latest information to you about – that man, in order to finally put your mind to rest."

"If I must hear it, I must," sighed Harriet. "But a ballroom is no place to talk of such matters."

"Then come with me to somewhere more private," he said halting abruptly. She was quite relieved to stop the dancing. He took her by the hand, which sent a frisson though her, and led her along the passage towards the library. "I trust the Carters have left us somewhere untouched in my own house."

Rupert found the barrel-roofed library relatively undisturbed and a low fire burning in the grate. He urged Harriet to sit on the ottoman in front of the hearth while he searched for some tapers, grumbling over the alteration to the placing of the furniture. Harriet wondered if something else was afoot besides his news and was surprised at Rupert being so ill at ease. She could still feel the warmth of his hand on her palm.

Eventually, with candles lit in the sconces and a lamp aglow on the desk, Rupert flipped up his tail coat and took a seat beside her.

"Harriet, I *am* pleased to see you again, though you are still pale and have lost a little of your bloom."

"Thank you kind sir," she said. Her lips twitched. He would always sacrifice tact to truth.

"Forgive me, I did not mean-. I merely voice my concern for your welfare."

"I assure you Mr Darville, I could not be in better spirits. Now, as you have come all this way from London to tell me what has *else* has happened to my kidnappers, I suggest you begin."

"Byrd is dead. *The Andromeda* docked at Freetown, Sierra Leone. Byrd got into a fight, he was robbed and beaten and died of stab wounds. We have Valentine's letter via a fast clipper and then the packet boat from Lisbon."

Harriet's hands flew to her cheeks. "Oh, poor Miss Finch! What will become of her?"

Rupert shrugged. "That's not our concern. Sir Hamish informed me that you already knew about Miss Finch." He looked offended.

She nodded. "He came down a few weeks ago and told me of her involvement. I'd already guessed, but couldn't be certain. And I did not want to betray someone whom I sure was innocent of any malicious intent."

"If you had spoken, I would have listened to you."

"Oh, do you really think so?" said Harriet in mild parody of Philippa.

Rupert looked awkward. "You seemed as persuaded as the others that there was no informant."

"I take it you are referring that afternoon in the study with Andrew and William? Yes, I admit I was trying to distract you, trying to convince you there were only three people involved in the robberies. You were right of course, there was another, but no good would have come of exposing poor Miss Finch *then*."

She gave him a moment to digest this.

"I confess that I was trying to stop you searching for another culprit. Can you forgive me? It was from the best of motives I promise you. And so, I now know, were Andrew and William; Sir Hamish had told them about Miss Finch on the day Byrd was captured, but he had sworn them to secrecy. It was something they did not want anyone outside the family to discover."

"So I am not to be trusted," said Rupert.

"None of us were, not me, not even Lady McAllister was told – until Miss Finch disappeared."

"Why did you want to delay the inevitable? The woman's relationship to Byrd was certain to come to light in time."

"I disagree! Who's to say that Miss Finch's gossiping would have *ever* been revealed beyond the gentlemen of the family? Sir Hamish intended to find an excuse to send her away to Scotland, where all would have been forgotten."

Rupert still looked stern. Harriet continued to justify her silence even though she didn't need to. She realised Rupert needed some excuse to salve his pride.

"Miss Finch was not to blame for the robberies, though I doubt if anything would convince her of that. If her past and the results of her foolish chattering became generally known, Lady McAllister would have dismissed her instantly. No one wanted that kind of public scandal! And what kind of life would she have had, thrown on the street? Discretion gave Sir Hamish time to decide on an alternative scheme - which would have been much the better if she had not made a different choice. In the end our silence provided an opportunity for her to follow her son. I wonder if she was looking for redemption by exiling herself to life in India? Or was it just mother love?"

They sat in silence for a while, contemplating the events of the past few weeks. Rupert had a lot to take in. In the end he said: "You should have told me Harriet, but I suppose it was my own fault that we did not then stand upon such terms of intimacy -."

"You did not need to be told. You had already worked it out for yourself. You were correct in your supposition of a fourth party. And the whole conundrum of the thefts and my kidnapping would never have been solved without your logic and systematic investigations – and your bravery."

Rupert stared moodily into the fire.

"So that is that?" said Harriet, drawing her shoulders back. "Byrd is dead. If this news is all you have to tell me Mr Darville, shall we return to the ballroom?"

"I have something more to say to you Miss Larkhill." She looked at him with polite anticipation. He looked like a man who was about to leap off a cliff.

"When I received your letter, thanking me for my efforts in securing your safe return, it gave me hope that you might think – kindly of me once more."

"I am *enormously* thankful for *everyone's* kindness. And even more for your efforts in rescuing me, Mr Darville. I am under an eternal obligation to you for my life! You would never allow me to express my gratitude properly and now you and Sir Hamish have settled every aspect of the matter most handsomely. That is what I call true friendship."

Rupert lowered his eyes. "You must know I acted out of more than friendship. When Beaumont showed me the ransom note I knew what I truly felt." He gave her a long look. She merely smiled. Gaining courage from her affability he ploughed on. "The truth is, Harriet, I don't want to lose you. I could not lose you twice. I – I do not want to imagine my future life without you." He leant towards her and took both her hands in his. "Can you ever forgive me for my clumsy and arrogant proposal by that cursed grotto?"

"I think we both behaved badly that day, and it is best forgotten."

Rupert drew back uncertain and then took another breath but held on to her hands. "Then allow me start again. Dearest Harriet, would you make me the happiest of men and consent to become my wife? Would you do me the honour of marrying me?"

She looked at his angular intense face and longed to take it between her fingers and kiss the anxious frown away. Like any woman she savoured her moment of triumph.

"And your family?"

His cat's eyes narrowed. "I do not need the approval of my family. I would marry you if the whole world were against us. Though if you need such reassurance, my Uncle Patrick is heartily in favour."

"And your mama?" she said almost laughing.

"My mother has hopes that Gerald will provide the title with a male heir. She has washed her hands of me. But she is fond of you, Harriet, you know that."

"And my newly acquired fortune, no doubt."

"I do not believe she knows of it yet. It is of no consequence to me and never has been! Give me credit for not being a mercenary man."

Harriet nodded as if considering the matter. He waited and then said desperately: "Will you say yes? Do you love me at *all*? Or do you delight in punishing me for my boorish behaviour, which God knows I deserve."

"But I heard you were going on another expedition – to Bogota?"

"Only because I despaired of ever winning you. If you refuse me now, then I embark next month," said Rupert truthfully.

"I would not wish to prevent any man from pursuing his profession," she said demurely.

"Dammit Harriet! Will you be my wife?"

"Tell me, Mr Darville, have you laid a bet on my acceptance at White's?" she said innocently.

He gave a great crack of laughter and pulled her roughly into his arms. "You minx! You delight in tormenting me."

"But I do make you laugh," she agreed.

"You make my heart leap whenever I see you."

She relented. "Yes, Rupert I will marry you."

In an instant he pulled her to her feet and crushed her into his arms, finding her upturned mouth and kissing her with passion. Reluctantly breaking away he brushed his strong fingers over her face. "You are the most bewitching of women! How could I have been so blind? It has always been you, Harriet." He bent to kiss her again.

At that moment the door of the library swung open to reveal Mr Carter and Sir Charles Durrington, disputing hotly. "But I tell you Carter I don't believe these steam ships will come to anything, at least not on the open ocean. Good Lord! Darville!"

"Miss Larkhill, Mr Darville. I do beg your pardon," said Mr Carter. "We had no notion anyone was in here-"

Rupert released Harriet with a broad grin. "Congratulate me Carter, Sir Charles. Miss Larkhill has just done me the honour of agreeing to become my wife." He took her in one arm again.

The two men, startled and embarrassed, managed to say all that was necessary and suggested they seek their wives to tell them the happy news.

Harriet came out of her daze. "I thank you but no, Sir Charles, please say nothing until I have spoken to Uncle John first, and Miss Humble." She looked up at Rupert for support.

"Of course, Miss Larkhill is right. We must observe the formalities," though he looked like a man who would whisk his bride away on the moment. "And we would not trespass on your kindness, Mr Carter. This is your party, your occasion. Our news must not overshadow your hospitality."

"Sir, your announcement would be the crowning glory of the evening," said Carter, "making it an occasion never to be forgotten. But we will respect your wishes – though what my wife will say when the news gets out - but I will not tell her until I hear it from others."

Harriet laughed. "She will always have the satisfaction of knowing the proposal took place in *her* library."

"*My* library," corrected Rupert automatically.

"Our library, my dear," said Harriet slipping an arm around Rupert's waist.

"It's quite fitting that you should offer for Harriet here under your own roof, Darville," said Sir Charles, shaking Rupert's hand. "Nothing could be more proper. But Lady Durrington is bound to tease the matter out before the evening is over. Your absence here will be noticed and both of you look like the cat that got the cream."

"Then I will beg your indulgence gentlemen, and take my affianced bride home to her family, before we betray ourselves further."

"And what are we to tell our wives?"

"That, gentlemen is your affair."

What was said between the lovers in the snug comfort of the barouche we will not go into. Suffice it to say that Jacob, on his master's orders, drove the mile or so to Larkhill Manor very slowly under a glowing hunter's moon.

It was agreed that Rupert would come as usual in the afternoon when Harriet had broken the news to Sir John and the rest of the household. Rupert left her at the oak door with a lingering kiss and then pulled the bell for Dunch. The butler stared at the early return of his mistress and the unexpected appearance of Mr Darville, both in such beatific moods. It was a pity that the rest of the household was abed, he reflected; he would have to wait until the morning to relay this interesting news. But he didn't give much for the curate's chances.

******

The following morning was full of smiles and tears.

Annie smirked at the news, handing her mistress a hair ribbon. "'Bout time, Miss, if you'll excuse me sayin' so. I seen it comin' for *weeks*. But Mr Darville be no different from my Jem, beggin' your pardon: a slow fuse but a powerful burn as Corporal Briggs used to say."

Harriet cavilled at this unexpected assessment of Rupert's character until she thought of Sir Hamish's account of Rupert's daring rescue.

"I wish Major Clement were here," she said suddenly. "And Aunt Betsy." Her hand could not quite tie the ribbon properly.

"Have you set a date, Miss?" asked Annie trying to be hearty.

"No, not yet," faltered Harriet. "We are to have *your* wedding first and see you and Jem settled. Mr Darville thought Christmas, perhaps, when all the details have been arranged."

Annie disappeared to the kitchen to break the momentous news to Cook and Janet and, with her superior knowledge, recount all the little London episodes that had convinced her of this happy outcome all along.

On being informed of her charge's change of status, Miss Humble clutched Harriet to her spinster bosom saying: "I always hoped, always dreamed, but it seemed so far away! Just like a fairy tale – so romantic!"

"Well, I have no time to be romantic now, we have practical decisions to make, and I have yet to tell Sir John my news." Harriet had lain awake most of the night becoming steadily more anxious about the future of Larkhill Manor. Rupert had been full of promises and she forced herself to accept that this was the strong shoulder she had yearned for.

Telling the squire her good news was as difficult as she had anticipated. When she informed her uncle of her engagement, he drew his bushy brows together. "Engaged? How can you be engaged to young Darville? Isn't he married to Sylvia? They ran off, didn't they? Is he back? Where is *she*?" He dabbed at his chin with a cotton handkerchief, angered by the effort to speak.

"Yes, Uncle, Mr Darville is home from his travels. He's a widower now and he wants to marry again. Me, I mean."

The squire pondered this. "Humph, sensible boy. You're not a bubble-head like your cousin. Every man should be married. Where's my wife? Where's Betsy?"

"She's busy uncle," soothed Harriet. "She'll be here soon."

"You don't have to treat me like a fool. I know she's dead. And what's going to happen to me?" he snapped, showing more animation than he had in weeks. "You're not going to leave me too, are you?"

"No, no, you must not worry so! Rupert will live here with us when he is in Wiltshire, though I daresay he will be spending much of his time in London, so you won't notice any difference. Nothing will change, except he will be able to take you out and about more often in his barouche."

This seemed to satisfy the squire until he said with a ferocious gleam in his eye. "And when is he going to ask my permission to pay his addresses to you? You are still my niece. It is still customary, I assume, to ask a young girl's guardian for her hand before embarking on courtship?"

"Mr Darville will be here this afternoon, Uncle," promised Harriet. The formalities were unnecessary but they would please the squire. She left him to Dunch who, as he held the door open for her, murmured: "May we wish you joy, Miss. Everyone below stairs is very pleased at the news, though of course rather desirous of knowing Mr Darville's and your plans."

"Thank you Dunch. Mr Darville will speak to you himself, I'm certain, as soon as matters have been decided. But I do not anticipate much change."

It was a relief to find Young Clem in the nursery feeding the parrot slices of apple through the bars of its cage. Taking the child on her lap, she explained the matter as simply as she could. After a moment's consideration the boy looked at her with Sylvia's cornflower blue eyes and said. "Does that mean Jacob will live here, too?"

Harriet smiled. "Why, yes, I suppose it does. Should you like that?"

"Of course. He can help me teach Captain Blood to hunt mice."

She gave him a sudden hug and said: "Then you can tell him yourself *after* your lessons as I daresay Mr Darville will bring Jacob with him when he comes to visit us this afternoon".

Young Clem gave a whoop of joy and Miss Humble, come to find her reluctant pupil, despaired of teaching him anything that morning.

Luncheon was a scrappy affair with Harriet, instead of attending to Miss Humble's extravagant wedding plans, straining to hear the sound of a horseman or a barouche on the gravel drive. After luncheon she tried to busy herself but her mind was like a butterfly, alternatively flitting with happiness and then alighting on some cause for anxiety. Having miscounted the sheets in the linen cupboard for the third time, she gave up the attempt and sought calmness of spirit in the garden. Her hope was that Rupert should find her there, picturesquely amidst the remainder of the roses. However, the Yew walk enclosed her and the shadow on the sundial seemed stubbornly set in one place. Would he never come? She found herself aimlessly circling the round basin fountain and counting the flagstones on the terrace.

Determined to put her fidgets to rest she returned to the house for her hat and coat, changed her shoes and started through the orchard to the road to the Downs. She would not tamely wait for Rupert. A thirty minutes brisk walk brought her to the stile in the hedge she knew well. Before her lay Lud's long barrow, somewhere she had not ventured since she was twelve years old but now felt drawn towards as if in some act of completion.

She trudged up the steep slope, feeling the absence of a dog at her heels. Why had they not found another dog when Beauty died? A puppy would be a companion for Young Clem and encourage Uncle John to walk again. She would speak to Rupert about it.

She puffed a little, not as fit as she was when a girl, and still weakened by her recent experiences. A few great lung-fulls of air set her on her way again and it was with joy and satisfaction that she crested the hill to see the green mound of the long barrow rising in front of her. It looked no different from ten years before, and no different from a thousand years before, with the daisies and vetch and clover dotting the rough grass like stars in a green firmament.

This time there were sheep in the field, munching and bleating vaguely at her approach. The wind soughing in the grass brought colour to her cheeks. Harriet took off her hat and untied her ribbon, letting her loose short tresses blow about her face.

She had no desire to explore the scene of her childhood adventure and avoided the standing stones at the entrance to the chamber. Instead, she hitched up her skirt and clambered to the roof of the barrow to spy out the land. Autumn was coming; the trees looked spent, their leaves tinged with yellow, the fields were brown and gold with stubble. A faint haze of bonfire smoke drifted up from Home Farm. She had a sudden wish for Lieutenant George's old telescope and wondered what had become of it. Young Clem would enjoy playing with it.

From her vantage point she could see the dome of the Darvilles' Temple of Athena. Who would be the new tenants of Quennell House, she wondered. And somewhere behind the trees lay the river and Bourne Park where Mr West dreamed of Jamaica and Mrs West plotted revenge.

Harriet stood up on tip-toe. She was grown tall enough now to make out the grey slates and the twisted chimneys of Larkhill Manor to her right, nestled in the valley. Something made her turn and look back down the slope of the field to the way she had come. On the old cart track, she could make out a tall man in a dark coat, striding purposefully towards the stile. As he put one hand on the gate and vaulted confidently over, he looked up towards the barrow and waved. She knew it was Rupert, come to find her.

THE END

EPILOGUE

Harriet and Rupert were married at Christmas in St Saviour's Church, Larkhill. Reverend Butterworth was a happy man and the young curate abjured women forever.

Everyone came to the wedding. Mr and Mrs Beaumont, newly returned from their honeymoon in Paris with Philippa, escorted by Mr Andrew McAllister in his capacity as acknowledged swain. Sir Hamish and Lady McAllister were prominent in the front pew, and Lord Patrick gave the proceedings an air of fashionable consequence. The district turned out in force despite the blustery weather. Sir John gave the bride away, his passage down the aisle one of the last walks he would make. Juliana Durrington was matron of honour and Young Clem, cherubic in velvet knee breeches was, with difficulty, persuaded against bringing Captain Blood.

Between mopping her eyes for joy, Miss Humble produced a commendable wedding breakfast and Lady Durrington, looking around the Great Hall, was happy to see the manor returned to something like its prosperous self.

"Betsy would have been so happy today," she allowed herself to whisper to Sir Charles.

Durrington wondered if, after all, George wouldn't have made a better matrimonial bargain by marrying Harriet. But then, as a besotted grandfather, he would never have had baby Georgiana to dandle on his knee.

Will Hinton was groomsman and a sprinkling of Rupert's London friends braved the muddy roads down to Wiltshire. Viscount Frodingham would ever after refer to Harriet as the 'Nut Brown Maid'. William, entertaining himself at the Three Crowns, beyond the reach of fussing women, was astonished to hear of the smuggling adventure of ten years before which had accrued even more high drama and inaccuracy in the interim.

Even the dowager countess dragged herself over from Ireland. Her wedding present was the Darville emeralds. She thrust the shabby cases into Harriet's reluctant hands.

"Here, you may as well have 'em, you saved them for the family after all."

"But what about the Countess of Morna? By rights these are hers! And what of the Ladies Sophia and Rosa, when they grow up?"

"I'll not have a Dublin barmaid flaunting the Darville emeralds about her neck! At least you've got good blood in your veins. Besides, that dreadful woman never leaves her bed nowadays. I'll outlive her yet!"

"And the little girls?"

"The stones pass through the male line and are worn by the wife of the title holder."

"The earl may have a son one day, and if not, there is your second son in Italy to inherit. I have no legal right to keep these emeralds."

"Harriet! Will you not cross me in this! I have nothing else to give you, and you would set the mind of a sick old woman at ease if you accept them. You kept your side of the bargain, now I'll keep mine."

Harriet resisted no more, but when she spoke to Lord Patrick on the matter, he looked sad. "Do not trouble your conscience dear girl. My sister-in-law is losing her wits as well as her health. Humour her in this. She will not remember, and if she does demand the emeralds back, I am certain you would always oblige her." He paused before continuing. "They are worth very little - you realise this don't you?"

"Oh yes. They are paste. I have known since the night of the burglary in Brook Street."

"You can afford to buy your own set of emeralds now my dear, none of this trumpery glass for you!"

Harriet held the jewel cases tight to her bosom and said in amusement. "Not emeralds but rubies. My Uncle Beaumont has given me an enormous blood-red stone on a golden chain for a wedding present. It is delightfully vulgar! But I assure you, Lord Patrick, that these pieces of 'trumpery glass' as you call them, are far more precious to me because of all the memories they hold."

The young couple took their bridal trip to the warmth of Italy and made a special visit to the English cemetery in Rome. A month later they returned to Quennell House and held a ball for the county.

The last word came from Lady McAllister. Elspeth wrote to welcome them home and enclosed a cutting from *The Morning Post*: "A marriage has been arranged between Miss Lavinia Charlotte Snoddie, eldest daughter of Doctor and Mrs Donald Snoddie of Edinburgh, and Mr Mortimer Shawcross, M.P. of Grantham Grange, Lincolnshire."

Watch out for 'Quennell House – part 3 of The Cousins' where, ten years on, Rupert and Harriet are confronted with a murder mystery.

Printed in Great Britain
by Amazon.co.uk, Ltd.,
Marston Gate.